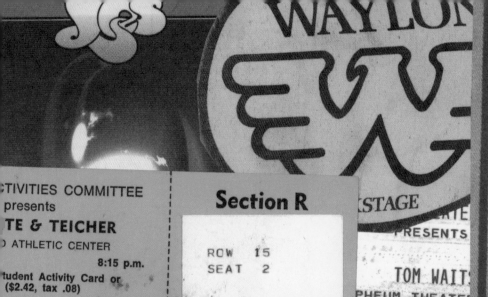

YES

WAYLON

Dolly Parton
RCA Records
BACKSTAGE PASS

ACTIVITIES COMMITTEE
presents
TE & TEICHER
ATHLETIC CENTER
8:15 p.m.
Student Activity Card or
($2.42, tax .08)
Concerts and Lectures

Section R

ROW 15
SEAT 2

BACKSTAGE
PRESENTS

TOM WAITS
ORPHEUM THEATER
THU OCT 11, 1979

ADMISSION 8.50 7 59262

OLE KING

6 K 60
AISLE ROW SEAT
Sun. Eve. ORCHESTRA
FEB. $4.15
18 1968
TICKET CO.
CHICAGO 95

POLIS TRIBUNE Feb. 4, 1968

ALL
ACCESS

Evening Star

THEATRE ROYAL
Drury Lane 265

EVENING
FRIDAY
MAY 11
Grand Circle
£25·00
A 24

NORTH GATE
DEC.
1967 19
11
SEAT
FLOOR
METROPOL
PRODU
ATTA
GUESTS
ES CLA
HIGHW

LIGHT F
-5-93
PERSONNEL

JUDY
COLLINS
FOLK-SINGER/GUITARIST

8 P.M. SUNDAY, FEB. 18
GUTHRIE THEATRE

TICKETS: $4.15-$3.10-$2.05 at
Dayton's, Field-Schlick, Guthrie
(377-2224). Order now; they'll
go fast.

PRESENTED BY
WALKER ART CENTER

3 B 4
Sec. Row Seat
RESERVED
DAYTON'S 8th FLOOR AUDI.
THURSDAY
EVG. AUG. 4
McGill Graphic Arts

ANNOUNCES
ERE PRODUCTIONS, INC. PRESENTS
EO SAYER
L GUESTS THE NEW COMMANDER CODY BAND

DRALION
CIRQUE DU SOLEIL®

O'SHAUGHNES
FRIDAY, JULY

STANDING

IN THE

WINGS

STANDING

IN THE

WINGS

MY LIFE ON

(AND MOSTLY JUST OFF)

STAGE

FRED KROHN

ISBN: 978-0-578-92968-2
LCCN: 2021911569

Book design by Mayfly Design
Edited by Marly Cornell
Index by Ina Gravitz

CONTENTS

vii   Dedication

xi   Foreword (Gordon Lightfoot)

xiii   Preface

1   Chapter One .... Early Stages

14   Chapter Two .... Judy

18   Chapter Three .... Big Name Events

23   Chapter Four .... Open-Air Celebrations

32   Chapter Five .... Cameo Roles Act I

62   Chapter Six .... Political Stages

64   Chapter Seven .... Dylan and the Orpheum

84   Chapter Eight .... Enter the City of Minneapolis

89   Chapter Nine .... Saving of the State

99   Chapter Ten .... Rebirth of the Orpheum

105   Chapter Eleven .... Lightfoot

111   Chapter Twelve .... Marlene

119   Chapter Thirteen .... Ella

123   Chapter Fourteen .... Miss Lee

127   Chapter Fifteen .... A Tale of Two Cities

131   Chapter Sixteen .... Cameo Roles Act II

161   Chapter Seventeen.................................... The Lion Roars

169   Chapter Eighteen .... Much Ado About Jackie Mason

178   Chapter Nineteen .... The Arena Shows

185 Chapter Twenty .... Pantages vs. Shubert

199 Chapter Twenty-One .... Cameo Roles Act III

243 Chapter Twenty-Two .... Attempted Steal of Home

248 Chapter Twenty-Three .... Theatre Management Roulette

251 Chapter Twenty-Four ...... My Departure and Return to my Roots

259 Epilogue

263 Acknowledgments

265 About the Author

267 Appendices

Appendix 1: Live Shows Presented by Fred Krohn   **267**
(Chronological order)

Appendix 2: Live Shows Presented by Fred Krohn   **313**
(Alphabetical order)

Appendix 3: Minneapolis Broadway Seasons   **359**

365 Index

DEDICATION

SO MANY PEOPLE HAVE SUPPORTED ME ON THE MANY stages of my entertainment life (See Acknowledgments), but the people to whom I most owe my success in a decidedly unconventional business are my mother, **Lucy Snyder Krohn**; my brother, **Frank Ronald Krohn**; and my sister **Lisa Ellette Krohn**. I am also indebted to **Lee Lynch** and **Tom Hoch** for their support over many years.

My mother Lucy figured out long before I did that the arts might be a better choice for me than sports. She encouraged me to join clubs, participate in high school drama, and generally spend time on or near stages. When she realized in junior high that I seemed lost and sad, she quietly arranged for me to work as a bit player at the Salt Creek Playhouse in Hinsdale, Illinois, an experience which totally changed the trajectory of my life. She and I went to a number of Broadway shows and concerts together—most notably a Judy Garland concert at McCormick Place Convention Center in Chicago. And finally at the start of my concert promotion career, she welcomed the chance to be my gofer, helping to round up the dressing room and catering items required by artist riders. She had all the charisma that I lacked, and she was always the most upbeat and well-loved person backstage.

Without my older brother, Frank, my concert promotion career would not have gotten off the

Lucy Snyder Krohn

Frank Ronald Krohn

Lisa Ellette Krohn with Kris Kristofferson

ground, and I would have had to resort to practicing law (and not enjoying a minute of it). Well into a successful law career of his own, Frank gladly invested in my early shows when others would not, sometimes losing substantial sums in the process. But he stuck with me over the early years and hopefully recouped his losses and made some money over time. To me, the financial details were not paramount. But Frank was insistent on financial accuracy. He taught me that people with money will not deal with people with grand ideas but little cash unless they are treated fairly over time. That's probably the most important rule that led to the success of my career.

My sister Lisa started her career as a horse trainer and show rider, traveling all over the country, winning national shows, and trailering six or eight horses at a time. When she tired of that life, I invited her back to Minneapolis and suggested that she help me with advertising and public relations for the shows I was presenting. Since 1995 she has worked with me, taking on more and more responsibilities, and since my retirement, has served admirably as the director of Theatre Programming at Hennepin Theatre Trust. No way I could have accomplished what I did without her skills and her unflappable demeanor.

No one understood and supported my vision for the Hennepin Theatre District more than Tom Hoch. He devoted the majority of his working career to the development and success of the three Hennepin theatres, and led Hennepin Theatre Trust to new levels of recognition as its president and CEO. He has great political sense and was an effective lobbyist for the many initiatives we fostered over the time we worked together.

Finally, my success in the later portions of my career owes much to the generosity and confidence of my long-time friend and business partner, Lee Lynch. He and his wife Terry were there in both bad and good times, supporting me financially when needed, lending me their credibility, and finally sharing in the success of Historic Theatre Group when it was sold to national entities.

FOREWORD

BY GORDON LIGHTFOOT

N JANUARY 1972, JUST AS MY MUSICAL AND RECORDING career was breaking in the United States, I performed at O'Shaughnessy Auditorium in St. Paul, Minnesota, for a new and unproven promoter. His name was Fred Krohn. Little did I know then that Fred and I would be working together for the next fifty years.

I could tell from those first shows that Fred sincerely admired and respected the artists he presented. He did everything he could to make sure their gigs were successful. He had a law degree, but being a live-music promoter seemed to be his chosen career.

Over the years since our first meeting, I have come to know Fred both as a show producer and as a friend. I have followed his quest to save, acquire, and restore the State and Orpheum theatres, and his efforts to operate the Orpheum with my friend, Bob Dylan, and his brother, David Zimmerman. I have seen his reputation grow as he brought hundreds of shows to the people of Minneapolis-St. Paul, and to the rest of the country, culminating in his involvement with the World Premiere of Disney's *THE LION KING* at the Orpheum in 1997.

Fred has been one of my most loyal and supportive promoters for over half a century. I've performed nearly 100 concerts for him throughout the United States, and I don't recall a date when Fred was not there in person, making sure that everything I needed for a successful show was taken care of. We've had some interesting times.

I salute Fred's amazing career in live entertainment, and I feel you will find his exploits in establishing the Hennepin Theatre District, and bringing a celebrated list of legendary artists to his three theatres, captivating in *Standing in the Wings*.

PREFACE

T HE HAND-ADDRESSED ENVELOPE FROM MARLENE DIETRICH is addressed to "Fred Krohn, Impresario." Not "promoter" with all its negative connotations, but "Impresario." The only true impresario I am familiar with is the great Sol Hurok, so I am honored to be placed in his company by Ms. Dietrich.

The year is 1974, and I am twenty-eight years old and trying to wrap up a lingering law school education at the University of Minnesota while supporting myself by promoting concerts at various venues in the Minneapolis-St. Paul area. I am tall, rail thin, and bearded, with shoulder-length hair. My usual uniform is jeans, a flannel shirt, and a jeans jacket. But Marlene Dietrich herself seems to feel I am an Impresario.

The envelope Dietrich sends me contains her detailed notes on how she expects me to produce her show at O'Shaughnessy Auditorium in St. Paul, and a quick reading indicates that she will be a perfectionist. She will come in two days in advance of the show, rehearse my local sixteen-piece orchestra for a full day, and have approval over every aspect of the show's staging. Little did I know then what a stickler for detail she would prove to be, and how closely I would work with her and learn her legendary backstage secrets.

Marlene Dietrich in the elaborate hand-beaded dress she needed to be sewn into

Producing concerts is very personal to me, and that will continue throughout my career. I work only with artists I respect and am fascinated by, and I manage every detail of their local appearance—from their plane reservations, hotel requirements, and limo transportation, to getting their trunks through local customs—everything. I even design their ads and silkscreen their show posters. I pride myself on the fact that for my shows, these details are most often handled with attention and style. I welcome the personal contact that I am granted with great artists and I relish being told, as I personally deliver them back to the airport, that my skills have allowed them to do their best work. I look forward to presenting my stable of artists year after year, and having them remember me and spend time getting reacquainted with me and my family.

Fast forward to 2018, as I take my final bows in the entertainment business I have worked in and built for more than fifty years. How could those years have passed so quickly? How did the profession I have loved evolve into what it has become? How could a business where each local concert promoter is king of his own fiefdom become a national monopoly? How could two or three vast faceless corporate conglomerates have taken control of the industry? How could the art and the artists become secondary to the quarterly bottom line of these public corporations? How could so many true artists I have known, loved, and respected—artists as diverse as Ella Fitzgerald, Peggy Lee, Waylon Jennings, Gordon Lightfoot, Dolly Parton, and Carol King—been replaced by "artists" created instantaneously on the web or via television exposure and so ill-equipped to perform live?

I'm sitting on my dock in Northern Wisconsin, sipping my second gin and tonic and conjuring up a time when artists were legendary, Broadway was at its peak, and the theatrical venues the shows were booked into had glamour and history.

"THE NUMBER OF PEOPLE WHO WILL NOT GO TO A SHOW THEY DO NOT WANT TO SEE IS UNLIMITED."

—OSCAR HAMMERSTEIN

ONE OF THE CARDINAL RULES OF STANDING BACKSTAGE IN THE WINGS: IF YOU CAN SEE THE AUDIENCE, THE AUDIENCE CAN SEE YOU.

—THEATER LORE

THERE ARE NO BAD SHOWS, ONLY BAD DEALS.

—PROMOTER WORDS OF WISDOM

CHAPTER ONE

EARLY STAGES

AS I REMEMBER IT NOW, I'M IN SIXTH GRADE AT THE Hinsdale Junior High School in Illinois, and at the moment I am on the auditorium stage in front of the entire school. I am blindfolded and have some sort of radar device in my hands, and headphones over my ears. The topic of this school assembly is how planes and ships navigate. My task is to listen to the radar signals and determine how to navigate from one side of the stage to the other. I got myself into this unfortunate situation by being chosen to be the head of the Assembly Committee, one of the more nerdy committees at the Junior High. (I am also head of the Projection Committee, which is the nerdiest.)

The paid presenter of this program is encouraging me to listen to the various tones and plot a course across the stage to the north-northwest. Of course in my panic, I understand nothing he is saying. I know I am making a fool of myself, but I try my best. Before he can stop me, I walk blindfolded directly up to the lip of the stage, walk right off and crash into the front seats. Laughs ensue, but no damage other than to my ego. This is the low point of my tenure as head of Assemblies. The high point comes a few weeks later when I have the honor of delivering the famed "Romanoff" Stradivarius violin to the violinist David Rubinoff, who is onstage to open the program he calls "Rubinoff and his Magic

Violin." I am relieved that I don't step off the stage lip on this occasion.

In addition to these biweekly assemblies, I am also the king of the after-school sock hops held in the gym. I credit myself with very hip musical taste and the ability to completely control the mood of the dancers with my choice of songs. The 45s I play most often (from the home collection I play on my Webcor phonograph) include "Come Softly to Me" by The Fleetwoods, "Venus" by Frankie Avalon, "Dream Lover" by Bobby Darin, and "Cathy's Clown" by the Everly Brothers. To really get the place jumpin', I play "What'd I Say" by Ray Charles. I try to create just the right make-out atmosphere (encouraged by my older friends) by pulling down all the blinds in the gym, shutting off as many of the lights as the teachers allow, and mopping the entire gym floor so the white socks worn by both boys and girls do not get too dirty. Students hand me 45s of their favorite songs, and I play those from the students I most like or want to hang with.

My Projector Club gig is also useful to my status in junior high. Most of the school's audio-visual presentations are delivered to classrooms via 16 mm projection film, and I quickly learn more about Bell and Howell projectors than anyone in the school including the teachers: how to run film, how to replace a bulb, how to set them up and tear them down. So when a teacher has a movie he or she wants shown, I am the obvious go-to. Which means I am much loved by all the school's teachers and given pretty much free rein to be anywhere in the school without the need for hall passes.

I am also allowed to leave the school to walk over a block to the Hinsdale Health Museum and run their films from a private projector room in the back of their small theater. Depending on the group, I show a sex education film (learning more than I maybe should) or a science film like the Moody Bible Institute's film *Red River of Life,* which promises in its promo flyer that "You will see what makes your blood, your lifeline, carry its precious cargo of oxygen to every corner of your body. More importantly, you'll learn how the shed blood of Jesus Christ is the source of life in the Spirit."

I do not notice how inappropriately the religious messages are being mixed in with the supposedly scientific ones. Finally after the film, and as the climax of my show, I reveal the star attraction of the Health Museum—*Valeda The Transparent Lady*. I raise the projection screen, press the button to open her curtain, and bring to life a full-size naked glass female. As she talks in soothing tones, she lights up each of her organs, tells you what each does, and revolves to make sure you can see each one.

This is astounding to me. No matter how many times I run this show, she always awes me. She evidently awes others as well. In June 1960 I have the honor of showing *Valeda* to the Aga Khan when he visits the Health Museum. I meet him after the presentation and am told in hushed whispers that his followers weigh him each year and give him his weight in gold.

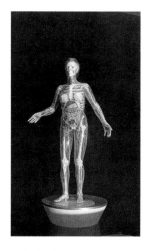

Valeda the Transparent Lady at the Hinsdale Health Museum

As a young kid, I am a paradox. I both crave attention and am scared when I receive it. I am charming and clever one-on-one and in small groups, but I panic when I have to interact with larger groups of people. I like attention but am also nervous when I receive it. These traits will follow me for the rest of my life.

I am the second of five kids, with an older brother, Frank, who is so handsome, talented, and athletic that it will always be impossible for me to compete with him. I realize I need my own skill set and find it not on sports teams but in music and theater. I love anything that might make me notable and interesting. I have three great younger siblings (Randy, Linda, and Lisa) whom I am close to. I take care of them most weekends while my parents are out socializing; and the four of us get into more trouble than my parents realize. One night we crawl up the exterior of our home all the way from the driveway, three floors up to the attic window of our large old house, and back down again.

I write many plays and skits for the four of us to stage for our parents. The most notable is a play adopted from the book, *Christmas This Way*, in which I as Santa (I give myself the best roles) sing out, *"Games and toys for girls and boys, I'll put them in my sleigh. There's work to do if I'd be through in time for Christmas Day."* The production is such an audience favorite that we stage it several years in a row.

Just before I turn eleven, I have another life-changing experience. I've lived for nearly five years in Hinsdale after moving from Pennsylvania. My mom is involved in a bunch of village projects, including the newly opened Hinsdale Community House and the Hinsdale Youth Center. She knows everyone. Right now the Youth Center, serving the junior high crowd, is in crisis with serious money problems, and it will either have to raise money fast, or close. The board decides to stage a concert by the beloved trumpet player, Louis Armstrong, at the Hinsdale High School gym. Students and their parents will have to sell the tickets ($3.50 and $2.25); and if the show does not make enough money to pay the Youth Center's budget deficit, it will have to shut down.

As the date of the show (March 20, 1957) approaches, there is a frenzy of selling, and finally the show sells out 4,200 tickets. My mom and I go over to the gym on the afternoon of the concert, and we work with others to set up the stage, arrange the folding chairs, and watch the contractor set up the sound and lighting. Then Satchmo and his band show up to rehearse and do a sound check.

They're all friendly folks, and we have a great time listening to them. Finally someone in the band asks whether I might be willing to help the maestro by handing him white hankies when he needs them. I'm told he will be working up a sweat during his two-hour show, and that he also needs to wipe his lips. Especially his upper lip, which has a large and noticeable callus on it from all the playing he does.

"Nothing I would rather do," I say.

I am given a pile of hankies, instructed to fold them into neat squares and place them on a small table just to the right of the two-foot-high stage where Satchmo will be playing. Armstrong says that he will come over to me between songs with an old hankie, and I am to take that and replace it with a clean folded cloth.

The show is amazing. Satchmo and his band play two complete sets and several encores. Armstrong goes through twenty or more hankies, all exchanged flawlessly. Having been so close to the stage, and with the rapport that I know Satchmo and I have developed, I am forever bitten by the kind of excitement that only a live show can generate.

I am the particular pet of my grandparents on my mother's side and often spend large chunks of my summers living with them in Bethlehem, Pennsylvania. My grandfather, Corson Snyder, is a Lutheran minister with his own church. Though I don't quite get religion, it's clear that he is the focal point of the church. I love attending his services with my grandmother, Lucy ("Big Lucy"). My mother is "Little Lucy." My job prior to each summer church service is to distribute paper fans on wooden sticks to the pews if it's forecast to be hot that morning. I then join Corson and Lucy in the church's sacristy while he dons his vestments and prepares for the service.

I really love the special access I have as a six-year-old to all the church's secret places. At the end of each service I stand beside of Rev. Snyder as the parishioners file out and greet him. I am not sure that "all the world's a stage," but I am pretty sure that my grandfather's church is.

After my grandfather retires, he becomes what he calls a "supply pastor"—a retired minister who serves rural Pennsylvania churches that do not currently have a minister. As kid of twelve, I travel with Corson and Lucy to small countryside parishes and, with large metal keys provided earlier in the week, open the church and conduct a service. Corson preaches, Lucy schmoozes with the churchgoers; there is no gossip that escaped her; she loved to talk. I run the church—ushering,

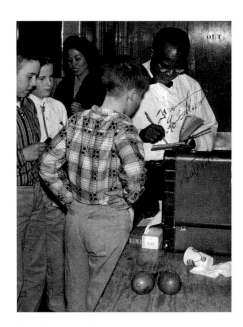

Satchmo signing autographs for my friends and me (PHOTO BY SWISS PHOTOGRAPHER MILAN SCHIJATSCHKY)

taking the offering, counting it, and then depositing it on the following Monday. Kind of a traveling religious show, and in retrospect much akin to running a theater.

My mom and grandparents encourage me to play music and sign up for school plays and musicals. My piano teacher, Wellington du Schiller, is a show biz vet who teaches me to play songs not by reading sheet music but via "lead sheets," which have only the melody and the chord progressions, and I ad lib the rest. He runs me through all the C chords (major, minor, diminished, augmented, major 7th, etc., and then does the same for the other piano notes, so I can play in any key. Later on I use these chords to recreate the tricky harmonies that my idol, Burt Bacharach, uses in his songs. My teacher is perfect for me, and I will play songs via lead sheets for the rest of my life.

In high school, I fall in with the artsy crowd and am involved in the Drama Club and the Marching Band. My most notable role in a school play is The Sewer Man in *THE MADWOMAN OF CHAILLOT*. Dressed in my dad's fly-fishing boots, which come up to my armpits, my character lives in the Paris sewers and helps the Madwoman, Countess Aurelia, fight off the forces that plan to destroy the Paris sewer system in order to get their hands on the oil that is supposedly under them. I am on stage at the start of the second act for only one fairly lengthy monologue, but it's funny and it usually gets me applause. However while I like being on stage, I know that I am far from a natural. I have stage fright before each show. Maybe just offstage is the place for me.

Our family always seems to have a dog, and I always seem to be assigned the responsibility of caring for it. Our first dog in Hinsdale is Pat, an Irish setter who is smart and affectionate, but loves to run away. She is gone for days at a time. I take her to obedience class to cure her of this habit, and in the process she becomes pretty skilled and obedient. My older brother, Frank, who it seems to me has not done a whole lot of her training, determines to enter her in Hinsdale's "Most Obedient Dog" contest, and he wins. Sadly, Pat runs away one fall day, and we don't

"Big Lucy," my grandmother; "Little Lucy" my mother; and Rev. Corson Snyder, my grandfather, with me in the summer 1950

see her for two weeks. Finally we get a call saying her body has been found in a cornfield and that it appears that she has been shot by a shotgun. Upon questioning, the farmer states that he did not know what kind of animal it was, and shot her. Very sad time for everyone in our family.

We get a new dog the next spring—our first of many golden retrievers—with the pedigree name of Lady Buffington of Scottwell. We call her Buffy. I latch onto her, take her to obedience classes, and train her until she's perfect. Then I enter her in the "Most Obedient Dog" contest. The event has become much more competitive since my brother and Pat won; it's obvious that there are some pretty smart dogs entered. But after three rounds of judging, Buffy and I are declared the winners. We get a nice article and photo in the *Hinsdale Doings*, the local paper. At the ceremony to present the trophy is one of my favorite actors, Leo G. Carroll, who stars in one of my favorite television shows, *Topper*. Mr. Carroll is appearing in a play at the Salt Creek Playhouse downtown.

On TV, Mr. Carroll plays Cosmo Topper, a bank executive, who buys a house that is haunted by George and Marion Kirby

Fred, his dog Buffy, and
Leo G. Carroll

and their alcoholic St. Bernard, Neal, who per the running joke
has a small cask of martinis around his neck. And only Cosmo
can see and hear these apparitions. His wife Henrietta can't, so
she can't figure out why objects are moving about her living room
on their own. Hilarity ensues.

Mr. Carroll agrees to pose for a photo with Buffy and me, and
later signs an autograph, "Leo G. Carroll, Topper to You."

Note: In March 2010, I brought legendary composer and lyricist Stephen Sondheim to Minneapolis for an onstage conversation, and two "six degrees" incidents occurred. I met him at the baggage claim, took him to his limo, and we rode to downtown Minneapolis together. On the way, I asked if he could guess what my favorite Sondheim work was, and he made several guesses. *WEST SIDE STORY? SWEENY TODD?*

I said no to both, and said my favorite was *Topper*. I happened to know the trivia that his first show-biz job was writing the first season of the *Topper* television show I loved. He was amazed that I knew. Later, when we were both backstage, talking with a local Broadway reviewer, the critic mentioned that my niece was Lindsey Vonn, the Olympic skier. Sondheim's reaction was instant and positive. He said his partner was a huge fan of Lindsey and was right then bidding on a ski gate on the internet. I told him that I had just been to the Winter Olympics in Vancouver and had several banners I had designed and waived on the day of her Downhill Gold victory, and that I would be honored to send one to his partner. There ensued several emails with Sondheim, and I got his New York address and sent it along.

During the summer of my sixteenth year, I find I have fewer friends and not much to occupy myself. My pals from grade school are transitioning to girls and dating, and I am not. My mom notices and, as per usual, figures out something I would never have been able to arrange, but which will change my life and generate a lifelong love of live theater. One afternoon in June she tells me that we are going to make a trip to downtown Hinsdale and meet some people she thinks I would like. We park in front of the Hinsdale Movie Theater, where my friends and I go to watch movies each Saturday afternoon. But each summer, the theater becomes the Salt Creek Playhouse, with live plays and musicals featuring B and C-level stars—a different show each week.

We walk from the lobby into the darkened theater. There on the stage are Imogene Coca, her husband King Donovan, and a small cast rehearsing a play for its opening in two days.

We walk slowly down the aisle and up to the front of the darkened theatre, trying to be as quiet as possible, and suddenly I step on something large. An animal death howl disturbs the quiet, the rehearsal stops abruptly, the lights come up, and Imogene and King come running down the aisle to see whether their black French poodle is okay. That's my introduction to a star I know and revere from watching television with my mom. Once they know their dog is not harmed, they greet us warmly and ask whether I might be the theater intern that they need to take a bit part in their show.

Before I can say anything, my mom says, "Why, yes, this is Fred."

Mom departs, and the show's stage manager hands me a script with my part marked up. The play is called *UNDER THE SYCAMORE TREE*. He explains that all the characters are Brown Ants, that Imogene is The Queen Ant, and King Donovan is The Scientist who is trying to destroy the ant colony with DDT. I will play The Queen's Guard Ant who, I am relieved to learn, has just a bunch of one-sentence lines, such as "As you command, my Queen," and "Yes, Your Highness." Playing Worker Ants are King Donovan's three kids, Mark, Josh, and Deborah Donovan, who are all around my age.

We go backstage and I am assigned a dressing room mirror and taught how to apply pancake makeup and eye coloring. And finally, I am given black tights, a black skin-tight top, a black head cover with little antennas, and a black-and-white-striped tunic. I am asked to change into the ant costume and come up to the stage to meet the other actors. The cast welcomes me, and I join their community for a week.

I quickly become fast friends with Mark, Josh, and Debb, and am invited to have dinner with them and their parents at a nearby motel. The place is pretty much a dump, and I call my

Fred on right as the Queen's Guard Ant

mom to see whether the kids can spend time at our house to let them escape. They come for dinner and end up staying with us all week. They put their stuff under our grand piano and sometimes one or more of them sleeps under there as well. The three are very much L.A. kids; they have a pretty liberal attitude and think they are way cooler than Midwest kids. If they like something, they say it's "bitchin'," which my mom at first does not approve

(*left*) Imogene Coca and King Donavan. (*right*) Margaret O'Brien.

of, but after Josh explains that it's not dirty, allows all of us to use the word by the end of their stay. I sense from our discussions that King and Imogene are thrilled to have their kids staying with us, so they can have some time alone.

Opening night goes well. I don't flub any of my lines or stage directions, so the leads and the stage manager are happy with me. We have a cast dinner after the show, and I am slipped a glass of white wine by one of the leads, even though I am only sixteen. The pancake makeup causes my skin to break out and gets all over the costume, but by the end of the week I get pretty proficient at keeping the layers very thin, and off my black turtleneck.

Josh, Mark, Deb, and I spend the week going swimming and to the movies, and I am able to drive them around in my mom's new light-blue Pontiac Tempest LeMans convertible. My mom insists that she take us into Chicago to see the Shedd Aquarium and the Museum of Science and Industry.

The loss of these new friends after just a week is hard on both Mom and me, but we stay in touch with the Donovans, and I continue to work at the Salt Creek Playhouse for the remainder of the summer. I have a bit role in the musical *GIGI* starring former child star, Margaret O'Brien (who I love from the Judy Garland film, *Meet Me in St. Louis*). She and that crew are as nice and welcoming as my first cast. After that summer, I conclude that Ethel Merman is right: there are no people like show people.

CHAPTER TWO

JUDY

N THE SUMMER OF MY JUNIOR YEAR IN HIGH SCHOOL, THE talk of my artsy crowd is that Judy Garland is bringing her renowned live concert to the Arie Crown Theater at McCormick Place. My mother and I both love Judy based on all the variety shows we watched together on television. Both of us want to be at the show.

I ride the Burlington commuter train to downtown Chicago early one Saturday morning, walk over to the Lyric Opera House, which is selling the tickets, and am among the first in line. I buy two top-price $10 tickets in Row AA, which I am certain is at the very front of the theater, but later find that it's the row after Row Z. I ride back to Hinsdale with my treasure and mark Wednesday, November 7 on my calendar. The *Chicago Tribune* reports that the show sold out in one day.

My circle of friends is pretty impressed that I have tickets to the show, and are disappointed that they did not have me buy some for them. Bill, a friend of mine, asks if I will take along a Garland photo for her to sign in return for his telling me some information that will allow me to go backstage with no one noticing. I agree, and he tells me that built into the audience-right proscenium of the Arie Crown Theatre is a small hidden door with no

Ad from the *Chicago Tribune*

handle that will allow me to pass quickly from the audience to the backstage wing. He tells me exactly how to find and activate it.

The day of the show finally arrives and, with Bill's photo and mailing envelope in hand, my mom and I drive to McCormick Place. Our seats are okay, on the main aisle about halfway back in the cavernous theatre. We arrive in plenty of time and I wander down front to casually scope out the existence of the door. I find the faint outline of what could be the door and lean into the area with my back. It moves!

The concert is all we had hoped for. Garland starts the show in seemingly poor health and weak voice, but with the spirit and determination she is known for, she turns potential disaster into triumph, with everyone in the hall pulling for her to succeed.

As the show is coming to an end, the orchestra is vamping "Over the Rainbow," and the audience is waiting to see whether Judy has anything left for encores. Gripping the photo, I join a throng of her fans who are moving down the main aisle to get closer to the stage. I sneak to the right, place my back against the secret proscenium door, and lean in. The small door springs open, I fall backward, and the door closes behind me.

I am totally alone backstage save a couple of stagehands, the onstage orchestra, and Judy in the wings on the other side of the stage. The vamp crescendos, and Judy rushes back onto the stage to a tumult of applause. By now the entire house is standing. Judy does two final encores, then totally spent, walks off the stage toward me. She stands offstage within ten feet of me, pauses, rushes back for one final bow, then rejoins me backstage, giving me a quizzical look. The main curtain closes. She runs her fingers through her hair and a cloud of white powder flies into the air. She goes to a table, picks up a pack of Salems, lights one, and smokes it for a minute while the last applause dies down and the house lights come up.

Finally she asks me what I am doing backstage. I tell her that I am a big fan and that I would like to talk to her and have her sign a photo. She motions for me to follow her into her dressing

Judy Garland

room and instructs me to sit in the outer area while she changes. Ten minutes later, she comes back out in a chenille robe with all her makeup removed. She looks very tired; any resemblance to the high-energy entertainer I have just witnessed is gone. The energy she has spent doing the show has completely drained her.

We talk for a minute about the set list and what I thought were the best songs, and then there's a knock on the door. Irv Kupcinet, the noted columnist for the *Chicago Sun Times*, kisses her check, and they begin talking. I sit quietly for forty-five minutes and take in the conversations; they hardly know I am there. Irv finally gets up, says goodbye, and leaves.

I rise as well, thank Judy for allowing me to stay, and ask that she sign my friend's photo. We find a pen, and she kindly provides her signature. I give her a hug, and then I'm back on the massive stage, now nearly empty. I leave via the stage door and find the parking lot. My mom's car is the only one left in the huge lot. She is cool about the long delay, and seemingly has not worried that something bad might have happened to me.

Even though I feel guilty, I decide then and there to keep my friend's photo. I have it to this day, still addressed to him with four uncancelled four-cent stamps on the envelope. If you read this, Bill, my apologies.

(*opposite*) Photo that Judy Garland signed

CHAPTER THREE

BIG NAME EVENTS

WHEN I ARRIVED ON THE CARLETON COLLEGE campus in the fall 1964, a new and challenging experience awaited me. In high school, I had been on the student council, was active in student activities, and took a number of advanced classes in order to get into a good college. But at Carleton, I was far from the brightest student, and had to start at the bottom rung in joining student activities. I applied to become a member of the Carleton Co-op Board (which basically ran everything on campus) and was not chosen. But because I seemed to know something about putting on concerts and large events, I was selected to head up the "Big Name Events" committee. That group was then more of a concert production and arrangements committee, helping stage the classical concerts that the college spoon-fed the students.

The first two shows I worked on during the fall semester were Indian Sitarist Ravi Shankar and jazz drummer Art Blakey and his Jazz Messengers, both in the Skinner Memorial Chapel. We had to set up the stage extensions to provide a larger performing space, and set up some rudimentary sound and lighting for each show. Both Shankar and Blakey were impressive shows (and I would work with both again over the course of my career), but our committee had little or no say in their actual bookings. The first artist we helped select was a very young Judy Collins in

January 1965. At that time she was touring colleges as a solo artist, playing only guitar and wearing a short cocktail dress and a semi-bouffant hairdo. Quite a different image from the long dresses and hippie Earth Mother hairstyle she wore during the many shows I booked her for after college.

We at Carleton were privileged to have as a benefactor the philanthropist Laura Jane Musser. Musser lived in Little Falls, Minnesota. Her father, lumber-baron Richard Drew Musser, had been on the Carleton Board of Trustees for many years. Laura Jane was musically trained and knew a number of classical artists, including Marian Anderson and the young Van Cliburn. Musser sponsored a number of classical concerts at Carleton, including a notable appearance by Cliburn in the new Carleton gymnasium in March 1965. Since the concert was certain to sell out, the Big Name Events committee had to figure out how to stage the recital with enough amplification to allow everyone to hear the piano, but not so much as to echo throughout the acoustically questionable building.

Cliburn and Laura Jane Musser appeared at the gym on the afternoon of the concert, Cliburn did a long sound check, and they determined that with his dynamic technique, his Steinway piano filled the space without the need for sound reinforcement. His concert was superlative.

The next thing our committee scheduled was jazz pianist Thelonious Monk, again in the new men's gym. We set the gym just as we had for Van Cliburn, used the same Steinway grand piano, and awaited Monk's arrival. I knew of Monk's reputation as a bebop piano genius, but I also knew that he could be moody and very eccentric.

He arrived alone in front of the gym and immediately wanted

Judy Collins at Carleton College, January 21, 1965. (Photo from Carleton Algol Yearbook 1965)

to try the piano and see how the acoustics were going to be in such a large room. He had a small goatee and was dressed sharply with a suit, sunglasses, and a skullcap. He had three or four rings on his fingers, including a large one on the little finger of his right hand. But something immediately seemed off to me. I took him into the gym and onto our little platform stage where the college's magnificent nine-foot Steinway grand piano had been positioned.

He sat down and started to play some modern jazz riffs. He seemed to have an amazing piano technique when he wanted to use it, but was more often aggressive and discordant. With each phrase, his loose rings, especially the one on his pinky finger, hit the keys and made distracting noises. When he approved of the piano, we headed to a lounge office, which was to serve as his dressing room. He was difficult to communicate with, and I did not understand his jokes or his behaviors. He said he wanted to take a nap on the sofa and asked that I check in on him an hour before the show.

When I came back, he was awake but appeared very anxious, pacing back and forth in the room. As the time for his performance ticked down, his anxiety continued. Thinking he needed some fresh air, I suggested that we take a walk outside the gym and down to the Canon River.

Without a word he put on his shades, and walked with me, holding my arm, out the back door and around the soccer field to the river. We walked and talked for forty minutes or so, and finally he seemed to be more relaxed.

I asked him to show me his rings (big bulky gold things). I suggested that it might be wise for him to put some of them—especially the large gold ring on his little finger—in his pocket while he played. I told him that the college was very sensitive about its Steinway, and it would be my neck if his rings chipped the keys. He agreed.

We got back to the gym just before the 8:00 start time. I cued the house lights and walked him to the side of the stage. He walked right up onto the small platform to great applause, sat down, and did a very hip ninety-minute bebop concert. I can't say that I understood everything he did; but when he was on, he was the greatest.

I later learned that Monk had a history of mental lapses while on tour, which some attributed to bipolar disorder, others to Tourette syndrome, and complicated by the therapeutic drugs he was prescribed and the occasional overuse of alcohol. I of course had no clue about the reasons for his unusual behaviors, but was glad he was able to deliver a concert that allowed him to exhibit his great talent to our audience.

Our remaining '65–'66 shows included Flamenco guitarist Carlos Montoya, and pianist, singer, and composer, Mose Allison. In '66–'67, our artist list included violinist Isaac Stern (again thanks to Laura Jane Musser); local favorites Koerner, Ray, and Glover (who I had to dig out of a snowbank just outside Skinner Chapel where they had passed out); and the Paul Butterfield Blues Band.

During that school year, famed futurist and inventor of the geodesic dome, Buckminster Fuller, spent time on the Carleton campus. At a convocation event I helped set up, he was introduced by college President John Nason as "Fuckminster Buller." Of course the whole audience, and Buckminster himself, broke up and didn't calm down for ten minutes.

In spring 1968, as my graduation swan song, I decided to book some artists that were currently on the Top 40 (which in our market meant that they were being played on WDGY or its rival, KDWB). I worked with my friend and promoter, Harry Beacom. We arrived at a co-billing of The First Edition, who had a Billboard #1 hit with "Just Dropped in To See What Condition My Condition is In," and English artists The Foundations, who had the current hit "Baby, Now That I've Found You." I did several PR swings around the Northfield area to drum up sales, including to the Shattuck Military Academy in neighboring Faribault, where I was the cadets' luncheon speaker and got to play a couple of records as a part of my promo.

Sales were good as the day of the show arrived, and The First Edition and their crew arrived and set up their gear. But as the day sped by, The Foundations were no-shows. I called Harry Beacom in a panic. He was told by their agent that this was the first time they had been in the United States, and they had no idea it was that big. We were assured that they were en route to Northfield and should be there soon. A half-hour before showtime, I checked in with The First Edition's leader, Kenny Rogers (yes, that Kenny Rogers), told him my issue, and asked if he would be willing to open, rather than close, the show. He graciously agreed. At 8:00 he and his band mates began their show and ran through an hour's worth of their songs to nice applause. Then Kenny stepped off the small stage and told me that he could do two or three more songs, but they hadn't much more material than that. He would have to end his portion of the show at 9:30 PM.

We agreed that if The Association had not arrived by then, I would take the stage and let people know that our second band had gotten lost, and that they would not be performing. Sadly, that's what I had to do. The audience was polite (mainly because The First Edition had done such a good show) and left the gym. At 9:40 PM a rented station wagon pulled up in front of the gym, and The Foundations came running into the building in alarm. Their leader told me that they had gone to Northfield, Wisconsin, and only upon arrival there had realized their target was Northfield, Minnesota. So much for their first gig in the US.

While I didn't realize it then, the shows I produced as head of the Big Name Events Committee got in my blood; and while I had trained for a career in law, what I really wanted to do was work in live entertainment. Luckily I got my chance, my legal training proved to serve me well as a concert producer and saved me from fatal mistakes on many occasions.

CHAPTER FOUR

OPEN-AIR CELEBRATIONS

N THE SUMMER 1971, I WAS THREE YEARS OUT OF GRADUA-
tion from Carleton College, and a year out of my job in the
Office of Minnesota Governor Harold LeVander. I was attending law school at the University of Minnesota, but my heart
was not in it. I could not see myself practicing
law and trying to solve other people's problems
for the next forty years. I was kicking around,
looking for something interesting to do, having
worked with my mentor and friend, Bob Reid, at
Met Center on some shows, but not sure what
direction to go. I had faked a "Nhork Syndicate" press pass (Krohn spelled backward, and
C.C.S.—my grandfather's initials) just before I
took my grandparents to Expo 67 in Montreal.
Amazingly the fair had issued me a photo I.D.,
which we used to go to the front of the lines at
all of the fair pavilions. Armed with the press
pass plus the Expo 67 photo pass, I got backstage at most of the concert venues of that era
and "interviewed" a number of artists. Such an
outlandish "press pass" idea would not work in
today's industry, but it sure worked well back
then. My sister Lindy and I used the press pass

The press pass Expo 67 issued and my fake
press pass

(before the Expo addition) to get into the Beatles' famous 1965 press conference. We got there early and set up the chairs like we thought they should be arranged. Then just before the event, the police swept through and kicked us out because we were not on the approved list.

One of my first successful backstage forays using the Nhork pass came in July 1968. WDGY was sponsoring an "Aquatennial Spectacular" starring the "Aretha Franklin Review" at the old Minneapolis Auditorium. For shows I really wanted to see, my *modus operandi* was to immediately buy the best two seats I could for the show, then hope that I could use my press pass to get backstage at some point in the evening. As I recall the night, several local bands were opening the show, so I determined to get backstage during these preliminary sets and see if I could talk to Aretha prior to her performance. At the stage door, I showed the guard my two tickets (second row center, I still have them) and then flipped him my press pass, saying that I hoped to interview Aretha for a "national story."

He let me through, and I went upstairs to the side of the stage and hung out. I soon ran into The Sweet Inspirations, which featured Cissy Houston (Whitney's mother) and several of Dionne Warwick's cousins. I chatted them up and got their autographs. They welcomed the attention from "national" press people, since all of them envisioned themselves as future stars like Dionne and Aretha.

Then events took an odd turn. One of the Sweet Inspirations told me that Aretha was not feeling too well, and asked if I might interview her while I walked her around backstage. It soon became clear that many in the entourage were worried about Aretha's ability to perform that night. My job was to keep her awake until her set began. I took her arm, and we walked around the large backstage area and talked for an hour or more. She slowly seemed to come back to life.

Finally after 11:00 PM, she took the stage to do her show, and I watched from the wings. I must have watched her whole show from backstage because my two tickets were never torn in half by an usher. While by no means a perfect show, I recall being awed by Aretha's immense talent. We knew we were in the presence of a major star.

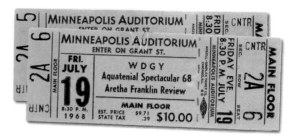

Aretha Franklin Concert Tickets

That period was when I got to know the only legitimate concert promoter in the area, Harry Beacom, who ran an organization known as Beacom and Associates. Harry was not a typical promoter type with jeans and a flannel shirt. He had more of a local businessman look, usually with nice pants, a dress shirt, and a blazer. Most of Harry's shows were at the old 8,000-seat Minneapolis Auditorium, and he seemed to handle all the artists I most respected. We knew each other pretty well from when I had bought some shows from Harry during my Carleton term as Big Name Events chair.

One night backstage, we discussed the possibility of an outdoor show that summer with a group of the most popular artists of the time. Although we had turned the corner from the '60s, there were still plenty of kids who liked '60's bands, and we felt they would come out for a full day's entertainment. We determined to do three shows during the summer 1971; and since Harry was working on marketing with Bob Dylan's brother, David Zimmerman, we thought it might be possible to get Dylan to participate.

We scheduled "Open Air Celebration I" for Saturday, June 26, after I persuaded the City of St. Paul to rent us the old Midway Stadium, a 30,000-seat facility, assuming we were allowed to fill the playing field with fans. Once we had the date and the venue, we started to find out who might want to play our show. To tempt Dylan to play the gig, we signed The Band as our headliner, then added John Sebastian, Delaney & Bonnie, Butterfield Blues Band, Muddy Waters, and local harp player, Tony Glover, who also MC'd. Unfortunately Dylan, despite having his band mates headlining the show, did not make an appearance.

We brought in a state-of-the-art sound system from Magnum Opus in Colorado, and built our own stage with four separate staging areas so we could be setting up the next artist while the current band was playing. We flew an ecology flag I designed and had custom-made, and we invited a number of Twin Cities peace groups, drug crisis experts, and community rights organizations to "table" in the stadium concourses, including American Friends Service, The Caucus to End the War, Planned Parenthood, and Minnesota Environmental Concerned Citizens. Finally, we set up a well-equipped and staffed field hospital with eight doctors and 130 medical and drug crisis experts for the day. Pharm House volunteers circulated through the crowd to spot problems.

Since we had all the concession rights (legal products only and no alcohol), I tried to bring in food items that our audience might like, including a lot of natural products. I even bought six juicers and huge bags of celery and carrots. I had my two sisters, Linda and Lisa, juice and sell various kinds of organic vegetables.

The result was an almost flawless day of music, which sold out 30,000 tickets. However, security outside for those who did not get into the show was more problematic. The St. Paul police had their hands full with gate crashers. We also had a guy climb the ecology flag flagpole, which was backstage. After taking in the view for ten or fifteen minutes, he took a dive onto the dirt forty feet below. I thought the worst as I saw him hit the ground like a rag doll and bounce around. But he was evidently so high that he felt no pain, and immediately got up and started to run around. We had him taken to a nearby hospital for observation, but we were told at the end of the day that he had no injuries or broken bones and was released to go home.

Our biggest logistics nightmare for these shows was getting all the artists and equipment to and from the airport. We had rented a couple of box trucks for equipment, and had a bunch of private cars and drivers to shuttle the artists and their crews back and forth. During Celebration II, my brother Randy had the task of driving Little Richard to the airport in my dad's 4-door

Delaney and Bonnie with The Band's Garth Hudson. PHOTO BY MIKE BARICH

Impala. Randy recalls that Little Richard sat in the front, was curious about his interest in playing drums, and was kind and low-key throughout. When they got to the airport, Little Richard reached into his sock and plucked out a $20 bill and handed it to him. Lifelong fan made right there.

One of my brother's friends had a little different experience driving one of the box trucks filled with equipment back to the airport. He took a side road out of Midway Stadium and tried to go under a circular train overpass. While the center of the bridge was high enough for the truck, the side was not. He slammed into the cement at a pretty slow speed, but fast enough to get the truck wedged in place. We got a tow truck to drag it free, and only minor damage was done to the band equipment. Luckily we had taken the insurance on the truck, so we escaped too much financial pain.

Based on the success with our first show, we moved ahead to "Open Air Celebration II 'Superball'" on Saturday, July 24. Our headliner this time was The Allman Brothers, which still included its all-star line-up of Duane Allman (killed in a motorcycle

John Sebastian at Open Air Celebration I. Photo by Mike Barich

accident later that year), Gregg Allman, Dickey Betts, Jamoe Johnson, and Berry Oakley. Filling out the bill were Poco, It's A Beautiful Day, Little Richard, Long John Baldry, Joy of Cooking, Redeye, and the Mike Quatro Jam Band. Again it was a sellout and a musical success (Duane Allman is quoted as saying it was the finest musical event he had ever seen). But again, the outside security was difficult, with those unable to get into the show throwing beer bottles at the St. Paul police. That coverage made it difficult for me to hold onto our lease for Open Air Celebration III, even though we had established such a good reputation among artists that we had been able to secure Jefferson Airplane to headline. Public reaction to the hippies and druggies making trouble finally caused then "super mayor," Mayor Charlie McCarty, to bow to some public pressure and pull the lease on our

third show. We attempted to move it to Met Stadium, but after controversy followed us, that lease too was pulled. We cancelled the third show.

I was never privy to Harry Beacom's internal finances, but after the Open Airs, I got the impression that cash continued to be a problem. We still promoted occasional shows at the old Minneapolis Auditorium and elsewhere, but Harry seemed to be going to his investors much more often. Since I might have been the most presentable staff member, other than Harry, I was often sent down the street a few blocks to get money from Harry's major investor, Morris Chalfen. Chalfen owned the *Holiday on Ice Show* and was a part owner of the Minneapolis Lakers. He was an interesting guy to talk to. I would walk in to his office and he would regale me with the latest ice show gossip or pro basketball

The Allman Brothers at Open Air Celebration II.
PHOTO BY MIKE BARICH

Promoter Harry Beacom with Little Richard at Open Air Celebration II. PHOTO BY MIKE BARICH

news, then say, "I suppose Harry sent you down here for more money?."

After I told him he was correct, we'd have a discussion about the next few shows we had on tap and argue about whether they were money-makers. Morrie did not follow the rock world, so his opinions were not based on knowledge. I think he was just testing me to see if I was really behind the acts we were promoting. Eventually Morrie would get out his big check book and write me a $10,000 check, which Harry was waiting anxiously for when I got back to the office.

Harry Beacom's financial downfall seemed to come with his decision to book an entire tour of the avant-garde trumpeter, drummer, composer, and bandleader, Don Ellis. He and his Don Ellis Orchestra had received some recognition for his score for the movie *The French Connection*, but Don was hardly a household name in 1971. His music was challenging, shifting keys and time signatures at will. I liked Don, but he proved too much for many of the cities Harry took them to, and the tour collapsed due

to poor ticket sales. So after several legal skirmishes, including working with noted attorney Melvin Belli on the aftermath of the Celebration III cancellations, Harry quit the business, moved to Los Angeles with his wife, Barbara, and got into the custom drapery business. In doing so, Harry created a vacuum that I sought to fill.

Beacom & Assoc. Staff at Minneapolis Press Club

CHAPTER FIVE

CAMEO ROLES ACT I

SOME OF THE ARTISTS I HAVE WORKED WITH MADE strong impressions. Below are my recollections of some of the most memorable of the shows and artists I worked with over the early years of my career. Other reminiscences are included in Cameo Roles Acts II and III later in the book.

DELANEY & BONNIE BRAMLETT

Very early in my career, I booked Delaney & Bonnie & Friends at O'Shaughnessy Auditorium. I had seen the Bramletts at the old Minneapolis Auditorium and loved the possibility that almost anyone, most notably Eric Clapton, might be one of the "Friends" at their show. They had such good ties to Leon Russell, the Allman Brothers, George Harrison, and many others, that it seemed like a good bet that someone amazing might show up at their gig. That was not to be, but they did have a great band. What makes the show memorable was their demand upon arrival that they would not do the show unless I scored them a certain quantity of an illicit drug. I was clueless and thought I was going to be screwed, but luckily one of my gofers knew someone who knew someone, and the show went on.

THE ALLMAN BROTHERS

One of the first acts I worked with Harry Beacom on was the first incarnation of The Allman Brothers: Duane and Gregg, Dickey Betts, Butch Trucks, Jamoe Johnson, and Berry Oakley. They were playing at the old Minneapolis Auditorium, and after a couple of long sets, they wanted to head to their favorite Mexican restaurant in Minneapolis, Little Tijuana near 26th and Lyndale. I was designated as their driver, and we loaded up the van and headed out. We arrived just before midnight, and they started to eat and party wildly. The restaurant owner got everyone but us out at closing time, but allowed the Allmans to continue to eat and drink well into the night. I tried to stay sober since I was their driver, but they insisted I join in. Finally at about 3:00 AM, I loaded them back into the van and took them to their hotel, the old Capp Towers on Nicollet, letting them know they would need to be ready for my airport pickup at 6:00 AM. I went back to Harry's office for a brief rest, and amazingly, when I arrived back at the Capp Towers, they were in front and waiting for me. They sure knew how to party. I worked with them one more time—the second Open Air Celebration in 1971. But since that was a daylight gig, and they were flying out right afterward, we did not get back to Little Tijuana. Only months later, I learned of Duane's tragic death in a motorcycle accident. The Allmans were, I think, the greatest live band I have ever witnessed.

JUDY COLLINS

I first worked with Judy Collins when she played the concert for me at the Skinner Chapel on the Carleton College campus—one of my first shows as head of the Carleton "Big Name Events" Committee. Judy was just developing a following. Her act then consisted of just herself and her guitar. She wore a tasteful blue cocktail dress and a very "straight" hairdo. Not much Earth

Mother going on then. But her voice was pure, and her songs were magnificent. The capacity crowd loved her. Once I started promoting shows myself, she was the third show I did after Gordon Lightfoot and Delaney & Bonnie. By this time Judy had a great band, long hair, and a very folky long dress. She played some new songs on the piano that were stunning. I was so impressed with her that weeks before her next show for me, I had a jeweler friend custom-make a cloisonne pendant for her that contained the Colorado state flower, the blue columbine. I gave it to her before the show, and she professed her admiration for the fine work and my thoughtfulness. But after she and her band departed, I found it in her dressing room. I have it to this day. Fifty years later, I am still disappointed that she left it behind.

KRIS KRISTOFFERSON AND RITA COOLIDGE

Backstage at the first show I ever promoted myself, I spent some time after the second of two shows with Canadian troubadour, Gordon Lightfoot. We had a couple of Irish whiskeys, and he was generous enough to share some career advice with me. He was also just starting his career but had already learned things about agents and record labels, which he shared with me. When asked who I should promote next, he gave me two names: Kris Kristofferson and Anne Murray. I immediately booked both, and his advice paid off well. Kris was touring with Rita Coolidge and a great band, and the sparks between Kris and Rita were obvious when they shared a mic and sang love ballads. I toured the Upper Midwest with Kris and Rita, and fondly recall a Sunday breakfast with everyone in a Duluth hotel coffee shop when Kris's song "Sunday Morning Coming Down" came on the radio. Amazing to be sitting with him at that moment.

Kris is the person who authored one of my favorite put-downs, which he used on the producer of *A Star is Born*, which Kris and Barbra Streisand starred in. At a press conference where producer

Kris Kristofferson and Fred Krohn backstage at the Pantages Theatre, 2017

and then-current Streisand squeeze, Jon Peters, got into a public argument with Kris, Kris reportedly responded by saying, "If I want any more shit out of you, I'll squeeze your head." I still use the quote in appropriate situations. Kris is hands down one of the greatest songwriters and most gifted performers I have worked with.

Anne Murray and Fred Krohn at O'Shaughnessy Auditorium, St. Paul, 1974

ANNE MURRAY

The second of Gordon Lightfoot's recommendations was Anne Murray, who was then referred to as the "Canadian songbird." She always won the Canadian Juno Award for female vocalist, and Gord won it for best male vocalist. They were two of the few Canadian artists gaining traction in the United States. She was, at age twenty-eight, one of the most wholesome and natural artists I had ever met. She had good business sense and surrounded herself with pros. Every show I ever did with her was a crowd pleaser, and she went out of her way to meet her fans after each show like old-school county artists always do. Early in her career, she had a lesbian following, and women always wanted to get closer to her. I recall one night when one of her band members brought a woman back to his room, and in the middle of the night the woman tried to sneak from his room to Anne's, only to be discovered by the band member. Anne was one of the nicest and most naturally talented artists I have worked with. I wish she were still touring, because her fans are still devoted to her.

LEO KOTTKE

I love folk and instrumental artists, and I often booked them into smaller college gigs so I could get to know them and handle their bigger shows. Leo Kottke was one of my favorites, both for his quirky but amazing guitar technique, and for his offbeat humor. I recall driving up to Duluth with Leo, doing a quick sound check at the Marshall Performing Arts Center, and then grabbing dinner at the Chinese Dragon, Leo's favorite Chinese restaurant in downtown Duluth. He always prefaced his order with a statement to the waitperson that he was very sensitive to monosodium glutamate, and that if he consumed even a small amount, he would get a severe headache, flushing and sweating. The cook came out of the kitchen and assured him personally that he would not use MSG in Leo's dish. But halfway through his show, Leo began to get very red and sweaty, and it was obvious to me that the cook's promise had not been honored. Leo was just able to finish the show, and I loaded him and his guitar into my car and got him to Minneapolis. He slept all the way back and was just starting to feel okay as I got him home. Skilled instrumentalist, sometime vocalist, and very funny guy.

CAROLE KING

When I brought Carole King to Northrop Auditorium in 1975, she was still riding on the success of her multimillion-selling *TAPESTRY*. The tour of college campuses was wildly successful, and we were able to sell out two shows at the (then) 5,000-seat venue. I still have some of the promotional paraphernalia for the shows that Lou Adler's Ode Records sent me. It consisted of what they mistakenly thought that college kids might want: pencils, tablets, and large sheets of heavy paper with her logo with instructions on how to fold them into textbook covers. How times have changed. I recall that Carole was shy, but in a great mood, and she had a very handsome young blond guy with her, who she referenced when she sang a song she had written for him. Something about a golden boy. Legendary composer, and despite a nice but hardly spectacular voice, *Tapestry* made her one of the first real female singer-songwriters.

JESSE COLIN YOUNG

Jesse, leader of the Youngbloods, was very popular in Minneapolis in the 1970s. He headlined the Northrop Auditorium several times for me, and was usually very nice and friendly per his song, "Get Together," which advocated that everyone "love one another right now." But on the afternoon of one of his shows, he walked onto the stage for sound check, saw that I had gotten him 3.2 beer rather than full-alcohol beer, picked up a six-pack, and threw it at me. It hit me in the back and crashed to the stage floor. In that moment, he did not quite measure up to the lyrics of his song.

THE MANHATTAN TRANSFER

In 1976, after several years of work and a personal cold call on their agent, Aaron Russo in Hollywood, after he refused to return my calls, I was able to book The Manhattan Transfer, a close-harmony quartet with style. Not the typical artists of that period, but unique and with broad appeal. Two guys and two girl singers plus a small supporting band. Very '40's arrangements and attitude.

They seemed to come out of the same place Bette Midler did, and they had the same manager. Perfect act for the venue I was using most often, O'Shaughnessy Auditorium in St. Paul. I decided to make a statement with all my arrangements for this show, giving the posters and programs a '40's look, and renting a vintage Packard limo to get the group from the venue to the after-party I had planned for them at the very Art Deco Scotties on 7th nightclub in Minneapolis. Their show over, I escorted the group to the Packard, parked in the quad in front of the theater. They got in, and the driver attempted to start the car. Nothing. The battery was dead. So all five of us got out of the limo and pushed it across the quad until the driver was able to pop the clutch and get it started. Then we drove, laughing, to the after-party. All agreed that it was one of my best promotional efforts to date.

TAJ MAHAL

In fall 1977, I booked the blues artist, Taj Mahal, into the brand-new, 400-seat West Bank lecture hall on the University of Minnesota campus. Seemed like a good idea at the time, but the gig almost got me kicked off the U of M campus. I had to bring in all the sound and lighting equipment I needed for the show, and it was time-consuming to supervise its setup and sound check in a room that had never been used for a concert. While we were completing these tasks, Taj and his band showed up, and I showed them to a nice glass-fronted faculty lounge with showers and toilets that the U had allowed me to use as a dressing room. It was one floor down from the stage entrance to the hall. Because the lounge was brand new, I insisted to Taj and his band that there be absolutely no smoking (even though I knew Taj's marijuana smoking was legendary). Everyone said they understood, and I went back to the tech setup. An hour later, I went back down to the lounge, and the front area of the room looked like a dense fog had rolled in. Inside, in front of the glass, Taj and band were smoking the largest spliffs I had ever seen. Acting fast to avoid the building manager, I got them outside and quickly aired out the room. Luckily, no damage had been done to the new furnishings, and no U of M officials showed up. But if they had, I'm sure I would have been excluded from any further U of M facility rentals. Great show however, so the smokes had their desired effect—and an iconic artist I have worked with on many occasions since then, most recently in 2017 in an amazing pairing with Keb' Mo'.

STEVE MARTIN

Steve Martin was just breaking big when I booked him into O'Shaughnessy Auditorium for a show. It was his balloon sculpture and arrow through the head period when he had some great exposure on *Saturday Night Live*. Steve arrived in the city alone, and since it was close to the airport, I booked him into the old Hotel Sofitel, which had a great reputation both for its rooms and its great restaurants. I picked him up at the airport personally, and he wanted to go directly to the theater. He was carrying his trademark banjo and a bunch of other novelties and magic tricks, which he laid out for use during the show. He was so funny and engaging that the audience would not let him go, insisting via long-standing ovations that he come back and do more material. Amazingly, when the show finally ended, Steve raced out the stage door, greeted his fans as they were returning to their cars, and did another half-hour of material from a small balcony just outside the backstage. He earned his catchphrase of a "wild and crazy guy" that night. The next morning, I met Steve for great breakfast at the Sofitel (something that would not be possible in these highly corporate and controlled times), and took him back to the airport for his flight.

WAYLON JENNINGS

Anything could happen at Waylon's live shows, which I found out during a ten-day tour with Waylon, his wife Jessi Colter, and Waylon's band The Waylors. Before this tour, I had promoted a sold-out Waylon show at Met Center (July 15, 1977), and the energy it generated teetered the show on the knife edge between amazing and dangerously out of control. (My dad was there with his second wife, Connie, who didn't feel safe in the crowd. So he took her home and came back alone for the remainder of the

Steve Martin and Fred Krohn backstage at O'Shaughnessy Auditorium, 1977

MUSICSPHERE IN COORDINATION WITH NEW COUNTRY WLOL 1330 RADIO PRESENTS

WAYLON JENNINGS
JESSI COLTER · THE WAYLORS

WITH SPECIAL GUESTS **ASLEEP AT THE WHEEL**

WLOL

MET CENTER · FRIDAY, JULY 15 · 8 PM
TICKETS $7.50, $6.50, AND $5.50 AT ALL DAYTON'S STORES, MSA TOO
IN COFFMAN UNION, AND AT MET CENTER BOX OFFICE (854-8585.

show). Waylon was on his game, and the Met Center show is probably second to The Allman Brothers in terms of my most-impressive bookings.

On the road with Waylon and his band and crew, the high point (pardon the pun) of the day was the arrival of a Fed Ex package addressed to me (?) at whatever venue we were playing. When it arrived and I delivered it to Waylon's road manager, the energy level increased substantially and never subsided until well after each show. On a subsequent tour, I was introduced to the same road manager, but he had a totally different name and hair color. He winked at me and said his "new identity" caused less hassle on the road.

I was required to settle in cash with Waylon himself right after each show, and I usually handed him $40,000 or $50,000 in hundreds, which he stuffed into his boots and left. Despite his demons, Waylon was always a prince to deal with, thanks mainly to the influence of his wife Jessi. He never gave less than 100 percent on every show I did with him. One of my heroes.

After that tour, I set up what should have been one of my biggest paydays—"Waylon's North Country Jamboree" at the old Midway Stadium in St. Paul on July 22, 1978. It was the home of our Open-Air Celebrations in 1971, so I knew the venue pretty well. Waylon still had a strong following, so I knew I could sell a lot of tickets. But what made the event golden was that I had persuaded the City of St. Paul to allow me to sell all the beer, which I felt would yield an extra $100,000+ in show profit. We brought in a stage and a great sound system, and everything was set on the morning of the show. Then a giant front came in and the rain started. I assumed it would let up in time for the show, but by noon the forecast was for heavy rain for the rest of the day and into the night. So I reluctantly moved the show indoors to the St. Paul Civic Center, which virtually sold out. But of course I did not have the beer concession in that venue, so I watched sadly as the very beer trucks that had been at Midway Stadium that morning pulled into the Civic Center and unloaded keg after keg for

(*opposite*) Newspaper ad for Waylon Jennings show, 1977

sale by the venue concessionaire. Money made, but not anything like the payday I and my brother Frank had been expecting.

DOLLY PARTON

My friend Fred Bohlander, who lived several blocks from me in Hinsdale as a kid, had discovered and booked a local band, The Buckinghams, whose hit "Kind of a Drag" had been a million-seller. Following that success, he formed Monterey Peninsula Artists, left Los Angeles, and moved to Monterey, California, where he operated for years—an ideal situation for him.

In 1977, Fred suggested I book a country artist who was about to break into the pop market: Dolly Parton. After a long and successful career as a duo with Porter Wagoner, Dolly made the decision to break from him and establish a solo career (She penned the song "I Will Always Love You" as a farewell to Porter), and as of 1977, she had had just modest success. But she had a new album with a very pop single I loved, "Here You Come Again," so I decided to take a flyer and book her for a show at O'Shaughnessy Auditorium. Wildly successful—the audience went nuts. And like an old-school country artist, she patiently met her fans in the lobby after the show. I wanted more of this artist, so I booked her for a mini-tour of the upper Midwest, nine or ten shows in middle markets. All were sold out and she really knew how to connect with her audiences.

Dolly was as nice and considerate an artist as I have ever worked with, and I got to ride between several of the dates on her tour bus. My dad, who once told me he was a "breast man," got to meet her and pose with his arm around her. Must have been a high point for him. On the last night of the

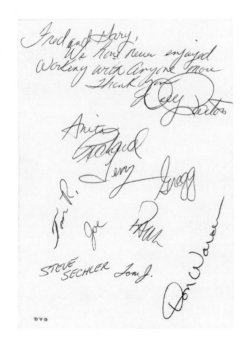

(*above*) Note from Dolly Parton to Fred Krohn and his staffer Gary Tassone on the last night of Dolly's Midwest tour. (*opposite*) Dolly Parton and Fred Krohn backstage at O'Shaughnessy Auditorium, 1977

tour, Dolly gave me a personal note that I still have. It said, "Fred and Gary—We have never enjoyed working with anyone more. Dolly Parton." And below, she had each of the band members and the bus driver sign the card. Truly one of the most sincere and friendly artists I have worked with. And she still has that reputation even with her current mega-star status.

HARRY CHAPIN

Harry Chapin's story songs were not instantly accessible. They were long, rhythmically complicated, and full of unusual instrumentation. He toured with a cellist rather than the usual rock band mates. You either loved Harry, or you thought he was pompous and unlistenable. I brought him to the Twin Cities three times, starting in 1977. I remember him being very intense—almost but not quite up to the intensity of Mandy Patinkin—but very sincere and likeable. He always wanted to greet his fans after a show, and his rider had a provision that his after-show process would not be interrupted or cut off. After one of his shows, his meet-and-greet having been in process for an hour and a half, the theater manager said they needed to close the hall and everyone had to leave. Harry got up, walked over to the manager, got right in her face, and very quietly said that he was going to leave, but it would be the last time he ever played her venue. Then he asked all his fans to join him out in front of the theater where he spent another hour with them.

AL JARREAU

A guy from Milwaukee who was friends with many Minneapolis-St. Paul musicians hooked me in the 1970s with his unique undefinable style—part R&B, part rock, and a lot jazz. He was unlike anyone I had heard. My theory then (later supported by a ton of research on ticket sales and record sales in my market) was that if I thought someone was interesting enough to listen to, then probably others did as well. Sheer hunches based on my taste only. In Al Jarreau's case, I was absolutely correct. He sold out his first show at O'Shaughnessy, sold out an Orpheum show and, then at the peak of his popularity, he sold out two shows at the old Northrop Auditorium. He was far bigger in Europe; no jazz festival was complete until they had booked Al to do the final show. Throughout the time I worked with Al, he was such a humble and modest guy that he became one of my favorite artists. After working with him in the 1970s and 1980s, I booked him into the Pantages Theatre in 2011 to give myself, and all the other Minneapolis musicians who loved and respected him, a chance to reconnect, and ultimately to say goodbye. Amazingly talented musician and vocalist. No one could do what he did.

DAVE BRUBECK

Early in 1979, I got a call from Columbia Records. They wanted a large stage to record an audiophile CD, using the new digital technology and wondered if they could rent the Orpheum stage for a few days in May. The theatre was open, so I replied positively. It turned out to be a project involving the legendary Dave Brubeck and his Trio, the Dale Warland Singers, the St. Paul Chamber Orchestra with Dennis Russell Davies conducting, and some noted choirs and soloists. They planned to record a new Brubeck composition, *La Fiesta de la Posada*, a depiction of the Mexican Christmas tradition of posada, Joseph and Mary's search for lodging just prior to Christmas Eve. Based on folk music, but with Brubeck's jazz flourishes. The producer of the disc was to be one of Columbia's most-noted talents.

Due to the extreme sensitivity of the digital recording technique, we were told that only the very minimum personnel could be in the audience for these sessions. They set up the SPCO and the artists on the Orpheum stage (pre-expansion, but still pretty large), rehearsed for a time, then did several takes of the piece. I witnessed the recording sessions, and the recording seemed destined to become a Christmas classic. The tunes, the Brubeck additions, the children's choruses, everything had an upbeat joy so appropriate for the holidays. Brubeck and the musicians seemed thrilled with the experience. But there seemed to be undercurrents of concern, which no one was willing to voice. At the time, I wondered whether they were unhappy with the acoustics in the Orpheum, but was assured that they were just fine.

Several months later, I learned the unfortunate truth. Unbeknownst to the record's producer during the recording sessions, the ballasts for the fluorescent lighting in the theatre lobby and/ or the theatre marquee left an electronic signature on all of the recording tape that could not be removed. So the record was either not going to be released, or released with some compromising flaws. Richard Ginell, in a review of the disc, said that "the sound is wiry and dim, mastered at a very low level on the CD (you really have to crank up the volume)." Obviously that was the only way to compensate for the sound on the tape. Sadly, if the producer had been alert to the problem while the recording was taking place, we could have shut off the interfering lighting. I still have the CD and play it each Christmas. I can only imagine what a hit it might have been if the recording had been pristine.

RICHARD KILEY (*MAN OF LA MANCHA*)

Early in 1979, as I was working with David Zimmerman on Dylan's purchase and refurbishment of the Orpheum, I got a call from Broadway producer and general manager, Chuck Eisler, who was interested in a "four-wall" (building only) rental of the Orpheum for his touring production of Richard Kiley in *MAN OF LA MANCHA*. He was planning a four-week run, which seemed wildly optimistic, even with the star of the original Broadway show. But

Chuck taught me some marketing lessons, many of which I was able to use for our *A CHORUS LINE* run later that year. When he visited Minneapolis, the first thing he wanted was to find a space for a "phone bank." I took him down to the bowels of the theatre and we found a large room that he said would do fine. He next had AT&T install forty lines with forty phones around the exterior, and had our carpenters build a ledge around the room for the phones and order forms to sit on. Next, he hired and trained a bunch of people to handle the phones. Finally, Chuck booked a shocking number of thirty-second television ads on all three (that's all there were then) television stations. When the day came for the first ads to run, we watched the television in the phone room. He told me not to worry if they got almost no calls when the first spot ran, that it took two or three impressions for people to act. His theory proved accurate. When the second spot ran, there were a few calls. But starting with the third spot, the entire forty lines lit up, and we could not take orders fast enough. Sales were brisk throughout the run, and Chuck's gamble in Minneapolis paid off. The production might look pretty stiff and low-key based on current Broadway standards, but Richard Kiley was the perfect Don Quixote. When he sang "The Impossible Dream," the audience was always on its feet.

THE CAST OF *A CHORUS LINE*

In July 1979, as I was installing the three-sheet posters in cases in front of the Orpheum just prior to the opening of *A CHORUS LINE*, a group of obviously not Minneapolitans walked up and greeted me. There was a very tall and lanky Black kid, a handsome dark-haired guy with a black mustache, a petite, perky woman with a great figure, and two of the most beautiful and fit young lovers I had ever seen. The *CHORUS LINE* cast had arrived. Rudy Lowe played Richie, the basketball player turned dancer. Stephen Crenshaw played Paul, the gay Puerto Rican.

Pamela Ann Wilson played Val, the singer of the "Tits and Ass" bit; and Wanda Richert played Cassie, one of the leads. The handsome guy with her, dressed in very short shorts and a bare midriff shirt, was Wanda's boyfriend. When they found out that I was the local producer of the show, we became instant friends and hung together for the next three weeks. They seemed to have the ideal jobs. They got paid well for doing something they love, and because of their generous per diems on the road, got to keep 100 percent of their salary for use during their down months. But on Thursday of the first week, I learned the downside to their jobs. Just before that show, the company manager informed the cast that show creator and producer, Michael Bennett, had arrived in town; and he was going to watch the show and give everyone "notes" afterward. I came to learn that one of the notes might be, "You're fired." All of my friends survived nicely, but one of the other cast members was let go, and his understudy went on for the next few days until Bennett could send a replacement from New York and have him "taken in" to the show.

A *CHORUS LINE* was the first national company we'd had in Minneapolis, and the difference between a typical "bus and truck" production and this show was night and day. A perfect set with rotating periaktoi (large vertical rotating triangles) lining the rear wall, which could instantly change from a mirror to a sunburst to black. A very small detail which was not used in subsequent productions impressed me. During the finale with the cast in full gold costume with top hats, as they are doing their final kicks, the lighting goes from full on gold, then morphs into silver white while they are still kicking, then fades slowly to black. For whatever reason that very quick lighting effect always made me tear up, as the most important show I had booked up to that moment faded to black as well.

In the middle of our run, it was announced that our Cassie, Wanda Richert, had been cast by Gower Champion as the lead in his new production of *42ND STREET* on Broadway. She became a part of Broadway lore. She and Gower were having an affair,

(left) A CHORUS LINE star Wanda Richert and boyfriend. (right) Stephen Crenshaw, Paul in A CHORUS LINE at the Orpheum, 1979.

and sadly Gower died on opening night. Legendary producer David Merrick kept the information from the cast, including Wanda, during the show, but then just after the show finale, Merrick came on stage to announce Champion's death, to the complete surprise of the entire cast, including Wanda, who burst into tears.

Others in our A CHORUS LINE cast ended up in the New York company, and when in New York, I often met them at the Shubert Theatre stage door after the show for a drink. I was especially close to Pam Wilson and Stephen Crenshaw. Pam was seeing the guy who ran the Bitter End folk club, so I sometimes helped her open the club and then stayed around to see who might be playing that night. I saw Steven Crenshaw several times when he returned to the Twin Cities to perform in A CHORUS LINE, and once drove him over to Stillwater Prison where his father had been incarcerated. He would not tell me what crime he had committed. As a gesture of our friendship, he gave me his top hat from the show, which I still treasure.

LIZA MINNELLI

One of the most polished and professional artists I booked during the Orpheum's Dylan era was Liza Minnelli. Maybe hard to believe now, but she was the most electrifying singer and dancer of that era. Her show came with a full set, a large orchestra, and four great male dancers. She worked as hard as any performer I have ever presented. We booked four shows, and they all sold out in advance. Her manager, Eliot Weisman, also managed Frank Sinatra.

Weisman had reportedly been charged with racketeering in connection with a Westchester, New York theater, reportedly along with some organized crime figures, and had been pressed repeatedly to snitch on Sinatra's mob ties. Weisman reportedly refused and was rewarded with the job of a lifetime—Frank Sinatra's personal manger. I knew nothing of the veracity of any of that story, but the chill that I felt when he walked into the room was palpable. He had a real presence and not necessarily in a good way. But I got along fine both with Liza and with Eliot, and the run was a complete success. It was such a crime that, with all her talent, Liza seemed to have the same self-destructive genes as her mother, Judy Garland. Liza would have likely had a much longer and more notable career if she could have kept herself together.

PETER PAUL AND MARY

Three of my folk idols were Peter Yarrow, Noel Paul Stookey, and Mary Travers. Their blend of great songs, great harmonies, and an activist mentality won me over when I was still in high school. So it was an honor to work with them later in my career. Their 1981 concert at the old Northrop Auditorium was memorable as it was the last time I worked with Mary Travers before her death. In her earlier years, Mary was rail thin and strikingly beautiful, especially in person. Her blonde hair and bangs were her trademark, as were her many amazing outfits. I can remember Mary coming up to me backstage with something in her fist, and asking me to guess what it was. No clue. It turned out to be a very thin and colorful silk dress designed by Emilio Pucci, which she planned to wear for the show. Wow. It left very little to the imagination and showed off her great legs and figure. I last worked with Peter and Paul in October 2017. I certainly agreed with them that finding a "replacement" for Mary would have been a mistake; Mary's contribution to the group can't be overestimated. Her unique and pure voice floating above Peter and Paul's was what made the group iconic.

DAVID LETTERMAN

Mark Zelenovich ("Mark Jr."), who I worked with during the Dylan period at the Orpheum, was nuts about a new comic with a late night show on CBS, David Letterman, and kept urging me to find a place for him on one of our shows. Since Letterman was then relatively new and unknown, I knew he could not attract a large audience, so he needed to be an opening act on a star artist's show. David's agent was interested, but for months I could not find an artist who needed a support act. Finally Nancy Wilson, the Black jazz and contemporary singer, became available, and her manager asked if I could find a comic opener, and he didn't seem to care who it was. I got back with Letterman's people, and they seemed to be fine as well. Thus occurred probably the most ill-conceived booking I have ever made. Mark Jr. and I picked up Letterman at the airport, had a great and funny conversation all the way to the hotel, and said we would pick him up just before the show. When he arrived, Nancy had done her sound check and was in her dressing room. I told David that he needed to do a half-hour minimum. Then we looked out at the audience from the wings. The crowd was almost completely Black and elderly.

David froze, realizing that his material would not connect with this crowd. But I insisted that it would, and after my introduction he walked out

Ad for David Letterman's ill-fated appearance

stage center to very light and confused applause. Sadly, David was right—his hip material went right over the heads of this audience, and dead silence greeted each of his jokes.

After ten minutes, he excused himself, walked off the stage, and pleaded with me that he could not keep going. I told him that Nancy's people insisted he do his half-hour, and he went back out. Rarely have I seen a comic bomb so completely, but David completed his thirty minutes and walked off to absolutely no applause. We laughed about it the next day on the way to the airport, but we had both learned a booking lesson the hard way.

TOM WAITS

On occasion, I booked artists who were both hip and in demand, as Tom Waits always was. A pretty nondescript guy with a pork pie hat and a rough and unpolished voice, his songs detailed the lives of junkies and the down-and-out urban characters that ironically we had hanging around the Orpheum in its early days. In fact one of Waits' most beloved tunes he wrote while in Minneapolis for a show at the Orpheum. It's called "Christmas Card from a Hooker in Minneapolis." It mentions 9th Street, and it well illustrates the shady underside of the holiday season. What made his live shows work was the combination of his gravelly voice, his perfect lyrics, and the many props he brought to add a touch of performance art to each of his songs. The image I most recall is a large, battered, nondescript garbage can which he placed center stage, I believe during his song "Trash Day." When he came to a certain lyric at the end of the song, he yanked the lid off the can and a blast of intense white light shot up from inside like a klieg light. Amazing, jarring image. Some artists sell tickets. Some artists are so ultra-hip that all the musicians and cool people in the city beg for tickets. Tom Waits was both, sold out multiple shows three times, and never failed to deliver.

LAURA NYRO

Laura Nyro was in a way similar to Harry Chapin. They both wrote great songs, but they were considered a bit too idiosyncratic for Top 40. Laura's songs were big hits for others in the late '60s and throughout the 1970s ("Stoned Soul Picnic," "Sweet Blindness," and "Wedding Bell Blues" for the Fifth Dimension, "And When I Die" for Blood Sweat and Tears, and "Eli's Coming" for Three Dog Night). But I happened to like Nyro's versions of her songs, with her great gospel piano and striking vocals, better than the cover versions. So she was always on my "ask about" list, and I hounded her agent for years to try to get a date. But in the late 1970s, Laura walked away from the business to raise her daughter and be with her family in the country. It seemed that her most creative and rewarding years might be behind her. But finally in the summer 1988 I was offered a date on her tour. I chose to book her for two shows at the new Children's Theatre near the Minneapolis Art Institute—the only time I used that facility. The shows were some of my most memorable, but even at this smaller venue, they did not sell out. She wrote some of the finest songs of that era, but I guess she was an acquired taste that not everyone loved. Sadly she toured less often after that, and died of ovarian cancer in 1997 at age forty-nine.

ROBERT GOULET (AND WIFE, VERA NOVAK)

When I booked Robert Goulet in the musical *SOUTH PACIFIC* in 1989, I had heard Broadway folklore about how hard he was to handle and keep on the straight and narrow. So I was pleasantly surprised that he was a prince (not Lancelot in this show, but Emile de Becque) throughout our run. The secret, I soon found, was his third wife, Vera Novak, who also served as his personal manager. She was originally from Macedonia, and has been variously described as an artist, a writer, an actress, and a Vegas

Robert and Vera's 1989 Christmas card

showgirl. She was pretty, she knew what Robert liked (fine wines for one), and made sure he had everything he needed to succeed. Both Robert and Vera had the old-school idea that they needed to keep the local promoter happy, since he/she would ultimately make the decision on whether they came back to a particular market. Robert did all the PR he was asked to do (unlike many Broadway stars), was always ready on time, and was always gracious to his audiences. They were right, I did like them, and did bring Robert back in the same show in 2002.

During the Christmas season following Robert's 1989 performances, I received a large and heavy envelope from "Rogo Rove," which turned out to be a Christmas card from Robert and Vera. And what a card! A very formal photo of the two of them dressed to the nines on the cover, and a second, more spontaneous photo of them on the card's interior. Very show biz, and very Vegas. The next year, a newly designed card arrived from them, and every year since then until Robert's death in 2007, our whole office anxiously waited for the "Robert and Vera" card—a highlight of our office holiday season. I still have all of them, and look through them each season to remember a Broadway legend and his vivacious wife.

MICKEY ROONEY

Having seen the original *SUGAR BABIES* production with Mickey Rooney and Ann Miller on Broadway, I jumped at the chance to bring it to Minneapolis with the original cast well after its New York run. Since I was "between theaters" in 1985, I determined to try my luck at Northrop Auditorium on the University of Minnesota campus, then a venue of nearly 5,000 seats with a huge proscenium opening. It proved not to be the ideal theater for a vaudeville show with lots of sight gags, mugging, and vintage jokes.

Both Ann Miller and Mickey Rooney were legends by that time, but much of their fan bases had apparently aged out of theatre-going—as I found to my dismay. Northrop, pre-renovation and modernization, was not an ideal fit for Broadway. Ann Miller was still trim and shapely, but Mickey had not aged well, and was almost as wide as he was tall by that time (He was 5' 1"). When he arrived to check out the theater, he immediately found several deal-killers. First, he said he would be unable to walk down a flight of stairs to use the toilet, and needed to have one installed on stage. Second, he needed a couch to sleep on between his stage bits and between shows on matinee days, since he got tired very quickly. I ended up getting him a very small and low to the ground porta potty (which was okay to him based on his small size). He wanted that placed just offstage right so he could use it whenever nature called (which was often). I asked if he wanted some drapes or other privacy, and he said that it was not necessary.

There ensued more calls of nature in a week than I have ever witnessed since, and the image of those calls is still stuck in my brain. But the guy was always upbeat and had an unlimited number of show-biz lore stories to tell based on an amazing movie career and his six wives. Very entertaining if they could be believed. Sadly, even though he had been one of Hollywood's highest-paid stars, he was then almost broke, having been ripped off, he alleged, buy his relatives. He died with a reported net worth of $18,000.

I also rented the large couch Mickey requested and had it delivered to his dressing room. He used it often, and I and his stage manager had to make sure he was up and ready for his stage cues. But what a trooper he was. He could go from sound sleep to full on singing, dancing, and dressing in drag in a heartbeat.

The show bombed, I lost big money, and to add insult to injury, the sofa I had rented for Mickey disappeared on the night of the load-out. None of the stage crew could tell me whether they saw it exiting the building, something that must have been obvious. Pretty hard to make a couch disappear unless you are David Copperfield. All in all one of my least-favorite experiences in show biz.

SARAH VAUGHAN

As a major jazz talent, Sarah Vaughan, "The Divine One," was to me second only to the "First Lady of Song," Ella Fitzgerald. It was like the rivalry between the "Queen of Soul" Aretha Franklin, and the "Godmother of Soul," Patti LaBelle. After presenting Ella on a number of occasions, I felt it might be appropriate for me to bring Sarah Vaughan to Minneapolis. The date was May 7, 1989, and Sarah was, at sixty-five, heading toward the end of an amazing career, and reportedly battling health issues. When she walked into the Orpheum with her band for her sound check, I was concerned, since she looked tired and very drained. The band did the sound check without her, which concerned me even more. So when the time came for her first set, and she had not come to the wings, I knocked on her dressing room door and heard a cheerful "Come in," which I did. I found Sarah in costume at her makeup mirror with a large pile of white powder, which I assumed was an illicit substance. She took no mind of my presence, and said she would be right out to do her show. That knowledge plus her earlier frailty told me that I should pray that she got through her show successfully. But minutes later she came out of her dressing room looking radiant and energetic, walked onto the stage, and did one of the most amazing shows I have seen—her voice as superb as I recalled it on record. After a standing ovation, she left the hall. Sadly, like Miles Davis, she would be gone mere months after her Orpheum show. She died of reported lung cancer on April 3, 1990, at age sixty-six. A tragic loss of one of the most-gifted jazz vocalists in history.

BONNIE RAITT (WITH JOHN RAITT)

I love unbilled surprise guests at shows. My favorite was at a Sue Weil show at the Guthrie early in my career. I thought Sue was one of the smartest bookers in the area, and her *Live at the Guthrie* shows (at the old Guthrie Theater) were often memorable. I first saw Elton John there, and her Sam and Dave Show (with all the instrumentalists lined up along the back wall and moving in unison) is still on my greatest shows list. She booked a young James Taylor, who was then married to the even more well-known Carly Simon, and we all hoped Carly might make an appearance. But we got to the encores with no sign of her. Then James and band went into his hit call-and-response song "Mockingbird," which we knew was a duet with Carly. When I heard the very beginning of that song riff, I just knew that Carly would appear. Sure enough, Carly sang the first few lines of her duet lines offstage, then walked onstage to join James for a tumultuous duet that went on for ten minutes. It was obvious the effect that James had on Carly. She had a reputation for nervousness and stage fright, but when she joined her husband, James Taylor, she was a totally different personality—outgoing and relaxed. A magic stage moment.

I had another such experience, which was almost as meaningful when Bonnie Raitt first played the State Theatre for me. As a Broadway aficionado, I knew that Bonnie's father, John Raitt, had been a huge Broadway star, most notably for his leading roles in *OKLAHOMA!* and *SOUTH PACIFIC*. So when a still-handsome older guy showed up with Bonnie for the show, I knew exactly who he was. So I was not surprised when, after a smoking blues set by Bonnie, she said she had a special guest to invite to the stage to join her for her encore. Thus she introduced her father, John Raitt, to the audience, to prolonged applause. They chose the song "Oklahoma" from the musical, and did a rousing rendition, which resulted in a standing ovation. Another magic stage moment.

Fred Krohn, Cary Maynard, and Andy Williams at the Sheraton Ritz Hotel, Minneapolis

ANDY WILLIAMS

When I was working for Harry Beacom, Andy was the king of what we would now call "adult contemporary" artists. Ferrante and Teicher, Glen Yarbrough, The Temptations, The Chad Mitchell Trio, Sonny & Cher, Bobby Darin, The Righteous Brothers, Tom Jones, you get the idea. An almost mandatory stop for this category of artists after their Minneapolis show was the cocktail lounge on the top of the now-demolished Sheraton Ritz Hotel, where radio celebrity Henry Wolf broadcast his late-night radio show. A more unlikely personality than Henry you would be hard-pressed to find. He was an older guy, and he spoke in a very thick German-Austrian dialect. His last name became "Vulfe," and I won't even try to tell you how he spoke phrases like "brought to you tonight by Schmelz Brothers Volkswagen." He knew his artists and their current hits and activities, and he was ready and willing to plug just about anything the star wanted hyped. And he allowed those who wanted to (Glen Yarbrough and Chad Mitchell for example) to bring their guitars and sing a song or two.

Harry Beacom came to some of these late-night interviews and let me handle many others. I recall inviting my friend, Cary Maynard, to one of these Henry Wolf shows after we presented Andy Williams for (as I recall) an outdoor Aquatennial concert at the bowl end of Metropolitan Stadium. It was in Andy's "Moon River" heyday, and he was becoming a big star. But his Wall Lake, Iowa, roots always showed through; he never argued with anything we suggested in terms of publicity. While he was much more famous than most of Henry's guests (and I had warned Andy about Henry's odd delivery), Andy gamely played along and did a gracious interview, then stayed to have a drink with Cary and me. Years later, in late November 1989, I brought Andy back to Minneapolis with his Christmas Show, which sold out instantly and brought audiences the same warmth and family charm that his annual Christmas shows did on television.

CHAPTER SIX

POLITICAL STAGES

WHEN I BEGAN MY STUDIES AT CARLETON COLLEGE, my plan was to major in Government and International Relations, attend law school after graduation, and find work in the public sector. I was a "liberal republican," which meant to me that I was very liberal on social issues and more conservative in the fiscal areas. North Oaks, the village north of St. Paul where I spent my high school years, was pretty conservative. Most families had some money and wanted to keep as much of it as they could. My parents were no exception. The republicans of the '60s and '70s were not anything like Trump republicans—they were pragmatic and able to work across the aisle.

The head of the Carleton's Government and International Relations Department was Professor Ralph Fjelstad. I immediately connected with him as a very practical and down-to-earth guy who could teach me things I could really use in the real world after my graduation. We both had an interest in state government, and he allowed me to travel up to St. Paul on a regular basis to follow the legislative sessions. While there, I began to admire the Cass Gilbert-designed State Capital Building, and especially the ornate governor's reception room. I decided during these early trips that it would be an exciting place to work. So after some discussions with Dr. Fjelstad, I determined to do a paper on the 1967 legislative session, since it fit nicely into the school's January to May calendar. A new governor, republican Harold LeVander, was to be sworn in on January 2, 1967, and since he beat former Governor Karl Rolvaag by tagging him as an ineffective legislative leader, I decided to focus my paper on new Governor LeVander's skills as a legislative leader during the 1967 legislative session.

At the start of the term, I traveled to the capital on a weekly basis; and by the end of the Session I was there almost daily. One of the people in the governor's office I worked closely with, and got to know, was the governor's research director, Archie D. Chelseth, a smart and generous guy who became a mentor to me. He and his secretary, Maureen Herbert, worked in the outer area of the reception room, and I was able to visit both of them often. I also got to know Barbara Miller, who worked in the press secretary's office.

Bottom line is that my paper, "The Role of Harold LeVander as Legislative Leader of the 65th Session of the Minnesota legislature" earned me an A from Dr. Fjelstad, an invitation from Archie Chelseth to intern in the governor's office during the summer between my junior and Senior years, and later an offer to work on the governor's staff full time. I served for the next several years, and was around in 1970 when Governor LeVander determined that he did not want to run again. When he left office in January 1971, I was still on staff and made sure some mementos of his term in office were saved. During those years, I made many close relationships that continue to this day: I wrote speeches with the governor's daughter, Jean LeVander King; I was given many staff assignments by the governor's administrative assistant, David Durenberger (who would later serve as a United States Senator), and I developed a strong admiration for Harold himself, who I felt was smart and an old-fashioned spellbinder of a speaker.

I also got to know many state legislators from both parties who were giants in state history. Names like Gordon Rosenmeier, Paul Overgaard, and Jerome Blatz. (As the Governor's legislative

Fred with the governor's daughter, Jean LeVander King

aide, I was allowed access to both the House and Senate chambers). I got to know Attorney General Doug Head, who worked right across the hall from the governor. Finally, I met a number of wealthy republican businessmen (Wheelock Whitney, Jim Binger, George Pillsbury, etc.), all of whom I was able to call on later during my live entertainment career.

Note Fred Krohn in the front row just right of the lectern

BALLOON BARRAGE . . . Thousands of balloons are released in the Minneapolis auditorium Tuesday night as Minnesota Gov. Harold LeVander (right) introduces Richard Nixon to a public rally of about 8,000 persons. Republican presidential candidate Nixon brought his campaign to Minnesota Tuesday, home state of Democratic nominee Vice President Hubert Humphrey. (AP Photofax)

I was flying high back then. Riding around in the governor's limo and parking my British Racing Green Corvette right next to the limo by the steps to the west wing of the capital. I didn't totally neglect my show-biz skills during this time. I staged many a state convention demonstration, and helped with dinners and rallies for President Nixon and President Reagan (and later, Johnson and Bush as well). Governor LeVander and I had attended the Miami Beach 1968 GOP Convention in support of New York Governor Nelson Rockefeller, who Nixon soundly defeated. But when Nixon came to the Minneapolis Auditorium in October 1968 for a rally, LeVander had no option as governor other than to introduce Nixon, and I supervised the logistics of the event, including a giant balloon drop, which I timed to occur when LeVander was on the podium with Nixon).

During my senior year at Carleton, and pursuant to a request from Carleton President John Nason, I invited Governor

Fred Krohn accompanying Governor LeVander to convocation speech. Governor LeVander and President Nason in front.

LeVander to deliver a convocation speech on the campus. I was honored that LeVander accepted, although his speech was a bit more conservative than my fellow students were expecting.

After leaving the Governor's Office, I finally graduated from law school at the University of Minnesota and passed the bar. Based on having little else to fall back on, I briefly determined to hang up my shingle and try practicing law as a solo practitioner. Finding clients was not difficult, but dealing with their problems was not something I relished. With absolutely no trial experience other than watching Perry Mason shows on television, I took on a jury trial (deteriorating concrete steps that a contractor did not stand behind), and a trial before a judge (termination of parental rights versus an attorney who is currently active in the area of

child abuse). I won both cases and also successfully represented myself in a case against a political lobbyist friend who had purchased my condo and later defaulted. With that, my legal career came to an end. I just did not find the stress of having others depend on me desirable. During this time I also got my real estate and brokers licenses and considered whether I might find buying and selling properties interesting; but I did not.

Only the theatrical real estate on Hennepin Avenue proved fascinating to me, so that's where I gravitated. During the years I was involved with saving and operating the Orpheum, State, and Pantages Theatres, I got to know each of the thirteen City Council members and several mayors as well, something that helped me round up votes for the many proposals I brought forward to

Fred Krohn, Minnesota Governor Harold LeVander, and Vikings quarterback Joe Kapp in the locker room after the Vikings defeat in Super Bowl IV in New Orleans.

them. I was especially close to flamboyant Council member, Barbara Carlson, and produced two of the most memorable fundraisers any Minneapolis CM has had: gala dinner events starring Peggy Lee and, later, Bobby Short.

During the 1980s, I promoted shows and dabbled in politics, and I got to know Arne Carlson, the ex-husband of Council member Barbara Carlson. Arne was smart as a whip and a great speaker, and I knew that he really wanted to be governor. He evidently thought I could help him because during the time he was serving as state auditor, he asked me to become his deputy state auditor, and I agreed. I had both statutory duties, and I moonlighted as a political advisor. But Arne was a moderate, and not a pure enough opponent of abortion for the Republican Party in the 1980s. So despite traveling all over the state and delivering amazing speeches, he could not get the GOP endorsement to run for governor. But in one of the real flukes of Minnesota history, John Grunseth won the republican endorsement for governor, but due to a scandal, he had to drop out of the race with Rudy Perpich nine days prior to the election. Arne stepped in at the last moment and won the race. He was sworn in on January 7, 1991, and served two very successful terms as Minnesota governor. He and his wife, Susan, loved Broadway shows, attended frequently, and had a number of gala theater events at the governor's mansion.

NOTE: In 2005, my friend Joan Mondale was awarded a "Sally" award for her contributions to the nation's Arts by my rival, the Ordway Music Theatre. Joan invited me to join her as her guest at the luncheon. It goes without saying that the Ordway officials were not ecstatic about my being at the head table for one of their most important annual events. But based on who I was accompanying, they had no choice but to welcome me graciously.

CHAPTER SEVEN

DYLAN AND THE ORPHEUM

D URING THE TIME I WORKED WITH PROMOTER HARRY Beacom, some of his advertising was handled through Bernard Productions, an ad agency run by Bob Dylan's brother, David Zimmerman. I'm sure Harry had the same idea as I did: work with David and maybe he can deliver some shows by his brother. Working in David's office were a couple of real characters, the father-and-son duo: Mark Zelenovich, Sr. and Mark Zelenovich, Jr. "Senior" came from the very old school days of Minneapolis advertising; he was a friend and contemporary of the legendary pitchman, Mel Jass, who pretty much owned daytime television advertising during the '60s and '70s. No matter what show we were advertising, Senior always wanted to have Mel Jass do live endorsements or rely on other old-school media outlets like WCCO AM. Mark Jr. and I were always on Senior's case to more appropriately fit the media outlet to the sort of audience we wanted to attract. Both Senior and Junior had hair-trigger tempers, and on many occasions discussions between the two ended up in fist fights.

Once Harry Beacom stopped promoting shows, David Zimmerman and his office needed shows to market, and somewhat against my better judgment,

Bob Dylan's brother, David Zimmerman

I determined to work with David on marketing and as a partner for some of my shows. Not a marriage made in heaven, but it allowed me to get to know David and learn more about his brother, the very-secretive Bob Dylan.

During the middle '70s, I was officing on the fifth floor of Butler Square in downtown Minneapolis in a one-room office. From there, I handled my concert promotions and studied for my law school classes. In mid-1977, David called me to see if I might want to work with him on his brother's new film, *Renaldo & Clara*, which Bob was completing the final edits on. Dylan's business advisors expected it to be a major hit, and advised Bob to take it to the Cannes Film Festival in May and sell it to European countries where Bob was worshiped by his fans.

One night David gathered a bunch of us in the viewing room of an old mansion on the hill above the old Guthrie Theater for a screening of the latest cut of the film. Bob would be there and would want our reactions to his creation. At that point, I recall that the film was nearly four hours long. Although I feigned interest, the whole thing seemed incomprehensible to me, and I'm sure that most of us slept through major portions of the film. It was shot during Bob's *Rolling Thunder Review*, but surprisingly, it contained very little music, just a white-faced Dylan as seen by a number of the cast members—most notably Joan Baez. I told David privately that I thought I could make a great movie if I could just gather up all the music scenes which landed on the editing room floor and splice them together.

Despite a rather lukewarm reception from our small audience, Dylan insisted that he could do some additional edits to shorten the movie somewhat, and have it ready in time for the Cannes Film Festival in May. David quickly formed Circuit Films to handle the project and decided to office in a space across the hall from my Butler Square office. Senior and Junior, as well as Junior's girlfriend, joined us in that new space, along with David's uncle, Mel Edelstein, who had run movie theaters in Bob's hometown of Hibbing (and whose son is film critic David Edelstein).

(*opposite*) Renaldo and Clara newspaper ad

CHAPTER SEVEN

RENALDO & CLARA

Starring

BOB DYLAN & JOAN BAEZ

"THE MUSIC LEAPS FROM THE SCREEN with a brilliance and power I've never seen equaled in a rock-oriented film."

CHRISTIAN SCIENCE MONITOR—David Sterritt

"DYLAN FANS WILL WANT TO SEE RENALDO AND CLARA AGAIN AND AGAIN to piece together this often dazzling puzzle."

"RENALDO AND CLARA IS ALIVE in a way that separates it from much of the passing Hollywood parade."

L.A. TIMES—Robert Hilburn

"DYLAN IS ELECTRIFYING."
"DYLAN IS A GENIUS."

NEWSWEEK—Jack Kroll

Written and Directed By Bob Dylan   *Produced by Lombard Street Films, Inc.*
Distributed Worldwide by Circuit Films   *Metrocolor*   **R** RESTRICTED

Fred Krohn and director Howard Alk in Cannes

Our first order of business was to arrange a screening for Dylan's Minneapolis fans in February 1978. I rented the Varsity Theater in Dinkytown (still a movie theater then) for the premiere, and since flowers were integral to the movie, we provided everyone who attended with a red carnation. The reaction of this first audience was less than glowing, but on to Cannes.

We quickly found that the main Cannes competition had already closed, but there was a possibility of the film being accepted in a sub-category called the *Quinzaine des Realisateurs* ("Director's Fortnight"), a competition for smaller films with well-known directors. We scrambled to get it entered, and just weeks prior to the Festival, we learned that the film was accepted. The first question from the Festival officials, of course, was when Dylan planned to arrive in Cannes to explain the film. They were shocked that Bob did not, in fact, plan to attend the Festival, instead sending his co-editor and cinematographer, Howard Alk. I had a number of conversations with Alk in my attempt to understand what Dylan was trying to say in the film, but I can't say that his explanations added much clarity.

Of course someone had to go to Cannes to sell the film rights to the many foreign countries that we were sure would be clamoring to exhibit any film by Bob Dylan. As an attorney, I was the logical guy to prepare the contracts and sell the film, but Mel Edelstein and his wife really wanted to travel to Cannes; so David Zimmerman decided they would go over for the first week, and I would handle the second. When I flew into Cannes, I met Mel and his wife at the airport, took over their rental car, and asked them how many countries they had been able to sell the film to. I was shocked to learn that the answer was zero, and I would have to do a full court press to salvage our efforts. I soon found that everyone wanted to book a film by Dylan, that is until they actually screened the film.

My Cannes Festival Pass (new photo added to old Mel Edelstein pass)

On my second night in Cannes, I was told that a high-level Los Angeles movie executive (we'll call him Howard) had been authorized by Dylan to attend the Festival and help with the rights negotiations. News to me. I learned that he had invited many of the prospective buyers to dinner at one of Cannes most-exclusive restaurants high on the cliffs overlooking the harbor the following night. I arrived at the place to find that Howard had hired out the entire premises, and had invited over thirty guests. After some cocktails as we admired the view, we all sat down to dinner. The food was excellent and the great French wines flowed generously. But Howard himself had not yet showed, and I began to get very concerned. Dessert arrived, but still no Howard. The event ended and I saw everyone out, thanking them for coming and setting up appointments to discuss the film rights in the next several days. Finally I was alone and the maitre'd arrived with the bill, which totaled over $7,000. Still no Howard. I cringed as I handed him my American Express card, fully expecting it to be rejected; but amazingly the charge went through. Howard showed up the next day with no explanation for his absence, and I let him know that his services were no longer needed.

Out in the Cannes Harbor were some amazing yachts, and the head of a major German studio I had entertained the night prior invited me out to the largest and most impressive of them for dinner and a discussion of Bob's film. The tender that took us out to the yacht was nicer than any vessel I had ever been on, and the ship itself was beyond amazing. It was filled with the "beautiful people" that Cannes was famous for. Topless women with heavy gold chains crisscrossing large breasts was the look of the period, and I saw many variations on that theme on the boat. After an amazing dinner with the guy and several associates, they signed a contract with me, making that my first success. He afterward told me that he hated the movie; but despite the provisions in my contract, he would cut it up and make a good hour-and-a-half music film out of it. I also completed a major deal with a British firm and five or six smaller countries while there. But overall the response to *R&C* was not good, and I realized that if I had been able to deliver Bob himself, I would have been able to sell the film to many more than the six or eight countries I ended up signing.

Arriving back in the US, we attempted to find a domestic distributor for the film, but due to its long length, that proved difficult. (Bob later edited the film to a more reasonable two hours). So we decided to promote a New York run ourselves to show potential distributors that the film could attract Bob's fans despite its length. New York, we figured, would support our project if any place would. We rented three of four classic movie theaters, several in Greenwich Village, where Bob had lived and performed in his early years. To make certain that the theaters paid us accurately, we hired film audience auditors to go into each theater and actually count the number of people watching each screening. We generated okay audiences for the early screenings, but word-of-mouth was not good, and sales quickly dropped off. I can recall talking to our film auditor the morning after a screening and being told that the film did screen as scheduled, but there were absolutely *no* patrons in the theater. Bob finally pulled the film, and my short career as a movie producer ended.

During this time, I was on occasion invited to Dylan's farm in Loretto, often to interact with Dylan's kids. I was never invited into Dylan's living quarters, and rarely did Dylan join us in our outdoor activities, like hiking or snowmobiling. I do, however, recall seeing some of Dylan's framed Gold Records in a cardboard box in his garage. When I told David Zimmerman that I was planning to see the legendary Russian pianist, Vladimir Horowitz, at Orchestra Hall, he asked me whether I would be willing to take Bob's daughter Maria with me. I was fine with that until the great musician came to his first encore, Chopin's "Polonaise in A Flat," my favorite piano composition bar none, and its difficulty the reason I had stopped considering a piano career. As Mr. Horowitz began the piece, Maria whispered to me that she wanted to leave. I told her that I wanted to stay until the end of the piece, but at that she got up and walked down the center aisle and into the lobby. I was forced to follow, missing the masterpiece. That was my final event with Maria.

While I had always loved Broadway shows, mostly as a result of spending summers with my grandparents and taking a bus from Allentown, Pennsylvania, to New York for matinee performances (including a very memorable *FUNNY GIRL* with new star, Barbra Streisand), the show that pushed me over the top in 1978 was *A CHORUS LINE*, which I felt was like no other show I had seen. I determined just after the curtain calls that I needed to bring that show to Minneapolis. But what venue could I use? Northrop was a 5,000-seat barn of a place, the St. Paul Auditorium theater was so decrepit that it had nets to catch falling ceiling tiles before they hit the patrons, and O'Shaughnessy had neither the capacity nor the stage size I knew *ACL* required.

The only option was the Hennepin Orpheum Theatre, which had been home to Broadway shows in the '50s and '60s, but had not been used much recently and was pretty run-down. But it was probably my only good option since it had a capacity of 2,600 and a fairly large stage house.

With more guts than brains, I flew out to New York and made

a completely cold call on Joe Papp at the New York Shakespeare Festival, which had produced *A CHORUS LINE*. I was told that Joe was "busy," but that I could talk to the show's general manager, Laurel Ann Wilson. I told her how much I admired *ACL*, and detailed my entertainment background, my legal training, and my desire to bring the show to the people of the Minneapolis area. I told her that I had some connections to the Orpheum Theatre, and wondered what the minimum technical requirements to produce *ACL* were. She was familiar with the venue, and said that it might be possible to do the show there, but a lot of upgrades would be needed. She went down the hall and got me the rider for the show listing all the deliverables she would need to do the show at the Orpheum. I knew right then that much work would be needed to get the theatre up to that "national touring company" level. I then asked the question I would use to leverage the deal that created the updated Orpheum: If I can deliver the theatre in the condition she required, would she commit to booking the show through me. Amazingly, she said yes.

As I was leaving, Laurel Ann took me down the hall, and we stepped into legendary Joe Papp's office for a quick meeting. He didn't make a good first impression since he was sort of unkempt, but when Laurel Ann told him what I wanted to accomplish, he said good luck, go for it. I left more determined than ever to somehow upgrade the Orpheum and bring *A CHORUS LINE* to Minneapolis.

Back in the Twin Cities, I tried to identify those who might have the cash and the interest in Broadway to partner with me on my project. After meeting with, and being turned down, by just about every wealthy businessman (and they were all men then), I hit on a very novel idea. I had learned that Bob Dylan really liked to own land, and in his drives to and from Hibbing, he often wrote down the telephone numbers on signs for farm land he liked the look of. In some cases, he bought the land. *Would Bob be interested in an investment in the Orpheum?* I wondered.

David Zimmerman and I talked. I could see that the idea was

very interesting to David, who was looking for something exciting to get involved with. He suggested that I put together a prospectus on the project he could show Bob. Thus began my very thorough review of the Orpheum physical plant and the costs to bring it up to the technical level I needed. At the time, the Orpheum was owned by local movie magnate, Ted Mann, and used only occasionally for first-run films. With his permission, I was given access to the theatre, and I brought in construction experts to assess its current condition. The costs to bring the heating plant, the available electrical power, the toilets, etc., up to national touring standards were substantial, but not impossibly so. Ted Mann indicated that he would be willing to part with the venue at a "reasonable" cost (meaning that he wanted to dump the place).

Armed with all this information, I prepared a detailed pro forma on the cost to acquire the Orpheum, the estimated costs of bring it up to Broadway standards, the costs of running the venue, and what a typical week of Broadway and a typical live concert might yield. I ended the document with the commitment of Laurel Ann Wilson to book *A CHORUS LINE* with me if/when we get the theatre ready for her show.

David was excited, and he promised to show it to his brother. At the time, Bob had a property in Loretto, Minnesota, a very small town a half-hour from Minneapolis. Bob's place had a variety of buildings that Bob had fixed up for himself. His brother David had a more contemporary house on the property just as you turned in the driveway.

Days passed, and I was worried that Bob would go back to his house in Malibu before we got a reaction from him. But one early winter day in 1978, I was told by David that Bob would like to sit-down with me the next day to discuss my proposal. Bob would come down to David's house and meet me there. I arrived at the scheduled time and was led into David's kitchen. There was Bob with a cup of coffee and a copy of my proposal. David and his wife Gayle then left, leaving me alone with Bob on a crisp, snowy morning.

We immediately launched into a two-hour discussion about the pros and cons of my proposal, and why I thought it could work. It became obvious early on that Bob had studied my projections carefully, had absorbed all my arguments, and was testing me on each of them. Bob immediately impressed me as someone who had substantially more real estate and business acumen than I had given him credit for. Finally, we talked about my background and legal training, and about the commitment I had received from the New York Shakespeare Festival to present *A CHORUS LINE* when the theatre was ready. (Amazingly, no one I made that claim to ever determined to confirm the commitment by contacting Joe Papp). At the end of the meeting, Bob said that he found the idea interesting and gave me the okay to talk to Ted Mann about what purchase price he would accept.

How to describe Ted Mann? Self-made cinema magnate. Married to movie star Rhonda Fleming. Owner of Mann's Chinese Theatre in Los Angeles. Short but imposing. Fan of polyester suits with contrasting piping. Totally full of himself but a good guy once you got to know him. Ted had an office above the old Pantages Theatre on Hennepin Avenue just down from the Orpheum run by his long-time assistant, Esther, who I had gotten to know. I learned long ago that to get to an important person, get to be on great terms with that person's gatekeeper.

Esther helped me set up a meeting with Ted, and I told him that I had an unnamed person who wanted to consider purchasing the Orpheum from him, but needed to know what price he would need to pay. Even though it was widely known that Ted wanted to either sell the Orpheum or tear it down and sell the land, Ted at first tried to bluff me with ridiculously high multimillion-dollar prices. I basically told him to get real quickly or the opportunity to sell would go away. After a lot of back and forth, we settled on $900,000, which I thought might be fair, based on the actual value of the nearly full-block land the theatre sat on. But I told him that I would need to have an appraisal done to verify the valuation.

The appraisers told me that since the theatre had not been

generating revenue for a few years, that the only valuation method they could use is the value of the land less the cost of tearing down the property. But their estimate came in higher than the $900,000 that Ted had agreed to accept.

Dylan thought the price we had set seemed reasonable, and said to get a purchase agreement drafted. Working with Bob's New York business advisors, Ben and Naomie Saltzman, and with his Los Angeles entertainment attorneys, we arrived at an approved document. Ted Mann signed, and the deal was complete. I called Laurel Ann Wilson, told her that Bob Dylan had bought the theatre and we were about to put money into getting it ready for her show. She said the run must be two or more weeks, and that she had an opening on her schedule from July 3 through July 21, 1979, she could offer us. Could we be ready for her by then? I immediately realized that the dates being offered were over the Fourth of July, a black-hole time for live shows in Minnesota since most people spent Fourth of July week at their cabins. Obviously this period was open only because any sane presenter would not accept the period.

But when told that there would not be another opening for the next year, we decided to roll the dice and accept a three-week run. The rapidly approaching run put a lot of pressure on us; could we get the theatre ready in six months? The answer, we would find, was yes, but we would be completing the last upgrades on the day of the show's opening night.

We immediately began the backstage upgrades: increased electrical power, more dressing rooms, repair to the very antiquated cold-water cooling system, etc. The main power for the backstage area was direct current rather than the now standard alternating current, and modern shows with hundreds of stage lights needed much more power than we could easily provide. Those issues took the lion's share of our budget.

In the hall itself, we pretty much did everything wrong. Since we did not have time to restore the vibrant colors of the original design, we just slapped some beige paint on everything and called it done. We had the main floor seats reupholstered with a tan cotton fabric, but we used cotton padding instead of foam, which within a year of use had matted to a very uncomfortable dense surface which people complained about. And because we used David's home interior decorator, we laid some very cheap and plain gray polyester carpet with a fine pattern that was just what the interior did not need. I called the decorating scheme "terminally beige."

On the day of our *A CHORUS LINE* opening, we were still laying carpet in the mezzanine area in front of our offices (later to become a large Women's Restroom area). The show's legendary press representative, Horace Greeley McNab, was presiding over continual rounds of press interviews in our office during the carpet laying, and I can recall with horror when a television personality came walking through the mezzanine heading to our offices and did not notice that not only was the carpet not laid just in front of our door, but that the floor had just been coated with carpet glue. The guy came up at a good pace, and before I could warn him, he hit the glue, fell, and slid more than fifteen feet on the slick surface, in the process coating himself with glue. He had to strip in our office and have someone bring him some fresh clothes. Not a happy guy, but we bought him a new suit; and he never sued us.

The easiest part of the opening was the "take in" of the show. The traveling crew had seen everything on the road, and even though we had a pretty green local crew, they made everything work, and the show itself was spectacular. But just twenty or so minutes into the first act, a rainstorm hit the area, and because we had not installed back-up valves on our sewer connections, the entire basement, with all the offices and dressing rooms, flooded with a foot of raw sewage and fecal material. It dissipated in five or ten minutes but the smell was not pleasant, and we had to spend the next day cleaning and disinfecting the area. Again, the national crew took it in stride.

Our sales lagged a bit over the Fourth, but because of the

quality of the show and the amazing publicity the show got, sales rebounded and the last two weeks of the run completely sold out.

Our lead Cassie, Wanda Richert, was sensational, and she went on to star in the Broadway smash *42ND STREET* and date the show's director, Gower Champion. On the opening night of the show, Gower died suddenly, but the show's producer, the legendary David Merrick, withheld the news from the cast until the curtain call, then came on stage and broke the news to Wanda, and to the stunned cast, crew, and audience.

Sadly, *A CHORUS LINE* would prove to be the most successful show in the Zimmerman era. There were just not that many A-level touring shows available, so we were relegated to booking "bus and truck" and "split-week" shows that did not come close to the quality of seeing shows on Broadway. More often than not, we got shows with bad sets (doors slamming wiggled the entire wall), poor sound systems, barely adequate casts, and over-the-hill C-level stars like Forest Tucker in *SHOW BOAT*. Predictably, we did not sell enough tickets to make money. Our few real successes included a sold out four-night run by Liza Minelli and a multi-show run by Lena Horne. But these successes occurred infrequently.

In those early days, booking a Broadway Touring Show was a whole different process. Theater executive Ernie Rawley had a pretty much one-person office in a beautiful brass-facaded building on Broadway near Sardi's that the touring industry had set up: the Independent Booking Office. Theater bookers from around the country would call to set up appointments with Ernie. Each year I would get an appointment scheduled and fly to New York to see what touring shows might be available in the coming year. The meetings started at 10:00 AM or so, and the first thing Ernie did was to offer me a Scotch, which he poured from a half-gallon bottle on a rotating stand which he kept on his credenza. And he would have one (or more) too. Then he'd reach for a bunch of leather-bound ledger books, each representing the route of a touring show, and check through his handwritten notes to see if or when it might "route" into Minneapolis. Then I would check with the Orpheum and State calendars I brought along to see how the offered dates would work. After a couple of hours work, I would okay four or five shows, and Ernie would enter them into the ledgers. Deals done. No price negotiation; you either approved his entire deal or it didn't go into the book.

Then we would descend to the street and walk over to Sardi's for a late lunch—at which time Ernie had several more Scotches, and between courses, we got up and walked around the restaurant, and I was introduced to many of the producers of the shows I had just booked. It was a small and exclusive club, and I was thrilled to be a part of it.

After my meeting, I'd see some shows compliments of the producers, and then I'd fly back home, receive some marketing materials, and go to work trying to market my "season." But the finances of touring Broadway were not at all stable and were dependent on each market performing well enough to keep the show on the road for the many weeks prior to my week. I read the *Variety* grosses religiously to see how each of my shows was performing, and whether it was likely to actually reach Minneapolis.

Along with B or C-level shows, also working against us was the fact that we really didn't have a working air-conditioning system, so summer dates proved spotty in terms of comfort. On the opening night of the Lena Horne show, the weather was blazing hot, and our "swamp cooler" system (cold water drawn up 300+ feet from our artesian well was misted and passed through big air ducts to cool the air) surrendered easily, and caused the humidity, especially in the balcony, to be jungle-like. I still have the vision of a Lena Horne fan in a tuxedo literally soaked to the skin with sweat running down his face.

Working for us was the fact that Dylan made a lot of money, and for ten years he benefited from the tax losses he could take from theatre ownership. But three years after our *CHORUS LINE* success, we had run through a bunch of money, and Bob's people decided to cut their losses. We ceased actively promoting shows, most of the staff, myself included, were let go, Orpheum Theatre Corporation was dissolved, and the theatre became a rental facility. Dylan later sold the Orpheum to Jerry Lonn of Seattle's Northwest Releasing on a contract for deed, but Lonn had as little success as we had, and defaulted the theatre back to Dylan within a couple of years. After that, David attempted to rent to venue to outside promoters, but with little success.

By the end of Dylan's ten-year tax advantage period, the Orpheum had returned to an unfortunate state of disrepair, having experienced some vandalism and some water leaks that damaged the balcony interior. Deferred maintenance was taking its toll, and the theatre was not generating much revenue. Rumors of Dylan's efforts to sell the theatre to a church or demolish it and sell the land revved me up. I realized that in the years since I had been absent from the Broadway business, the industry had changed for the better. British shows like *PHANTOM* and *CATS* had arrived, and the overall quality of the touring shows had become much better. This time, rather than trying to find a private investor, I decided that I could make a strong argument to the City of Minneapolis that the Orpheum was a city treasure and a potential downtown economic development tool, and they needed to work with me to save it rather than letting it be torn down. Enter the Orpheum's savior, the head of the Minneapolis Community Development Agency (MCDA), James Heltzer.

NOTE: In August of 1992, I promoted what many say were some of Dylan's best shows—five sold-out performances at the Orpheum. Each show featured a different set list, and the mysterious thing about these gigs is that he didn't seem to stay at his Loretto farm between shows. In fact not even his band members admitted to knowing where he was, and each night we waited anxiously just before showtime for his arrival. But he always arrived and these shows were magical.

CHAPTER EIGHT

ENTER THE CITY OF MINNEAPOLIS

THE CONDITION OF HENNEPIN AVENUE IN 1988, AS DYLAN looked for a way to rid himself of the Orpheum Theatre, was somewhere between grim and dangerous. You might walk safely down the east side of the street, but venturing onto the west side, with its dive bars like Moby Dick's, Brady's, and Mousey's was risky. Moby's, with its "A Whale of a Drink" slogan, was thought to be the most fearsome. But the whole street was unsavory, from the music venues to the porn theaters. How Schinder's survived on the corner of 7th and Hennepin was a mystery to me. If Hennepin's west side was wild, venturing west on foot any farther than that was unwise. Having the entire Orpheum block dark and unused added to the city's concern. It seemed like a perfect time for a discussion about how the City of Minneapolis might work with me to reopen the Orpheum.

My partner at the time, Tom Hoch, worked for the Minneapolis Community Development Agency (MCDA), the development arm of the city. That seemed as good a place to start as any. I waited until the press reports of Dylan's efforts to sell the building to a church grew strong, then set up a meeting with MCDA head, Jim Heltzer, to urge him not to allow the city to lose the irreplaceable asset that was the Orpheum.

I prepared a packet on how many other old vaudeville theaters were being restored and returned to action as homes for Broadway shows. At that point, it was the opinion of many downtown movers and shakers that Heltzer had more power in the city than either the mayor or any council member, so his interest was crucial.

Heltzer requested that David Zimmerman give us access to the Orpheum so we could assess its current condition, and he reluctantly agreed to do so. (Since moving my stuff out of the Orpheum, I had not talked to David. I'm sure he blamed me for our failure to make the theatre work). Heltzer had a bunch of city engineers go through the building and make cost estimates. Meanwhile he and I did our own research. I recall meeting Jim at the Intermission Lounge, a dive bar next to the Orpheum, at 8:00 AM one morning to check it out. Amazingly, most of the bar seats were already occupied. We sat down, had a beer, and talked with the patrons for the next hour. Heltzer was able to blend in perfectly and have some great conversations.

Our investigations indicated that the Orpheum faced a great likelihood of being torn down unless the MCDA intervened to save it. I had learned from other cities that unless and until the theatre is seriously threatened, city governments refused to act. So Heltzer and I both sounded the alarm and got the City Council's attention.

Obviously the key to the Orpheum's success was product—the successful booking of live shows to generate revenue for the MCDA effort. So we needed to put forward a scenario for the successful reuse of the building. Since I had a reasonably successful concert and Broadway promotion career on my resume, I believe Jim Heltzer felt I would be a good partner in his effort to save the venue.

Certain members of the City Council were receptive, and Heltzer was a master at lining up votes based on the financial incentives he could dole out to each Council Ward. Heltzer got the votes even though he as yet had no plan for reuse. But faced with the threat of losing the Orpheum, the city bought it. The deal was completed on June 25, 1988, at a purchase price of $1,400,000. Bob Dylan signed the purchase agreement in New York. His signature was notarized by his assistant, Naomi Saltzman. Heltzer signed on behalf of the MCDA, and the deal was complete.

While the MCDA proceeded with the upgrades that Heltzer and I had talked about to return the Orpheum to operational status, the question of theatre management needed to be determined quickly, and in a fair and unbiased way. Following their usual procedure, the MCDA issued a request for proposals. Four entities responded: Company 7/Jam Productions, The Palmer Group (developer of the LaSalle/State Theatre block), the Minnesota Timberwolves, and The State Theatre Group/Fred Krohn. I had formed my newest entity to save and manage the State Theatre; but that decision was down the line, and it seemed likely that one entity would ultimately manage both the Orpheum and the State Theatres. So I aggressively sought the Orpheum contract. I had already done so much work on the Orpheum and, since I had promoted shows there in the past, I knew far more about the facility than the rest of the proposers.

As I expected, the MCDA chose me for a one-year management agreement, beginning October 11, 1988. I was quickly added to the MCDA task force on the Orpheum, and began working with a great team of staff members to get it ready to open. The deal I negotiated did not require the MCDA to pay me any guaranteed amount. Rather, I proposed to take a percentage (originally 26 percent) of the combined revenues I was able to generate. I was to handle ticketing, bar operation, the stagehand contract, and all other aspects of the theatre operations through my entity, but provide the MCDA with monthly updates on revenues and an annual audit of operations. The fact that I was confident enough that I could generate cash that I did not require a guaranteed fee from the City of Minneapolis was one of the deciding factors in this RFP and the many that would follow in the coming years.

I had a phone installed, rented some office furniture, and

began a very stressful first year, attempting to convince outside promoters and the artists I worked with that they could move to the Orpheum successfully. My only company in that dark and spooky theatre was my German shepherd dog, Max. Because the utilities were so ancient, I often found myself shoveling coal into the two boilers on weekends when our custodial person was not working.

The theatre was still terminally beige, the seats were not very comfortable, the backstage was nasty, the electrical power inadequate, and smoking had been permitted in the theatre for so long that it reeked of tobacco (something I immediately vetoed). I had large no-smoking signs hung everywhere, and it still took years for people to accept that change.

The dreary vaudeville dressing rooms were stacked within the stagehouse on seven levels with no working elevator, and the artists didn't believe they had to use such decrepit rooms. I clearly recall walking up four or five levels of dressing rooms to settle with one of my first artists, Emmylou Harris. Other artists I managed to sign that fall were The Nylons, Kenny Loggins, Robert Palmer, a multi-show David Copperfield run, Cheap Trick, and *SOUTH PACIFIC* with Robert Goulet.

During these early days, I had to continually battle the negative elements on the street, including a very active "sauna" next door. I observed the operation for several nights and saw a surprising number of men entering the establishment surreptitiously in the dark of night. The next day I hatched a plan: I ran an extension cord up to the Orpheum marquee overlooking the sauna entrance, wired up several bright theatrical lights, and aimed them at the front door of the sauna so no one could enter without being seen. Then at about 10:00 PM, I turned them on and watched for a while. To me it seemed that men were walking up but, because of the bright lights, were reluctant to enter. The next day the proprietor of the sauna, a small Asian woman I had met before, called me on the phone and yelled, "Mr. Klone, Mr. Klone, turn off the frucking rights!"

Sauna next door to the Orpheum Theatre, early 1980s

Note: When one of my business partners, Lee Lynch, eventually bought the sauna building and the remainder of the corner, he and I had the opportunity to go into the sauna. As expected, we found a warren of small rooms with cot-like beds, but we were startled to find that on the wall of each room was a poster of the girls of the *LENINGRAD MUSIC HALL*, a show we had promoted at the Orpheum a couple of years earlier. We had thrown out all the posters the company supplied since they had very visible pubic hair coming out of their skimpy costumes. But obviously the sauna thought it appropriate for their clientele. We also found five or six rotting four-foot carp in the small enclosed courtyard in back of the building.

CHAPTER NINE

SAVING THE STATE

WHILE TRYING TO FIND LIVE EVENTS FOR THE OR- pheum, my concern was also with the future of the State Theatre across the street. It had for a few years been the home of the Jesus People Church but it was now vacant and unused. The church had made some possibly substandard technical upgrades in order to produce their very successful Christmas production of *THE GOSPEL AC- CORDING TO SCROOGE* each Christmas season. Since a major development was looming for the State Theatre block, I decided that getting more familiar with the venue could be an asset down the line when discussions of its future were being considered. I thought it might be interesting to promote a couple of shows in the venue so I could see how the acoustics were and gain some firsthand promoter cred. In August 1988 I brought Ray Charles, The Raelettes, and his band to the State. I had to recreate all the things a theatre is usually equipped with, including stage rigging, sound and lighting, a box office, concessions, dressing rooms, and ushers. There was also the odd problem of the large full-immersion baptismal font where the old orchestra pit used to be (left over from the Jesus-people era).

Two strange and memorable things happened at that concert that still stick in my mind. Since there were no decent dress- ing rooms on site, I had to access a closed hair salon within the building, tape brown paper on the windows for privacy, and thoroughly clean up the space. Ray arrived at the stage door, I took him down to this ad lib dressing room, helped him get his tux out of its bag, hung it up, and showed him where the toilet and sink were. When he said he would be fine, I left him to get ready for his performance. When I came back a half an hour later, Ray was in his boxer shorts changing into his tux, and a small crowd had gathered at the windows.

Much of the paper covering the window glass I'd taped up had fallen off, and those on the sidewalk were getting more of a show than the one Ray thought he would be giving. I helped Ray get dressed, helped with his tie, and hustled him out of there before he realized he had an unexpected audience.

For his soundcheck, our experienced sound crew had set up mics throughout the band area so we could achieve a good mix of the many band instruments. When Ray and I arrived, Ray insisted that ALL of the mics be removed, because that's the way he had always done things. Predictably, the resulting sound was muddy, with some instruments too hot and some almost inaudible. Finally I went up to Ray, told him what I was hearing from the audience, and suggested that we try the mics again to see whether he thought they helped. After some argument, he agreed, but told me in no uncertain terms that if during the show he did not like the sound, he would walk off the stage and not return. My sound crew and I were on pins and needles for the whole show. But the sound was excellent, and Ray seemed to be having a great time. Afterward, he told me that it sounded okay, but his band members privately thanked me, saying that they had wanted to insist on the mics for months, but were too afraid to cross their boss.

A month later I brought in The Robert Cray Band at the height of their initial fame. They sold out and performed a very impressive show, which led me to believe that Robert was the next Eric Clapton— something that for whatever reasons did not pan out.

After this sold-out two-show experiment at the State, it was obvious to me that the venue had great natural acoustics (as many of the wonderfully designed vaudeville theatres were blessed with) and decent sightlines. Certainly the State deserved to be saved and operated as part of a Hennepin Theatre District. The experience I gained promoting these two pop-up shows allowed me to make that argument several years later.

As I struggled for a couple of years trying to return the Orpheum to service, the debate I knew was coming over the future of the State finally hit. As the LaSalle project was nearing approval for tax increment financing, David Frauenshuh, the developer of the project, was proposing to tear down the State Theatre and use some of the artifacts to provide a 200-seat recital space within its development as a substitute. The State had reached the danger zone, which demanded action. Once again I went to the MCDA and the City Council to strongly suggest that the State could also be part of a revived Hennepin Theatre District, and should be preserved in full.

Realizing that I needed some business and financial credibility, I enlisted three powerful and respected city titans: former Honeywell chief and Broadway theatre-owner, James Binger; Carmichael Lynch advertising head, Lee Lynch; and attorney and former Minnesota Attorney General Douglas Head, to join me in this effort. Brett Smith and others had begun the battle to prevent the State's demise, but I brought in the heavy artillery and began an aggressive lobbying campaign.

All three of my partners in "The State Theatre Group" were very generous in their participation since, for many months, the odds of persuading developer David Frauenshuh to preserve the entire State Theatre seemed remote. Mayor Don Fraser had made major contributions to Minneapolis both as 5th District congressperson and as mayor, but theatre was not his thing. His aide, Jan Hively, seemed to me to be tied to the established arts groups like Northrop Auditorium, the Walker, the Guthrie, and the Minnesota Orchestra. None of those folks wanted any additional competition for their programs and existing venues. I recall hearing about a meeting of arts movers and shakers scheduled in

Jan Hively's City Hall office that I was not invited to. Despite my shyness, I barged in, sat down, and joined the conversation, much to Hively's displeasure.

I did, however, have allies on the City Council—most notably Sharon Sayles Belton, and we were able to convince others to join our cause. In order so show council members other successful theatre districts, Jim Heltzer and I arranged a junket to show interested council members the successful theatre districts in Chicago and Cleveland, each of which had beautifully restored theatres that were operating very successfully. They had been spearheaded by Ray Shepardson, who had singlehandedly saved many old vaudeville theaters and would later work with us on both the State and the Orpheum restorations. Ray was a unique guy—think Harold Hill in *THE MUSIC MAN*—and he really impressed the City Council. Once they could see what my vision for the State was, four or five council members became strong advocates.

We also lobbied developer David Frauenshuh, attempting to persuade him that a restored State Theatre could be a major asset for his project rather than the dead zone he assumed it would be. At first Frauenshuh refused to even give me access to the theatre, but as pressure built and preservationists and downtown business leaders rallied to the building's cause, he relented.

One of the major sticking points in the discussions with Frauenshuh was my insistence that the State Theatre stagehouse (the sub-building housing the stage and the fly space) was too small, and the shallow stage depth would not accommodate most Broadway shows. We needed to back the rear wall up about ten feet, taking that space away from the LaSalle project's main and second-floor lobby space. Frauenshuh was adamant that his plans would not allow that. I recall a winter day when we invited David to lunch at the Carmichael Lynch offices, which were then housed in several magnificent old mansions just north of the Minneapolis Museum of Art. Lee Lynch had arranged an intimate lunch in the Pillsbury Mansion in front of its massive stone fireplace, and I think Frauenshuh was impressed. He was under

Tom Hoch, Fred Krohn, and Ray Shepardson during State construction

great pressure to complete his negotiations with the MCDA so his project could proceed; and I think he finally saw allowing the full State Theatre to be included in his development as the tipping point of his efforts. Ultimately the City Council gave Frauenshuh an ultimatum: include the full State Theatre in your plans or project approval would be unlikely, and Frauenshuh buckled. The Council subsequently approved his project with a full-size State Theatre included.

Soon after that approval, the MCDA set up a design-build team consisting of MCDA staff, me and my staff, Ray Shepardson, staff architects from Hammel Green and Abrahamson, sound and lighting consultants, and members of the LaSalle project staff. While all were very skilled and professional, HGA and the consultants had little expertise with Broadway and professional concert venues, having worked mainly on college "performing arts" centers. That left Ray Shepardson and me to advocate for the things that would allow the theatre to operate efficiently with so many shows loading in and out frequently. Rather than the permanently installed sound and lighting systems HGA and the consultants were used to, we persuaded the group to have sound, lighting, and electrical power access panels on the side of the stage, so shows that were carrying their own sound and lighting could plug into our speakers and lighting instruments from the stage rather than having to run their own cable, lighting instruments, and speakers into the theatre. Ray and I were confident that we had saved substantial show costs by insisting on these design adjustments.

We got our extra ten feet for an expanded stage and, while not optimum, it proved to be just enough extra space to accommodate most Broadway and concert attractions. We also got a beautifully restored theatre interior, new theatre seats with greatly improved sightlines, and a great selection of the theatre sound, lighting, and equipment required to operate a first-class Broadway touring venue. The colors chosen by designer Tony Heinsbergen, Jr. (whose father had been the State's original interior designer) were perfect, and made the State a very desirable venue to play. As the State approached its reopening in early 1991, I took much personal pride in the work I had put into making it very functional, and a unique and stunning venue.

After a very successful run of opening shows at the State (*CAROUSEL*, Harry Connick, Jr., Mannheim Steamroller, Anne Murray, among others), I faced the daunting task of finding enough shows to fill both the Orpheum and the State. There was some interest from New York Broadway producers; but they were booking out a year or more, and we could not afford to leave the State empty for months at a time.

Then lightning struck and the result would change the developing Hennepin Theatre District for decades to come. I recall sitting in my office in the State Theatre basement with several staff members and my dog, and getting a phone call from Garth Drabinsky in Toronto. The call was brief. "I have been reading about your new Minneapolis theater and might be interested in renting it. Can you meet me in the lobby at 10:00 AM tomorrow so I can take a look at it?"

I vaguely knew Garth's name but had no idea what he might want. But I of course I said I'd be happy to meet him.

The fully-restored State Theatre. PHOTO BY GEORGE HEINRICH

The next day precisely at 10:00 AM, a limo pulled up in front of the State and a large man with a cane and a decided limp crawled out and walked up to the front doors, where I met him. He walked into the newly gilded lobby, looked around quickly, then proceeded into the theatre. He walked down the main aisle with difficulty, looked around quickly, the walked back up the aisle, saying nothing to me.

I asked him whether he would like a tour of the backstage area and he said yes. After a quick discussion of the available power and stage equipment, we walked back to the lobby and he said, "I'll take it, assuming you have the dates I need."

When I asked him what date he needed, he said, "I need it for eighteen weeks this fall," which floored me. I had no idea what he had in mind. "I need a place to launch my tour of *JOSEPH AND THE AMAZING TECHNICOLOR DREAMCOAT* starring Donny Osmond, and this theater and market seem perfect to me."

I told him I thought I could make his dates work. He said he would call me tomorrow to confirm, and he walked out and got into his waiting limo.

Since the State had barely opened, I had no difficulty moving a couple of tentative holds and blocking off the dates Garth wanted. But I was a little apprehensive in doing so, since I could not conceive of any Broadway show running for that many weeks in the Minneapolis-St. Paul market, and I did not want to face a cancellation which might leave so many dark weeks with no show product.

Garth called the next day, I told him the dates were his, and he asked that I immediately prepare a lease agreement for his signature. He said I needed to be quick because he was going to announce the booking in several days with Sir Andrew Lloyd Webber participating in the press conference. After some quick conferences with Lee Lynch, Jim Binger, and MCDA staff, we decided to roll the dice and see what happened.

True to his word, Garth signed and returned the lease, and had a very splashy press conference in Toronto with ALW present. I immediately got scores of calls from my entertainment industry friends asking how I pulled off such an amazing coup. "Right place, right time, I guess," I said. But Garth's unexpected visit had changed everything—we had gone from a new theatre with few bookings to the hottest venue in the country in just two days. I felt like the luckiest guy in the world.

As the opening night of *JOSEPH* approached, the production and the long run dominated the media. Garth's press staff were pros, and Donny Osmond proved to be the most friendly and cooperative star we have ever had in any of the theatres. The entire run was nearly sold out by opening night, and Andrew Lloyd

Andrew Lloyd Webber
at the opening night of
JOSEPH

Weber showed up, putting things way over the top. I can recall talking to him at the after-party at Palomino Restaurant after the opening night performance. "I think my little show will settle into your theatre nicely," he said. That was an understatement. The show sold out, generated nearly $7,000,000 in ticket sales, and resulted in a rebooking before the original booking was finished.

Our only stress came during the few shows that Donny Osmond was unable to perform. He had gotten such good reviews, and we had marketed him so aggressively, that people were often in tears when we told them that the understudy would be going on in his place, and that there were no tickets available for any of the later shows.

Note: During the second and even longer run of *JOSEPH* in 1995 ($10,000,000+), Donny had obviously had his fill of the show, and would fly home to be with his family during the three days we had scheduled off at the end of each week. When he returned, it was obvious that he really didn't want to do the show. I often had to go to his apartment near the theatre just before the first show and beg and persuade him to come to the theatre and get into costume. Since there was a backstage door near his apartment, I gave him a key to make it as easy as possible for him to perform. It's still referred to as the Donny Door.

CHAPTER TEN

REBIRTH OF THE ORPHEUM

NOTHING SUCCEEDS LIKE SUCCESS, AND THE STATE HAD delivered success in spades. But as great and popular as the State proved to be, it still had some obstacles that made it difficult for me to land other Broadway shows: at 2,100 seats, it was larger than the Ordway, but still pretty small by touring Broadway standards. Even with the extra ten feet of stage depth, the stage and wings (the offstage spaces on either side of the main stage) were too small. So to accommodate the "mega" touring shows, I determined to try to rehab the Orpheum, hopefully greatly expanding the stagehouse so virtually any Broadway show could be produced at the venue. I needed a restored 2,600-seat venue with a very large stage, greatly expanded chorus and star dressing rooms, and a lobby that could provide concessions and restrooms for sellout crowds.

This time I did not have to ask city leaders to imagine what an economic development tool a restored theatre could be. They had all marveled at the *JOSEPH* crowds, and were ready to take the dream even farther. But in order to get the project moving, I needed to land another *JOSEPH* to push things along. Beginning with the 1992–1993 Broadway season, I was working with Jim Binger's Jujamcyn organization, which was co-producing a Twin Cities Broadway season with the Ordway Music Theatre. All of us brainstormed about what mega-show might be available

Fred Krohn and *MISS SAIGON* producer
Cameron Mackintosh

to reopen the Orpheum if I could get funding to re-furbish that venue. We decided to go after producer Cameron Mackintosh's next show: *MISS SAIGON*. We got a relatively favorable initial response from his people, and I used that to sell the Orpheum project to the city. That sale was much easier than selling them on the State.

In April 1993, Cameron Mackintosh came to Minneapolis to tour the Orpheum and review our designs to upgrade this space. The Hammel Green and Abrahamson firm was again chosen to work with us on the Orpheum, and they provided a large number of drawings, color samples, and swatches for Cameron to review. I walked him through our plans, and all seemed fine until he got to the swatch for the seating fabric and an artist's rendering of the main floor with our chosen blue upholstery. He stopped dead, looked me in the eyes, and said, "My theaters do not have blue seating fabric. That color is too cold. My theaters have rich burgundy color seats."

Without losing eye contact, I told him that we had just de-cided to swap the blue color for his preferred rich red seating. He seemed pleased with the decision, and later that day con-firmed that he would approve our booking of *MISS SAIGON* for a seven-week run with a January 11, 1994, opening night.

The Orpheum restoration proceeded with the same excel-lent team that had been involved with the State, and things went well. Once again Ray Shepardson, Tom Hoch, and I advocated for design revisions that would make the venue more efficient and functional for large Broadway shows and concerts.

One disappointment was that Tony Heinsbergen, whose ge-nius for color had made the State a showplace, was unable to work on the Orpheum. A comparison of the two theatres' color palates shows how much he was missed.

Just as we were discussing the need to push out the back wall

(*opposite*) Restored Orpheum Theatre interior. PHOTO BY GEORGE HEINRICH

CHAPTER TEN

of the Orpheum stagehouse to increase its stage size, yet another amazing and fortuitous thing happened. Before I could even broach the idea of moving Tenth Street, which then tightly followed the rear stage wall, I got a call from the head of Minneapolis Public Works wondering if I would mind if they straightened out Tenth Street, giving us an additional thirty feet at the rear of our building. I gave him an enthusiastic yes.

With that extra space, we were able to remove the back wall of the theatre and increase the size of the stage, making it one of the largest of all the touring Broadway theaters. This extra space allowed us to book a number of pre-Broadway shows, including the world premiere of Disney's *THE LION KING*.

For the Orpheum, instead of installing new heating and air-conditioning equipment, we determined to connect the Orpheum up to Minneapolis Energy Center, which provided heat and chilled water to many of the downtown office towers and was just a block and a half from the theatre. (Ironically, a new chiller we had just installed in the Orpheum was used for only a matter of weeks prior to the restoration, and we determined that it would cost more than its $40,000 price to remove it and reuse it elsewhere. To this day, the unit has sat in the bowels of the Orpheum basement virtually unused).

The technical requirements of the *MISS SAIGON* production were massive. It would prove to be the largest show we ever booked (and most likely ever will again), and would require two weeks and seventy-one 18-wheel trucks to load the set pieces into the theatre. The entire stage had set pieces, which raised it from a few inches high at the front of stage lip to more than six feet at the rear. It was in fact so tilted that it was difficult to walk on, but created a very dramatic image when the Vietnamese army was marching down and right toward the audience. It gave "raked stage" a new meaning. The full-size helicopter that appeared backstage-left was a magic theatrical moment in each show. Not until *LION KING* did we have a more impressive production.

MISS SAIGON opened on January 11, 1994. While the run was

(*opposite*) Restored Orpheum Exterior with new marquee. PHOTO BY GEORGE HEINRICH

successful, demand weakened after the fifth week, and we had to work to sell the final shows. But like *JOSEPH,* it put the theatre on the national map and allowed us to book some impressive Broadway seasons going forward. However the developing rivalry between Theatre Live in Minneapolis and the Ordway in St. Paul nearly brought our success to a halt.

CHAPTER ELEVEN

LIGHTFOOT

ONE OF THE MOST ENDURING ARTISTS I HAVE HAD THE privilege of working with is "Canadian troubadour," Gordon Lightfoot. Our involvement began in 1972 and continues to this day.

It began early on, before I promoted a single show on my own, as it became more and more obvious to me that Harry Beacom's finances had become precarious, and he might not survive as a promoter. Harry had recently tied his wagon to Don Ellis, a very talented but somewhat inaccessible rock "big band" leader, and had agreed to promote him for twenty or more dates across the country. When none of the dates were successful, Harry effectively stopped promoting shows, moved to Los Angeles with his wife, Barbara, and began a new career selling custom draperies.

Beacom's demise had opened the way for me to enter the promotion business on my own. Working alongside Harry, I had worked with a bunch of artists I really respected; and I felt I could do the same things I'd done for Harry—this time as my own boss. But the first question was: Where would I find the investors I needed to underwrite my shows? Who would be my Morris Chalfen?

After talking to a few wealthy people, including Minnesota North Stars owner Walter Bush (I had worked one summer at Met Center and helped promote shows out there) I came up empty. No one was too interested in doling out money to a young and inexperienced promoter like me.

My answer came close to home. My brother Frank, associate general counsel for Waste Management, Inc. in Oak Brook, Illinois, had the capital I needed if I could persuade him that his investments would pay off. He suggested that I find a show and prepare an investment pro forma, and he would consider it.

For my first show, there was no question who I would choose: the Canadian folk artist, Gordon Lightfoot. I had been mesmerized by his sold-out concert at the Guthrie for Sue Weil, backed only by guitarist Red Shea. It seemed to me that anyone who saw him there would want to see him again. I called the Millard Agency, and they quoted me a fee of $9,000, plus $500. for Gord's sound system, for a show at the then brand-new O'Shaughnessy Auditorium on the campus of the College of St. Catherine in St. Paul. The agent said Sunday, January 23, 1972, might route on Gord's calendar, and I went to work on the details.

Issue #1 was that, at a $9,000 guarantee, I would need to do 7:00 and 10:00 shows on a Sunday night to cover costs, which didn't seem ideal to me. But I moved ahead and reserved the date at the venue after the agency agreed that Gord would do two shows in one night. I then gathered my expected costs and calculated what the promoter profit might be—approximately $5,000. I proposed that I would split 50/50 with my brother. Frank agreed that we should go ahead.

I did everything myself: I designed the print ads and the program. I silkscreened the posters. I set up the catering and coordinated all the venue issues. I handled the tickets (which then were "hard tickets" that were distributed and sold at all Dayton's stores). I worked with the MSA Student Store in Coffman Union, and with the Electric Fetus record store to sell tickets. I had to count tickets in and out, make sure they were kept safe at both stores, and finally do a cash settlement with each outlet just prior to the show.

Both shows sold out. Gord had just released "If You Could

Read My Mind," and it was rising on the *Billboard* charts, so that attention helped generate sales. Gord and his band were great to work with and very supportive of my efforts. In fact Gord suggested the next two acts I promoted: Canadian singer Anne Murray, and singer-songwriter Kris Kristofferson. Little did I know on that night that I would work with Gord and his band for another ninety-plus concerts over the next fifty years.

Per my predictions, we made $4,592., so Frank received a profit check of $2,296. Both of us were ecstatic, assumed that there was virtually no risk involved in the entertainment business, and determined to move forward with a series of other concerts.

On the Monday after the show, I got a call from a Catholic

Fred Krohn with Gordon Lightfoot, his band, and Jeffrey Siegel in clown costume sister at The College of St. Catherine, where O'Shaughnessy was located, and I was asked to report to the theater lobby at 11:00 AM. When I arrived, she and the president of the college took me through the theater, counted every cigarette burn, and said they would have to bill me for each at five dollars per burn. And that if it happened again, I would not be able to rent the theater going forward. After that, I had my ushers police cigarette smoking much more rigorously. (It's now hard to believe that smoking in a theatre was ever allowed).

Based on the success of the O'Shaughnessy shows, Frank and I decided that Gord might also do well in other Upper-Midwest markets. I tried him in Duluth, Madison, Milwaukee, Fargo, Grand Forks, and Rochester. All these shows virtually sold out, so every year or two, I booked a swing through these markets. Routing them on successive nights, as Gord requested, was easy for him, since he had a small jet to get him and his band from one city to the next. But I and a couple of informal staff members (Gary Tassone, Jimmy Allen, Ann Laughlin, and others) had to close each show, settle with the venue staff, make sure Gord's equipment truck was packed, and depart each show late at night. Then we had to drive most of the night, get to the next venue, and be there for the next day's load-in. We would sleep for a few hours and get back to the theatre in advance of Gord's arrival. This wore me down after a few days—definitely a young man's schedule, which I had to cut back on as I got older.

When I first knew Gord, he had a liking for Irish coffees prior to his shows. When he did two shows in one night (which was often in those days), I worried that he might mess up his late show due to too much whiskey. Things sometimes got especially bad when we were touring with an opening band that he knew. I recall a night in Duluth with Gord and openers, The Good Brothers, when, during Gord's second show, one of the Brothers came out on stage and "helped" Gord play his 12-string guitar. Gord strummed and the brother handled the frets, to the astonishment and confusion of the audience.

Gordon Lightfoot
backstage with Fred Krohn

Things seemed to get the wildest in Duluth for some reason. We always stayed at the Duluth Radisson Hotel, and Gord and his band and I made it a point to have an after-show drink at the hotel's revolving restaurant and bar on the top floor. One night long after the band members had gone to bed, Gord and I closed the bar after consuming a bunch of White Russians. When we got up to leave, it seemed that the restaurant was spinning at a high speed, and we both had to approach and step off the carousel portion of the room very slowly and carefully.

Gord had an eye for the ladies during that period. His sister Bev (who ran his business, Early Morning Productions, for years) once had to call me to request that I not give a backstage pass to an ex-girlfriend who had been stalking Gord from city to city.

For more than fifty years, I worked successfully with Gord on dates throughout the country—more than ninety total, and Gord has never let me lose anything on his shows. Most did well, but when I tried a new market unsuccessfully, he insisted that I pay him only what I could afford without a loss. I consider him a true friend, and I sense that the feeling is mutual. In the book accompanying his four-CD *Songbook* release, I am listed just after Bob Dylan and Kris Kristofferson as one of the "fine people I have known and/or worked with over the years." An honor.

Gord's tour managers and band members also became family. My mom and sister Lindy always baked special brownies for their Minneapolis shows.

Bassist Rick Haynes and drummer Barry Keane still tour with Gord, and I especially miss guitarist Terry Clements and long-time tour manager, Barry Harvey. Great guys, and always fun to be on the road with. No doubt that if I had to single out one artist I feel is responsible for my long career as a promoter, it is Gordon Lightfoot. He was the first artist I promoted, he gave me great advice on other artists, and he stuck with me for over fifty years. Gord is a consummate singer and songwriter who I am honored to have worked with.

CHAPTER TWELVE

MARLENE

I N THE EARLY PART OF MY CAREER, THERE WERE ESTABLISHED local promoters who "owned" their local markets, and it was very difficult for a new and unproven promoter to break into these fiefdoms. So when I started in the promotion business, I had to prove myself with artists the established Twin Cities presenters had passed on. Not many rock artists were available to me, but there were plenty of folk, jazz, and middle-of-the-road artists I *might* be allowed to work with. My only competition for these categories on occasion was Sue Weil at the Guthrie; but she and I were close and I considered her a mentor. Since my musical tastes were pretty eclectic, the artists I was offered fit me just fine.

The first shows I promoted were folk artists like Gordon Lightfoot, Judy Collins, Leo Kottke, Steve Goodman, Harry Chapin, and the like. I drifted into jazz, mainly because of the many hours my mom and I had spent watching variety shows on TV with some of the jazz greats like Ella Fitzgerald, Oscar Peterson, Sarah Vaughan, and Peggy Lee. From there my choices went farther and farther from the usual concert fare—my only requirement was that I must respect the artist's skills and talent.

One of my most out-there choices occurred in May 1974 when I determined to present legendary movie and cabaret star, Marlene Dietrich, at the O'Shaughnessy Auditorium in St. Paul. I was familiar with the glamour of her many films, and her somewhat

Marlene Dietrich return address card

eccentric talk-singing style. But the thing that convinced me was that one of my favorite artists and composers of the period, Burt Bacharach, had gotten his start as her conductor and arranger. Few of my fellow promoters thought promoting Marlene was a smart idea (and they proved to be correct), but I felt it was a live show that could be totally unique and memorable.

As with many other artists, the fee itself was not excessive, but the rider requirements greatly added to the show's costs. I needed to provide a first-rate local sixteen-piece orchestra (not difficult in Minneapolis-St. Paul due to the presence of both the Minnesota Orchestra and the St. Paul Chamber Orchestra), and make them available for a minimum of twelve hours of rehearsals. I needed to provide Ms. Dietrich and her conductor with hotel rooms for three nights. I was required to provide a very specific set of sound equipment and special mics. And I needed to hang a number of special lighting instruments per the lighting design plot I was provided.

I was told that the Dietrich was in Los Angeles at the Beverly Hills Hotel, and she would send me a packet with her detailed instructions. When it came, hand-addressed by her to "Fred Krohn, Impresario," I was shocked. No lighting gel in the United States would be adequate. She needed a special English "Bastard Amber" gel which was twice as thick (and twice as expensive) as its US counterpart. I needed to pay the shipping on her eight trunks worth of costumes and set pieces. She needed to be driven anywhere she wanted to go for the three days she would be in town to rehearse and perform. That might be the norm for the European impresarios she had worked with; but for me, these extra requirements meant the difference between making and losing money on the show. I quickly determined that I would not skimp, and would treat her with the respect she was due as a major star. But that meant that I would have to do virtually everything myself since I had no staff at that stage.

Marlene Dietrich's reimbursement for special lighting gel

The May morning of her arrival, I borrowed a new Lincoln Town Car from my parents' car-dealer friend, cleaned myself up a bit, and drove to the airport to pick her up. Many of her trunks had been shipped in advance and were at the theatre, so I expected just a piece or two of luggage. But I was told at the gate that she had five pieces of luggage that needed to go with her to the hotel. I grabbed a porter and cart.

When she deplaned, I walked up to her with my hand extended. She took one look at me and said, "Where is Mr. Krohn? He should be here to meet me personally."

When I told her that I was, in fact, Mr. Krohn, she looked dumbfounded. "Why do you want to work with the Dietrich? You are too young to know of me."

I told her that I greatly respected both her amazing film career and her later cabaret work; and in addition, I had a great admiration for her former conductor, Burt Bacharach (admiration she shared). At that moment, I won her over. She smiled and said she looked forward to working with me in the coming days, and that she would teach me all about her art form. I would find that she was true to her word.

We walked slowly to the Lincoln with the porter following us with the luggage, and I opened the rear door for her. She said no, that she would sit in the front seat with me. I helped her buckle her seat belt, and we began our short drive. When we reached the Hilton, where I had reserved the six-room penthouse suite, the hotel staff were at the ready and showed us to the top floor. The

Dietrich took one look at the grand space and told the staff to close off half the rooms—that she did not want me to have to pay the huge cost of such a grand suite.

I put her Louis Vuitton bags where she wanted them and helped her hang up the many outfits she brought along. Finally I noticed that the hotel had provided a chilled bottle of Champagne and some glasses, and I suggested that we try some. She agreed, and I opened the bottle carefully (turn the bottle not the cork) and poured two glasses. Ms. Dietrich took hers, I toasted to a successful engagement, and we both took a sip. She immediately put hers back on the table and said one word: "Mouthwash."

She said that she would like to rest for a while after her flight, but would like to be picked up at 2:00 PM to make a visit to the theatre.

I picked her up at the hotel (where her presence in the lobby was causing quite a stir), opened the front seat, buckled her in, and we made the short drive to O'Shaughnessy Auditorium, and 1,800-seat theater on the campus of the College of St. Catherine. We pulled up to the stage door, and I opened the door for her. But she could not release her seat belt. Nor could I even after several minutes of trying. So without any request for help from me, she slacked up the seat belt and crawled under it. I thought I might be in trouble, but she smiled as if to say "no problem," and we went into the hall.

The next morning at 8:00 AM we began a full day of rehearsals. Stan Freeman, her conductor following the departure of Burt Bacharach, worked with the local orchestra for an hour while Marlene was in her dressing room with her dresser. When she came onto the stage (to applause from the band members and stagehands), she put everyone through a rigorous day of rehearsals. Each cue was rehearsed over and over until both the stagehands and the players could do everything in perfect unison. The one she seemed most concerned about was an encore cue that required the two spotlight operators to hit her hand perfectly as she reached between the closed curtains. We must have repeated that for half an hour until it could be done without any unnecessary movement of the spots.

Dietrich insisted that no one, and she meant no one, was to be allowed in the hall during these rehearsals. But my dad, Herb, snuck into the third balcony to watch her in action. His stories about his experience always ended with how many times Marlene yelled, "Schtop, Schtop, Schtop" while he was there.

At noon, everyone took a break, and we went to the nearby Cecil's Deli for lunch. The Dietrich did not eat much, but she regaled the crowd with stories and could swear with the best of them. She was seemingly not on good terms with her conductor, Stan Freeman, both because she wanted Burt Bacharach to return to her to conduct, and possibly because, a year earlier, during the encore of a show in Washington, DC, Stan had fallen off the piano bench he was standing on while shaking her hand and yanked her into the orchestra pit. It took her months to recover from the severe injuries she sustained, and she almost lost her leg in the process.

On the day of the concert, the Dietrich arrived at the hall at 2:00, and she and her dresser allowed me to witness every detail of her transformation from seventy-three-year-old German hausfrau to the most glamorous and mysterious woman in the world- still one of the most miraculous illusions I have witnessed.

First on the pre-show agenda was Dietrich's version of a facelift. She removed her usual wig, glued thin gauze to the area behind both ears, and with the help of her dresser, attached the cloths to the skin of her scalp with needles. She seemed to have holes much like ear lobe piercings in her scalp, because there was no blood when the pins were inserted. The effect was instantaneous. Her face gained twenty-plus years in thirty seconds. There followed more than an hour of facial and hand makeup with colors that did not look too natural in close-up, but when viewed from a short distance looked perfect.

She then looked over to her custom-designed beaded dress, and showed me how heavy it was. I found it amazing that with her thin frame, she could wear such a substantial dress for such a long time. Next she showed me her two white floor-length swans-down capes, which she wore for her entrance and encores. She asked me to feel both and tell me the difference between the two. They looked identical, yet one felt much fluffier and more luxurious. She said I was correct, that the more opulent of the two was made from male swan feathers, and was worth twice what the second one, made of female feathers, was worth. She said she planned to wear the male swans down cape for that night's show, and instructed me to make certain that the stage floor was spotless so it would not be ruined.

After resting for a period, it was time for her to put on her beaded dress. She said that there were no zippers or buttons—that to achieve the perfectly smooth look on her body, she needed to be sewn into the dress each time she wore it. Dietrich stepped into it. The dresser pulled it up to her shoulders, and then began the sewing process, which took all of forty-five minutes. By this time it was one hour prior to curtain, and the orchestra was arriving and tuning up. Ten minutes prior to curtain, her dresser added the *pièce de résistance*, which completed her illusion—her wig made of silky Russian hair.

As the overture played, her dresser draped the male swans-down cape over her shoulders, and Dietrich was ready for her entrance. She walked out from stage right and there were audible gasps from audience members. They were enchanted with her myth creation and gave her a prolonged standing ovation.

There followed more than an hour of her legendary songs: "Lili Marlene," "Johnny," "The Boys in the Back Room," and many others—all with the arrangements by Burt Bacharach I had heard so many times on record. Finally she left the stage to a standing ovation as the orchestra vamped her overture again and again. As the applause crescendoed, she gave the audience one more song, her trademark "Falling in Love Again." A rain of flowers were thrown on the stage, and she personally accepted several bouquets from the front row. Then she was gone, the "Falling In

(*opposite*) Marlene Dietrich in the full-length swansdown cape she wore for her entrance and encores. Photographed by Milton H. Greene (c) 2021 Joshua Greene www.archiveimages.com.

Love Again" vamp of the orchestra repeating over and over to loud applause while the curtains slowly closed.

The vamp went on for several minutes, and I was worried that she was pushing the audience too far. But with perfect timing, she gave the signal for the much-rehearsed encore cue. She walked inside the closed curtain to the center of the stage, found the seam where the curtains parted, and reached one hand out for the audience to see. The two follow-spot operators hit her hand perfectly with a small circle of light, and after pausing for thirty seconds to let the excitement build, she threw open the curtain and revealed herself back in her swans-down cape. The place was pandemonium for ten minutes while she took her final bows and left the stage.

By the time I rejoined her backstage she had removed her wig, unpinned her scalp pins, been cut out of her dress, and was in a sort of sailor suit. Obviously the show had tired her. I immediately drove her to her hotel. In the morning, on the way back to the airport, she thanked me for having faith in her when many of her other US impresarios had refused to book her. I insisted that the pleasure was mine, and that the insights she had given me were going to influence my career for my entire life.

CHAPTER THIRTEEN

ELLA

SOON AFTER MY 1974 MARLENE CONCERT, I HAD MY FIRST opportunity to work with a totally unpretentious but prodigiously talented woman who certainly deserves her title of "The First Lady of Song," Ella Fitzgerald.

Like many jazz artists preferred to do back then, Ella decided to come into Minneapolis-St. Paul several days early to rest in her hotel and do some advance press prior to her concert. Bob Protzman, the St. Paul *Pioneer Press* music critic, and very knowledgeable on all things jazz, gladly accepted my invitation to do one of the interviews, and promised to get it published on the day prior to Ella's concert. My only "staff member" for this show was my mother, Lucy, who enjoyed every minute of her work assisting me with catering, travel arrangements, and artist relations. She was loved by every star she worked with. (My mother's career in my business would be cut short by her untimely death in May of the following year, leaving me with a void that remains impossible to fill).

We had booked a suite at the old Radisson Hotel for Ella, and I arrived there three days prior to the show to let her know that her 1:00 PM interview was in the lobby. I noticed that she had all three of

Ella Fitzgerald

Poster for her 1974 show, designed by Fred Krohn

her television sets tuned to a popular daytime soap opera and seemed entranced by the show. After several minutes, she asked me whether the writer would mind waiting for a few minutes while she watched the end of her favorite show. "We women have our programs," she informed me.

After the delay, Protzman connected with Ella, had a magical hour-long interview, and impressed Ella with his vast knowledge of her career.

With Ella, there was no need to rehearse; she was so on top of her game, and so naturally gifted, that too much rehearsal might only stifle her talent. So great was her reputation that she had her pick of top musicians. For my show, she brought along the legendary Roy Eldridge, who joined her regular trio consisting of Tommy Flanagan, Keter Betts, and Bobby Durham. They all referred to me as "boss," as many jazz artists seemed to do back then. The group set up and did a sound check so that Miss Fitzgerald could just walk in and do her show.

Like I did for all my shows back then, I designed, laid out, and silk-screened the posters advertising my concerts, and I personally found prime locations for them to be displayed prior to each event. They were usually nice enough so that salons, stores, and restaurants were happy to have them (and many were framed once the show occurred). My paper of choice was silver Mylar and the ink was usually black—somewhat of an art deco motif. I liked the 36"x48" Ella Mylar posters so much that I determined to use the same paper and graphic on the show programs, which were also a trademark of my shows. But when my mother tried to pick them up from the printer a day prior to the show, she found that the ink was not drying well, and it smeared when touched. She left them at the printer overnight to finish drying, then picked them up just prior to the show. They seemed dry, but unfortunately when handled by warm moist hands, they still smeared, and after a number of complaints from audience members, we had to discontinue their distribution. And we had to pay more than a few dry cleaning bills as well. Lesson learned.

Ella's show was amazing. It highlighted her uncanny ability to scat, to bend tempos and rhythms, and to ad lib a lyric to meet any need. She did "A-Tisket, A-Tasket," "Satin Doll," "Miss Otis Regrets," and selections from Cole Porter, Duke Ellington, and Harold Arlen, a generous tour of the American songbook, and made each song her own. No frills or choreography. Just spot-on interpretations of great songs made even greater by Ella.

At the end of the show, during one of several standing ovations, my youngest sister, Lisa, was tasked with bringing a bouquet of roses to the stage to present to Miss Fitzgerald. She ran down the main aisle to the front of the stage and raised the arrangement up to Ella. But diabetes had already started to claim Ella's eyesight, and she did not notice my sister through her thick glasses. Lisa screamed, "Miss Fitzgerald, Miss Fitzgerald," but was not able to get her attention. Finally one of her musicians intervened and got the roses to Ella.

The show ended, and it was obvious that the band members were not interested in the task of babysitting Ella. Instead, they all wanted to gig at a local jazz club. They asked me whether I would mind driving Ella back to the Radisson, and I gladly accepted. They packed up and left, and now only Ella and I remained backstage. After a few minutes, Ella appeared in her street clothes, topped by an exceptional ankle-length Russian sable coat. Even then, I was not a fan of fur, but I had never seen such a luxurious coat. I praised it, she asked me to feel the quality of the fur, and told me with her usual simplicity that it cost her $60,000. It looked all of that amount and more.

We drove back to the Radisson, and Ella suggested that we have a nightcap. We went to the Haberdashery, a funky "peanut bar" on the first floor of the hotel. We had a couple of drinks while she shyly told me about her childhood, her marriages, and her family. Finally she said she was tired. I walked her up to her room and said good night.

As I was driving home however, I suddenly got the sick feeling that Ella did not have her sable coat when I dropped her off at her room. I sped back to the hotel, left my car at the curb, ran into the bar, and hurried to the area where we were sitting. Under our table, on the floor and covered with peanut shells, was her $60,000 sable coat. I returned it to her the next morning as I was taking her to the airport. She had not missed it and seemed unconcerned.

Over the next few years, I was honored to present Ella in additional concerts, including one with Ella, pianist Oscar Peterson, and guitarist Joe Pass at Northrop Auditorium. During those years, it was always my pleasure to reconnect with her and find out what was new in her life. She had such a pure and childlike grace, and I was greatly saddened when I learned of her death in 1996.

CHAPTER FOURTEEN

MISS LEE

I N AUGUST 1987 I BOOKED ONE OF MY MOM'S FAVORITE singers, the Incomparable Miss Peggy Lee, for six shows in the Scandinavian Ballroom at the new Radisson Hotel. Miss Lee liked the idea, since early in her career she came from her home in Jamestown, North Dakota, to the original Radisson for a successful gig. Miss Lee (her band members suggest calling her "Peggy" would be too informal and is reserved only for her good friends) was then sixty-seven years old, had had more than her share of physical ailments, and performed mostly sitting down after walking in with the aid of a rhinestone-encrusted Lucite cane.

I was concerned about her health, about her stamina in undertaking six shows, and about whether I would be able to pull off an A-level show in a new hotel space with no concert equipment. I brought in an elaborate lighting system, two follow spots, and a state-of-the art sound system. We designed a ramp that allowed Miss Lee to walk onto the stage rather than be wheeled on in a wheelchair.

As was then pretty standard for jazz stars, Miss Lee arrived in Minneapolis several days early, along with four or five trunks for her costumes and props, and settled into a large suite in the brand-new Radisson Hotel.

We set rehearsals for the next day, and I mistakenly assumed that due to her frail health, she would not want a long rehearsal.

Miss Peggy Lee
promotional photo

Instead, she had her quintet of A-level players (Grady Tate, Emile Palme, Jay Leonhart, John Chiodini, and Mark Sherman) and my technical staff rehearse for the entire day. Each song was staged with its own lighting effects and band intros, and each had to be done over and over until everyone has them down cold.

The one I was most impressed with was the opening of one of her classic songs, "Fever," which was similar to Marlene Dietrich's encore cue. From a completely blacked-out room, her band started the familiar "Fever" vamp. She raised her hand up and started finger snapping to the beat. At that exact instant, the two follow spots must hit her hand with tight beams of light, illuminating only her long elegant fingernails and an impossibly large diamond solitaire on her ring finger. If the two spot operators don't hit the mark perfectly, the illusion would be shattered. If the spots bounce around trying to find her hand, the bubble would have been burst. When I later remark that the "Fever" cue is stunning, she reiterated one of her famous quotes: "Perfection is made up of trifles, but perfection itself is no trifle."

Beginning when she was the lead singer for the Benny Goodman Orchestra, Miss Lee always sang with understatement and

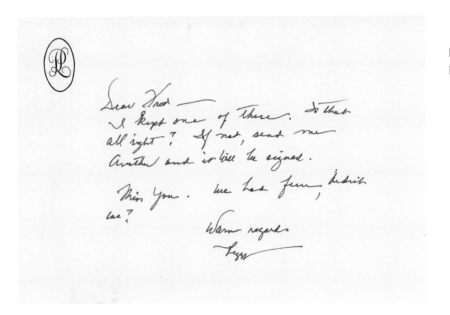

perfect diction. But her recordings do not do justice to her live voice—so easy and flexible and clean with a quality that no one else has ever had. Both her speaking voice (she told wonderful stories between songs) and her singing voice were incredible, and her sense of time was the equal of Ella's, I thought. She might appear frail offstage, but when the lights hit her perfect skin, she came alive.

Miss Lee performed six very generous shows, and included different songs in each set. Her quintet had played with her for so long that they had a seamless bond with her and could almost anticipate which song she would want to play next. She did many of the songs she was known for, including "Fever," "Is That All There Is," "It's a Good Day," and the one that I liked best, "I'll Be Seeing You," and many she wrote herself, including a selection of her songs from the Disney feature, *Lady and the Tramp*.

After the final show, she asked that I come up to her room and wait while her dresser helped her into bed. After about twenty minutes, I was ushered from her living room into her large bedroom suite. There was Miss Lee, propped up in her queen-sized bed, still in complete makeup, her trademark large platinum blonde wig, and in a beautiful silk nightgown and feather-trimmed robe—all of which personified the glamour of a bygone age. For the next twenty minutes she regaled me with stories of her life experiences and thanked me for making it possible for her to return to Minneapolis. Noting that she was looking sleepy, I thanked Miss Lee for her consummate star performances. She paused, then said, "Please call me Peggy."

"My honor," I returned.

I corresponded with Peggy for many years after these shows. Her handwritten notes were on Crane stationery and contained only an engraved "Miss Peggy Lee" or a PL monogram at the top. I still treasure those times, and was sad when she died in 2002.

CHAPTER FIFTEEN

A TALE OF TWO CITIES

I N OUR EARLY BROADWAY SEASONS, THE BROADWAY partnership between Jujamcyn Productions (owned by Jim Binger and Jujamcyn in New York) and the Ordway Center seemed to be working well. Because the Ordway was first and foremost a home for its principal tenants, the Minnesota Opera, the St. Paul Chamber Orchestra, and the Shubert Club, it did not have many weeks available for Broadway shows. So by necessity the partnership booked most of its shows into the (then) two Minneapolis theatres, the State and the Orpheum. The 1992–1993 season contained a long run of *JOSEPH AND THE AMAZING TECHNICOLOR DREAMCOAT*, and the 1993–1994 season featured the Orpheum's opening show, *MISS SAIGON*. The 1994–1995 season did not have a real blockbuster, but it was more than adequate in terms of shows and show weeks in Minneapolis vs. St. Paul. But as the 1995–1996 season began to be booked, the Ordway, which was then booking the season shows, began to favor its own venue over the two Minneapolis theatres, and made clumsy efforts to bring more of the season shows to the Ordway. This culminated when they at the last minute moved a twelve-week run of *SHOW BOAT* from the Orpheum to the Ordway, angering Minneapolis officials. In forcing their principal tenants to reschedule performances in order to accommodate *SHOW BOAT*, the Ordway also greatly annoyed their own important partners. To me, Bill Conner and the Ordway board and supporters seemed arrogant and tone-deaf to the criticism they were getting from all sides.

In the interim, Jim Binger, owner of Jujamcyn Theaters and Jujamcyn Productions, seemed to become more and more disenchanted with his Ordway relationship. The Ordway booked the shows (with Jujamcyn's input), marketed the shows, sold the tickets, decided where each show would play, and kept the lion's share of the net proceeds. When a more beneficial deal could not be negotiated, Binger determined to exercise an escape clause and end the Ordway/Jujamcyn relationship as of June 30, 1995. This seemed to catch the Ordway people by surprise, and they launched an effort to mend fences and continue the partnership. There followed a lot of "St. Paul and Minneapolis are really one united community, and we should put the interests of the citizens of these cities first and present just one unified Broadway season" discussions. Both mayors seemed at first to buy into this sentiment. They finally persuaded Binger and the Ordway to negotiate a new one-year extension with a potential second-year extension. So the entities booked a joint 1995–1996 season.

From the start, things did not go well. Binger still had the same problems with the relationship, and in an effort to improve things, he sent the Ordway board a list of eleven proposed changes to the agreement between them. All eleven suggestions were rejected by the Ordway at almost the same time as the Ordway unilaterally yanked *SHOW BOAT* from the Orpheum to the Ordway. The die was pretty well cast. Binger terminated the extension after one year, ending the Ordway/Jujamcyn relationship as of June 30, 1996.

This time, Mayor Sharon Sayles Belton and MCDA head Rebecca Yanisch had apparently had enough. While there was talk of once again attempting to put Humpty together, it was clear to insiders that Minneapolis officials disliked the Ordway's arrogance and its underhanded efforts to pull shows to St. Paul. They would forge a new Broadway season agreement with Jujamcyn

Productions and a nonprofit I had started, Theatre Live! Inc.

On February 7, 1995, Yanisch informed the players that the MCDA would award an exclusive Broadway deal to Theatre Live! and Jujamcyn Productions. On February 23, Ordway President Bill Connor resigned and took a position at Live Entertainment of Canada in Toronto.

We had to scramble to put together the 1996–1997 season. We had already agreed on a major tour of SUNSET BOULEVARD and a replay of SHOW BOAT at the Orpheum, so we built on those two anchors.

The Ordway leadership, it seemed to me, had caused their own downfall, and were now in a weak position. They professed their determination to book a St. Paul-only Broadway season. but they seemed at a severe disadvantage in that they had a single theatre that was smaller than either Minneapolis theatre, their playing weeks were limited by the calendars of their principal users, and the vast majority of Broadway patrons resided in the western suburbs, far from downtown St. Paul. The culture at the Ordway conveyed a sense of superiority to everything around them, that they deserved to get exactly what they wanted from those they dealt with. One example was when they sent their ushers over to our Minneapolis show houses. Their supervisors dealt with our well-trained ushers in condescending ways that alienated our people. So we could not allow them to supplement our ushering corps.

The Ordway's major miscalculation was when they failed to realize that the City of Minneapolis had developed the State and Orpheum not to further the arts scene but as economic development tools to support the viability and safety of their downtown. When the Ordway started to move shows from Minneapolis to St. Paul, it hindered the repayment of the bonds the city had issued to restore the theatres, and irreversibly damaged their relationship with their sister city. Had they been willing to tone down their egos and compromise some of their aggressive positions just a bit, they might have been able to stay involved in future Broadway seasons.

For the next few years, the Ordway tried to develop its own Broadway seasons that competed with ours, but it became clear that we had the better downtown, better venues, and, with Jim Binger, the Broadway clout that even New York producer-turned-Ordway President Kevin McCullum could not match.

CHAPTER SIXTEEN

CAMEO ROLES ACT II

B ELOW IS ACT II OF A REVIEW OF SOME OF THE ARTISTS I have worked with over the years, with others included in Act III of this book. I begin with one of the two Olympic Gold Medal winners I have worked with. (The other is my niece, Lindsey Vonn.)

DOROTHY HAMILL

I have seldom met a more charming wheeler-dealer than Dick Oszustowicz. He was treasurer and finance VP for Abbott North-western Hospital (as it was known then), and he had somehow ingratiated himself with skater and Olympian, Dorothy Hamill. He was not your typical hospital executive. Rather he should have been in show biz, because that's where his interests seemed to lie. Dick had gotten to know Minneapolis City Council member Walter Dziedzic, a friend of mine, and both of them came to me in the summer 1989 pushing Dick's idea.

He wanted to stage a show that had been done only in San Francisco up to that point, *DOROTHY HAMILL'S NUTCRACKER ON ICE*, at the Orpheum Theatre. He suggested it could be a joint venture between my company, Historic Theatre Group, and Abbott Northwestern. He envisioned that the show would play

Dorothy Hamill in
Nutcracker On Ice

during the Christmas seasons of 1989, 1990, and 1991. His hospital would advance $600,000 in production money and in return would share in the show profit with my company (but I would absorb any loss).

I was originally skeptical; since while everyone loved Dorothy, it had been thirteen years since she won Gold at the Innsbruck Olympic Games, and I was not sure she could still skate. But Dick had two effective weapons in his arsenal: first, he had a video of her San Francisco production, which showed that Dorothy was indeed still a skilled and talented skater. Second, he had Dorothy herself. He flew her into town for a lunch with Lee Lynch and me, and we were sold. She still had every bit of the charm she had shown at the Olympics, and even had the same short wedge haircut she had then. She seemingly had not aged a day since her Gold.

Lee and I decided this was a natural Minnesota holiday

production, and that it was, as our marketing tag line said, "A Great Tradition in the Making." We negotiated a three-way contract between Dorothy, Abbott Hospital, and Historic Theatre Group, and began our planning. Meanwhile, Dorothy hired a bunch of world-class skaters to fill out her cast and found a company to install a large sheet of ice over the large stage floor at the Orpheum. Everything went perfectly for the 1989 run. Dorothy charmed the media and got the show great PR, ticket sales were good, the show appeared on national television, and everyone made money. Dorothy and her family were in Minneapolis a lot and became good friends with all of us.

So everyone decided that we should exercise our option to do it again in 1990. After all, what could go wrong? The reviews and audience reaction to her initial shows had been overwhelmingly positive. But when we put the 1990 shows on sale, there was almost no reaction. And the more we pushed sales, the less successful we were. It became painfully obvious that while Twin Citians had liked the show, they wanted to move on from it and try something else in 1990.

Fast forward to December 23, the final day of the run, and the date set for a financial settlement with Dorothy, who was self-managing the show with her husband, Ken. At the matinee, Lee Lynch had joined me in my second-floor office (after the Orpheum's restoration the space became the large Women's restroom) when a faxed demand letter came from Abbott saying that they knew the run was in trouble, and they would sue us if we tried to stiff them. Just at that moment, Dorothy Hamill, in full costume and skates with skate guards on, walked into the office. We had to tell her that due to poor sales, we would not be able to pay her her full guarantee, and that all the parties needed to share in the pain.

Pain was not something she was expecting, and she became very upset. I told her I would write her a check for her fee less $20,000, because that was all the cash I had, and that we could discuss it further once she returned to her home in Palm Desert.

She tearfully accepted the offer and went backstage to do her final show. Not a nice way to spend the day before the day before Christmas.

A check of the books after the run indicated that Historic Theatre Group owed Abbott Hospitals roughly $100,000, and we were able to pay that amount back over time thanks to some forbearance by Abbott, and some cash infusions from Lee and his wife Terry. It took us over a year to get these losses off our books. So much for "A Great Tradition in the Making.

In 2000, Chip Davis, who I had worked with for many years as the leader of recording artists, Mannheim Steamroller, determined to tour a Mannheim version of Dorothy's *NUTCRACKER ON ICE*, this time for arenas. He asked me to work with him on a Target Center run. Since I had always made big money with Mannheim, I said yes. What I had hoped for in the process was some sort of reconciliation with Dorothy. I had hated to have had to reduce her guarantee and hoped that by then she would understand that I had no choice. But on the afternoon of the sold-out Target Center show, I was told by the Mannheim people that Dorothy had requested that I not be allowed backstage because she did not want to see me ever again.

So Dorothy, let this be my apology to you. On occasion things don't work out as I had hoped, but I still respect and admire you.

MILES DAVIS

I had been impressed with Miles Davis's music for years, and in addition awed by the mystique of his persona. Thanks to Sue Weil, I saw him several times at the Guthrie; but since then he'd had an up-and-down performing career, and seemed to have been plagued by periodic health issues. Despite how often I asked his agent for a date on one of his tours, I was always turned down with an "it's only a short tour and Minneapolis is not a city he's interested in playing right now" response.

Finally in early 1990, I was able to secure a booking. Miles was frail by that time, and we were all worried about his ability to do the show. He and his band arrived and did an engaging mix of music from a number of his eras. What I most recall about the show was his aloofness. What he had to say he said with his trumpet, and he faced away from the audience for most of the night. It became pretty obvious that he was not feeling well, and he left quickly after the end of the concert. But it was an honor to have worked with him. Sadly, he died just a bit over a year from our show, on September 26, 1991.

DAVID COPPERFIELD

When I first became interested in the Orpheum Theatre, I was fascinated by the many legendary vaudeville acts that had performed on its stage. The Marx Brothers opened the theatre, and major artists like Jack Benny, George Burns, and Fanny Brice performed there over the years. The stories that most intrigued me were the tales of legendary magician Harry Blackstone. In the theatre's basement under the stage were large metal cages, which I was told were to house the live animals in many vaudeville acts, including Blackstone's. He evidently made elephants, lions, and tigers appear and disappear in his act, and they had to stay somewhere. So when I started booking the theatre, I very much wanted some classic magicians on our schedule.

The first major magician I booked at the Orpheum was Doug Henning, a diminutive guy who had had major Broadway and television success. The show ran for a week and did great business, but the animal cages in the basement did not get any use. Only when Harry Blackstone, Jr., appeared did we have one tiger in one of the cages, and when the Orpheum was refurbished, the cages were a casualty.

Starting in 1988, I began booking the greatest, richest, hardest-working magician on the planet: David Copperfield. The guy was absolutely amazing, both in his sleight of hand tricks, and his gigantic fill-the-stage illusions. He was very secretive about how they were created. Everyone backstage, the promoter, the stage-hands, the security people, were required to sign an agreement wherein at penalty of law they promised not to reveal how his tricks were accomplished. The load-in of David's show did not start until everyone had signed up. After that, no one new was allowed backstage.

David always wanted to do more and make more money, since he seemed to feel that his gigantic show grosses proved his importance. If we had sold out two shows in a day, he would want us to add a third. We sometimes started by advertising five or six shows and ended up with eight or ten.

Everyone wanted his autograph, and at one Saturday matinee, he determined to set the world record for the most autographs in a half hour. He placed himself on a table in the lobby and rehearsed with our ushers how to line up audience members and instruct them that they should just walk by the table with their programs and not stop to talk to Copperfield as he signed. Virtually everyone in the audience wanted to try to participate in setting a Guinness World Record, so right after the show, we got them lined up, got Copperfield on his table, then rushed everyone past the table as David did a quick "DC" on each program. He set a record with 2,100 signatures.

David was a pretty shy and low-key guy, but his skills and money seemed to attract beautiful women. I can recall him leaving the stage door between shows and getting into his limousine with two knockout females.

David was a staple on my schedule over the years, appearing for me in 1988, 1990, 1993, 1995, 1996, 2000, 2002, 2003, and 2006. We still have his yellow lines and arrows on the floor passageway from backstage to the front of house. I could tell you what David used them for, but I am still sworn to secrecy.

BOBBY SHORT

Bobby Short

I've had a love affair with the Great American Song-book for years, as many of my artist choices would confirm. The American Standards of Noel Coward, George Gershwin, Cole Porter, Irving Berlin, Jerome Kern, Harold Arlen, Johnny Mercer, and Richard Rodgers seem, both in melody and witty lyrics, to be among the finest songs ever written. When I began making regular trips to Manhattan for my Broadway-booking and Tony-voting responsibilities, one of my not-to-be-missed stops was always the Cafe Carlyle to take in a cabaret show by the inimitable Bobby Short. After I got to know him a bit, he always saved a small table very near the piano when he knew I was coming in.

No one did Cole Porter better in my opinion than Bobby and his two side men, Beverly Peer on bass and Robert Scott on drums. When I first met Bobby, he had already been to Minneapolis several times. He fondly recalled the food he ate at the Market Barbeque on Nicollet Avenue. So each time I visited him at the Carlyle, I brought him several bottles of the Market's famous barbeque sauce, which he seemed to treasure. I presented him to Twin Cities audiences twice in the '80s, the first time at O'Shaughnessy Auditorium, and the second for a cabaret run at the now long-closed Yvette on the Mississippi. One of the shows was a benefit for my friend and City Council member, Barbara Carlson. The flamboyant BC is most probably the only City Council member who had fundraisers by the likes of Bobby and Peggy Lee. Great memories of Bobby and the elegance he brought to his music. Without doubt the king of cabaret—a seemingly lost art.

HARRY BELAFONTE

Harry Belafonte, of the "Banana Boat" song (*"daylight come and he wan' go home"*), had a touring review in the 1980s that seemed popular with female audiences of a certain age. And he was a civil rights activist whose positions I agreed with.

In 1990 I booked his review at the Orpheum and did near-sellout business. Harry was in good shape and his voice had not diminished much since his heyday. But when I brought him back to the State in 1993, his sales were not quite as good, and his voice was starting to develop a hoarseness that was difficult for audiences to accept.

Finally, in 1997, I brought him back for a third time, and both the show and my relationship with Harry were disappointing. The show seemed less a review and more of a low-key concert. Harry's voice was not in good shape and was not miced well—just a part of the production issues I had setting up this show. Harry had played Milwaukee the night prior, and the truck with his set and equipment was scheduled to arrive at the State Theatre in time for a noon load-in. In order to get the stuff out of the truck, on stage, and set up, I had a union crew of twelve ready at the stage door and on the clock at noon. But no truck arrived.

I called Harry's nephew, who was the tour manager, and he told me that things were a little behind schedule, and that they "might" get there by 2:00 PM. I told him the noon schedule was not just a hoped-for time, and that his lack of concern was unprofessional and did not reflect well on Harry. Meanwhile, I had twelve stagehands milling about the stage, getting paid, with nothing to do. When the truck finally arrived at 2:30 PM, I told Harry's nephew that the delay had cost me $400. in stagehands costs, and that since I was losing money on the show, I'd have to take that amount out of his uncle's guarantee. He told me (rudely) that was not going to happen, and Harry would not do the show unless he was paid everything he was due per the contract prior to the show. He said that if I didn't like that, I could talk to Harry directly.

When Harry arrived later in the afternoon, I asked if I might have a quick word with him. He said yes, come on into the dressing room. I explained how his nephew seemed very unconcerned about the two-and-a-half-hour truck delay, and I suggested to Harry that such unprofessional conduct did not reflect well on him.

To my surprise, Harry was very quick to defend his nephew, and to say that $400 was such a small amount it was of no concern to him. I responded that it may not be to him, but to me, it was a substantial amount—especially since I was already losing money on his show. That seemed to piss off Harry; he reached into his wallet, drew out four $100 bills, and threw them on the floor in front of me. He may not have thought I would grovel for them, but I immediately dropped to the floor and gathered them up. Not surprisingly, that was the last show I ever did with Harry Belafonte.

YANNI (AND LINDA EVANS) / BURT REYNOLDS (AND LONNIE ANDERSON)

There are a couple of sets of artists I think of together, not because they ever performed on the same stage, but because of their offstage similarities. In the case of Yanni and Burt Reynolds, it's because each had beautiful, high-profile female companions who all but stole the stage from these stars. Yanni had moved from Greece to Minnesota to attend the University of Minnesota, and had been the leader of local rock band Chameleon. He returned to Minnesota as a headliner to play the Orpheum for me in May 1991. He brought along his live-in girlfriend, television star Linda Evans, who was universally known for her portrayal of Krystle Carrington on TV's *Dynasty*. She was amazingly beautiful and dressed like a diva. Yanni asked that I seat Evans in the fifth row center on the aisle. I knew she would create more of an audience stir than Yanni's music might, but I complied. As I predicted, when she walked in, the entire audience rose and applauded. But Linda was not willing to just sit quietly. She had semi-pro video equipment (which we would not have allowed anyone else in the audience to have), and she was determined to do a video of the entire concert. She got up often, walked down to the very front of the stage, and videoed incessantly. Gawkers got their money's worth that night.

A month after the Yanni show, Burt Reynolds brought his *CONVERSATION* to the Orpheum, bringing along his then wife, Loni Anderson, who had played receptionist Jennifer Marlowe on the sitcom *WKRP in Cincinnati*. She was blonde, beautiful, and voluptuous. Anderson was born in St. Paul, and had appeared in many shows at Excelsior's Old Log Theatre (along with fellow alum Nick Nolte). She had many local friends and fans. I recall strolling down Hennepin Avenue with her to Schinders to buy a magazine; she really drew a crowd. As a famous Minnesotan and friend of Dave Moore, she got far more PR than Burt was able to generate.

DIANA ROSS / BARRY MANILOW

My second odd pairing is Diana Ross and Barry Manilow. Both were superb performers who I worked with on several occasions, but each was a bit eccentric backstage. When Barry Manilow performed three sold-out shows at the State soon after it opened, he insisted that we build a sort of cocooned tent all the way from his lower-level dressing room to the stage right wing area so he could walk back and forth without anyone staring at him. Diana Ross's rider contained a provision that all those who were allowed backstage during the time Miss Ross was on premises must "avert their eyes" when she passed by. Despite these quirks, both artists proved charming in person and hugely talented on stage.

MELISSA MANCHESTER

In the fall 1991, we were just putting the final polish on the newly restored State Theatre prior to our gala opening-night party, scheduled for Friday, November 1. Caterers, many bottles of champagne, and a performance by singer Melissa Manchester were scheduled, all at some substantial cost to my management firm, Historic Theatre Group. But on the evening of Halloween, as kids got ready to trick or treat, a massive three-day snow storm hit the Twin Cities, virtually closing down the Twin Cities area. As the snow continued to pile up, it became less and less likely that we could pull off the opening event; but with Melissa safely in her dressing room, we decided we had to go ahead.

By the time we opened the State Theatre doors for the event, twenty-eight inches of snow had fallen, and traffic was at a standstill. Melissa did a great show, and I think everyone who was able to get to the theatre had a whole bottle of champagne to themselves. But rather than the 800 people we expected, only 150 made it. I left the theatre at about 11:00 PM after getting Melissa back to her hotel (via the skyway system), then faced the task of driving home in my two-seat, low-to-the-ground Mazda Miata. With some difficulty I reached the alley behind my garage, but it had not been plowed and there was absolutely no street parking possible. So I turned around and drove back to my office parking ramp and decided to find a hotel for the night. I walked the skyway to the IDS Center, got a room at the Marquette, then ventured into the first floor bar. There was only one other person having a drink, and it turned out to be my brother-in-law, Allan Kildow, who also had difficulty getting home. A memorable night.

PATTI LABELLE

I have two lasting images of Patti LaBelle. The first is Prince on stage with her playing with her band. The second is her stage entrance from the rear of the Orpheum Theatre—possibly the second-most amazing start to a show after the parade of animals at the start of *THE LION KING*.

During the 1990s, we often received calls from Prince's handlers asking if he could stop in and check out an act we had booked, and we never said no. When we got the call, it usually meant that we had to take the house right box seats (18 total) off sale and hold them as comp tickets for Prince. We had to provide security for Prince and his entourage of eight or ten people while they were in the building. Obviously at some cost to us, but it was hard to say no to a legend, and there was always the hope that he would join the band on stage. But most of the time he came in, watched ten or fifteen minutes of the show, and then left. But on one of the five or six LaBelle shows I promoted over the years, he brought his trademark guitar, walked on stage unannounced, and surprised Patti, joining her and her band on several songs. The fans went wild, of course.

At another of the Orpheum shows, Patti told us she was going to enter from the rear of the main floor with a wireless mic, singing as she walked down the main aisle and onto the stage. But when she got to the front of the stage, there were seats in the orchestra pit, and no stairs from the house to the stage. Undeterred, Patti, with some help from patrons, climbed up onto the narrow railing of the pit and, with ultra-high heels, walked forty feet along the pit railing and onto the stage, all the time singing perfectly. She finally stepped gracefully onto the stage to thunderous applause audience. I had never seen anything like what she did, even in Olympic gymnastics competitions. Much better than an early Bay City Rollers concert at the Orpheum—when fans pushed on that same pit rail and it collapsed, sending forty or fifty of them ten feet down into the empty orchestra pit. Lawsuits ensued.

SHIRLEY CAESAR

I've always loved music that takes over my spirit, let's me forget about whatever might be dragging me down, and thrills my soul. From my early days watching Marian Anderson and Mahalia Jackson on television, to seeing The Barrett Sisters at a church in downtown St. Paul, I have loved gospel music. Aretha Franklin and Whitney Houston started in gospel music, and it formed the core of their huge talents. The problem for me as a concert promoter was that gospel did not have the best track record for ticket sales, at least not in my market. So I was always looking for gospel artists I respected who might have a chance to at least break even in a live concert. The few I tried performed great shows, but consistently lost money for me. Artists like The Winans, Kirk Franklin, CeCe and BeBe Winans, and Mary Mary.

The one gospel artist who sold enough tickets to rebook, and lifted the roof off the State Theatre, was Grammy and Dove award-winner Shirley Caesar. I booked Shirley for Easter Sunday, April 19, 1992, and paired her with the noted local gospel group, The Sounds of Blackness. The headline on Jon Bream's review said it all: "The Queen of Gospel on Easter Night: Heavenly."

As Bream observed, "Caesar turns her concerts into church. Last night she preached as much as she sang. The Hammond organ swelled, and the piano and cymbals shimmered as this pugnacious bundle of energy started preaching."

And later, "Caesar was as mesmerizing, electrifying, and amazing as James Brown."

While things seemed spontaneous, Shirley was always in complete control of her singers and band members, and of the entire audience. They were on their feet for the entire concert. Luckily for me (since I paid her entire fee in advance), I was able to watch this show from the fifth row. So glad that while she asked many around me to join her in singing, she did not get to me. This concert remains on my Top-Ten list as one of the live shows I am most proud to have presented.

WAYNE NEWTON (AND ANGIE DICKINSON)

In June 1992, I experimented to see if there was a market for Las Vegas talent by booking Mr. Las Vegas himself, Wayne Newton. Seemed there was only a medium market, but those who came to the show really adored Wayne. His was a full Vegas review with a band and show girls and, while it was not my sort of show, he received several standing ovations (which he milked unmercifully).

After the show, Wayne said he wanted to have a small party to entertain several guests, and I said fine. We had the gathering of about twenty people in my old office on the mezzanine of the Orpheum (now the large Women's restroom). Wayne's people brought his guests up, including then US Senator Rudy Boschwitz. A half-hour into the party, the theatre phone on my desk rang, and a female voice asked for Wayne. They talked for several minutes, then Wayne said he had a guest at the now-dark front doors of the theatre.

I went down to the lobby, unlocked the doors, and found Angie Dickinson outside to meet me. I always liked her, and all the more so because she was married to one of my idols, Burt Bacharach. She began to introduce herself, but I interrupted her by saying I certainly knew exactly who she was. I was also able to figure out why she was in Minnesota. I knew that Angie and Burt's daughter had health issues and was being cared for at a hospital in Faribault. Angie and I went up to meet the other guests. Needless to say she was the hit of our party and certainly brought her Rat Pack cred with her. She was still stunning, and her legs were fabulous.

BURT BACHARACH AND DIONNE WARWICK

During my high school years (this seems such a distant memory now), I went to the Village Record Shop in Hinsdale to buy the latest 45s (single records with the big hole in the center). I

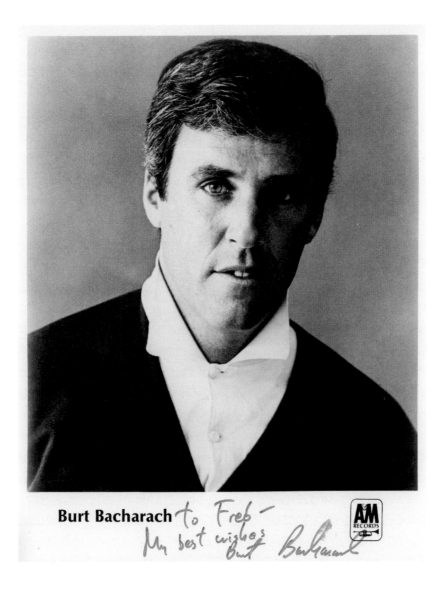

Burt Bacharach

Burt Bacharach to Fred –
My best wishes
Burt Bacharach

played play them on my Webcor record player. When I thought a song might be good for me to play on the piano, I bought the sheet music for the song and tried to learn it. I began to notice that many of the songs I liked the most were sung by Dionne Warwick and written by a young composer named Burt Bacharach. What I liked most about his songs were the major seventh chords that allowed me to make my piano arrangements sound much more like the records than the stock chords most sheet

Dionne Warwick ticket

music allowed. In addition, Burt was a handsome guy with what seemed like a great Los Angeles lifestyle that I coveted. So began my lifelong love of Dionne and Burt, which continues to this day.

My first encounter was with Dionne. During the early '70s, the Dayton's department store executives were determined to project a hip, fashion-forward image for the store. They brought a series of pop stars to town for appearances in their "8th Floor Auditorium." Using my Nhork Syndicate press pass, I had already seen and talked to Spanky and Our Gang and the very young Simon and Garfunkel (Art signed his name "Arthur"). When Harry Beacom was asked to book Dionne Warwick for an appearance in the Dayton's Sky Room, the luxurious restaurant on the top floor of the store (and later the home of the famous salad bar), I wanted to be involved.

The Sky Room had a cute little stage at one end, which I had noted but never seen used. But on November 21, 1972, we scheduled a 9:00 PM show for Ms. Warwick and her trio of musicians. Since Dionne's agent wanted more money than Dayton's could afford to pay based on the small capacity of the room, we arrived at a deal whereby Dionne would receive half her pay in cash, and the other half in merchandise credit at Dayton's. So on the afternoon of the show, Dionne and I, and an executive from Dayton's, met on the first floor and began a shopping spree. As I recall, Dionne was so slim that the dresses in the Oval Room did not fit her, so most of the stuff she chose came from the shoe department and the jewelry department. She had a great time making the selections, and she was fawned over by her fans as she shopped. Her show was well-received. We suggested other potential acts to store execs, but we never used the Sky Room stage again.

I first encountered Burt at about this same time. I was visiting my grandparents in Allentown, Pennsylvania, and Burt was appearing at the *Great Allentown Fair*. Once again, I flashed my Nhork press pass and had a few minutes with him after his show.

Burt's musical, *PROMISES PROMISES*, had had a successful run on Broadway, and thanks to my grandparents I had seen it, so we talked about that show and anything else I could think to ask about. Then I got his autograph on the sheet music for one of his songs. (I did not have any idea at that point who Marlene Dietrich was, and what her connection to Burt might be, so that topic did not come up.)

Burt was about as cool and Hollywood as anyone I had by that time met, and he was married to Angie Dickenson, so I'm sure I was tongue-tied. Twenty years later, I was able to book Dionne Warwick and Burt Bacharach on a co-bill at the Orpheum with an orchestra, and the show was a personal high point. I just wish my mom, Lucy, could have been there to see it.

GEORGE BENSON

I booked George Benson into Northrop Auditorium at the height of his popularity in July 1981, and he sold out 4,810 seats. Great show ("Give Me The Night" was #1 on the charts), but the thing I recall most is our trip to the Calhoun Beach Club. George asked me when he arrived whether I had a gym where he might lift weights. I said I was planning to visit the Calhoun Beach Club myself that afternoon. So he joined me, and I got him a guest pass and a padlock for his locker.

After an hour, he was done (he obviously lifted on a regular basis—he was extremely fit and cut). But when he opened his locker after our session, he immediately let me know that his four-carat $10,000 diamond solitaire ring was missing. I had noticed it earlier; it was hard to miss. We got the Club to call the police, and George filed a report. No one could figure out how someone might have gotten a duplicate key for his padlock, but George said the ring was insured, and didn't seem overly upset. I thought I might have been asked some further questions by his insurance people, but I never heard anything more about the loss. When I asked George about it when I brought him back to Minneapolis many years later, he did not recall anything about the loss of his ring.

JOHN DENVER (CHAD MITCHELL TRIO)

I loved folk artists in the '60s and '70s, artists like Ian and Sylvia, Judy Collins, Peter Paul and Mary, We Five, and of course Gordon Lightfoot. I had worked with Harry Beacom on a couple of Chad Mitchell Trio shows, and gotten to know Chad and trio members Mike Kobluk and Joe Frasier. In 1965, when they were booked at St. Olaf College while I was across the Cannon River at Carleton, I volunteered to help organize the show. It sold out quickly, but as the date approached, we were told that there might be a new Trio member, and that Chad might be leaving the group to go solo.

The night of the show arrived, and Mike and Joe showed up, but Chad was nowhere to be found. They had a new member, the shaggy-haired John Denver, who had kicked around Minneapolis a bit but was totally unknown back then. He had a great voice and played a skilled guitar. But I thought he was a bit dorky and smiley, and didn't bring the same social gravitas to the group that Chad had brought. Of course as a solo artist, those dorky traits worked to his advantage, and he became a huge star. I brought his Christmas Show to the Orpheum in 1993 for a multiple-sellout engagement less than four years before he died piloting his own experimental plane in 1997. John had been married to Annie Martell ("Annie's Song") from St. Peter, Minnesota, and they lived in Minnesota for a time, so he had many friends and fans in the area. Trite as this may sound, he was the same sincere guy offstage as he appeared onstage, and he was ahead of the curve on environmental concerns.

MIKHAIL BARYSHNIKOV

One of the biggest stars I've ever worked with came to me thanks to my friend and mentor, Sue Weil. Sue may not realize this, but I thought she was the best promoter of live music and dance I had ever seen. I rarely missed one of her *Live at the Guthrie* shows. Luckily for me, Sue was more a discoverer of talent than a repeat booker, and she rarely presented the same artists for recurrent concerts. So that allowed me to attend her shows and attempt to rebook them myself for their second plays in our market. Nine times out of ten, I loved her choices.

I was there when she brought in Canadian artist Gordon Lightfoot with amazing guitarist Red Shea, before Gord had become popular in the United States.

I was in the front row right behind Elton John at the piano when he got up quickly and in the process pushed the piano bench down two steps and into the audience.

I was there at a Carly Simon show when her new husband, James Taylor, joined her on stage for her finale.

I was there when she brought in soul group Sam and Dave, who performed with their band standing along the back wall and moving in precision.

Sue had unerring taste, and stands at the head of the Twin Cities concert promoter class as far as I am concerned. After a long run at the Guthrie, Sue moved to Washington, DC, to head up dance programming for the National Endowment for the Arts. Then she moved to PBS and worked for Robert Redford at his Sundance Film Institute. Sue was close to choreographer Twyla Tharp, and Twyla introduced her to Mikhail, who asked Sue to help him pull together a new dance idea, White Oak Dance Project. Based on her long history in Minneapolis, Sue wanted to make certain the troupe played Minneapolis, so she called me to determine my interest.

She explained that after a long career dancing a classical repertoire, and having gone through a couple of knee surgeries, Misha at

forty-six had transitioned into a more modern repertoire, which relied on his dance technique rather than classical leaps. He had chosen eight of the premiere modern dancers in the world to join him, as well as a quintet of musicians. The terms for the booking were staggering, and dance is known by concert promoters as financial poison; but this was not just any dancer, it was the world's foremost dancer, with a following well beyond dance. Or so I reasoned. I decided that I would take a gigantic flyer in order to work with Sue and Misha.

In 1994, the *StarTribune* newspaper was still a major marketing vehicle, and I decided to go big, with a full-page opening ad for the run. I felt we needed to let Minneapolis-St. Paul citizens know that this was a major show for our market, and not to be missed. The gamble worked; we sold out six shows at the Orpheum and grossed nearly $500,000. Despite the modern rather than classical repertoire, audiences loved the chance to witness Baryshnikov. As reviewer Mike Steele said, "(H)as there ever been a dancer as totally adored as Baryshnikov? It's doubtful," and observing that "(I)f the dancers are sensational, Baryshnikov is chief among them, and he doesn't let us down."

During the run, Sue asked me if I could get Misha onto a specific private golf course that required a member to sponsor and accompany guests. My business partner, Lee Lynch, was able to accomplish this, and I decided to join the foursome, as did my sister Lisa. A decision I soon regretted.

Misha was just taking up golf seriously and, as would be expected, he brought a grace and skill to his game. He was not a large man, but could drill the ball down the fairway beautifully. I had never been much of a golfer, but was determined to show Misha that I could compete. After the first three or four holes, Misha took me aside for a short golf lesson, which ended with the suggestion that I not try to kill the ball, but just glide into each shot. After his gracious advice, I did a bit better. I was at least able to keep my ball within the appropriate fairway. While Lee and Lisa played well, Misha won by eight or ten strokes.

(*opposite*) Mikhail Baryshnikov press photo

I brought Baryshnikov back to the Twin Cities in 1996, 1998, and, with Walker Art Center in 2003. But I never had the nerve to golf with him again.

MANDY PATINKIN

In the 1990s, Broadway star Mandy Patinkin made a number of tours with his one-man musical show, mostly to theatres that hosted Broadway shows. Mandy had originated the role of Che in *EVITA*, and the role of Georges Seurat in *SUNDAY IN THE PARK WITH GEORGE*. He was a regular on the television show *Chicago Hope*. His shows were heavy on Broadway, especially Stephen Sondheim. But what stood out was the shear intensity he brought to each song. The commitment to lyrics was almost painful. In Rodgers and Hammerstein's "You've Got to Be Carefully Taught" from *SOUTH PACIFIC*, the message that parents teach kids to hate was conveyed so pointedly that the audience seemed subject to his judgment. This was no waltz through pleasant show tunes. Each song was chosen for its message, and delivered with a plea to end whatever evil the song contained. One year his main cause was gun control, and after several long monologues during his show on the evils of guns, he ran down the main aisle after his encore, met the audience with a large cardboard box, and made it difficult for people to leave until they contributed. Some commitment.

Mandy Patinkin with the gun control cash he collected at end of his show

Adding to his intensity was a sound system that intensified his voice—not loud, just sharp and focused. His sound engineer was the eminent Otts Munderloh, who I had gotten to know during the original run of *A CHORUS LINE*. Most of Mandy's required equipment was not available in Minneapolis, so it had to be shipped in, making the rentals double or triple what they would otherwise be. The last time Mandy appeared for us was a benefit at the State Theatre for Theatre Live!, our nonprofit presenter. We scheduled a VIP reception on the stage immediately after Mandy's show. We cleared the stage quickly after the show, and all was going well until a bartender with a tray of fifty flutes of champagne attempted to walk up the stairs from the main floor to the stage, tripped, and hurled the tray in the direction of our main benefactor, James Binger. I can still see the glasses in the air and remember thinking how much noise and disruption they were going to create when they hit the stage floor.

CHRISTOPHER PLUMMER IN *BARRYMORE*

During our 1996–1997 Broadway season, a show cancellation forced us to find a replacement very quickly. We landed on *BARRYMORE*, a one-person show highlighting the life of actor John Barrymore and starring the noted Canadian actor, Christopher Plummer. We banked on his movie role in *The Sound of Music* opposite Julie Andrews to sell tickets. Despite a ton of marketing, we were not making headway as the show's opening night approached. Mr. Plummer was in town, he had done a sound rehearsal and seemed in good spirits. So on the afternoon of the first show, when his assistant invited me down to his dressing room for "tea," I was thrilled. The man is legendary for his movie roles and for his Shakespearean acting chops.

I went down to his room in the basement of the State Theatre, knocked on his door, and was greeted by his imposing figure. A full English tea set had been set up, and he cordially invited me to sit down, offered me some cookies, and poured some tea. When we were both seated, he put down his cup, smiled at me, and said he had one question. In a loud and menacing voice he said, "Mr. Krohn, what the FUCK are you doing with advertising? I have not seen one ad since I arrived in Minneapolis. Are you trying to keep this show a fucking secret?" He picked up some local entertainment papers and magazines he had collected, and threw them at me. "Not one thing about the show in any of these. What's wrong with you people?"

His lines were all the scarier coming from one of the foremost actors of our time. I started a rundown of how much we had spent to advertise the show, and where we had spent it. But he was having none of it, so it seemed prudent that I excuse myself and exit the tea party. He was a prince for the rest of the run, and later admitted that he had seen a lot of TV spots and a couple of print ads for the show.

Ten years later, I was staying at the Renaissance Millennium Hotel in Manhattan and I was joined by Mr. Plummer in the elevator. I reminded him of his Minneapolis run, and I was pleased that I got positive comments rather than a further venting of frustrations.

RIVERDANCE

One of the biggest risks I ever took on a show resulted in the most beneficial and financially rewarding relationship I've ever had in this industry. In 1996 William Morris agent Clint Mitchell (thank you, Clint!), who I had known as a rock agent, tried to persuade me to book an Irish show which was based on a seven-minute segment on the 1994 Eurovision Song Contest, and starred then-unknown Irish dance sensation Michael Flatley. The show was called *RIVERDANCE*. It was doing well in Dublin, but it was hard to see how it might sell tickets in the US. I liked the Irish immigrant story it told, and it had great music and some compelling dance from around the world, so it was worth considering. The company was quite large and the staging quite complex, making the guarantee substantial, but I determined to roll the dice and become one of the initial US promoters of the show (most American promoters had turned the show down, and the eight promoters who first booked it had carte blanche from the show producers from then on). The rest, of course, is history.

I brought *RIVERDANCE* in for an initial three-week run in February 1997, and it became a phenomenon, selling out every seat in advance and grossing nearly $2,000,000. While the initial run was still playing at the Orpheum, we put a longer 1998 run on sale, and it sold over $4,000,000 in tickets with almost no advertising. Since then, Riverdance has returned to the Twin Cities many times and never failed to make money. It in fact became an annuity for me, and for Theatre Live!, and later for Hennepin Theatre Trust, most recently in 2020 when my sister Lisa brought it in for a successful run on the show's twenty-fifth anniversary.

I hate to gloat, but the most rewarding aspect of the *RIVERDANCE* saga was that Jujamcyn Productions, my usual Broadway co-presenter, turned down working with me on that first run of *RIVERDANCE* (they had a right of first refusal for any Broadway shows I presented), and I made it clear to them that if they turned me down initially, they were also turning down any repeat bookings of the show as well. So for all the years since the original 1997 run, I and our nonprofit partners have owned the show with no financial involvement by Jujamcyn Productions and their successors. *RIVERDANCE* is still one of my favorite shows.

BARRY HUMPHRIES (DAME EDNA)

As a rule, I am not a fan of drag entertainers, but Australian comic Barry Humphries' creation, *DAME EDNA*, won me over. I saw the Dame's original show in New York, and her quick wit and faux celebrity shtick got to me and was so refreshing after seeing some of the usual Broadway fare before and after it. When I learned that the show wanted to tour, I argued (as I always did) that it should launch the tour in Minneapolis at the State Theatre. The Jujamcyn folks agreed, and we worked with the producers to make a two-week tour premiere in the Twin Cities happen.

Dame Edna greeting Minneapolitans on the "Spoonbridge and Cherry" sculpture. Photo by Judy Griesedieck, Minneapolis Star Tribune via Getty Images.

Having only seen Barry in Dame Edna drag, I had no idea what he might look like; and when he walked into the theatre to start rehearsals, there was nothing feminine about him. Good-looking older man in tweed with an Australian accent. But funny and fun to be around in or out of drag.

As the opening night in October 2000 approached, we decided to have one huge press day for Dame Edna in character, planning on-camera appearances in all three network studios, radio interviews, and a bunch of print media interviews. We started early in the morning, and by midafternoon they were complete. The *StarTribune* wanted something more, so we decided that since she was new to town, that I would give Dame Edna a tour of Minneapolis hot spots, followed by a *Strib* writer and photographer.

For the next hour, we strolled downtown, hitting the Nicollet Mall, and walking through the makeup area of Macy's. I recall the double takes we got, especially from the MAC Cosmetics department folks, who remarked that they had never seen hair in quite Edna's shade of lavender. We then ventured over to the Walker Art Center Sculpture Garden and made a beeline for the Spoonbridge and Cherry sculpture.

Dame Edna quickly climbed onto the spoon handle, and we got a bunch of iconic photos prior to the arrival of the guards, who said that no one, not even Dame Edna, was allowed to sit on the sculpture. The photo appeared on the Friday *Variety* cover, and the show was launched. Barry remains one of my favorite personalities—an amazingly quick and funny mind.

BOBBY CALDWELL

For a brief and not-so-shining moment in 1997, a smooth jazz format station ruled the Twin Cities airwaves. KJZI-FM played artists like Boney James, Dave Koz, Kenny G, Brian Culbertson, and Spyro Gyra. These artists rapidly developed strong followings in our market. I was never too fond of most of their roster, but the station discovered and popularized an artist that I really liked and respected—the Sinatra wannabe, Bobby Caldwell. I loved classic American Songbook songs, and loved Sinatra, but most of those who tried to sing Sinatra songs had no sense of Ol' Blue Eyes' rhythm and delivery, and they sounded like trash. Bobby Caldwell came closest to me, and his *Blue Condition* CD became one of my favorites. So when KJZI played the heck out of his song "Beyond the Sea," and then set up a promotional lunch and show for Bobby, my sister Lisa and I signed up. We were impressed with his style, both on the classic Sinatra songs, and the songs he wrote during his earlier R&B career, including the classic "What You Won't Do For Love." His voice was so soulful that when he toured with Natalie Cole, the audience was surprised to learn that he was White.

(He also wrote hits for other artists: "The Next Time I Fall" for Peter Cetera, and "Heart of Mine" for Boz Scaggs, among others).

Bobby's *Blue Condition* CD blew up in the Twin Cities in the fall 1997, and Bobby began to find a national following. Seemed like a good time to bring the guy in for a show. We landed on a New Year's Eve show at the State Theatre, and determined to make it a gala affair with champagne, optional formal dress, and a VIP reception. Tickets to the first show sold out immediately thanks to the built-in KJZI audience, and we added a late show with a champagne toast at midnight, which also sold out quickly.

Since these shows were some of the most important Bobby had done, he asked if he could add musicians and some props and really make the shows memorable. I said sure, and we added a big band for the Sinatra stuff and, at his direction, I got a bunch of props including a streetlight and a park bench.

Bobby wrote a complete script with stage cues, and he came in early to rehearse it with his players, the hired local musicians, and our stagehands. We even made Bobby Caldwell merchandise and sold it in the lobby. Pretty amazing to come from an almost complete unknown in fall to a star with two State Theatre sellouts on New Year's Eve. The shows were impressive, and the audience reaction was stellar. Sadly, Smooth Jazz KJZI changed its format, and we suddenly had no easy way to connect with Bobby's fans. He still did well when I booked return gigs, but he never reached the level of his first concerts.

MITCH HEDBERG

Short and sweet. Mitch Hedberg was the sharpest and funniest comedian I have ever worked with. He was born in St. Paul, and I worked with him several times over his too-short career. What made him great was that he was totally unique. His deadpan style and out-there, but so logical, humor did not remind you of anyone but Mitch. Unfortunately, one of his most famous lines was

Mitch Hedberg, Fred Krohn, and staffer Steve Weiss

also one of the saddest: "I used to do drugs. I still do, but I used to too." He died of a drug overdose in 2005 at age thirty-seven.

ROB BECKER IN *DEFENDING THE CAVEMAN*

Rob Becker had absolutely the best gig in show biz. He was a stand-up comic with a routine about coexisting with his wife, and over three years he developed his act into a theatrical show which he called *DEFENDINGTHE CAVEMAN*. It became the longest-running one-person show in Broadway history, having played to more than eight million people in forty-five countries. Rob got the lion's share of the money the show generated, since he was performing his own material, and there were no other cast members. I can't even imagine what his income might have been during the Broadway run and subsequent tours.

I was concerned when we first booked the show in 1997 that our audiences would not pay Broadway money for what was basically a stand-up routine. But the show was wildly popular, grossing close to $1,000,000 each time it played the State Theatre. It depended in large measure on Rob's large stature and gentile

Defending the Caveman Broadway logo

demeanor, which allowed him to discuss the differences between how he viewed life, and how differently his wife did, without offending the predominantly female audiences (and the husbands that they dragged along to the show).

The greatest thing about the show for Rob was that there was no need for any makeup or costume—he always wore old baggy jeans and a dark T-shirt, and those were exactly what his onstage character (which was basically him) wore. Rob and I often had dinner at Palomino restaurant, right next to the theatre, before his shows, and at about 7:55 PM we were still sitting at our table. I'd ask whether he wanted to do the show that night, and he would say sure, let's go. We'd finish our glasses of wine, get up, walk around to the stage door, and Rob would walk in, walk right onto the stage without hesitation, and begin the show. I've only seen one other artist pull that off. Frank Sinatra's people had everything timed so perfectly that for each of the shows I was backstage for, I saw Frank's limo pull up, Sinatra got out without any stress, his people would hand him a wireless mic, and he walked right up the steps to the stage with the overture for his show at exactly the correct cue for his entrance.

Great gig if you can get it both for Frank and for Rob.

CHAPTER SEVENTEEN

THE LION ROARS

AFTER THE DEPARTURE OF THE ORDWAY JUST BEFORE THE 1996–1997 Broadway season, I had the ultimate responsibility not only for managing the three Hennepin theatres, but also for the nonprofit I was involved with, Theatre Live!, which after the Ordway's departure had stepped up to serve as the presenter for the Broadway season. It immediately became obvious that there were conflicts in the two roles, so I decided to concentrate on theatre management while my key staff member, Tom Hoch, took a more active role in the operation of Theatre Live!. At that time, we were working closely with Mike Brand and Jim Sheeley at Jujamcyn Productions on the season, and the four of us pretty much ran the Minneapolis Broadway market.

From the start of my involvement with Broadway, I was determined to differentiate our market from others, and to make certain that we got shows at the start of their tours rather than at the end, two or three years later, when they were tired and on their fourth of fifth cast changes. One way to do that, it seemed to me, was to offer our theatres as pre-Broadway tryout theatres. The premiere North American booking of *JOSEPH AND THE AMAZING TECHNICOLOR DREAMCOAT* in 1992 had been a bit of a fluke, but it really cemented the reputation of the State Theatre in short order. So when I learned of new productions

that were being planned, I always offered up the Orpheum or the State to Broadway producers.

One problem with this approach was that the producer almost always needed a number of dark weeks prior to opening to build, tech, and rehearse their show, and these weeks were expected to be provided rent-free. Another difficulty was that the stagehands union contract mandated a four-hour minimum wage for each stagehand call. That meant every time the producer stopped a rehearsal to adjust lights, change a set, etc., the hands felt they should be paid for a separate call. In order to make the union costs more reasonable, I drafted and negotiated a "production rate" for stagehands with a higher hourly wage, but with a provision that allowed the hands to be paid solely by the hour to do any rehearsal, build, adjustment, etc., that the producer needed to do, and to switch from one to another at the direction of the show's tech people. I argued to the stagehands' union that we would be able to generate many more shows if they accepted my provision. To their credit, they agreed. That flexibility really made our market much less costly for producers to load-in and rehearse a show, and was a prime reason we were able to book so many pre-Broadway productions.

Since I handled the rentals of the Orpheum and State theatres, it became my task to negotiate theatre rental agreements with show producers considering Minneapolis for their pre-Broadway tryouts. I obviously needed to find a balance between charging the standard rent for the dark weeks, and appearing to provide a generous deal that was better than what other markets were offering. Since I was working with the MCDA (and later CPED), I needed to get their approval for the deals I was cutting. Luckily our market was gaining the reputation for smart and adventuresome audiences, so I did not have to sell producers on that aspect of the deal.

Using both the production rate argument and the quality of the Twin Cities audiences argument, and with the help of the Jujamcyn staff, I was able to negotiate pre-Broadway deals for a

(OPPOSITE) Orpheum marquee for the world premiere of *THE LION KING*. PHOTO BY GEORGE HEINRICH

Fred Krohn's Disney University graduation photo

surprising number of shows, most notably *VICTOR/VICTORIA* starring Julie Andrews, *SMOKEY JOE'S CAFE*, *SWEET CHARITY* starring Christina Applegate, and *DAME EDNA*.

But the tour premiere run that most set us up for success with the Disney execs was the booking of Disney's *BEAUTY AND THE BEAST*, which opened at the Orpheum on November 7, 1995. I sold the Disney tech people on the benefit of the production rate, and gave them free rent for their dark weeks. I also enrolled all of our executives and head ushers in Disney University, a one-week course at Disney World that teaches corporate types the mentality of the Disney culture (those attending are "guests" rather than just ticket buyers, etc.). The result was a successful tour launch for a show that had been a bit problematic for Disney on Broadway. Everyone from Disney head Michael Eisner on down professed to having had a great experience in Minneapolis at the Orpheum.

When Disney announced that they planned a theatrical production of their mega-hit animated feature *THE LION KING*, it seemed to most that we had a leg up for the pre-Broadway tryout. But there were a number of major markets that really wanted this production, and were willing to offer sweet deals to Disney to land it. For me, the main issue was that Disney needed ten weeks in the theatre prior to opening for their build and rehearsals, and I was concerned that other markets might offer them free.

Luckily I had made some friends at Disney who could guide me. I had the knowledge that Disney really liked the production rate deal, which would result in substantial savings on stagehand costs during the long take-in period. Negotiations went back and forth for weeks, and the Disney production crew came in to figure out whether the stage would be able to accommodate a 25'x35' hole for Pride Rock.

While they were in Minneapolis, I found them rehearsal space for their dancers, help with their puppets, and we found them a potential promotional sponsor, Dayton's Department Store. Finally on November 6, 1996, Disney announced that the Minneapolis Orpheum would host the world premiere of their new musical production of *THE LION KING*. It seemed big then, but in retrospect it was maybe the biggest announcement in touring Broadway history. None of us realized how important this show would become. The production is still running on Broadway and is the highest grossing Broadway show of all time.

While we were all thrilled with the announcement, we had no idea whether Disney planned a literal adoption of the animated feature a la *BEAUTY AND THE BEAST*, or whether they planned something more innovative and theatrical. The announcement that Julie Taymor would direct should have given us an early clue. Taymor, a MacArthur "genius" grant recipient, was known for her innovative productions and her work with masks and puppets. Broadway insiders were surprised at Disney's choice, but felt it had promise.

In May 1997, a large crew of production people and creatives descended on the Orpheum and immediately began to remove the large I-beams from the stage floor to accommodate Pride

Rock, a technological wonder that would corkscrew up from a flat stage to form a promontory high above the stage floor. The tech folks had some ideas about how this might work, but admitted they had no idea what they would ultimately end up with. The guts of Pride Rock filled the large room directly under the stage, and the clearances as it rose up needed to be less than a half-inch.

After weeks of work, Pride Rock functioned perfectly and became the majestic icon of the Simba birth announcement scene. I fondly recall sitting near the guts and computer controls below stage with legendary star Glenn Close, who was dating one of the Disney stagehands, and watching with awe as it climbed upward—almost more amazing from below than it was on stage.

When Julie brought out the masks and headdresses, told us that they would be worn by the actors over their heads, and that they would move forward to interact with other actors, we were at first skeptical. But once we saw how easy it was to suspend disbelief and buy into the characters, we found them mesmerizing. The various animal "costumes" were awesome. The first time I saw the Circle of Life intro to the show I have to admit, I cried. I made sure I was at every show to see it again and again. Without any doubt the most amazing ten minutes of theatrical magic I've ever witnessed.

As the first previews were approaching in early July, things were really getting hectic, and changes in the show were being made on an hourly basis. We were shocked to learn that Julie Taymor had had emergency surgery to have her gallbladder removed and it was not known how long she would need to recoup. Worried Disney faces, since the show was not yet close to ready. But at the next rehearsal, there was Julie in a Lay-Z-Boy recliner mounted on a platform over the front seats, continuing her directing tasks.

By the first previews, everyone in Minneapolis knew something amazing was happening, and wanted to get a first peak at the show. Both national and local press hounded us, as did the local downtown business community. With the approval to Disney,

Minnesota Governor and Mrs. Arne Carlson at opening night party with star Jason Raize

I was able to take small groups up to the balcony on rehearsal days to quietly watch the show. They were amazed.

At times during several of the preview performances, there were technical glitches and the show needed to pause to correct them. During those delays, Peter Schneider and Tom Schumacher, heads of Disney Theatrical Productions, did what could only be described as stand-up comedy to entertain the audiences while repairs were made. They were both disarmingly charming, and audiences were made to feel that they were present at the creation of a major new production.

Finally, late in the run, the opening night of *THE LION KING* on July 31, 1997: the biggest night in the history of the Orpheum Theatre. Michael Eisner. Local media. New York critics. International critics. City politicians. Governor and Mrs. Arne Carlson. (Elton John was a no-show). When at the start of Circle of Life the animals paraded onto the stage, they received a standing ovation. The climax of that scene—the arrival of the elephant on stage as Pride Rock rose majestically from the savanna and Simba's birth was announced—brought tears to many. The show ran perfectly and was a complete success. Mike Steele of the Minneapolis *StarTribune* called it "an evening of almost pure delight."

THE LION KING opening
night curtain call

Dayton's exec Michael Francis was a perfect promotional partner, and he put on an amazing after-party for the cast, crew and VIPs in Dayton's 8th floor auditorium, which had been transformed into an African grassland and catered with appropriate native dishes. I had my sisters and several of their kids with me, and my fourteen-year-old niece, Lindsey (before she became the most successful skier in US history) did what no one else at the party seemed brave enough to do. She walked right up to Michael Eisner's private table and began talking to him about the show.

THE LION KING world premiere became the high point of my Broadway career—there would be nothing that could top that experience, and it put the Orpheum in the pantheon of Broadway history. While the Orpheum was once again chosen to host Disney's next Broadway production, *AIDA*, in 2001, a great production, nothing could top our *LION KING* experience.

CHAPTER EIGHTEEN

MUCH ADO ABOUT JACKIE MASON

A JEW AND A GENTILE WALK INTO A BAR. STOP ME IF you've heard this. The Jew is a former Rabbi and now a famous comedian from New York. The Gentile is a concert promoter from Minneapolis. They have decided to have a drink after the comedian's opening night at the Music Box Theatre in March 1997. And the bar is the Palomino near the State Theatre lobby.

Thus began a most unlikely friendship and business relationship that would take the two of us to shows in Toronto, London, and Las Vegas, and to a Broadway opening night in New York. The comic is Jackie Mason. And I am, of course, the concert promoter.

I admit that, as a kid, I was not that fond of what was called Borscht Belt humor; I much preferred the great singers that Ed Sullivan had on his show to the old school comics like Myron Cohen, Shecky Greene, and Alan King. But I did like Jackie Mason. The rhythm and timing of his jokes was perfect, and he was unlike anyone I ran into in Hinsdale, Illinois. To me he personified New York.

Fast forward to Minneapolis. Jackie's opening night show of a two-week run I booked was funny, and my Jewish friends *and* my Gentile friends seemed to like his material and timing.

Jackie Mason

Jackie periodically did one-man Broadway shows, and he told me he took my gig because he wanted to try out material for his return to the New York stage. I saw most of his Minneapolis shows and was happy to provide my opinions on which jokes seemed to land best with his audiences. He kept up on current events and wove them into his routines, which I liked. So many of the comics I worked with to that point had their spiels down, and the jokes never changed. I liked that Jackie had such a quick mind that he could ad lib new stuff so easily. We went to the Palomino bar after each show and had discussions. Others who recognized him joined us, and he regaled us with his Catskills stories. Why a politically incorrect Jewish comic related to someone who was his polar opposite in so many ways always mystified me, but we really seemed to click.

A couple of months after the Music Box Theatre run, I got a call from Jackie's manager (and wife), Jyll Rosenfeld, asking me if I would be interested in becoming involved with Jackie's next one-man Broadway show, which he was calling *MUCH ADO ABOUT EVERYTHING*. Since Jackie's 1986 show, *THE WORLD ACCORDING TO ME*, had won a Special Tony Award, an Outer Critics Circle Award, an Ace Award, an Emmy Award, and a Grammy Award, it seemed prudent to at least discuss what might be involved in such an investment. But I was hesitant, since the risk of putting money into a Broadway show is notoriously huge.

Since I was a Tony voter during that period, I went to New York a lot, so I set up an appointment with Jyll and Jackie in their condo near Carnegie Hall to discuss their proposal. It seemed per Jyll that my task was to either put my own money into the show, or find investors to put in the money, in return for an above-title "executive producer" credit along with Jyll. Since the show was basically stand-up, we needed some sort of set but didn't require the multimillion-dollar capitalization of a typical Broadway show. I figured that since I had some available cash, and I knew some rich folks in Minneapolis who might find this sort of investment interesting, and since I was probably not going to get any other invitations to invest in a Broadway show, I agreed right there to get involved.

The next year was spent getting the paperwork set, and visiting Jackie at some of his gigs to see how the new material was developing. One of my most memorable nights was flying to Vegas and staying at the legendary old Sahara Hotel (run down and sad for years), and spending time with Jackie in the dressing room that was used by Frank Sinatra and so many early Vegas stars. I could sense the ghosts, and it gave me chills.

We previewed *MUCH ADO* in London at the Playhouse Theatre (I was unable to attend), and at several other theatres in the US. I also brought him back to Minneapolis, this time at the State Theatre. I thought the new material was funny, and it was obvious that he already had many more clever bits than he could fit in a two-hour show.

When the ink had dried on our *MUCH ADO* deal, Jyll and I were over-title executive producers. Jackie's close friend, attorney Raul Felder (more about him later), and Florida concert promoter Jon Stoll were producers, and Howard Weiss, Henry Handler and Jam Theatricals were associate producers. I brought in Minneapolis artist Ward Sutton to do the ad art after not being impressed with anyone our ad agency, Spotco, had come up with. (Ward Sutton was already well known on Broadway, having designed the iconic artwork for John Leguizamo's show *FREAK*). Minneapolis rock and roll lighting designer, Stan Crocker, came in to help with the set design and lighting.

We felt the show needed to go into a smaller, but well-located Broadway Theatre, and because of Jackie's track record, the Shuberts welcomed us into the John Golden Theatre, an 804-seat venue in the heart of Broadway on West 45th Street. The Golden had a great pedigree, having been the home to many Tony and Pulitzer Prize shows (*MASTER CLASS* and *AVENUE Q* among them), so we felt we were in the right theatre. The smaller capacity allowed us to sell out the early shows and thereby create demand for the rest of the run.

I went to Manhattan for a couple of weeks in November 1999 prior to our first previews. I still recall the morning when I first saw John Golden Theatre with Jackie's show artwork installed on the theatre facade. The display case on the left had a large poster; at the top it said, "Jyll Rosenfeld and Fred Krohn Present." I really felt I had made it to the Broadway elite at that moment. I had a theatrical credit in the top theatre town in the world.

Choosing an opening night was our next decision. For a show like Jackie's, which has just one star and hopefully does not require last-minute rewrites, two or three weeks of previews are usually sufficient, after which an opening night is informally scheduled with the Theatre League. Thursday is usually the most desirable night to open, so the reviews can be in the Friday papers (Critics are allowed to attend a few days early if they agree to hold their reviews until after opening night).

For reasons not very clear to me, Jackie kept postponing opening night; but finally, nearly six weeks after the previews began, we set a Thursday, December 30 opening night, which didn't seem ideal to me. Many critics would be seeing one of the last previews (to write their reviews) and most likely would also attend on December 30. I recall the backstage concern when legendary critic John Simon walked down the main aisle to a front seat at the last preview. I had read his reviews for years and well knew how stinging and vicious they could be.

Broadway's John Golden Theatre exterior

To my amazement and appreciation, Jackie rose to the challenge. His last week of previews and his opening night performance were all excellent and well received by his audiences. So when we nervously gathered the Friday reviews after opening night, we were thrilled when the show received all nine favorable (or as *Variety* calls them "Pro") reviews. Most importantly, Lawrence Van Gelder in *The New York Times* wrote, ". . . give thanks that Mr. Mason (if all goes well) is around to make the twenty-first century safe for democracy and for those who cherish a good laugh."

Such positivity is almost unheard of on Broadway. No "Con." No "Mixed." All "Pro." Sales responded accordingly, with virtually sold-out houses for the first few weeks of the run. Ultimately, *MUCH ADO* ran until July 30, 2000, grossed $5,303,427, and ran

Jackie Mason Playbill

at an 85 percent+ capacity. *Variety*, in its summary of the 1999–2000 Broadway season, called out only three hit shows that had recouped their capitalizations and could be called hits: *TRUE WEST, DAME EDNA: THE ROYAL TOUR,* and *JACKIE MASON: MUCH ADO ABOUT EVERYTHING*. All the other shows in the 1999–2000 season were in the "Maybe" or "Misses" categories.

I enjoyed my time as a Broadway producer, visiting the show, taking guests backstage to meet Jackie, eating lunch at Sardi's, and actually having other Broadway types greet me. I can recall Jujamcyn head, Rocco Landesman, who I knew via Jim Binger, come up to congratulate me, saying he greatly admired Jackie's skills.

As the show headed for its closing night (our marketing people felt that getting the production through the rest of the summer was going to be difficult), Jackie, Jyll, close friend Raoul Felder, and I began discussing where we might tour the show, and what sort of vehicle we should consider for Jackie's next Broadway adventure. They felt that nothing less than a *SUGAR BABIES*-type burlesque show with a supporting cast, sets, and musical numbers would do. I agreed to consider such an idea, but privately saw many difficulties. I was also reluctant because my dealings with my Minnesota partners were made more difficult because the paperwork Jyll and her New York attorney for the show provided me did not cover out-of-state investors. So I had to spend some of my profit on forming a New York limited partnership and complying with all sorts of tax and securities regulations, which per my lawyer should have been taken care of in Jyll's documents. My investors were happy (one wrote, "I like the way you do business—direct, timely, as promised, and friendly professionalism. Keep me in mind for future deals"). But without my last-minute legal fixes, they would not have been.

Raoul Felder also had another show idea that intrigued me. Raoul was one of the country's most famous divorce lawyers, having represented everyone from Mayor Rudy Giuliani, to Carol Channing, legendary producer David Merrick, and Mrs. Martin Scorsese. But he was also the younger brother of one of Tin Pan Alley's most famous lyrists, the legendary Doc Pomus. Among the hundreds of songs Doc Pomus penned were "A Teenager in Love," "Can't Get Used to Losing You," "Little Sister," "Save the Last Dance For Me," "This Magic Moment," and "Viva Las Vegas." He wrote with all the greats of the era, including Mort Shuman, Dr. John, and Jerry Lieber and Mike Stoller. His life had been almost as colorful as his songs. He grew up in working-class Williamsburg and had polio as a kid, spending the rest of his life on crutches or in a wheelchair. But he still hung out and performed in blues clubs and got to know many performers. He lived across from the legendary Brill Building in Manhattan, and started writing lyrics to many rock and roll songs. He died from lung cancer in 1991, and has been inducted into the Rock & Roll Hall of Fame. He was a great, if then unknown, personality whose life story Raoul felt would make an ideal "juke box" musical.

We discussed this project for years, but could never figure out a script angle to showcase his many memorable many songs. We knew that despite Doc's songwriting credits, the complete rights to his songs (a veritable history of the era) might be difficult to secure. Ultimately we were unable to achieve liftoff on this project, but it remains intriguing.

Once MUCH ADO closed, we took the show to Toronto and back to London, with only moderate success. I was able to travel to London for opening night, and it was another gala evening. Afterward, I accompanied the group to a swank casino where Jackie and Raoul seemed to have many fans and friends.

As discussions for Jackie's next show progressed, we began to explore who might write an appropriate script for a SUGAR BABIES-type show. We determined to go to that show's writer, Ralph Allen, who said he might be interested with the right deal.

But others who I did not know kept popping up in our discussions and, with a show capitalization of $2,500,000 or $3,000,000, I quickly got cold feet and determined to bail on my participation. It just didn't feel right to me to start putting money down on an idea that had no solid stars (other than Jackie), and no proven creative team. That might work for a one-man show, but I got very nervous that our little team did not have the skills to put together a show of this complexity. With my decision, Jackie and Jyll unfriended me. Nothing said. Just radio silence.

Jackie did one more solo show, *PRUNE DANISH* in 2002, and then announced that he would be producing and starring in a *NEW COMEDY MUSICAL REVUE*, which flyers described as "all comedy, tons of Jackie's shtick, lots of music." It was to be called *LAUGHING ROOM ONLY*. The book was to be written by Dennis Blair and Digby Wolfe, with music and lyrics by Doug Katsaros. The show featured a cast of six. Jyll and Jon Stoll seemed to be the only holdover producers from *MUCH ADO*, along with four or five new names. No "Raoul Felder" anywhere I could see.

Reviews for *LAUGHING ROOM* were brutal. *MUCH ADO* got nine "Pros" in *Variety's* "Crix' Picks" column. *LAUGHING ROOM* got nine "Cons." Charles Isherwood's *Variety* review said, "Mason trots out the same shtick in his new show that he served up just last fall. To camouflage the absence of new material, he has spliced some feeble musical comedy numbers into his regular standup. The result is a staged throwback to TV variety shows, the lesser ones." Bruce Weber's *New York Times* review was even worse. It stated that the show's original material was "some of the trashiest musical comedy ever written for the Broadway stage." And later, ". . .in the interest of consumer advocacy, it needs to be said that by conservative estimate, half of Mr. Mason's solo material has been recycled." And finally, *Stage Magazine* said, "Jackie Mason's musical (*oy*) went over like a week-old knish." The show closed after thirty-one previews and fourteen performances.

What happened between my very successful Jackie show in 1999 and this apparent fiasco in 2003 is unknown to me. But I can assure you that I feel blessed that I do not know. Seems that all the pitfalls I envisioned when I bailed on the show came true, with devastating financial consequences to the producers. It saddens me to have Jackie's Broadway career potentially end in such unfortunate fashion. He's still a good friend and a great talent.

CHAPTER NINETEEN

THE ARENA SHOWS

URING THE LATE 1960S AND EARLY 1970S, I BOMbarded the folks at the newly opened Metropolitan Sports Center with offers of help in producing their live concert events. Bob Reid, the administrative director of the North Stars hockey team, finally responded and offered to talk to me. As a part of his duties, Bob headed up the rock stuff, mostly hall rentals by outside promoters. He took me under his wing and allowed me to see how the backstage of the Met was run. It started off as more of an unpaid internship than an actual job, but I shadowed Bob and learned a ton about how large venues were run. Bob was a straight-laced guy with a great baritone speaking voice that was famous as the voice of the high school tournaments for forty-two years. Not many people recognized Bob, but everyone knew his voice. He was a great mentor, but the thing I recall most about Bob was that, well before his time, he was a recycling fanatic; he set up a program for Met Center and insisted that it was followed with precision. The others on the small Met Center staff were very friendly, and welcomed me warmly. Team owner Walter Bush was just down the hall, and hockey legend John Mariucci officed next door, with cigar and pipe smoke floating out into the hall. Jack Larson, who currently runs Xcel Center in St. Paul, was also on staff back then.

(*opposite, top*) Tiny Tim and Fred Krohn. (*opposite, bottom*) Tiny Tim, Fred Krohn, and The Young Rascals.

The odd thing about the arena shows in the late '60s was the weirdness of the billings. The only common denominator for the acts was that they had a hit on either WDGY or KDWB. The first show I recall was Sergio Mendes and Brazil '66 with opening act, Glen Campbell (a new artist with one hit I was really impressed with). In March 1968, we had a WDGY show that headlined Wilson Pickett, The Hollies, and Strawberry Alarm Clock. I can recall Pickett coming on stage in full regalia with a flashy three-piece suit, a long matching floor-length cape, a fancy cane, and a large hat made of the same material. He had an onstage assistant who took first the hat, then the cape and cane, then jacket, then vest, with Wilson indicating he was working so hard, he was getting overheated. Finally at the end of his act, while his band vamped his theme song, he had worked so hard that he "collapsed" on the stage floor and had to be helped off stage by his assistant (a schtick I'd seen James Brown use).

The strangest billing though, came on October 18, 1968, and featured Joe Tex, Tommy Boyce and Bobby Hart, The Young Rascals, and Tiny Tim. Oddly to me, the groups all really wanted to meet and hang with Tiny Tim. So I got the very shy Tim to come into the adjoining locker room to meet the Rascals and pose for some photos (note the jockstrap hanging on the wall).

I witnessed the amazing precision of a Frank Sinatra show in July that year. Just before showtime, Frank's limo pulled into Target Center and right to the back of the stage. His assistant handed Frank a newly developed wireless mic as he got out of his limousine. Frank immediately walked onstage, did his show, and was in his limo and heading back to his jet before the audience's standing ovation died down.

The openers for that show were Frankie Valli and the Four Seasons, who I would work with on many occasions. Frankie had a rare Bulova Accutron Spaceview II watch, which kept time via a small tuning fork. I was wearing an identical one (given to me by my dad for my twenty-first birthday), so we had something to talk about backstage. (The only other celebrity I ran into who had an identical watch was noted attorney, F. Lee Bailey, who I met after a law school lecture Bailey flew in for in his own Lear jet).

The Met Center show I most recall was The Who concert in March 1968. It might seem tame by current standards, but I remember that the fans were out of control, pushing down our front-of-stage barricades and otherwise rioting—all with the approval and encouragement of the band.

Working on arena shows taught me several things: they lacked any sort of intimacy for the bulk of the audience (no giant video screens at that point), the sound quality (especially back then) was usually not ideal, and it was difficult to control 15,000 fans if they did not want to be controlled. I had always preferred shows in intimate venues like the Broadway theatres that my grandparents took me to as a child. Arena shows didn't work for me unless I had tickets in the first ten or so rows. I resolved to concentrate on theatre shows when possible rather than promoting in larger venues.

The last time I worked at Met Center before it closed and was torn down resulted in one of my most memorable live shows: Waylon Jennings, the Waylors, his wife Jessi Colter, and Asleep at the Wheel. As I describe elsewhere, the show was completely sold out, and the audience and the artists were there to have a good time. Much beer was consumed, and my control of the venue balanced on a knife edge. But Waylon and his band were awesome, and he had the audience in his complete control. Certainly one of the shows I am most proud of.

Once the State and Orpheum theatres were up and running, I had enough to do keeping both (and later the Pantages as well) busy, so I rarely promoted arena shows in either Minneapolis or St. Paul. Only on occasions where an artist's popularity had increased so much that they had outgrown a theatre play did I take artists to arenas. Some of those were Mannheim Steamroller, Lord of the Dance, and the Dixie Chicks. And it happened with one of the best double billings I was ever blessed with: N'SYNC with opening act Brittany Spears, at the Orpheum on December

Governor Jesse Ventura, Kevin Dochtermann, Fred Krohn, Terry Ventura, and Dana Warg

27, 1998. Of course neither of those acts were that big then, so I didn't know what a killer show I had.

In the late 1990s, I got to know Dana Warg, who was then managing Target Center, and he suggested that we co-promote some arena shows together. Of course what he was mainly interested in was to work with Theatre Live! in order to indirectly benefit from its nonprofit tax status, since any shows presented by Theatre Live! were exempt from sales tax on tickets. At that time, the Minneapolis sales taxes were higher than those at Xcel Center in St. Paul, so Dana was at disadvantage competing for shows. I partnered with Dana and Target Center on a number of very successful arena shows (Tina Turner, Janet Jackson, N'SYNC, Backstreet Boys, Elton John, and Billy Joel (for two arena shows), U2, Cher, Dave Matthews, etc.). When it became clear that I and Theatre Live! Inc. were at the very center of the rivalry between

Target Center and Xcel Center, I decided that discretion was the better part of valor. The nonprofit exemption from sales tax that Theatre Live! and other major nonprofits were granted was so important to the success of the Broadway season and other live events at the Hennepin theatres that it seemed very risky jeopardize that status by being the lightening rod between the two cities on the arena sales tax issue. So I, Theatre Live!, and Hennepin Theatre Trust opted out of presenting shows at either arena (with only one or two exceptions) after 2001.

One thing I learned from producing large-venue shows was that the arena promotion business was far more cutthroat than promoting shows in theatres, especially when two arenas in one market are competing for the major shows. I recall Dana Warg telling me that Elton and Billy Joel's agents said we could have the show, but that whatever our two-show gross with venue

Fred Krohn, Dana Warg, and Kevin Dochtermann with N'SYNC

expenses might be, Elton and Billy would want all of it plus $100,000; and we as promoters would have to make all of our profit on our share of concessions and merchandise. Crazy, and a good reason, I felt, to back out of that arena (so to speak). I could sustain a major theatre-level artist's losses, but the potential magnitude of an arena loss could finish me off in one night.

CHAPTER TWENTY

PANTAGES VS. SHUBERT

W ITH CONSTRUCTION AT THE ORPHEUM FINALLY complete, and with its relaunch in January 1994 with a spectacular production of *MISS SAIGON*, I finally felt that a Hennepin Avenue Theatre District was now more than just the abstract concept Tom Hoch and I once envisioned. We had a first-class 2,650-seat Broadway theatre capable of accommodating virtually any touring show that producers could conceive of. We had a slightly smaller and more intimate 2,100-seat theatre that was perfect for smaller touring shows and live music and comedy acts. We had a solid management agreement with the city to operate both. We were content, and set about filling both venues. But as happens, events intervened and we were dragged into a bizarre Tale of Two Theatres that no one in the city or the entertainment business anticipated.

Act One of the Tale. The Pantages Theatre: Tom Hoch and I were quietly advised by several city officials that Ted Mann, the owner of the Mann (originally Pantages) Theatre a block down Hennepin Avenue from the State Theatre, planned to demolish the long-closed Mann and turn it into a parking lot so he could generate revenue from the property. We'd had our eyes on the Mann Theatre for several years, so following my theory that the best time to save a theatre is when it is in the most danger, we began some quiet conversations. Unfortunately one of our greatest

Although hidden by gray paint, the remaining details of the Pantages Theatre were very clear

allies, the head of the Minneapolis Community Development Agency (MCDA), Jim Heltzer, had left that position. While the agency had a great number of skilled and sympathetic staff people (and a few who were not so sympathetic), the agency seemed to lack the sort of decisive leadership that Jim Heltzer had provided, and which was so crucial to the success of the State and Orpheum projects.

One of our first city allies on the Pantages Theatre project (we refused to refer to it as the Mann Theatre) was City Council President Jackie Cherryhomes. She liked the vitality that the Orpheum and State brought to the downtown area, and was determined not to allow Ted Mann to tear down the Pantages and replace it with surface parking. She first authored a moratorium on the creation of additional downtown surface parking lots, then she began the process to designate the interior of the theatre as historic, preventing a short-term demolition.

During these early times, we had a number of discussions with Kelly Lindquist and Tom Nordyke of Artspace Projects regarding the potential of their organization working with us on the building surrounding the Pantages Theatre. Their well-respected non-profit managed the Hennepin Center for the Arts just down the street from the Pantages on Hennepin Avenue, and provided artist live-work spaces, and rehearsal and office spaces for nonprofit arts groups. All four of us envisioned that Artspace might work with us to manage the retail and office portions of our Pantages project. So during 1996 and 1997, we shared the details of the Pantages project with Kelly and Tom at Artspace.

In May 1996, I went public with my desire to save and restore the Pantages, and operate it as an off-Broadway and music venue, supplementing what the State and Orpheum could offer. The original *CityBusiness* and *Skyway News* stories emphasized my amazement that so much of the decorative plaster and the original stained-glass skylight were still intact. When questioned about the Pantages, MCDA economic development director, Terrell Towers, said he would be fine seeing it restored, but would "rather not" help finance the project. I said it would take broad interest and support to save the theatre. "My only objective here is to point out to people that this is a pretty magnificent theater," I was quoted as saying. Our then rival at the Ordway, Kevin Mc-Cullum, sniped in *CityBusiness* that "I think (Krohn) should sell out (shows in) his other theaters first."

To head off our effort to save the Pan, Ted Mann in 1997 hired "architectural historian" Charlene K. Roise to conduct an assessment of the "Landmark Potential of the Pantages (Mann) Theater." I assumed at the time that Ms. Roise was well aware of Mr. Mann's objectives for her engagement. In a murder trial, the prosecution does not hire an expert witness whose opinions will free the defendant. Ms. Roise's report was issued in May 1997 just prior to the Historic Preservation Commission's May 20, 1997, hearing on landmark designation. After a bunch of the usual historical boilerplate designed to add credibility to her work, Ms. Roise concluded that (1) the Pantages was not a prime example of theater development in the early twentieth century,

(2) the Pantages did not have an important-enough association with the lives of historic personages or events with strong ethnic, community, or city identity to qualify for landmark designation, (3) the Pantages interior did not display enough of its original plasterwork and detailing to qualify for landmark designation, particularly when compared to the neighboring State and Orpheum theatres, (4) the Pantages was a relatively unimportant example of theatre architect Marcus Priteca's work, and so much of Pritica's original design has been severely compromised by alterations that the property was not eligible for landmark designation, and (5) in summary, the Pantages had been so severely compromised by alterations to both decor and configuration that the property did not warrant landmark designation. She concluded that "(G)iven the unfortunate lack of architectural integrity of the Minneapolis Pantages Theater, it does not merit landmark designation under the city's guidelines."

We of course strongly disagreed with what we felt were Ms. Roise's convenient and self-serving conclusions, and we conducted a series of theatre tours with greatly enhanced theatrical lighting powered by an electric generator to illuminate the ceilings and walls and illustrate just how much of the original plaster and stained glass were still extant. Council President Cherryhomes was able to keep Ted Mann's proposed demolition at bay and, in May 1997 the Heritage Preservation Commission (HPC) voted to give the interior of the Pantages local landmark designation. That got Ted's attention, and Ted and his attorney agreed to meet with Tom Hoch and me in Jackie Cherryhomes' office.

Jackie told Ted that the city wanted to buy his property, and asked me to outline our plans. After our meeting, she teamed up with us to bring the rest of the City Council along. Mayor Sharon Sayles Belton was her usual supportive self, having seen by then how shows like *THE LION KING* could bring vitality to her downtown. The city purchased the Pantages and the surrounding Stimson Building in 1998 and spent another chunk of money to fixing the areaways under the sidewalks and stabilizing the structure while the development process could be finalized. It also directed the MCDA to commission a "market impact study" on the Pan. The agency engaged Maxfield Research and arts consultant, Bradley Morrison, to do this work, about which the less said the better. It was done on the cheap ($20,000), and in my opinion its recommendations were not even worth that paltry budget. Morrison is quoted in *City Pages* as saying that the Pantages' "shoebox" design is a problem that makes for a bad view from the back of the hall. "In my opinion," he said, "the Mann (Pantages) Theater is of no use whatever as a legitimate theater venue. It is not suitable for any kind of contemporary theater productions. I think it is very unfortunate the city decided to buy this property."

Luckily the City Council considered the credibility of the "experts" involved in the study, and what we felt were their obvious bias and lack of knowledge on the study's topics. They balanced their findings against our past success with the Orpheum and State theatres. We also pointed out to the City Council that Morrison had been responsible for a prior report that advised strongly against saving the State Theatre, and had expressed many of the same misinformed opinions about the State in his prior report. Thus in May 2000 the Council voted 10–2, over the objections of MCDA leadership, to grant my company, Historic Theatre Group, Ltd., exclusive development rights to both the Pantages Theatre and the surrounding Stimson Building.

We quickly went to work putting together a finance plan for the Stimson while at the same time preparing for the redevelopment of the Pantages itself. We envisioned that the Stimson Building would be condominiumized so that the city would initially own the Pan, and a private entity we'd form would own the Stimson portion of the property. This the MCDA project manager refused to do. (The PM is unnamed in this chapter since too much time has passed to hold grudges—I'll just refer to him as PM.)

PM insisted that much of the Stimson's second floor be devoted to a skyway connection, and the connection absolutely needed to run along the front windows of the property. Which of

course greatly reduced the revenue we could potentially generate from the second-floor space. PM continually attempted to poke holes in our proposed financing plan and play down our success in managing the State and Orpheum theatres. The final blow was that, despite a City Council mandate for our participation in the development of the MCDA financing plan for the project, we were afforded no input. The agency's plan was not even provided to us until one day prior to our deadline to show the MCDA our leases and financing commitment. In December 2000 we informed the City Council and mayor that Tom Hoch and I would be declining any additional participation in the Stimson project.

We continued to work with the MCDA on the Pantages Theatre itself, but our relationship with PM proved to be an ongoing problem. He constantly tried to limit our participation in theatre decisions. He wanted to put his personal image on this, his final major project. PM, along with a female architect, literally had plaster casts of their faces added to the cherub faces on the front edge of the balcony—something I insisted be removed.

We fought to stay involved, and I believe the design and functionality of the Pan were much improved because of our input. We were proud of our work when the Pantages reopened to rave reviews on November 8, 2002. But even when the Pantages Theatre was given a Heritage Preservation Award in May 2003, PM, I believe, kept the Hoch and Krohn names, and that of Historic Theatre Group, off the award. Only when someone stood up at the lunch and asked why we were not included, since we had done the lion's share of the work, did PM have to agree that we deserved some of the credit for the award.

Sadly, the leadership at the MCDA was not strong enough to rein in PM even though they reportedly had heard many suggestions from other staff people that PM was not working effectively with us. Even well after the Pantages was completed and turned over to us as managers, we discovered that PM still had some theatre keys and was entering the facility without our knowledge. The State and the Orpheum restoration projects were so

(*opposite*) The resplendent Pantages Theatre on opening night. PHOTO BY GEORGE HEINRICH.

collegial that it was disappointing that the partners in the Pantages restoration could not have worked better together.

Note: In October 2015, when I was retired but still booking some shows for Hennepin Theatre Trust, my sister, Lisa, who was still at the Trust, received an email from PM. It suggested that he had in his possession "an original, signed, and fully executed purchase agreement of the Orpheum with notarized Dylan signature."

PM told her that he didn't know how to reach me, but that he wondered whether I would be interested in "acquiring the document that represents the first major step in developing the Minneapolis Theatre District."

After the email was forwarded to me, I responded to PM that I might well be interested in the document, and asked what PM might be willing to sell the document for. PM said that he was thinking in the $2K/3K range, and said his ask was $2,500. I responded that "I am a bit concerned about the chain of title of this document, and why it would not be the property of the MCDA or its successors."

PM responded that he had saved this 1988-dated document from the shredder during one of their periodic office clean-ups at the now-nonexistent MCDA.

I bought the document from PM for $1,500, but the whole thing still feels a bit unseemly to me.

Chapter Two of the Tale: The Shubert Theatre versus The Pantages. I had often encouraged public officials to "Save the Pantages—the last Broadway theatre on Hennepin Avenue," but events intervened and a second theatre was soon moving in the direction of that Hennepin Avenue distinction. The city had acquired and demolished most of the property on Block E (the block bounded by Hennepin Avenue, Sixth Street, First Avenue North, and Seventh Street), and had gone through a series of negotiations with several real estate firms to redevelop the block into a retail showpiece for Minneapolis—something that would compete with the Mall of America and bring people to the center of the downtown.

During the time that Brookfield Management held the development rights, it insisted that the last property on the block, the long-dormant Shubert Theatre, needed to be demolished before Brookfield could complete any redevelopment of the block. They were adamantly opposed to incorporating the Shubert into their proposed project. The decision to demolish the Shubert became for a time an either/or decision: either the Pantages or the Shubert. We felt like the answer was simple: the Pantages should survive if only one theatre could. The Shubert had a nice facade, but behind it, the theatre was in a much worse state of disrepair than the Pan with virtually no remaining decorative plaster. The "stacked balcony" configuration (two steep but narrow balconies stacked one on top of the other) ruined the sightlines in all of the second balcony and a big portion of the first balcony. Yes, audience members were close to the stage, but they were either looking up at the balcony overhang above them, or looking down on the tops of the heads of the artists. The extreme steepness of the balcony aisles was intimidating to many audience members.

As discussions began, we felt these flaws would become self-evident, especially since there was a twin Shubert (now Fitzgerald) Theatre in St. Paul that had the same flaws, and could be examined by anyone who cared.

The Minneapolis preservation community, for whatever reason, seemed to rally against the Pantages and for the Shubert, based mainly on the Roise Report. In a 1997 comment letter from Britta Bloomberg, deputy State Historic Preservation officer at the Minnesota Historical Society relative to the Pantages local designation, stated that the Charlene Roise report was a "well documented and thorough addition to the draft local designation form. . .," and that "(O)ur review of the 1996 draft material concluded that the Pantages Theater had been altered to such an

extant [sic] that the architectural integrity had been compromised, thereby preventing it from being eligible for designation under the local ordinance."

In a 1996 tour of the Pan, Susan Roth of the Minnesota Historical Society had, per our notes, said she had "some reservations about the Pantages." Specifically, she was concerned about the physical integrity of the building, and the exterior, the interior, and the house. But of course preservation officials just loved the Shubert, which was in much worse shape and had almost no remaining decorative plaster. Ironically, preservationists seemed to buy the argument that the Shubert's stacked balconies brought the audience closer to the stage (ideal for dance, they said) and improved the theatre's acoustics. The National Register document praised the Shubert as "Minneapolis' only extant two-balcony theatre."

With development of Block E (and potentially a wider swath of Hennepin Avenue) at a standstill while a decision on the Shubert was worked out, my theory of only being able to save theatres that are in serious danger reared its head. Proponents, in order to solve the Block E problem while still saving the Shubert, proposed what I found a preposterous idea: the move of the Shubert across the empty block to a position aside of Artspace's Hennepin Center for the Arts. The strongest proponents of this idea seemed to be our "partners" on the Pantages Theatre and the surrounding Stimson Building—our friends at Artspace. Many of the City Council members seemed desperate enough to finalize the Block E project to give the move idea some credence.

In April 1998, Artspace commissioned a Shubert Theatre "Needs and Use Assessment" prepared by Dewer & Associates and Sutton & Associates. The report was based on moving the theatre (sans stagehouse) across Block E to within fifty feet of Hennepin Center for the Arts, and connecting it to the HCA via an atrium. The theatre would be configured as a 500-seat, 750-seat, or 1,000-seat venue depending on how many of the stacked balconies were retained. The report however stated that "the ability

(*opposite*) Historical photos of the Shubert Theatre, Minneapolis, c. 1997

The completed Pantages Theatre. PHOTO BY GEORGE HEINRICH

for the theater to effectively operate as a three-tiered auditorium assumes that upon completion of renovation all seating will have unimpaired sight lines"—something that later proved impossible. It also concluded in its financials that "rates for stagehand labor assume that the Shubert will be a non-union house." Nothing in the report seemed to identify sources of funding for the move and the restoration of the theatre.

In July 1998, Artspace prepared a "Shubert Theater Development Proposal" that detailed their plan to move the Shubert (sans its stagehouse) to a space just north of the Hennepin

Center, lease with option to buy the land in Jim Binger's parking lot where the theatre would be situated, and once the theatre was in place, fundraise to secure the nearly $26 million they estimated to be required to complete the project.

Since the Block E timeline was so tight, Artspace obviously needed to move the theatre first, and then, with the theatre sitting in its new space, raise the funds needed to complete the project. They agreed to Jim Binger's demand that he could require the demolition of the theatre and a return of his land if the option to buy was not exercised within three years. So once the

The completed $42,000,000, 505-seat Shubert Theatre

theatre move began, there was no easy way for Artspace to back out of the project if its fundraising did not pan out, since the nearly $5 million in city moving costs would have been sacrificed if the theatre was demolished after the move.

The City Council really wanted to see the Block E project move forward; and for that to happen, the Shubert either needed to be demolished, or it needed to move off the block per Artspace's proposal. Despite the huge cost and the shear impracticality of the move, many Council members seemed captivated by the idea that the move would set a record for the heaviest building ever moved. The city approved $4.65 million for the move, and in February 1999 the Shubert made its two-week voyage to its new site.

Despite several target reopening dates, fundraising proved more difficult than Artspace envisioned. The theatre reopening was delayed for twelve years—it finally opened on September 9, 2011. During those years, the cost of the project rose from Artspace's original estimate of $26 million to a staggering $42 million (an unfathomable $83,168 per seat vs. $8,167 per seat for the Pantages). In the process, the Shubert lost much of its historical significance, and the original interior configuration was greatly revised. The original stagehouse did not make the move. Both of the highly touted stacked balconies were jettisoned (lowering the capacity to 505).

CHAPTER TWENTY-ONE

CAMEO ROLES ACT III

INALLY, CHAPTER THREE OF THE TALE, HIGHLIGHTING eleven more of the amazing cast of fine artists I have had the privilege of working with over my career.

FAITH HILL

I was certainly familiar with Faith Hill as one of country music's stars, and her tour with Tim McGraw, I knew, had led to their marriage. Her first major single, "This Kiss," made her a more mainstream artist. When I was offered the chance to promote the first solo show of her career, I jumped at the chance. Faith played the Orpheum for me on April 9, 1999, and the show was an instant sellout. Since I knew how close Hill and McGraw were, and how they had pledged never to be separated for more than three days, I guessed that Tim was a cinch to be at her first solo concert, and most likely appear as an unannounced guest. I nosed around the backstage area to see if McGraw was anywhere to be found. I sadly concluded that he had not made the trip. Faith's show was beautifully presented, and she was one of the most natural and wholesome artists I had worked with—obviously destined to be the major star she later became.

LORIE LINE

When I first became aware of Lorie Line, she was playing a beautiful Steinway grand piano on the first floor of Dayton's Department Store at Christmastime, and selling CDs of her holiday music. She would become one of my highest grossing artists in the 2000s. What I liked most about Lorie were her business smarts. Rather than signing with a record company, she and her husband, Tim, kept her recording and publishing rights and her touring—meaning she had total control of her career and business.

Lorie's Dayton's gigs became such a holiday tradition that she and Tim self-produced a Christmas show with some success, playing some smaller Twin Cities venues. I was constantly looking for a holiday show that I could bring back over and over, as I had done with Mannheim Steamroller very successfully since 1989, and Lorie's show popped up. Lorie, Tim, and I had a discussion, and we determined to try the show at the State Theatre in December 1998.

Since Lorie and Tim owned every aspect of their business, they did not pay booking agent or management fees on their live shows. They were able to spend what they thought was needed on their production. Hence an orchestra of twelve, master vocalist Robert Robinson, amazing fashions (Lorie usually changed outfits two or three times), and a beautiful, festive set. Fans loved the show, and we were able to bring it back on consecutive Christmas seasons from 1998 to 2007. In its peak run in 2002, we sold out twelve shows and grossed almost $800,000. Not bad for a pianist who started at Dayton's.

One of Lorie and Tim's problems became how to top the prior year's already over-the-top production. I think they finally stretched so far that the shows became, in my opinion at least, a bit too "out there" for Lorie's audiences, who would have been fine with staying closer to the wholesome holiday spirit of her first few years.

Lorie and Tim knew their way around public relations. When

Jesse Ventura was elected Minnesota governor in 1999, I was not surprised to meet the new governor and his wife Terry backstage before our opening show. Lorie had gotten to know Terry and had pledged to do a fundraiser for one of Terry's favorite charities. Later in the run, I was invited to dinner at Lorie and Tim's palatial home on Lake Minnetonka for dinner with a small group of their friends, including Governor Ventura and his wife.

After dinner, Jesse asked if anyone would like to join him on the dock for a cigar, and I was the only one who accepted. I had really never smoked a cigar before (which I'm sure was obvious to Jesse). But how could I pass up some good face time with one of Minnesota's most unique and legendary of politicians? As I discussed Minnesota issues and the WWE with him, I realized he was clearly much more logical and intelligent than many Minnesotans gave him credit for. While in office, he proved adept at choosing skilled administrators to fill the gaps in his knowledge of our state. If he could have controlled his ego a bit and 86'd the beads in his beard, he certainly had the potential to win a second term and become one of Minnesota's more successful governors. His greatest asset, in my opinion, was his fine wife, Terry.

TONY BENNETT

Growing up in Hinsdale, Illinois, and North Oaks, Minnesota, Tony Bennett was one of my mom and dad's most-revered artists. I was often around during my parents' dinner parties (think many cocktails, a nice dinner, and more cocktails a la television's *Mad Men*). After dinner I was usually asked to play a couple of things on the piano for the guests, and then DJ the stereo, playing the most popular long-play 33 RPM records of the day. Often they were comedians such as Bob Newhart, Jonathan Winters, or JFK impersonator, Vaughn Meader. Then I went to the more serious stuff—artists everyone loved, like Ella, Sinatra, Judy Garland, and show tunes. By far the most popular in my parents' circle was

(*left*) Tony Bennett music. (*right*) Tony Bennett and Fred Krohn.

Tony Bennett. Sometimes his songs were requested for an hour or more. I had to play "I Left My Heart in San Francisco" three of four times during the evening.

I first worked with Tony Bennett when Harry Beacom brought him in for a Minneapolis Aquatennial event in the early 1970s. That was the first of my ten-plus shows with Tony over the amazing span of six decades. My last show with Tony prior to my retirement was in 2016. He was still going strong and performing amazing shows at age eighty-nine. He's been back since, performing for my sister Lisa. Tony can, of course, command the best musicians in the world to accompany him, and his style and voice continue to hold up well. When he arrives at the theatre stage door in a track suit and running shoes, it's a bit of a surprise. But when he comes out of his dressing room in a perfectly tailored tux, you absolutely know he's the real thing—the guy even Sinatra called "the best singer in the business."

Tony loved playing the old vaudeville theatres because of their great acoustics. On most of his stops at the State Theatre, he commented first on how beautiful the venue was, and rhapsodized about the wonderful sound. He then, without any announcement to the audience, laid down his mic on the piano, stepped to the edge of the stage, and did a complete song without amplification. Pure magic.

Tony is certainly one of the most talented and gracious artists I've worked with. Each time, it was an honor for me. A true legend.

KIDS IN THE HALL

I don't recall too much about these shows (for the reason I will describe). I worked with Sam Kinken (he must have been with Jam Productions, Ltd., at that point, but he moved around to a couple of other big promoters over his career) to bring in Canadian comic troupe, Kids in the Hall, at the height of their popularity in 2000. We sold out four shows at the Orpheum. Sam knew that the group loved to drink, so he thought that spending some of our substantial profit to make them happy was a great idea. So we developed our idea for the "Orpheum Martini Bar."

We took a fairly large onstage production room, brought in special lighting, décor items, a juke box, and many bottles of vodka, gin, and vermouth, and opened an after-hours speakeasy bar. After the 10:00 PM shows ended, we all piled into the bar, and consumed martinis. I was not a martini fan, so I had just one, but the rest of the guys hit the liquor table pretty hard, and it was difficult to persuade them to get into their limo and return to their hotel. That usually happened by about 3:00 AM. Sam and the guys could sleep all day, but I had to show up at work, so these late-night escapades were hard on me. Funny guys. Skilled drinkers.

CAROL CHANNING

I doubt I've worked with a bigger Broadway legend in my career than Carol Channing. We had many *HELLO DOLLY* productions

Carol Channing and
Fred Krohn

at the Orpheum over the years, but only one that really mattered—the run in 1994 starring Carol Channing. Hard to explain her effect on audiences because she certainly did not have a real Broadway voice or the kind of dynamism some stars have. But when she walked out on the stage, she just radiated energy and star quality. She owned, and will always own, the role of Dolly Levi. Not even Streisand or Bette Midler could top her.

Later in her life, after she had pretty much retired from the Broadway stage, Carol determined to put together a little review consisting of a few songs and many reminiscences of her long career. She had a very old-school agent who very likely had not booked a show in many years, making the process of getting Carol signed up difficult. Very antiquated contract blank, no fax or scans, just the US mail. We settled on a date in the fall 2004, and I began to work with Carol on her production needs. As might be expected, she was funny but a bit vague on the phone. Her husband, Harry Kullijian, quickly came to her assistance as they plotted out the content of the show. Carol had just reconnected with Harry, who was her junior high sweetheart many decades earlier. They had been married for just over a year when I booked her. When they arrived at the airport for the show, it was obvious that they were still very much in love in their late eighties.

The show itself was still a work in progress, since she had really only performed it two or three times prior to the Minneapolis date. But Carol was so charming that, even when she forgot where she was, the audience pulled for her. At the end of the show, after the requisite "Hello Dolly" number, she invited her new husband Harry to join her on stage, and they told their romantic tale of meeting after sixty-plus years of being disconnected. Tears flowed.

After the show, I invited Carol and Harry to join a small group of us for dinner at the Graves 601 Hotel where they were staying. Carol was very careful with what she ate—it had to be simple and organic. We had a great time. She shared many more of her legendary stories. A great and charming First Lady of the Broadway stage.

BOB NEWHART

When I booked Bob Newhart at the State in 2003, I expected just the usual stand-up comic requirements (follow spot and mic on a stand). But Bob had other ideas. He wanted a band to play him on and off the stage, and do some of the themes of his television shows. Obviously a throwback to his days playing Las Vegas. So I got him a killer group of local musicians who were thrilled to be working with one of their favorite performers.

While Bob did have some new material, he seemed to want to revisit the stand-up fame of his 1960 LP *The Button-Down Mind of Bob Newhart*, which I and most audience members knew by

Bob Newhart and Fred Krohn

heart and didn't mind hearing again fifty-plus years later. His polished recreations of those bits, most notably "Driving Instructor," took all of us back to our younger years. His stories about his two classic television shows were also welcome. The most surprising thing to me was Bob's physical stature. When I watched him on television, his size relative to the other actors was not noteworthy. But he was fairly diminutive in person.

CIRQUE DU SOLEIL

Early in 1999, I learned that the famed Cirque du Soleil in Montreal was looking for locations for their newest touring show, *DRALION*. I made some inquiries. I found they had already started the process of finding an appropriate Twin Cities site for their big blue tent, *Le Grand Chapiteau* and had already gotten the Minneapolis Community Development Agency involved in the search. Since landing this attraction would be a coup for Minneapolis, I joined the effort. It turned out that they were not only looking for a site, but were also looking for a local partner who could assist in their marketing and work with them on the governmental aspects of their run. Our nonprofit presenter, Theatre Live!, proved to be just the partner they were looking for.

Well before the new Guthrie and all the luxury apartments began to fill the south bank of the Mississippi River, that area was empty, flat, and close to downtown—a perfect location for the Cirque big-top tent. After many rounds of negotiations, Cirque determined to go forward, and set an opening date for their show of August 17, 2000. We knew the show would be spectacular, but witnessing the Cirque folks working with our skilled Local 13 stagehands to create the venue and all its support tents from scratch was magic. The chapiteau was state-of-the-art. Comfortable seating, beautiful sightlines, air-conditioned, and with all of the trappings and artistry that Cirque was known for. It became one of my favorite venues and I was always awed by it, whether with a full house when a show was being performed, or when the tent was completely quiet and empty. The culmination of a circus tradition that dated back to the 1800s, and by far the most impressive tent I'd ever been in.

The Cirque producers understood that their tickets were pretty pricey, and they allowed Theatre Live! to offer complimentary tickets to many large groups of school-age kids and their parents when the tent was not sold out. A great experience that I'm sure those families will not forget. Theatre Live! employees and their guests were often invited to the Cirque VIP preshow tent for dinner, cocktails, and show merch. Certainly Cirque du Soleil was masterful at taking care of its guests.

One of the high points of Theatre Live! involvement was a staff trip to Montreal to meet with Cirque's production and marketing staffs to determine how to best sell and operate the show. Included in the junket was an insider's tour of Cirque's campus to see how they develop all of their amazing acrobatic and clown artists, who are at the very pinnacle of skill. That night, at a superb dinner in old Montreal, I got to use my French language skills.

GREGORY PECK AND VERONIQUE

In the mid-1990s, I got a call from Nancy Nelson, a woman from Massachusetts who specialized in "conversations" with famous television and movie stars. Her meal ticket for much of the 1980s had been Cary Grant. After Cary died, she signed one of my most beloved male actors, Gregory Peck. I had two catalysts for my law career (both of them a bit lame in retrospect)— Perry Mason and Atticus Finch, the small-town lawyer played by Mr. Peck in *To Kill A Mockingbird*. The opportunity to meet this legendary actor very much appealed to me. The event would consist of a video montage of memorable moments from his film career; anecdotes by Mr. Peck on his movies, colleagues and family; and finally, a period of question and answers. I immediately said yes.

While Nancy sent me all the press stuff and contract riders, Mr. Peck obviously must have had time on his hands. He was on the phone from Beverly Hills on many occasions to ask questions of me and offer his suggestions on how the event could be best marketed and produced. Very old-school star, and very generous attitude. It was hard to fathom that the man on the line was one of Hollywood's greatest stars.

With the event approaching, Gregory and his wife, Veronique, arrived a day early. My sister Lisa and I picked them up at the gate with an electric cart and got them and their luggage quickly into their awaiting limo. Veronique was beautiful, vaguely exotic, and had the most beautiful French accent I had heard. They were an amazing couple; and to our surprise, they seemed to like us as well.

On the day of the event, they asked to be picked up early so they could settle into the dressing room. The twenty-minute video started, and the audience loudly applauded each film, culminating with several scenes from *To Kill A Mockingbird*, which the whole audience stood for. Mr. Peck then walked quietly onto the stage. The audience gave him a five-minute ovation before he had said a word. He was obviously a beloved part of the life of each person in the room.

His comments, as expected, were understated. He was a major star and had no reason to hype himself in any way. Very gracious and low key. During the anecdote section of the event, Mr. Peck invited his wife to join him on stage and discuss how they had met. She had been a Paris news reporter who interviewed him when *Roman Holiday* was released. They'd been inseparable ever since, and married on the day after Peck's divorce from his first wife was finalized.

After the Q and A and final standing ovation, Mr. Peck and

Fred Krohn and
Gregory Peck

his wife moved to a private reception for Theatre Live's most important benefactors, for whom they had generously agreed to make an appearance. But of course every one of the one hundred or so guests, including my sister Lindy, insisted on an autograph or a photo. I could tell that Gregory was tiring a bit. But he stuck it out and made each of our guests feel they had left as friends. Again what one might expect from a legendary old-school star.

The next day, Lisa rode with them in their limo back to the airport, helped them onto their electric cart, and onto the plane. In the airport drive, and while riding to the gate, Lisa and Gregory and Veronique exchanged contact information and vowed to stay in touch. Gregory told Lisa to let him know if she was ever in California, so she could come and visit. So when Lisa accepted a judging job at a horse show in Santa Barbara the next summer, she sent him a note letting him know, and he immediately

375 NORTH CAROLWOOD DRIVE
LOS ANGELES, CALIFORNIA 90077

August 1, 1995

Mr. Fred Krohn
President and General Manager
Theater Live! Inc.
c/o The State Theatre
805 Hennepin Ave.
Minneapolis, MN 55405

Dear Fred,

I have to write at once to tell you how
much we enjoyed meeting you and your family.
This was an extraordinary visit for us.
Veronique and I fell a little bit in
love with Minneapolis. It must be because
of the people. What an invigorating
change from life in L.A.

Please express our appreciation to the stage
crew. This was easily the most skillful,
expert operation we've encountered.

My thanks to you for encouraging us to come,
and for receiving us so warmly. We both
send fond regards, and our love to that
adorable horse trainer.

Sincerely,

Gregory Peck

insisted that she stop in. She arrived at his Beverly Hills home in the morning, greeted Veronique, then spent the next four hours with Gregory, including a nice lunch. Gregory's son Carey visited, and talked about his effort to set a world record for the most

CHAPTER TWENTY-ONE

DENNIS BROWN
1921 NORTH KENMORE AVENUE · 8
LOS ANGELES, CALIFORNIA 90027

August 6, 1995

Dear Fred,

One week has now passed since we were in Minneapolis, visiting your beautiful theater. You're now up to your neck in female arachnids, and we're ancient history. Nevertheless...

Just wanted to drop you a note to say thanks again for taking such good care of us...and me, in particular. Driving me over to St. Paul was above and beyond, and your generous nature did not go unappreciated.

I had a thoroughly enjoyable time in Minneapolis, and I think the Pecks did too. True, he worked like a dog, and he gave every person at that reception extra value for their extra money. And I know that he got exhausted...he let that on to me, more so than usual.

But even so, he never uttered a single word of complaint. To the contrary, the only word of complaint I heard from him had to do with the fact that he was unable to spend more time with the people at the reception, because he liked them so much, and found them so interesting to talk to.

In addition to the patrons, Veronique especially enjoyed talking to your sister with the triplets. But the topper...their *very* favorite person...was Lisa. They both thoroughly enjoyed the drive out to the airport with Lisa. As we rode to the airline holding room on the cart, the two of them kept trying to top each other in their descriptions to me of how charming they had found Lisa...which in turn led to another account of how much they liked the people of Minneapolis.

I just thought you'd like to know.

Dennis

people in a sky-diving formation, which was to happen later in the week. As he walked Lisa to her car, Gregory told her how lucky he was to have a friend like her.

Obviously a major memory for Lisa.

TAP DOGS

Another show I successfully took an early flyer on was Australian choreographer Dein Perry's *TAP DOGS*. It would be an understatement to say that I had not at that point had a lot of success promoting shows with tap dance content. Until Savion Glover updated tap for a contemporary audience, tap was harder to sell to audiences than any other dance form. *TAP DOGS* was obviously different: it featured six or eight hunky Australian boys in jeans and boots, and was a very macho combination of construction site and things from the show *STOMP*. I knew right away that I could sell it to younger audiences of both sexes. The guys could relate, and the girls would find the young stars irresistible. But the show was a totally unknown quantity, so we would need to spend some television money explaining the show to Twin Cities audiences. In order to have sufficient marketing money, we needed to book the show for multiple nights—a risky proposition if it didn't sell. But as we did with *RIVERDANCE*, we rolled the dice and plastered the airwaves with thirty-second television spots. We had all sorts of contests ("Win Blundstone boots!") and Meet-and-Greet opportunities.

The guys came in early and did round after round of daytime TV shows. By opening night, the hype we generated was palpable. Although the opening show was sold out, we had hundreds of fans show up to try to buy tickets. Of course with no other alternatives, they purchased tickets for the remaining three shows. In my career, I can't recall another instance where we had to turn that many interested fans away. But scarcity creates its own demand, and the run became sold out very quickly, grossing nearly $500,000. Sometimes it's smartest to be in all the way instead of just playing it safe.

THE VAGINA MONOLOGUES

I'd venture a guess that there's not a stage show out there that I related to less than Eve Ensler's *THE VAGINA MONOLOGUES*. The work consisted of short essays on a variety of topics such as consensual and non-consensual sexual experiences, body image, genital mutilation, menstrual periods, etc., all explored through the experiences of a wide variety of women. This sort of exploration of real topics was hot in the mid-1990s, with plays such as *ANGELS IN AMERICA*, and *The New York Times* critic Charles Isherwood had called *MONOLOGUES* "probably the most important piece of political theater of the last decade." So it seemed like I could find an audience for the work. I determined to book it into the intimate 400-seat Woman's Club Theatre in downtown Minneapolis near Loring Park, which I was attempting to book more often.

One of the most interesting aspects of the play for me was that I, as the show producer, had to find local celebrities to fill some of the monologue reader slots (the show was like the play *LOVE LETTERS* in that there were no sets, just three actors with scripts on stands. I first thought of two women I admired and respected: Joan Mondale and her daughter Eleanor. The Mondales lived in my neighborhood, and I had become friends with Joan over the years due to our mutual love of the arts. I called Joan. While she was not too optimistic that it would interest her, she and Eleanor both said they would read the play and determine if any of the monologues might work for them. I dropped off a copy. Both declined after looking it over.

My next idea was even more outrageous based on the politics of the time. Democrat turned republican Norm Coleman was mayor of St. Paul, and obviously had his eye on the governorship or the US Senate. His attractive wife, Laurie, was from a theatrical family and had done some television and movie work. Obviously *MONOLOGUES* did not fit the conservative stance that Norm was then trying to sell to the public, but from the minute I contacted

Laurie, she seemed very interested in participating, and very open about the content. She finally agreed to participate for one of the three weeks of the run. To his credit, Norm did not try to persuade Laurie not to do the show. In fact he showed up on opening night and watched the show backstage with me, praising Laurie's work after the curtain call. An important show, and one that fit the Woman's Club perfectly, both in clientele and aesthetics.

JOHNNY MATHIS

Another old-school star I watched on *Ed Sullivan* and worshiped as a kid was Johnny Mathis. Our family had two "go-to" Christmas LPs that were played over and over during the holidays: *The Andy Williams Christmas Album* and *Merry Christmas with Johnny Mathis*. I think I felt especially close to Johnny as a kid because he seemed "sensitive" (the true meaning of which I did not understand at the time).

Johnny had always been on my short list of artists I wanted to be involved with; but he took few dates, his agent asked top dollar for his appearances, and he required major production and a thirty-piece orchestra. When I did make Christmas offers, he said that he preferred playing warm climates where he might golf during his free time. Finally in December 1997 I made a two-show Christmas offer that he could not turn down. Both shows immediately sold out, the local orchestra, augmented by his great players and conductor, was perfect. Johnny was in great spirits and voice. Two of my top-ten shows.

Backstage, Johnny was friendly and a bit shy, with a hint of melancholy, I thought. He had a young male assistant with him who I thought was disrespecting him a bit, and that made me sad. But what a life and what a career. I worked with Johnny for three additional concerts over the years, and all were stellar.

DAVID SEDARIS

Early in my booking career, I determined to present major au-
thors, poets, and media personalities more often, because I
thought they would sell and because I was interested in meeting
them. One agency and one agent, stood head and shoulders over
the rest of the pack: Steven Barclay at the Steven Barclay Agency
in Petaluma, California. Steven's roster of personalities was major, and he always advocated for them and helped me figure out

how to best market to each. Over the years, I booked everyone from *Fresh Air*'s Terry Gross to historian David McCullough, poets Billy Collins and Mary Oliver, *This American Life* creator Ira Glass, composer and lyricist Stephen Sondheim, commentator Fran Lebowitz, and writer Frances Mayes. But the most lasting and important to my presenting career was a quirky writer and sometimes radio contributor, David Sedaris.

I first heard David on *National Public Radio* reading an essay he called "Santaland Diaries." I found it one of the most odd and endearing things I had heard. A bit later, I heard him read equally funny stuff on Ira Glass's radio program, and I was hooked. My friends had been asking me if I had heard of this guy David Sedaris. I bought several of his books, then realized that David's stuff was twice as good on his audiobooks, where his quirky inflections and voice added to the experience. Seemed to me that a live reading would sell tickets. I might have known that David would be on Steven Barclay Agency roster.

When he first showed up at the State Theatre in April 2001, David had not yet blossomed into the Mark Twain-level performer he became. He was shy, read from his past and future books without much comment, answered a few audience questions, and left the stage. But that was only the beginning. Next came the after-show book and audio sales, and autographs and time with David for a vast portion of the audience. They were willing to stay as long as it took to have a couple minutes of face time with David and possibly receive a small gift—usually consisting of miniature hotel toiletries, stickers, or (for some younger fans) a condom. That first year, while I was warned that these events could go on for hours, I doubted our audiences would have the patience to wait around. Boy, was I wrong.

I presented David annually for the next fifteen years, and the shortest meet-and-greet session was two-and-a-half hours. The longest was three-and-a-half hours. Since I make it my responsibility to get all my artists back to their hotels safely, I always stayed around until the bitter end, and usually ended up buying

David Sedaris

David's latest book and asking him to sign it for me. I typically asked David (and his local friend, Dawn) what they might want to eat while David signed, and went to a neighboring restaurant to pick it up for them.

One thing I learned quickly from listening to David's conversations with his fans was that he had a purpose in these long sittings with them: he was mining for new material for his lectures and books. On a couple of occasions, something funny that a fan had said in Minneapolis ended up either in his readings or his next book.

Over the time I've known him, David Sedaris has blossomed from a quirky shy guy to a writer and humorist who is a national treasure. I am honored to have worked with him over those many years.

JIM BAILEY

There are just a few artists whom I very much regret not having the opportunity to work with. At the top of that list are Dusty Springfield, Gene Pitney, and Nat King Cole. But at the very summit of that group is Judy Garland. I felt she was the finest singer America had ever seen. She had the singular ability to grab and hold a live audience like no other performer. As I plotted my future career in the entertainment business, I just knew I would work with Judy at some point soon. After leaving Harry Beacom at age twenty-two, one of my first calls was to Judy's management company to see when she might be planning a US tour. Sadly, those discussions had just begun when she was found dead of a barbiturate overdose in her London hotel room on June 22, 1969. Her tragic death left a blank spot in my career that I tried without success to fill.

Her daughter Liza was great at her peak when I booked her, but she did not in any way replace Judy for me. The closest I came was my booking of Jim Bailey, who was able to not so much impersonate Judy as to channel her almost perfectly. Many artists, male and female, have tried to do so, but only Jim Bailey succeeded. He was friends with Judy and had access to all the great Mort Lindsey arrangements she used in her classic Carnegie Hall concert. More than that, he was able to capture every nuance of Judy's voice, and every one of her gestures, better than anyone.

When I booked Jim, I was given the choice of having an entire show featuring Judy Garland, or a two-act show featuring both

Judy and Barbra Streisand. I decided to try to recreate the Carnegie Hall show, so I stayed solely with Judy.

I have always felt blessed that, due to the Minnesota Orchestra and the St. Paul Chamber Orchestra, the range and quality of the instrumentalists I could engage was superb. There have always been great jazz horn players as well (think The Hornheads as the best example). The thirty-piece orchestra we put together for Jim was just magnificent. What a pleasure it was to hear them rehearse the Mort Lindsey arrangements (surely some of the best *American Songbook* charts ever written), even without Jim on stage. When Jim came out of his dressing room for his final rehearsal dressed as Judy, the effect was magic. I had seen Judy live only once, but I was convinced that she had been reborn when I saw Jim sing "The Man That Got Away."

The show followed the general format of the Carnegie concert, and Jim was even able to recreate the Judy quotes that those of us who love the LP recall so well (*"I'll sing 'em all and we'll stay all night"*). After the show at a small reception for Jim, he remained in his Judy costume (but not the Judy persona). I was amazed at how many local theatre artists showed up to see whether Jim lived up to the hype. I recall Jungle Theatre head, Bain Boehlke, saying that the way Jim totally inhabited Judy was theatrically beyond anything he'd ever seen. Sadly, this show was as close to booking Judy as I was able to come, but much closer than I had any reason to hope for. A *tour de force* performance.

RAUL MALO AND THE MAVERICKS

If I had a choice of what band I would like to watch live in a club or an intimate venue, hands down it would be The Mavericks. Led by Raul Malo, who possesses one of the most pure and empathetic voices in whatever style he is working in (only Roy Orbison can compete with him in my opinion), the guys just always seem to be having fun. Get me to Austin, Texas, put a cold long neck in my hand, put me in front of the stage, and I would be in heaven. Their material is uniformly great. No other band delivers it with the commitment the Mavs do.

I first worked with them in 1996, when they had a couple of charted country hits ("All You Ever Do Is Bring Me Down" and "What a Crying Shame"). Their State Theatre show was energetic, but they did not really catch on. They seemed too far from the stuff that was being played on country radio then. They were more Tex-Mex and western swing than country. Despite some minor hits, they really didn't catch fire. They disbanded, and Raul Malo pursued a solo career, putting out some amazing, but hard-to-classify, CDs. I followed Raul, but didn't feel there was enough of a market for his solo work to warrant a live show.

After many years of Mavs anonymity, I got a call from one of my agents in 2013 offering the reformed group for a live show. He sent me a copy of their new CD, MONO, as well as a couple of their most recent albums. I was hooked. They were at least as good as back in the 1990s, and amped up with the addition of killer-guitarist Eddie Perez and keyboardist Jerry Dale McFadden. They seemed to deserve a new chance to connect, so I booked them into the Pantages. They sold out almost instantly, there followed two more Pan shows, and then they moved up to the State for what have become almost annual shows. Most amazingly, their audience consists of an older demographic but, boy, can they party. They stand for the entire show, and are into the band to a degree I've not seen even with younger fans. Star Tribune reviewer Jon Bream loves them as much as I do, always referring to them as "America's best dance band." Long may they reign.

LORD OF THE RINGS PREMIERE

Common among many Carleton College students during the years I was there was high intellect and a quirky uniqueness that seemed to make socialization more difficult. For whatever

reason, most of us played bridge, read and loved the *Lord of the Rings Trilogy* by J.R.R. Tolkien, and spent our days plotting to find and reclaim the bust of Schiller, which was in hiding, and which by its rules had to be shown in public on campus periodically in order to be retained. There were some all-American sports jocks who were pretty normal and admired by all; but the rest of us were pretty odd and nerdy, it seemed to me.

When I started thinking about attending Carleton, the go-to Twin Cities guy to find out about the school was John Stout. He had adopted the bow tie as his trademark and was almost never without one, even when everyone else was in sweats. A bit full of himself back then, but a smart and unique personality. I have known John since college, and he has been instrumental in guiding me through some pretty rough spots in my entertainment

LORD OF THE RINGS producer Barrie Osborne (white scarf) and our group of Carleton College graduates

career. He's been on my nonprofit boards, and provided me with valuable legal advice.

Late in 2001, John came to me with some surprising information: fellow Carleton graduate Barrie M. Osborne was one of the lead producers of the soon-to-be-released series of *Lord of the Rings* movies, which had been filmed in New Zealand. John and Barrie thought we could do a Twin Cities premiere to benefit Carleton, screening the first of the three films at the State Theatre. Without thinking too much, I assured them that we could pull it off.

What was I thinking? Yes, the State had a large projection screen, and yes, the State had two movie projectors, but they were from the 1940s and hardly fit for screening the current generation of film technology. Confronted with these difficulties, most film moguls would have bailed, but Barrie brought in a projection consultant from Los Angeles, and he completely rebuilt our two projectors and added state-of-the-art Dolby sound. We brought in a modern, very reflective, movie screen to brighten the images. The result was amazing. The metal-to-metal clanks of the swords were startling, and the shear brightness of the projection was astonishing when compared to our prior screenings of vintage films. The sellout was a great victory for the Carleton nerds who had worshiped the Tolkien novels so many years prior. Sadly, the projection improvements were removed the next day and shipped back to LA, which pretty much ended our presentation of current cinema at the State Theatre.

RAVI AND ANOUSHKA SHANKAR

After having worked with sitar player Ravi Shankar at Carleton in the 1960s, it was a special pleasure to welcome him to the State Theatre in 2002, this time with his prodigy daughter, Anoushka. Their concert rider required that we construct a 12'x12' draped platform about a foot off the stage floor, and provide woven rugs for the playing surface. The rider specified that we light only the platform and no other area of the stage. The effect was magic; when the two were playing their beautiful, hypnotic ragas, they seemed to be levitating off the stage and into the universe. Amazing sitar masters but as I watched them, I have to admit I was wondering how one of Ravi's daughters became such a sitar virtuoso, and his other daughter became the multitalented pop singer, Norah Jones. Obviously genes matter, no matter what discipline you go into.

THE BLENDERS

After the holiday success of Mannheim Steamroller and Lorie Line beginning in 1998, I began to look for other artists who could build a loyal Christmas audience and become annual attractions. I was lucky enough to hit the jackpot with The Blenders, an a cappella vocal quartet from Fargo. Consisting of Tim Kasper, Ryan Lance, and Darren and Allan Rust, the guys had a lot going for them, including a pretty strong fan base. They had toured colleges extensively and opened for a number of national performers. All they needed, it seemed, was a hit record, and they got that with "I'm in Love With the McDonald's Girl." They had great songs, great arrangements, great blending of voices, and great stage presence. Most of us thought that national stardom should follow. But for whatever reason they never broke out like they deserved to do.

They self-produced several excellent Christmas CDs; and starting in 1999, the group and I worked out a deal for multiple-show runs at the Pantages just before Christmas each year—a tradition my sister Lisa continued after my retirement. I've watched all four of them mature, have families and kids, and become more skilled each year. They don't phone it in. Their shows are perfect in every detail, and I could not have found a more talented and loyal quartet to work with. My holidays would not be complete without attending their shows.

Marcel Marceau's backstage drawing at the Pantages Theatre. (Photo by Steve Olson

MARCEL MARCEAU

In 2003, I was not exactly a huge fan of mime. Nor did I know many who were. But legends are legends, so when I was given the opportunity to present the celebrated mime artist, Marcel Marceau, I could not say no. And I was rewarded with a sold-out run of shows at the Pantages that blew away my mistaken impressions about the discipline. Marceau as his stage persona, Bip the Clown, illustrated his complete mastery of the art. He was without doubt the maestro of mime—as he called it, "the art of silence."

As Marceau entered the theatre and began down the stairs to his dressing room one night, I asked if he might honor us with his signature on the stairway wall—something of a theatre tradition at our three theatres and throughout the world. He said he would be happy to, and asked for some Sharpies. When I returned a half-hour later, I found he had added a whole scene to the wall—just like his images from the children's books he wrote. It's still there, and I hope that it remains as long as the Pantages stands. A true master, who made me a mime fan in spite of myself.

ELAINE STRITCH

At the height of my success at the three Hennepin Avenue theatres, I had the luxury of being able to bring in shows I pretty much knew were not money-makers. I knew that, while I would lose money on the promotion itself, wearing my theatre-manager hat I would be able to make up the loss via the rents, ticket commissions, and bar and merch sales. It allowed me to bring in shows that had great artistic merit, but that most promoters in other cities were passing on. One such show was *ELAINE STRITCH AT LIBERTY*, which I booked at the State for a multi-show run in June 2003.

Elaine to me was Broadway personified, with a storied career beginning in the 1940s. I was a Tony voter at the time, and I was absolutely blown away by her Broadway show. Great unexpected anecdotes. Magnificent signature numbers from *BUS STOP* to her signature song, "The Ladies Who Lunch" from Sondheim's *COMPANY*. And who has ever looked better at age seventy-six in a simple, long white shirt and form-fitting black tights?

While the set looked very minimal in New York, recreating its plain brick back wall proved costly and time-consuming (even though the actual back wall of the State is brick). Bottom line is that we got to the week prior to opening, and it became obvious that not as many people as I had hoped knew what a legend Elaine was. We needed to cut back a week-night show or two that were not selling. Elaine was well aware of my low ticket sales, and did as much press as we were able to arrange for her. She had real old-school star power, and media types were awed by her. She got great press coverage, and sales picked up somewhat. I lost money on the run, but it was still one of the shows I will always remember most fondly.

MICHAEL BUBLÉ

One of my dreams over the course of my entertainment career was to find and popularize "the next Frank Sinatra." I thought Sinatra was head-and-shoulders above any other male jazz singer (with the exception of Tony Bennett, of course), and I loved the great songs and arrangements he always chose. Over many years, I made it my business to listen to any new artists who might fit the bill (on LPs first, then cassettes, then CDs). Over the years, I did okay, listening to and booking such artists as Michael Feinstein, Jamie Cullum, Harry Connick, Jr., Bobby Caldwell, Curtis Stigers, Jimmy Scott, Manhattan Transfer, and Steve Tyrell. But I can claim to have "discovered" and been the first promoter of only one artist who has reached even close to the Sinatra level of acclaim: Michael Bublé.

In the 1990s and early 2000s, artists toured to hype their CD sales. Their money was made on record sales and touring was only a means to that end (Now it's just the opposite). Back then, local record company reps provided a never-ending supply of the latest CDs, and were always willing to work with promoters who agreed to bring in their artists. The two standard measures of promoter support were a box of CDs for radio giveaways prior to a show, and a ticket buy of 60–80 tickets for the show, allowing the rep to wine and dine radio jocks in an effort to get them to play their artists.

In early 2003, I was provided with a self-titled CD by a Michael Bublé, who appeared to be a nice-looking Canadian guy who loved both hockey and *The Great American Songbook*. It had been produced by a great judge of talent, David Foster, and was full of standards and a couple of contemporary tunes arranged in timeless style. The CD immediately got a lot of play in my car CD player as I drove around town, and it grew on me. Problem was, the CD was not getting any play on local radio stations, and no one had ever heard of the guy. Michael's agent assured me there was about to be a national PR campaign for Bublé, and my early vote of confidence would be well-rewarded down the line. So I booked a show at the Pantages on July 19, 2003.

Once Michael appeared on the *TODAY* show that February, he developed a small but rabid following, and his Pan show sold out in advance. Wow, was the show impressive. Michael had worked in many a club, lounge, and cruise ship, and he had some of the funniest between-song patter I had heard. He was so cute and funny, yet so such a skilled singer, audiences could not resist him. I immediately rebooked him for a November date at the Pan, and that also sold out. But that was it. His career blew up from there. My "reward" for my early support was that his agent gave Michael's entire touring schedule to another promoter. But thanks, Michael, for your loyalty.

ANITA BAKER

Anita Baker's *RAPTURE* CD remains one of my most-admired albums. The songs are moody and romantic, and her voice and physical presence are awesome. When I was offered a chance to work with her in 2004, I could not say no, even at the substantial guarantee her agent was asking. Then I got her rider, one of the most costly and elaborate I had seen. Full orchestra, special guest artist, I had to rent her large chandeliers and ship them from Detroit to Minneapolis, catering for sixty, etc. All these costs meant I needed to sell out every ticket in order to keep the show in the black. Not at all guaranteed for a market with only a relatively small African American community.

The show sold out, and all went well on the day of the concert. Anita seemed in a good mood. She did a long sound check with the orchestra and her special guest. Then she retired to her dressing room. As show time approached, no one on her large staff indicated that there were any problems. But as the orchestra and her players assembled on the stage, there was no Anita to be found. I asked her people where she was, and was assured that she was just completing her costume change and would be out in a moment. But twenty minutes after the scheduled curtain time, she had still not made an appearance. The audience was getting restless and applauding in unison for the show to start. Now even her assistant was getting nervous. She was seen going in and out of Anita's dressing room on a frequent basis, each time assuring me that it would be only another minute or two.

At 8:30 PM, I went out on stage and assured her fans that she was, in fact, in her dressing room, and would be out to do her show momentarily. I called her agent at home and let him know what was happening, and he tried to make some calls to her manager. Finally at 8:50 PM, I knocked on Anita's door, which she did not open. I informed her through the closed door that if she were not on stage and starting the show in five minutes, I would have no option but to go on stage, cancel the show, and send the audience away, and then sue her for breach of contract.

No response from within, and the countdown began. Just as I was about to reenter the stage to give the audience the bad news, her dressing room door opened and, without saying anything to me, she walked directly on stage, surprising her conductor and orchestra. But they got things together and the show went on. And what a good show it was.

Afterward, Anita left immediately, and neither her agent nor her manager ever told me what was causing her difficulties, although there was some vague talk about stage fright. One of those backstage mysteries that was never solved.

LINDA EDER

In 1988, Linda Eder, a girl from Anoka, Minnesota, received some acclaim for winning the talent show *STAR SEARCH*, and I took notice. But in those days, such wins were not the ticket to instant fame they seem to have become. Linda continued to work locally but wasn't finding a fan base as far as I could tell. The next time I heard her name was in 1997. She was dating Broadway composer, Frank Wildhorn (who she later married), and starring in his production of *JEKYLL & HYDE*. As a Tony voter, I saw the show, was impressed with her big voice, and was quite surprised that she did not garner a Tony nomination. We played *J&H* at the Orpheum in 1999, but by that time Linda had left the company.

While I had expected her to repeat her Broadway success in other shows, she instead became a daytime talk show regular and began touring the country doing a solo show. I first booked her in December 2001 for a holiday show, and it sold out, leading to regular appearances at the State and Pantages over the next ten or twelve years. By this time she had developed a rabid fan following, especially within the gay community, and her shows were much anticipated. But as her Broadway reputation faded, so did her fan base, it seemed. After her divorce from Wildhorn in 2004, she toured less and less, content it seemed to stay home and take care of their son, Jake. Another artist with a magnificent voice who did not quite make it to the level of stardom I had anticipated for her.

KATHY GRIFFIN

Never in my career has an artist blown up so quickly. And never (with the possible exception of Bill Cosby) has an artist crashed and burned so ignominiously. Kathy Griffin appeared on several television shows, and had a popular reality show of her own, *My Life on the D-List*, but she was hardly a household word when I booked her into the Pantages in April 2006. But boy did she have some rabid gay fans. The show sold out, grossed $28,000, and we immediately rebooked her at the State two months later. That show sold out and grossed $60,000. So for her next tour in 2008, we booked her for two shows at the Orpheum, and they immediately sold out. So we added two more shows, and they sold out. Then we added two more shows, and they sold out. Then we added a final seventh show, and that sold out as well: 18,000 tickets sold. Gross in excess of $500,000.

I had never been so successful with a comedian, even with artists like Jerry Seinfeld. We brought her back several more times, and she sold out multiple shows, but never again at her 2008 record level. Within this success seemed to lurk a need on Kathy's part to keep topping her last outrageous actions, which led to her being banned from appearances on her stock shows: *The View*, *Ellen*, and *The Tonight Show*. But what led her to be a toxic performer was her posting in 2017 of a video of her holding a mask styled to look like the severed head of then-president, Donald Trump. All hell broke loose after that. I found I was unable to justify a rebooking due to the controversy. While Kathy apologized for the posting, saying she went too far and begged for forgiveness, that and other controversies damaged her drawing power, at least for the moment. Funny comic but prone to self-inflicted damage.

CAROL BURNETT

In early 2010, I got a call from Nancy Nelson (not the Twin Cities actress and TV personality, but the agent I had worked with on my earlier Gregory Peck event) asking if I would be interested in working with legendary television stage and movie star Carol Burnett. She would screen a twenty-minute video of her career highlights, then for the remainder of the event respond to audience questions as she had done on her iconic television show from 1967 to 1978. To me Carol seemed like the most-beloved star on television. I had no doubt that her legion of fans would do anything for a chance to see her in person. But her rider demands once again meant that I had to sell out every ticket in order to make money. Carol insisted on transportation via a $35,000 chartered jet, a five-star hotel suite, and meals at the finest restaurants in town. This sort of show, where the artist really has no past touring history, makes the booking a crap shoot; and when these shows go off the rails, the crash can be substantial. But it seemed like a perfect State Theatre show, so we went forward.

Carol and Nancy came in a day early, held a long rehearsal to make sure the video worked and all the stagehand cues became automatic, and then retired to dinner at 510 Groveland and her Graves 601 hotel suite. On the day of the show, she came in early, went over the cues a second time, and worked with our ushers to make certain that they understood how the Q&A would be handled. Then in a very generous gesture, posed for photos with each stagehand and usher and said a personal hello to each. By the end of the rehearsal she could have been elected president with ease. Beloved indeed.

The show itself was where Carol really worked her magic on her fans. No matter what was asked, she had the perfect retort, one that responded perfectly to the question and also revealed her life and personality. I have never since seen anyone in such complete control of an audience of 2,000.

Carol Burnett and
Fred Krohn

CHAPTER TWENTY-ONE

We repeated the show in 2003, and the event sold out even more quickly than it had in 2010. The quality was just as good even though Carol was by then in her early eighties. Several years later, without any advance comment from Carol or her agent Nancy Nelson, I opened the Sunday Minneapolis paper to find a large ad for the same Carol Burnett show as we had presented twice, but now in the hands of another promoter. To add insult to injury, it had been booked into our State Theatre.

I of course immediately called Nancy Nelson at her home to ask how this could have happened, but Nancy refused to take the call, and in fact failed to return any of my calls leading up to the show. Calls to Carol's office also went unanswered. I later found that she had done the same thing to many of the other performing arts venues who had earlier risked their money to bring her into their cities. Nancy Nelson, please return my call. I have a question from an audience member I would like to ask Carol.

ANTHONY BOURDAIN

On June 8, 2018, my sister Lisa, her son Cody, and I were at the airport about to fly to Tucson to visit our 102-year-old father, Herb. We were on a long moving walkway heading to our gate when Lisa spotted a friend of hers going the other direction. Upon seeing us, she immediately shouted out, "So sorry to hear about Tony Bourdain. So sad." As she passed, we asked her what she was talking about, but she went by quickly and was unable to relate the details. We hustled into a restaurant to get some breakfast, and immediately saw that every television in the airport was delivering the breaking news that author and travel documentarian, Anthony Bourdain, was dead, and speculation was that he had taken his own life. Lisa and I immediately both felt there must be some mistake, that the Tony Bourdain we had come to know would never be capable of something like that. He seemed far too stable and self-confident to end his life when everything seemed to be going so well for him.

Lisa and I had worked with Tony on three occasions (April 2010, May 2013, and July 2015) and had hung out with him after each event while he did VIP meet and greets. We loved his television travel/food shows like *No Reservations* and *Parts Unknown*. The episode where he ate in a Saigon noodle shop with President Barack Obama was to me the pinnacle of his craft. He was a person of strong opinions but, throughout his world travels, he was always able to relate to his hosts and bring the world together. In person, he was just as you hoped he would be. I recall his discussion with his friend and Minneapolis resident, Andrew Zimmern, about their past drug use. Both were frank and honest and pulled no punches. While he had strong opinions on almost every subject he was asked about, his responses always showed that he had wrestled with them and given them much thought. You could not help admiring Tony and falling into the gravity of his personality. The guy was just magnetic, and one of my great regrets is that I will not be able to work and hang out with him again.

ED SHEERAN

During the years that I wore the hats of both the concert promoter and the venue manager, I always attempted to persuade artists and Broadway producers to originate their tours in one of my venues. More rent, and it helped me generate additional wages for our stagehands. I gave them a good rent package, and most artists really liked the Twin Cities. Most wanted to head out to Paisley Park to hang with Prince. For musicians, these rehearsals and shows were often classic "underplays," live shows in venues much smaller than the artist could almost be guaranteed to sell out. They wanted to try out new material, develop an optimum set list, reestablish their musical chops, and build buzz for their upcoming arena tours. I worked these underplays with a number of groups, including Bob Dylan, Sting, and Florence+The Machine. But the biggest underplay I was ever involved with was Ed Sheeran in September 2012.

Sheeran's first two CDs had just been released, and they exploded internationally. He could have toured sold-out arenas. But his manager and agent felt he needed some time to develop his live show; so they booked him into a few theatres, one of which was the State. Tickets at $22.50 and $18.50. Artist guarantee to Sheeran, an amazingly low $10,000. Fans loved him and he immediately went on to large venues. He set touring gross records around the world. No doubt the best deal I ever got for an artist of his stature.

ALICE COOPER

Booking agent John Dittmar called me out of the blue in early 2013 and asked if I wanted to book one of his artists, Alice Cooper, into the State or Orpheum. Odd idea, I told him, since I knew Alice's shows, even after decades, still consisted of the "shock rock" elements he was famous for, including many set pieces like electric chairs, boa constrictors, and pyrotechnics. I asked John if the show would be cut down for such small venues. He assured me that the show would be identical to what Allice was currently putting into his arena tour. John sent me a copy of the rider, and it was massive. The pyrotechnics cost alone appeared to total $7,500+, and that would be *if* I could get a local pyro operator and city permit. The sound and lighting rentals were just as impossible, meaning that my stagehand bill would also be massive. But I do like a good challenge, so I decided to give this "School's Out For Summer" artist a very rare theatre play. It proved to be an excellent call. The first show at the State immediately sold out, and we added a second show, which also went clean.

Now all I had to do was produce a very elaborate and set-based show on the relatively small State Theatre stage. For the next few weeks, I was on daily calls with Alice's production team to figure out how we could fit everything on the stage, and also where we could store the large props when not being used. Most importantly, how we could do a major pyro display within the State without burning it down. My friends at the city were skeptical; but based on my track record, they allowed me to proceed.

A large portion of the audience at both shows had obviously been at Alice's first arena shows, and appeared frozen in time, wearing the same T-shirts and leather jackets, and sporting the same mullets I would have expected during the "chicken incident" days. But they loved the show, setting records for the Alice Cooper merchandise they purchased. The pyro was just awesome, and safely detonated. Alice came in early and I was able to get him on several tournament-level local golf courses (he's a scratch golfer), so he was in a great mood.

In 2015 I brought him back to the State. While the show went fine, the date got all messed up with a rescheduled arena show (with Mötley Crüe) that Alice was set to open just a couple of weeks later. The Target Center was so insistent on having Alice on that show that they agreed to subsidize any loss I might suffer because of the date conflict. Luckily I made money, but we did not roll into a second show this time. Great artist who is far more savvy than most folks give him credit for.

WOODY ALLEN

I first recall seeing Woody Allen as a very talented stand-up comic on *The Ed Sullivan Show* and other variety shows of the time. His style was more monologue than typical setups and punch lines, much like the conversational style later developed by Jerry Seinfeld. His persona of the insecure intellectual nebbish was completely different than other comics like Don Rickles, Jackie Mason, or Rodney Dangerfield. And he didn't delve into the issues of the day like Mort Sahl. I seem to recall seeing Woody at a Northrop

Auditorium appearance soon after we moved to the Twin Cities, and having the feeling that the guy was really different—in a very good and talented way. I later loved his movies, and was fond of quoting my favorite lines in college (like his line to Diane Keaton in *Annie Hall* when she parks her car almost in the middle of the street and he tells her, "That's okay, we can walk to the curb from here"). I was always intrigued by my friends in Manhattan telling me that Woody was an excellent clarinet player, and had a regular weekly gig with a small band. What I did not understand was the very complicated dynamics of his family life, and the allegations which would tarnish his reputation.

In 2015, I was offered a tour by Woody Allen and His New Orleans Jazz Band, which had toured Europe but had not played many gigs in the United States. It was immediately obvious to me that the booking was fraught with potential problems. While the Me Too Movement had not yet arrived in force, there were definitely those who felt there must be some truth in the allegations against Woody; I foresaw the potential of demonstrations in front of the theatre, or worse. Despite the accusations against him, Woody had never been charged and, at that point, based on my legal training, I felt he should be presumed innocent until proven guilty. I booked the show, it found an audience, and Woody proved to be a pretty-darn-good clarinetist, and just the sort of charming nebbish I had expected him to be for years.

RINGO STARR

On August 21, 1965, the Beatles were booked to play a Met Stadium show. I had four good tickets, but decided I needed a much more up-close-and-personal experience. My sister Linda and I drove out to Met Stadium on the afternoon of the show. I successfully presented my Nhork Syndicate press pass, and we headed for the room where a KDWB pre-show press conference was scheduled. It proved to be a small cafeteria-style room with clunky wooden bar chairs and tables, and it had not yet been prepped for the coming press event. Linda and I decided to set things up as we would envision them: we placed two tables with four chairs at the back or the room, then moved the rest of the tables to the side and arranged the remainder of the chairs for the press. As we were waiting for the event to happen, a police officer came into the room and asked for our credentials. I showed him my press pass, and he nicely told us that for this event, we needed to be on his advance list, or we needed to clear out.

Obviously we were not on the list, and were asked to leave. We reluctantly agreed, but ducked into a bathroom and into several stalls in the hope that we could hide out and rejoin the participants once the Beatles arrived. No such luck. Someone came in to use the stalls and discovered us. This time they took us all the way to the parking lot. So much for meeting the Beatles. The show itself was an anticlimax—such subpar sound, and such loud screaming, it was hard to know what songs the boys were singing. And a very short thirty-five minutes in length.

Fifty years later, I finally got to meet at least 25 percent of the Beatles. I booked *Ringo Starr and His All-Starr Band* at the State (in a twist of fate, Dave Hart, who managed Linda Eder, had one other major client: Ringo Starr). When Ringo's limo pulled up to the State Theatre stage door, I was ready. Ringo jumped out of the car, informed me that he did not allow photos, did not shake hands, and did not do autographs. He elbow-bumped my elbow, and went into his dressing room, not to be seen again. My one and only brush with a Beatle.

LINDSEY VONN

My experiences growing up with my niece, Olympic ski star Lindsey Vonn, are for another book. As a kid she was a challenge to babysit, as were her younger siblings, including a set of triplets. Lindsey was always plotting some wild adventure for all of them.

Lindsey Vonn and Fred Krohn on the night of her Olympic Gold

Even as a very young girl, she had absolutely no fear. One of the high points of my life was being in Vancouver with her mother (my sister Lindy) and our family when Lindsey won Gold in the Olympic Downhill. Things just don't get more exciting than that.

But while Lindsey is still famous, especially in and around the Twin Cities where she grew up, I had never envisioned that she would become a celebrity I would welcome to one of our theatres. But in September 2019, at the urging of the Trust's media partner, the Minneapolis *Star Tribune*, my sister Lisa booked Lindsey at the State as part of their *Inspired Conversations* series. It was pretty wild to see her name on our marquee after nearly fifty years of seeing non-family members up there.

As usual, Lindsey was on her game, looked stunning, and answered her questions in her customary friendly and disarming way. A great night, capped by a family dinner at the Capital Grille next door. Can't wait to see where Lindsey's life goes next.

STEVE WINWOOD

British singer, songwriter, and multi-instrumentalist, Steve Winwood, has been my constant musical companion over my entertainment career, and his. Whether as a solo artist or during his years with The Spencer Davis Group, Traffic, or Blind Faith, he always elevated the music he was involved in. He and Clapton are at the top of my musical honor roll.

Soon after I moved up to the Twin Cities with my family in 1966, I saw an ad in an obscure magazine announcing an appearance by The Spencer Davis Group at a small and rarely used space in East St. Paul that was once a schoolhouse. I bought a ticket and, after getting lost several times, found the building, and went inside. The crowd was sparse, but the band was amazing. They had two very recent million-selling singles, "Gimme Some Lovin'" and "I'm a Man," both of which were just raw energy live.

In 2015, nearly fifty years after I saw Steve playing with The Spencer Davis Group, I had the opportunity to bring him to town as a solo act. A local promoter had brought him in several years earlier and done practically no business with Steve, and his agent wanted someone else to take a crack at promoting him. (Turns out that, per my conversation with the promoter, her people "forgot" to advertise the show).

We advertised, and the show sold out. And what a show it was! Winwood played his Hammond B-3, several guitars, and a mandolin, and his singing was still spot on. He and his band rocked through a career of memorable songs with his fans standing throughout.

After the show, as I was packing up my things in the dressing-room area, Steve walked into my office, and we talked for a few minutes. I told him how much his songs had meant to me, related my early experience seeing The Spencer Davis Group, and how impressed I was with his playing back then. Steve paused for a moment as if thinking over his answer, and then told me he hated to spoil my forty-seven-year-old memory, but he had left that group just before they had done that United States tour. He had not been in the band when I saw them. We had a laugh. But I sensed that, nice guy that he was, he had considered just letting me keep my memory rather than bursting my balloon.

BETTE MIDLER

Ever since Guthrie Theater booker, Sue Weil, brought Bette Midler to that venue in 1973, I tried to rebook her at one of the Hennepin theatres. Despite cold calls on her manager in Los Angeles and scores of unsolicited concert offers, I had nothing to show for my efforts. Then, of course, she outgrew my theatres and headlined arenas. Over the years, she rivaled Judy Garland for "artist I most wanted to work with but did not."

Fast forward to the Barack Obama presidential campaign. I was helping to raise money for Barack when my friends Sam and Sylvia Kaplan called to ask if I would help them produce a fundraiser for Obama at their large Minneapolis townhouse. The star attraction, they told me, was to be Bette Midler. They needed someone to work with her people to bring in a grand piano, arrange for sound reinforcement, and set up the condo so that as many people as possible could see and hear Bette's performance.

Instant yes, of course. Her people sent me a list of the things Bette would need, and I went about securing them. I brought in our head stage person from the Pantages Theatre since he was an expert sound technician. I rented a nine-foot Steinway and, with Sam and Sylvia, we determined where it should be placed. We did some subtle sound and lighting and arranged the furniture to allow the best vantage points for the guests.

Bette showed up with her assistant and accompanist for a

sound check the afternoon of the event and was as chatty and friendly as she was talking to Johnny Carson during her many *Tonight Show* appearances. She sounded great. Of course we were on a similar high, as all of us in the room felt that Barack would win, and that a new era was in store for our country. Great to have worked with Bette, and even greater that it was in support of one of our greatest presidents.

CHAPTER TWENTY-TWO

ATTEMPTED STEAL OF HOME

W**ITH THE SUCCESSFUL RE-OPENING OF THE PANTAGES** Theatre in 2002, Hennepin Avenue had indeed become the theatre district we and the City of Minneapolis envisioned when we first purchased the Orpheum from Bob Dylan in 1988.

While it was widely perceived that I, through Historic Theatre Group, Ltd., had held the management agreement for the three theatres for years without any real competition, in fact, I and my firm had gone through a series of short-term management agreements that did not allow much long-term investment or planning on our part. We were granted a management extension for the Orpheum and State in 1991, gone through a successful RFP for that management in 1994, and given one-year extensions of the management agreement in 1994, 1996, 1997, 1998, 1999, and 2000. Finally in November 2001, Historic Theatre Group, LLC, was given a five-year management agreement for all three theatres.

During that same time, Theatre Live, Inc., the nonprofit presenter of the Broadway season, was awarded a "master use agreement" giving it the right to co-present a Broadway season with Jujamcyn Productions through June 30, 2004. In 2002, due to some very unfriendly last-minute legislation passed by the Minnesota Legislature, Theatre Live! was forced to assign its rights in the master use agreement to Hennepin Theatre Trust, a new 501(c)(3), which became the new co-presenter of the Broadway seasons.

By this time, the City of Minneapolis had issued bonds for the restoration of all three theatres in the total amount of over $25 million, and since the theatres were generating positive cash flow, two things happened: (1) the City Council and mayor determined that a study should be done to determine the best long-term management and operation of the three theatres, and (2) the Ordway, still smarting from its rejection as Broadway season co-presenter after the 1995–1996 season, began pressure to regain a Broadway foothold in Minneapolis.

In May 2004, after mandating and receiving a Theatre Study Committee report on the three theatres, the City Council directed CPED, the development arm of the City, to prepare and issue a request for proposals for the management and booking of the three theatres. In August 2004, an RFP was issued by CPED, with responses due by October 15.

Initially, seven different entities expressed some interest in responding to the RFP, but in the end, there were only three responders: (1) The Ordway Center for the Performing Arts, (2) Theatre Dreams out of Chicago (dead at the outset since they had never promoted a single show in Minneapolis), and (3) our joint incumbent proposal with partners Historic Theatre Group, Ltd., Hennepin Theatre Trust, and Clear Channel Entertainment.

While it was obvious to most observers that the City Council and mayor were very unlikely to turn over their three gems on Hennepin Avenue to a competing St. Paul entity (especially after their past history of stealing the *SHOW BOAT* run and moving it from the Orpheum to the Ordway), the Ordway leadership seemed oblivious to that logic. They began a full-court press, lobbying anyone they could think of with a connection to Minneapolis city officials.

In a patently transparent move, the Ordway proposed to reconstitute itself as "The Twin Cities Theatre Alliance" and move its headquarters from St. Paul to Minneapolis. From there, they would book their two theatres as well as Minneapolis's three theatres, under a "coordinated, one-season model," which many felt would eliminate competition and reduce rather than increase the number of shows in the market. They offered the city $2,222,500 in 2006 as a purchase option, vs. a $500,000 deposit as a rent option; but didn't seem to make any financial guarantees beyond these initial cash payments, and could leave after ten years at their sole option. And they did not seem to have a solid plan for ongoing capital improvements.

While the Ordway stressed its financial strength in its response, many pointed out that their 2001–2003 deficit had totaled $3,255,000, and their programming deficit for the same period was $5,886,764. Finally, they threw out the claim that they could increase attendance at the five theatres to 613,600, but their prior track record did not support their projections.

Our proposal, in contrast, seemed to respond to each of the city's concerns as detailed in their RFP. Since the length of the term allowed via the current tax-exempt theatre bonds was limited when for-profits were involved, we proposed to convert the bonds from tax-exempt to taxable in order to allow a thirty-year term. Historic Theatre Group would continue to run the theatres, and Hennepin Theatre Trust would continue to book Broadway seasons and concerts into the three theatres. Finally, Clear Channel Entertainment would co-present the Broadway seasons with the Trust, and in addition would provide letters of credit sufficient to guarantee the taxable bonds and the capital improvements over the entire thirty-year term. And at the end of the thirty-year term, when the bonds were completely repaid, Hennepin Theatre Trust (and not Clear Channel) would acquire title to the three theatres. Unlike the Ordway proposal, ours would take the city completely out of any financial risk for the thirty-year term and continue the A-level bookings we had achieved over the past decade.

As the date for Council action approached, the Ordway

Historic Theatre Group partners Lee Lynch and Fred Krohn at the execution of the sale documents

got more and more desperate, and its lobbying efforts became much more harsh than expected, pitting St. Paul business people (many of whom lived in Minneapolis) against the Downtown Council and Minneapolis leaders. In the last few days before the city's decision, the Ordway resorted to an unattributed email saying that the city was turning over the three Minneapolis to the mega-for-profit Clear Channel, which would ultimately own them—an obviously false claim. When that email was traced to the Ordway itself, they were forced to apologize, and their tactics were used by our supporters on the City Council to rebuke them.

It was thus not much of a surprise when the City Council majority chose our response and gave us 120 days to negotiate a long-term contract with CPED. Complicating things a bit was the announcement that Clear Channel Entertainment planned to spin off its "theatrical assets" from its radio assets; for a time during our negotiations with CPED, we had to call our partner "CCE Spinco." It later became Live Nation, and both old and new entities were required to post identical letters of credit to protect the City of Minneapolis.

After months of serious negotiation, and the review of lots of bond documents, the parties arrived at a lease of the three theatres by Hennepin Theatre Trust, a management agreement between the Trust and Historic Theatre Group, and really stringent financial guarantees by both Clear Channel and Live Nation. As previously discussed with the Council and mayor, Live Nation became the 51 percent owner of my entity, Historic Theatre Group, and I continued as its president and CEO.

All seemed pleased with the deal and the financial protections it offered the city, and the City Council approved the lease and related documents on April 15, 2005.

CHAPTER TWENTY-THREE

THEATRE MANAGEMENT ROULETTE

OVER THE COURSE OF MY NEARLY FIFTY YEARS IN THE live entertainment business, I have operated or worked with others under many different corporate guises. Below, to the extent that I can recall them, are a listing:

Beacom & Associates
Theatre Live! Inc.
Concert Tour, Inc.
TheaTour, Inc.
Theatre Live! Inc. (again)
Orpheum Theatre Corporation (Zimmerman/Dylan)
Marland Productions, Inc.
State Theatre Group, Inc.
Historic Theatre Group, LLC
PACE Theatrical Group
CCE Spinco
SFX Entertainment
Live Nation
Clear Channel Entertainment
Hennepin Theatre Trust (as concert booker)

In looking at that list, I am reminded of my friend and fellow promoter in the 1970s and 1980s, Dick Shapiro. He was fond of telling anyone who would listen that he named his most current company, "Company 7," because he had bankrupted out the first six of his corporate entities. Luckily I did not have that problem. Only once did I resort to the protection a corporation allowed. I booked a production of *SUGAR BABIES* starring Mickey Rooney and Ann Miller into Northrop Auditorium. The run proved to be a fiasco, and I was forced to stick producer Alan Wasser with a portion of the loss. Something that would haunt me for years afterward. I wish Alan were still around—he deserved at least an apology from me, if not a settlement.

The earliest names, all related to live entertainment in theatres, were used depending on who was partnering with me on a given show. I most preferred the name Theatre Live! Inc., used it early in my career, put it on the shelf for years while I worked with Dylan and his brother, and brought it back for an encore as I began my work with the refurbishment of the three Hennepin Avenue theatres.

From there it gets more complicated. In the late 1990s, I was one of a whole bunch of local and regional promoters, and we all pretty much stuck to our own concert markets. When we had "history" with an act, the national agents didn't allow other promoters to come into our market and steal our acts. There were exceptions, mainly with the major acts like Elvis or the Stones, but we could normally hold onto our stable of artists if their history with us was successful.

Enter a dude called Robert F.X. Sillerman, who began to acquire regional promoters and merge them into a national promoter entity, SFX Entertainment. When he first started his acquisitions, he was paying crazy prices, as he had to do in order to interest the regional majors like Delsner/Slater in New York, Contemporary in St. Louis, and DiCesare Engler in Pittsburgh. A few of the independents resisted, like Jam in Chicago, but most took their incredible money and ran. At that point I was not a big enough fish to interest Sillerman, so I just kept promoting on my own and with Jam on occasion. No one seemed to know what Sillerman had in mind. Was he rolling this up in order to package and sell? Or was he planning to actually operate the mega-entity to try to dominate the entire US promotional market?

The answer came in February 2000, when radio giant Clear Channel Communications purchased SFX Entertainment for a reported $3.3 billion plus the assumption of $1.1 billion in SFX debt. CCE cited "cross-promotional synergies" between its radio stations and the concerts generated by SFX, but many analysts found that justification questionable.

SFX had earlier acquired PACE Theatrical, so with the CCE purchase it acquired PACE's 50 percent of Jim Binger's Jujamcyn Productions (the Minneapolis entity) and later acquired the remaining 50 percent. So as we were responding to the City of Minneapolis's RFP in 1995, we were doing so via our new Broadway partner, CCE.

Just as we were in the thick of our negotiations, CCE announced that it planned to spin off its entertainment division, both concerts and theatrical, to an as-yet-unnamed entity we were forced to call CCE Spinco. As discussed earlier, that allowed the city to demand full letters of credit from both CCE and the newly named Live Nation. Thus for a time, Live Nation became our Broadway partner.

Finally in January 2008, Live Nation determined that their people knew concerts, but really knew very little about the Broadway market, and determined after a bidding process to spin off its North American theatrical assets to Key Brand Entertainment, owned by British theatre producer, John Gore. KBE was later renamed The John Gore Organization.

My relationship, personal and corporate, with John Gore was complicated, as I will discuss next.

CHAPTER TWENTY-FOUR

MY DEPARTURE AND RETURN TO MY ROOTS

BETWEEN 2000 AND 2005, MY COMPANY, HISTORIC THEatre Group, and our nonprofit partners Theatre Live, and later Hennepin Theatre Trust, had a bunch of partners to deal with, and those relationships were at times rocky. We were fine dealing with Jujamcyn Productions, since it was owned by Jim Binger, someone we trusted, and it was a local entity. And also because Jujamcyn mostly kept to its own business and didn't try to mess with ours.

The key to the financial success of my company, Historic Theatre Group, in those years was that it (1) had its own contract for ticket sales directly with Ticketmaster, and (2) had a local bank account which it used to hold, and earn interest from, the advance ticket sales that Ticketmaster provided under our direct contract. When we had a blockbuster show on advance sale, HTG's account could be earning interest on $15 million to $20 million at a time. Sometimes a producer, most notably Disney, required us to share that interest, but even a part of the funds these advance sales generated was fine with us.

> **Note:** Only Live Entertainment of Canada, Garth Drabinsky's company, required us to wire each day's advance sales to their bank, and to do so by 10:00 A.M. Minneapolis time. It soon became obvious to us that Garth was being pressured by his bank to make these deposits, since I often got calls from his Toronto banker. If I or my bank was five or ten minutes late in making a daily wire transfer, I got a call from Garth or his associate Robert Topol asking, "Where the fuck is our money?" Drabinsky was obviously under substantial financial pressure, and would later be found guilty of fraud and forgery and incarcerated. Sad, because his shows were among the best produced that we presented over the years.

Historic Theatre Group also received income from theatre rentals, local box office charges, merchandise sales, and bar and concession sales. All these streams of cash allowed HTG to invest in shows, even break-even or losing shows, in order to keep the theatres active. I as president and CEO of HTG oversaw the operation of the company, including finance, human resources, bank relationships (including check signing), the administration of our local Ticketmaster contract, and HTG's relationship with our nonprofit partner, Hennepin Theatre Trust.

But all of this began to change in late 1995, when Historic Theatre Group, Hennepin Theatre Trust, and PACE Theatrical Group/SFX Entertainment entered into a number of agreements with the City of Minneapolis wherein (1) the outstanding bonds and debt of the Orpheum, State, and Pantages theatres were wrapped together and refinanced, with the Trust having the ultimate responsibility for the bond payments; (2) the three theatres were leased to Hennepin Theatre Trust for a thirty-year term, after which the Trust would own them; (3) SFX Entertainment guaranteed the repayment of the new bonds by providing a series of letters of credit in favor of the city in case of default; (4) PACE Theatrical (owned by SFX) was given the exclusive right to work 50/50 percent with Hennepin Theatre Trust on the annual Broadway season; (5) PACE acquired 51 percent of my company, Historic Theatre Group, and HTG continued to manage and operate the three theatres on behalf of the Trust; and (6) I continued to serve as the president and CEO of the HTG at a very generous salary.

Going into this many-faceted deal, I as majority owner of Historic Theatre Group (Lee Lynch was the minority partner) well realized that a 49 percent ownership was not an ideal position to be in, especially after controlling everything for so many years. But I also realized that without the involvement of PACE and SFX, the city deal would not go through, since the city absolutely required a financial heavy hitter to guarantee the bonds in order to close the transaction and put Hennepin Theatre Trust in ultimate control. Neither the Trust nor HTG had the kind of balance sheets the city required.

Despite the needed participation of PACE and SFX, all the local parties (city, MCDA, Hennepin Theatre Trust, and Historic Theatre Group) wanted to make certain that neither PACE nor SFX, nor any other for-profit successor, had any opportunity under the documents to acquire any ownership or title to the three theatres. That's why we designed the documents to place the Trust in the ultimate ownership position. And that proved prescient since, on several occasions after the original deal, the PACE/Clear Channel/Live Nation/Key Brand Entertainment entities made strong overtures to purchase the Orpheum, efforts always rebuffed by city officials. (They didn't seem interested in buying the State or Pantages, I assume since they had no one on staff that had any experience with concert and live show booking to generate revenues from those venues).

While we were spending literally months to draft the city documents, I quietly negotiated with PACE on a purchase price for 51 percent of Historic Theatre Group. Lee and I wanted to set a price that was high enough to cover us should the new 51 percent owners turn out to be unacceptable or untrustworthy, and make our remaining 49 percent worthless. We realized that whatever we arrived at for 51 percent might well be all we got. We eventually reached our price.

The very complicated deal (there were twenty or more documents plus the actual bond documents) finally closed in December 2005. Lee Lynch and I had the pleasure of receiving a call from our bank informing us that a multimillion-dollar deposit had just been wired into our HTG account.

With all the transactions complete, including the Clear Channel spin-off of its concert and theatrical assets to Live Nation, the main players starting in 2006 were: (1) Hennepin Theatre Trust, lessor and ultimate owner of the three theatres and 50 percent partner in the annual Broadway Seasons; (2) Historic Theatre Group, LLC (now owned 51 percent by PACE/Live Nation) as manager of the three theatres with me at the helm; and (3) PACE/Live Nation, as both 51 percent owner of Historic Theatre Group and 50 percent "consultant" to the Trust relative to the Broadway seasons.

It soon became clear that Live Nation was a rock-oriented organization and really had little interest in theatre management or Broadway seasons. In a way however, that was a relief, since Live Nation pretty much left us alone and allowed to continue to do what we had been doing before the mega-deal.

But in late 2007 I began to hear rumors of Live Nation's interest in selling its theatrical assets and concentrating solely on its concert business. There began some internal discussion of potential suitors for the theatrical assets. In the end, there were six or seven bidders, and I was enlisted to promote the value of the Minneapolis assets to three or four of them.

I participated in several long-distance conference calls, and very soon afterward I got a call from a John Gore in England, who said he was one of the bidders and was traveling to the US to check out his potential assets. He asked that I give him a tour of the three theatres and have lunch with him. I found John a quiet, smart guy who I thought I could work with—an impression I would not continue to hold for very long.

John Gore's acquisition of the Live Nation theatrical assets was announced on January 24, 2008. He called his company Key Brand Entertainment (now The John Gore Organization). From the start I could tell that his people planned to aggressively take control of HTG and try to move as many aspects of the Trust's and HTG's businesses as possible to New York. Almost immediately, his people sent in their auditors and conducted a protracted and accusatory review of our finances, stressing out our staff and causing our acting CFO to develop a severe case of shingles and resign. It seemed to me that the audit itself was to be expected, but the harsh tone of the auditors and the KBE employees was not.

Next Gore fired our remaining finance and human resources people and moved those functions to New York. All we really had left on our local staff were several functionaries who were tasked with scanning documents and emailing them to those in New York who were now running most of the former HTG functions.

Gore's next move was to close the local Ticketmaster Agreement HTG had been working with for years, and move HTG's Ticketmaster relationship to his national contract. Of course with that move, my local control of the advance ticket sales, and their revenue streams to HTG, came to an end.

Finally, even though it seemed like the management agreement and our sale documents prohibited it, he moved the HTG bank account to New York and kept the substantial interest earnings that HTG had been receiving. Despite insisting that Gore show me where on the HTG spreadsheet that missing interest income was shown on the HTG books, he was never able to do so to my satisfaction. I felt he was merging HTG into his company rather than treating HTG as an independent subsidiary, stripping HTG of its appropriate revenues, and burdening HTG with expenses that were really those of Gore's organization. After months of unproductive discussions, I finally had to sue his firm for the production of documents on these topics. But it quickly became clear that Key Brand had very deep pockets and could keep fighting me on these issues until I ran out of money.

The ultimate indignity however was that, while he continued my employment, he stripped me of my usual duties as president and CEO of my company, never consulted me on anything, and forced me to spend my days preparing impossibly complicated Excel spreadsheets on my projections for the business. Since my employment contract provided financial redress if my responsibilities were diminished, I resolved to sue Gore, hopefully with more luck than my initial suit.

In sum, I felt that Gore had reneged on our agreement to continue to operate Historic Theatre Group as an independent entity, had systematically stripped HTG of its most important revenue streams, had moved most of its staffing to New York, and had burdened HTG with Key Brand Expenses that should by rights have been paid by his company. In the process, of course, he had totally devalued our 49 percent interest in HTG.

Finally, the stress and boredom of my job became impossible for me. Over a weekend in August 2009, I quietly moved my important papers and office items to my condo and drafted some emails to my agent friends, city officials, and key employees and friends in preparation for my resignation as president and CEO of Historic Theatre Group. On Tuesday, August 25, to the surprise of everyone in my office, I did not show up for work, and instead fired off the emails I had drafted. I told my city allies and friends that I had, for a number of months, had serious differences of opinion with John Gore and Key Brand over how to operate HTG, and I had finally determined that it was not possible for me to serve both as an officer of the company and to represent the concerns of the 49 percent owners. I stated that after taking some time off, I would "determine how I might most effectively deal with Key Brand to assure that the Hennepin Avenue Theatres can remain well-managed and successful."

I was not in the mood to provide a statement or discuss these issues with the press, which was probably a mistake, since I know it irritated several newspaper writers who had supported me for many years. I then spent many additional unproductive months plotting how to support the position of HTG's 49 percent owners and regain the revenues I felt were due us.

While I felt the facts were on our side, Key Brand was a very large company, and nothing I tried seemed to force them to yield to my positions. So I came away only with a nice settlement of my employment-related legal issues, and finally a marginal offer from Key Brand to purchase the remaining 49 percent of HTG. At that point I decided to pack the many boxes of HTG/Key Brand files away, shed the stress they had caused, and move on. I wanted to find some sort of job that would allow me to work until my Social Security benefits were maxed out at age seventy, and then chuck everything and travel to the many places I had dreamed of visiting.

Tom Hoch was then heading up Hennepin Theatre Trust, and my sister Lisa was handling the Trust's Broadway and concert marketing (Key Brand had tried without success to move all of the Trust's marketing activities to New York, as it had done for many of its other markets). I had been promoting an occasional show in coordination with the Trust. So I discussed with Tom and Lisa my proposal to formalize our relationship and promote live shows at the three theatres on a 50/50 percent basis, sharing the profit or the loss from each show we worked together on. At the same time I would work with my sister Lisa in anticipation of her taking over my promotion activities for the Trust. I felt more shows certainly benefited the Trust, and that my willingness to share both the profit and the loss from each show protected the Trust from my booking weak concerts. I certainly had a good knowledge of artists, agents, and marketing, and I welcomed working with Tom and my sister once again. So began a mutually beneficial partnership that lasted until April 2018, and resulted in more than 300 shows at the three theatres.

Promoting shows is where I started and, as it turned out, where I ended my entertainment career as well. My last show, on April 21, 2018, featured Berlin singer and band leader Max Raabe and his Palast Orchester, doing very stylized arrangements of '20s and '30s songs with a contemporary twist. A welcome addition to the local music scene, but not something any of the national concert promotion firms would have touched. An appropriate and suitably eclectic final artist in my eclectic promotion career.

EPILOGUE

I N APRIL, 2018, AS MY WORKING CAREER CAME TO AN END, I was for the first time in years able to relax and enjoy life without having to worry each day about how ticket sales for the many shows I had were doing. And I could end my effort to research artists, listen to CDs and streaming sites, and find the next generations of artists I "should" be booking. Welcome back to iTunes and the great artists I genuinely enjoy listening to.

I had pretty much achieved my pre-retirement goals: work until age seventy to maximize my Social Security benefits; review and organize my fifty years of concert and business files with the thought of a book in mind, and prepare them for eventual donation to the Performing Arts section of the Elmer L. Andersen Archives at the University of Minnesota; pack away my Broadway Across America/John Gore Organization files, along with the stress they had been causing; work with my sister, Lisa, to convey any wisdom I might have to offer her as she so successfully took over my booking duties at Hennepin Theatre Trust; and finally begin an intensive period of world travel that brought me to Manchu Picchu, Antarctica, Iceland, China, Italy, Germany, Croatia, and mini-countries like Monaco and Liechtenstein. Foremost among my travel destinations was a two-week safari to tented game camps in Kenya and Tanzania. My informal motto at this point in my life became, "I haven't been everywhere, but it's on my list."

In March 2019, my sister Lisa and her son Cody were about to join me on a trip the island of Aruba just 40 miles from the coast of Venezuela when the world slammed shut. After watching news videos of packed airports and cruise ships full of sick passengers trying to find a port which would accept them, we abruptly cancelled our trip and began to hunker down in our homes. Little did we know that the COVID pandemic would disrupt our lives for the remainder of the year and beyond, and virtually shut down the live entertainment industry.

As I contemplated my exit from that industry in 2018, I have to admit that the business had evolved so much that it did not hold as much allure to me as it had during my early years. It had become much too corporate, and controlled by executives who seemed to have no noticeable love for the product they were putting on their stages. But what I could not even contemplate was the shutdown of the entire concert and Broadway business for such a prolonged time.

At first the idea of holding meetings and concerts on Zoom seemed novel and convenient. But as weeks and months slowly went by, I began to miss the in-person interactions I had experienced for my entire educational and work career. After watching hours and hours of streamed concerts and shows, a truth I already knew came into sharp focus: there is NO substitute for being in a room with a large group of other people and participating in a live concert or Broadway show. Listening to CDs and streaming concerts is normally a solitary exercise. But live music and theater has the exhilaration of the collective crowd energy, the connection between the artist and the audience, and a sense of shared community with other audience members. When it's live, something new and absolutely unique is created by the actor or musician; you witness a moment of creation that will never be exactly the same again. No matter how good the recording, it will never have the presence and sonic impact of a live performance.

Sadly, the live performances I love most are the ones that will be the last to return. Broadway and live concerts are costly to produce, so the revenue from mandated quarter-filled houses will not be sufficient to sustain tours. Not until audiences are once again willing to attend sold-out theaters will concert and Broadway producers be able to return their shows to the road. That is not likely to happen before a substantial portion of live entertainment fans receive vaccinations, and the country reaches some sort of herd immunity. Hopefully nonprofit presenters like Hennepin Theatre Trust will be able to survive until then. As entertainment executive Tim Leiweke observes, "It's not our timeline but the virus's timeline, and until we get the virus under control, we're just not going to be in business."

Once again, I find myself on my dock with only the resident loons for company, contemplating my fifty-year career in the live entertainment industry, and wondering whether the theatres I love will fall victim to these difficult times, or whether they will survive and thrive after the world pandemic has had its way with us. To lose the musicians, artists, and the amazing venues I have cherished would greatly diminish the joy of life. Because, as I know from years of experience, *THERE'S NO BUSINESS LIKE SHOW BUSINESS!*

ACKNOWLEDGMENTS

I N ADDITION TO THOSE TO WHOM THIS BOOK IS DEDICATED, and those who are mentioned elsewhere, the following friends and associates have made major contributions to my success in the entertainment business, and I thank each for their assistance over the years:

David Allen

Jimmy Allen

Monica Bay

Harry Beacom

Peter Bell

David Bennett

James Binger

Jon Bream

Vallie Brewster

John Camp (now John Sanford)

Arne and Susan Carlson

Bill Carlson

Archie Chelseth

Burt Cohen

David Durenberger

Bob Dylan

Ira Glass

James Goetz

Sam Grabarski

Dick Guindon

Douglas and Martha Head

Frank Holley

Loyce and Lise Houlton

Sam and Sylvia Kaplan

Jean LeVander King

Mark Kroening

Randy Krohn (brother)

Ann Laughlin

Larry Leventhal

Lindy Lund (sister)

David Marietta

Roseanne Monten

Steve Olson

Rohan Preston

Bob Protzman

James Ramstad

Graydon Royce

Ray Shepardson

Jeff Siegel

Clarence Spartz and Family

Mike Steele

Scott Stein

John Stout

Gary Tassone

Sue Weil

Steve Weiss

Wheelock Whitney

David Zimmerman

CITY ALLIES

Sharon Sayles Belton

Scott Benson

Barbara Carlson

Jackie Cherryhomes

Walt Dziedzic

Lisa Goodman

Barb Johnson

Lisa McDonald

Sandy Colvin Roy

RT Rybak

Dennis Schulstad

Van White

MCDA / CPED ALLIES

Denny Daniels

Kevin Dockry

Robert Dronen

Phil Handy

James Heltzer

Jay Jensen

Chuck Lutz

Jim Moore

Jane Peterson

Dick Victor

Rebecca Yanisch

ABOUT THE AUTHOR

FRED KROHN, A LEADER IN THE PERFORMING arts industry for more than fifty years, started in concert promotion and theater management in the 1970s while still a student at Carleton College. Though he obtained a law degree at the University of Minnesota, his passion for music and theater led him to a career that resulted in the transformation of Hennepin Avenue in Minneapolis from a blighted and unsafe area into a vibrant theatre district.

Krohn was instrumental in the purchase of the Orpheum Theatre by Bob Dylan and his brother David Zimmerman in 1978, and a subsequent upgrade and reopening of the theatre with a successful run of *A CHORUS LINE*, demonstrating the potential for first-run Broadway theatre in the Midwest.

His key role in the preservation of the theaters continued with spearheading the effort to save and completely restore Hennepin Avenue's State Theatre. The multi-week sellout run of *JOSEPH AND THE AMAZING TECHNICOLOR DREAMCOAT*, starring Donny Osmond in 1992, and Krohn's other promotions at the State Theatre led the City of Minneapolis to finance a complete restoration of the Orpheum Theatre and award the management of both theatres to Krohn's company, Historic Theatre Group. Krohn reopened the Orpheum in 1993 with one of the first engagements of the Cameron Macintosh blockbuster, *MISS SAIGON*.

Fred Krohn with panda

He led the negotiations with Disney to host the world premiere of *THE LION KING*, which went on to be the most successful Broadway show in history. Krohn attracted other US and world premieres to the Orpheum, including Julie Andrews in *VICTOR, VICTORIA* and Disney's *BEAUTY AND THE BEAST*.

In 2002, Krohn worked with Hennepin Theatre Trust's Tom Hoch to persuade the City of Minneapolis to save and refurbish Hennepin Avenue's 1,000-seat Pantages Theatre, completing the Hennepin Theatre District.

As president, general manager, and co-owner of Historic Theatre Group, Krohn managed three historic theaters—the State, Orpheum, and Pantages—and presented hundreds of Broadway shows and concerts by entertainers from a virtual *Who's Who* of multi-generations and genres, ushering in a lively new era of theatrical entertainment in downtown Minneapolis.

Retired since 2018, Fred Krohn has traveled to all seven continents and supported organizations that are working to save the world's wild creatures, including Kenya's Sheldrick Wildlife Trust for elephants and rhinos, and China's Conservation and Research Centre for the giant panda.

APPENDIX

----

267   **APPENDIX 1**

Live shows presented by Fred Krohn
January 23, 1972 through April 21, 2018.
(chronological order)

313   **APPENDIX 2**

Live shows presented by Fred Krohn
January 23, 1972 through April 21, 2018.
(alphabetical order)

359   **APPENDIX 3**

Minneapolis Broadway Seasons
1992-1993 to 2009-2010

APPENDIX 1

LIVE SHOWS PRESENTED BY FRED KROHN

JANUARY 23, 1972 THROUGH APRIL 21, 2018

TOTAL GROSS: $394,331,896.40

(CHRONOLOGICAL ORDER)

CONCERT NAME	CONCERT DATE	CONCERT VENUE	CONCERT GROSS
BAND (THE BAND)	June 26, 1971	Midway Stad	$174,300.00
BUTTERFIELD BLUES BAND	June 26, 1971	Midway Stad	SEE THE BAND
CROW	June 26, 1971	Midway Stad	SEE THE BAND
DELANEY & BONNIE	June 26, 1971	Midway Stad	SEE THE BAND
JOHN SEBASTIAN	June 26, 1971	Midway Stad	SEE THE BAND
MUDDY WATERS	June 26, 1971	Midway Stad	SEE THE BAND
TONY GLOVER	June 26, 1971	Midway Stad	SEE THE BAND
ALLMAN BROTHERS	July 24, 1971	Midway Stad	$175,000.00
IT'S A BEAUTIFUL DAY	July 24, 1971	Midway Stad	SEE ALLMAN BRO
JOHN BALDRY	July 24, 1971	Midway Stad	SEE ALLMAN BRO
JOY OF COOKING	July 24, 1971	Midway Stad	SEE ALLMAN BRO
LITTLE RICHARD	July 24, 1971	Midway Stad	SEE ALLMAN BRO
MIKE QUATRO JAM BAND	July 24, 1971	Midway Stad	SEE ALLMAN BRO
POCO	July 24, 1971	Midway Stad	SEE ALLMAN BRO
REDEYE	July 24, 1971	Midway Stad	SEE ALLMAN BRO
GORDON LIGHTFOOT	January 23, 1972	O'Shaughnessy	$18,668.80
DELANEY & BONNIE	February 22, 1972	O'Shaughnessy	$5,115.92
JUDY COLLINS	December 6, 1972	O'Shaughnessy	$17,837.00
AMERICA	February 6, 1973	Northrop	$12,500.00
GORDON LIGHTFOOT	February 11, 1973	O'Shaughnessy	$17,998.68
KRIS KRISTOFFERSON	March 31, 1973	O'Shaughnessy	$17,792.70

CONCERT NAME	CONCERT DATE	CONCERT VENUE	CONCERT GROSS
DUELING BANJOS	May 5, 1973	O'Shaughnessy	$3,401.91
JUDY COLLINS	October 19, 1973	O'Shaughnessy	$19,302.00
KRIS KRISTOFFERSON	November 30, 1973	O'Shaughnessy	$18,078.00
GORDON LIGHTFOOT	February 16, 1974	Duluth Aud	$11,516.66
GORDON LIGHTFOOT	February 17, 1974	O'Shaughnessy	$27,178.89
ANNE MURRAY	March 8, 1974	O'Shaughnessy	$8,292.98
MARLENE DIETRICH	May 26, 1974	O'Shaughnessy	$13,396.75
ANNE MURRAY	August 16, 1974	Duluth Aud	$11,720.00
ANNE MURRAY	August 17, 1974	O'Shaughnessy	$15,488.00
ELLA FITZGERALD	September 13, 1974	O'Shaughnessy	$16,512.00
KRIS KRISTOFFERSON	September 27, 1974	Milwaukee	$20,080.00
KRIS KRISTOFFERSON	September 28, 1974	Duluth Aud	$16,304.50
KRIS KRISTOFFERSON	September 29, 1974	O'Shaughnessy	$19,409.00
BILL COSBY	October 13, 1974	O'Shaughnessy	$7,564.00
GORDON LIGHTFOOT	February 8, 1975	Duluth Aud	$24,101.50
GORDON LIGHTFOOT	February 9, 1975	O'Shaughnessy	$47,567.00
ANNE MURRAY	March 21, 1975	Northrop	$14,683.00
ANNE MURRAY	March 22, 1975	Duluth Aud	$10,158.00
SHAWN PHILLIPS	April 11, 1975	Duluth Aud	$11,764.00
LILY TOMLIN	May 2, 1975	O'Shaughnessy	$10,083.00
SHAWN PHILLIPS / HALL & O	November 3, 1975	Duluth Aud	$9,317.00
LEO KOETTKE	November 8, 1975	Duluth Aud	$8,214.00
CAROLE KING	November 16, 1975	Northrop	$28,000.00
CAROLE KING	February 1, 1976	Northrop	$41,538.14
JESSE COLIN YOUNG	April 8, 1976	Duluth UMD	$6,472.00
JESSE C YOUNG / P CRUISE	April 9, 1976	Northrop	$26,677.00
GORDON LIGHTFOOT	April 24, 1976	Northrop	$48,075.00
NITTY GRITTY DIRT BAND	July 9, 1976	O'Shaughnessy	$7,637.00
JUDY COLLINS	July 31, 1976	Northrop	$23,379.85
GORDON LIGHTFOOT	October 22, 1976	Duluth Aud	$30,000.50
MANHATTAN TRANSFER	October 24, 1976	O'Shaughnessy	$11,568.00
JOHN PRINE	October 31, 1976	O'Shaughnessy	$10,554.50
STEVE GOODMAN	November 6, 1976	UMD Kirby	$1,869.90

CONCERT NAME	CONCERT DATE	CONCERT VENUE	CONCERT GROSS
TAJ MAHAL	February 5, 1977	UM W Bank	$6,860.00
LEO KOETTKE	February 25, 1977	Duluth UMD	$6,302.00
STEVE MARTIN	February 27, 1977	O'Shaughnessy	$9,320.00
JESSE COLIN YOUNG	April 3, 1977	Northrop	$18,914.00
JERRY JEFF WALKER	April 7, 1977	Duluth Aud	$14,013.78
JERRY JEFF WALKER	April 8, 1977	Northrop	$27,754.00
GORDON LIGHTFOOT	April 15, 1977	Northrop	$58,922.00
GORDON LIGHTFOOT	April 17, 1977	Fargo NDSU	$22,983.50
AMAZING RHYTHM ACES	July 10, 1977	O'Shaughnessy	$4,282.00
WAYLON JENNINGS	July 15, 1977	Met Center	$72,500.50
JUDY COLLINS	July 16, 1977	Northrop	$28,123.00
LEO SAYER	July 27, 1977	Northrop	$11,361.29
NATALIE COLE	July 28, 1977	Northrop	$29,417.00
KRIS KRISTOFFERSON	August 13, 1977	Northrop	$32,444.00
DOLLY PARTON	August 15, 1977	O'Shaughnessy	$12,260.00
DOLLY PARTON	August 17, 1977	Duluth Aud	$14,459.50
DOLLY PARTON	August 19, 1977	S Bend, Ind	$12,112.00
HARRY CHAPIN	September 8, 1977	O'Shaughnessy	$13,710.00
STEVE GOODMAN	October 7, 1977	O'Shaughnessy	$7,592.00
AL JARREAU	October 9, 1977	O'Shaughnessy	$10,999.00
GATO BARBIERI	October 14, 1977	O'Shaughnessy	$8,791.00
DOLLY PARTON	October 26, 1977	Fargo Aud	$15,856.50
DOLLY PARTON	October 27, 1977	Rochester Aud	$17,249.00
TAJ MAHAL	October 29, 1977	O'Shaughnessy	$17,708.00
WAYLON JENNINGS	October 29, 1977	Ann Arbor MI	$32,179.00
WAYLON JENNINGS	October 30, 1977	Grand Rapids MI	$31,184.00
KEITH JARRETT	November 14, 1977	Northrop	$15,193.00
CRYSTAL GAYLE	November 19, 1977	O'Shaughnessy	$12,359.00
MICHAEL JOHNSON	November 25, 1977	O'Shaughnessy	$20,285.00
GORDON LIGHTFOOT	March 10, 1978	Northrop	$59,139.00
GORDON LIGHTFOOT	March 11, 1978	Duluth Aud	$30,491.00
TAJ MAHAL	March 26, 1978	O'Shaughnessy	$7,151.00
LEON RUSSELL	April 21, 1978	Northrop	$18,089.00

CONCERT NAME	CONCERT DATE	CONCERT VENUE	CONCERT GROSS
DOLLY PARTON	June 27, 1978	Duluth Aud	$19,066.00
YVONNE ELLIMAN	July 19, 1978	O'Shaughnessy	$2,698.00
MANHATTAN TRANSFER	July 21, 1978	O'Shaughnessy	$22,236.00
WAYLON JENNINGS	July 21, 1978	Duluth Aud	$35,111.00
WAYLON JENNINGS	July 22, 1978	St. Paul CC	$109,499.00
JOHN PRINE / L. REDBONE	September 22, 1978	O'Shaughnessy	$25,055.50
MICHAEL JOHNSON	October 6, 1978	Duluth Aud	$7,476.00
MICHAEL JOHNSON	October 14, 1978	Northrop	$24,151.00
JESSE COLIN YOUNG	November 11, 1978	Orpheum	$13,896.00
AL JARREAU	November 24, 1978	Orpheum	$18,716.00
JANE OLIVOR	March 17, 1979	Orpheum	$13,000.00
JUDY COLLINS	April 1, 1979	Northrop	$33,723.00
EMMY LOU HARRIS/GOODMN	April 21, 1979	Orpheum	$22,030.00
GORDON LIGHTFOOT	April 27, 1979	Northrop	$73,517.00
GORDON LIGHTFOOT	April 28, 1979	Duluth Aud	$24,118.00
JERRY JEFF WALKER	May 5, 1979	Orpheum	$38,262.00
DAVE BRUBECK (RECORD)	May 7, 1979	Orpheum	$-
MAN OF LA M (KILEY)	May 15, 1979	Orpheum	$750,000.00
DOUG HENNING MAGIC	June 22, 1979	Orpheum	$90,646.00
NATALIE COLE	June 30, 1979	Orpheum	$15,436.00
A CHORUS LINE	July 3, 1979	Orpheum	$835,877.50
JOAN BAEZ	July 14, 1979	Northrop	$35,159.00
CRYSTAL GAYLE	July 27, 1979	Orpheum	$21,193.00
ROBERTA FLACK	July 29, 1979	Orpheum	$17,500.00
BEATLEMANIA	July 30, 1979	Orpheum	$900,000.00
ANDRAE CROUCH	August 26, 1979	Orpheum	$9,620.68
JOHN PRINE	September 30, 1979	Orpheum	$24,000.00
TOM WAITS	October 11, 1979	Orpheum	$37,000.00
LIZA MINNELLI	October 13, 1979	Orpheum	$490,000.00
TIMBUKTU! (ERTHA KITT)	November 7, 1979	Orpheum	$350,000.00
JERRY JEFF WALKER	March 28, 1980	St. Paul CC Th	$37,000.00
WAYLON JENNINGS	June 7, 1980	Met Center	$111,000.00
AIN'T MISBEHAVIN'	June 10, 1980	Orpheum	$40,000.00

CONCERT NAME	CONCERT DATE	CONCERT VENUE	CONCERT GROSS
BEST LITTLE WHOREHOUSE	August 19, 1980	Orpheum	$250,000.00
A CHORUS LINE	September 9, 1980	Northrop	$689,482.04
ANNIE	October 16, 1980	Orpheum	$157,449.00
OKLAHOMA!	June 23, 1981	Northrop	$425,000.00
GEORGE BENSON	July 15, 1981	Northrop	$108,000.00
GORDON LIGHTFOOT	October 2, 1981	Northrop	$42,997.00
GORDON LIGHTFOOT	October 3, 1981	Duluth Aud	$20,102.00
PETER PAUL & MARY	October 3, 1981	Northrop	$67,000.00
GORDON LIGHTFOOT	October 4, 1981	Madison CC	$19,891.00
AL JARREAU	May 22, 1982	Northrop	$45,000.00
A CHORUS LINE	June 15, 1982	Orpheum	$480,000.00
GORDON LIGHTFOOT	October 15, 1982	Madison CC	$21,387.00
GORDON LIGHTFOOT	October 16, 1982	Duluth Aud	$15,874.50
GORDON LIGHTFOOT	October 17, 1982	Northrop	$45,570.50
GORDON LIGHTFOOT	March 18, 1983	Milwaukee	$27,017.00
GORDON LIGHTFOOT	April 20, 1984	Madison CC	$20,238.57
GORDON LIGHTFOOT	April 21, 1984	Duluth Aud	$14,108.50
GORDON LIGHTFOOT	April 22, 1984	Northrop	$46,844.00
GORDON LIGHTFOOT	April 23, 1984	Milwaukee	$24,975.47
GORDON LIGHTFOOT	June 9, 1984	Kansas City MO	$20,899.00
R. E. M.	July 5, 1984	Orpheum	$79,000.00
NANCY W / D LETTERMAN	October 7, 1984	Orpheum	$23,000.00
SUGAR BABIES	July 30, 1985	Northrop	$260,000.00
GORDON LIGHTFOOT	August 19, 1985	Milwaukee	$21,321.24
GORDON LIGHTFOOT	June 6, 1987	Milwaukee Riv	$31,323.15
GORDON LIGHTFOOT	June 7, 1987	Northrop	$58,966.00
PEGGY LEE	August 15, 1987	Radisson Mpls	$50,000.00
TOM WAITS	November 1, 1987	Orpheum	$39,391.50
MEL TORME	March 17, 1988	Radisson Mpls	$45,098.00
HARRY CHAPIN	August 6, 1988	O'Shaughnessy	$33,000.00
LAURA NYRO	August 9, 1988	Childrens Th	$27,117.00
RAY CHARLES	August 11, 1988	State Theatre	$37,925.50
ROBERT CRAY	September 6, 1988	State Theatre	$38,110.50

CONCERT NAME	CONCERT DATE	CONCERT VENUE	CONCERT GROSS
MIDNIGHT OIL	October 20, 1988	Orpheum	$29,000.00
GORDON LIGHTFOOT	November 5, 1988	Milwaukee Riv	$34,202.09
GORDON LIGHTFOOT	November 6, 1988	Northrop	$59,439.00
NYLONS	November 11, 1988	Orpheum	$31,000.00
KENNY LOGGINS	November 17, 1988	Orpheum	$48,000.00
ROBERT PALMER	November 26, 1988	Orpheum	$61,000.00
DAVID COPPERFIELD	December 11, 1988	Orpheum	$160,000.00
CHEAP TRICK	January 3, 1989	Orpheum	$51,000.00
SOUTH PACIFIC (R GOULET)	February 21, 1989	Orpheum	$220,000.00
BRUCE COCKBURN	March 14, 1989	Orpheum	$21,000.00
DURAN DURAN	March 17, 1989	Orpheum	$65,000.00
LITTLE FEAT	March 31, 1989	Orpheum	$25,000.00
LOU REED	April 7, 1989	Orpheum	$55,000.00
BUNNY WAILER	April 20, 1989	Orpheum	$12,000.00
MIKE & THE MECHANICS	April 22, 1989	Orpheum	$14,000.00
SHARON LOIS & BRAM	April 27, 1989	Orpheum	$24,000.00
EDIE BRICKELL	May 3, 1989	Orpheum	$36,000.00
MICKEY ROONEY	May 5, 1989	Orpheum	$28,000.00
SARAH VAUGHN	May 7, 1989	Orpheum	$37,000.00
BONNIE RAITT	May 10, 1989	Orpheum	$87,000.00
MUSIC OF A L WEBER	May 27, 1989	Northrop	$201,000.00
GYPSY (TYNE DALY)	June 27, 1989	Orpheum	$429,000.00
NAPOLEON (MOVIE)	July 14, 1989	Orpheum	$18,000.00
BILL GAITHER TRIO	July 29, 1989	Orpheum	$37,000.00
BLACKSTONE (MAGICIAN)	July 30, 1989	Orpheum	$61,000.00
EVERLY BROS	August 5, 1989	Orpheum	$57,000.00
k.d. lang	August 19, 1989	Orpheum	$63,000.00
ELLA FITZGERALD / OSCAR P	August 21, 1989	Northrop	$57,000.00
JOE JACKSON	September 13, 1989	Orpheum	$32,000.00
RAY CHARLES	September 15, 1989	Orpheum	$47,000.00
JAMES TAYLOR	September 16, 1989	Orpheum	$148,000.00
BO DEANS	September 21, 1989	Orpheum	$49,000.00
BOB GOLDTHWAIT	September 28, 1989	Orpheum	$27,000.00

CONCERT NAME	CONCERT DATE	CONCERT VENUE	CONCERT GROSS
KEN HILL PHANTOM	October 3, 1989	Orpheum	$523,640.00
RED ARMY CHORUS	October 12, 1989	Orpheum	$71,000.00
ANDREAS VOLLENWEIDER	October 13, 1989	Orpheum	$23,000.00
GORDON LIGHTFOOT	October 22, 1989	Chicago Symp	$36,578.00
GLADYS KNIGHT	November 2, 1989	Orpheum	$43,000.00
GORDON LIGHTFOOT	November 2, 1989	Milwaukee Riv	$20,688.13
GORDON LIGHTFOOT	November 3, 1989	Duluth Aud	$22,595.52
GORDON LIGHTFOOT	November 4, 1989	Orpheum	$71,604.00
MANNHEIM STEAMROLLER	November 24, 1989	Orpheum	$202,000.00
ANDY WILLIAMS	November 27, 1989	Orpheum	$107,325.00
DOROTHY HAMILL NUT ICE	December 4, 1989	Orpheum	$643,000.00
LASER LIGHT SPECTACULAR	January 26, 1990	Orpheum	$12,000.00
PINK FLOYD LASER SHOW	January 26, 1990	Orpheum	$17,000.00
MELISSA ETHERIDGE	February 10, 1990	Orpheum	$39,000.00
PATTI LABELLE	February 11, 1990	Orpheum	$67,000.00
FIDDLER ROOF(TOPOL)	February 20, 1990	Orpheum	$532,624.00
ERASURE	February 26, 1990	Orpheum	$31,000.00
LAURIE ANDERSON	February 27, 1990	Orpheum	$23,000.00
AIR SUPPLY	March 9, 1990	Orpheum	$21,000.00
CULT	March 14, 1990	Orpheum	$68,000.00
JOE SATRIANI	March 18, 1990	Orpheum	$49,000.00
JOAN JETT	March 23, 1990	Orpheum	$37,000.00
SAM KINISON	March 25, 1990	Orpheum	$43,000.00
KITARO	April 12, 1990	Orpheum	$29,000.00
SHARON LOIS & BRAM	April 21, 1990	Orpheum	$22,000.00
MILES DAVIS	April 27, 1990	Orpheum	$55,000.00
CAB CALLOWAY	April 28, 1990	Orpheum	$24,000.00
MAZE	May 13, 1990	Orpheum	$41,000.00
MICHELLE SHOCKED	May 15, 1990	Orpheum	$38,000.00
LITTLE FEAT	May 16, 1990	Orpheum	$44,000.00
ANNE MURRAY	May 17, 1990	Orpheum	$67,000.00
DAVID COPPERFIELD	May 19, 1990	Orpheum	$155,025.00
GEORGE CARLIN	June 2, 1990	Orpheum	$31,000.00

CONCERT NAME	CONCERT DATE	CONCERT VENUE	CONCERT GROSS
LENINGRAD MUSIC HALL	June 8, 1990	Orpheum	$73,736.25
JERRY SEINFELD	June 9, 1990	Orpheum	$41,000.00
ELAYNE BOOSLER	June 23, 1990	Orpheum	$17,000.00
GORDON LIGHTFOOT	June 27, 1990	TEMPE AZ	$33,041.00
ETTA JAMES	June 29, 1990	Orpheum	$29,000.00
SINBAD	July 7, 1990	Orpheum	$43,000.00
HARRY BELAFONTE	July 27, 1990	Orpheum	$77,000.00
EVERLY BROS/C PERKINS	August 3, 1990	Orpheum	$89,000.00
K. T. OSLIN	August 17, 1990	Orpheum	$43,000.00
MIDNIGHT OIL	September 12, 1990	Orpheum	$31,000.00
O'JAYS / REGINA BELLE	October 13, 1990	Orpheum	$63,000.00
HARRY CONNICK, JR.	October 21, 1990	Orpheum	$162,000.00
STEVE LAWRENCE / E GORME	October 23, 1990	Orpheum	$107,000.00
GALLAGHER	November 9, 1990	Orpheum	$129,000.00
ROBERT CRAY	November 13, 1990	Orpheum	$55,000.00
KEN HILL PHANTOM	November 16, 1990	Orpheum	$364,640.00
PENN & TELLER	November 21, 1990	Orpheum	$60,000.00
COCTEAU TWINS	November 28, 1990	Orpheum	$23,000.00
ICE CUBE / TOO SHORT	November 29, 1990	Orpheum	$63,000.00
DOROTHY HAMILL NUT ICE	December 6, 1990	Orpheum	$420,000.00
A CHORUS LINE	January 8, 1991	Orpheum	$276,564.00
SLAYER	January 30, 1991	Orpheum	$44,400.00
VANILLA ICE	February 3, 1991	Orpheum	$45,860.00
REPLACEMENTS	February 7, 1991	Orpheum	$97,832.00
NELSON	February 19, 1991	Orpheum	$43,067.50
HAIR	February 24, 1991	Orpheum	$46,690.50
HALL AND OATES	March 12, 1991	Orpheum	$38,947.50
TIM ALLEN	March 23, 1991	Orpheum	$47,196.00
PET SHOP BOYS	April 3, 1991	Orpheum	$29,960.00
EDIE BRICKELL	April 9, 1991	Orpheum	$45,454.50
DENNIS MILLER	April 28, 1991	Orpheum	$43,683.00
GEORGE THOROGOOD	April 28, 1991	Orpheum	$98,300.00
HOWIE MANDEL	May 1, 1991	Orpheum	$46,450.00

CONCERT NAME	CONCERT DATE	CONCERT VENUE	CONCERT GROSS
BO DEANS	May 2, 1991	Orpheum	$51,000.00
TODD RUNDGREN	May 5, 1991	Orpheum	$28,700.00
BOB WEIR	May 17, 1991	Orpheum	$59,085.00
FRED PENNER	May 18, 1991	Orpheum	$3,755.50
YANNI	May 21, 1991	Orpheum	$99,321.00
BURT REYNOLDS	June 5, 1991	Orpheum	$49,220.00
JERRY SEINFELD	June 7, 1991	Orpheum	$45,144.00
BILLY SQUIRE	June 23, 1991	Orpheum	$23,000.00
STYX	June 25, 1991	Orpheum	$53,527.50
K. T. OSLIN	July 18, 1991	Orpheum	$38,752.50
BRUCE HORNSBY	July 21, 1991	Orpheum	$41,867.50
NELSON	July 24, 1991	Orpheum	$28,175.00
ROSEANNE BARR	July 25, 1991	Orpheum	$35,249.00
AIR SUPPLY	July 26, 1991	Orpheum	$16,029.65
DAVID SANBORN	August 8, 1991	Orpheum	$41,341.50
DIANA ROSS	August 12, 1991	Orpheum	$86,140.00
CROWDED HOUSE	September 18, 1991	Orpheum	$34,835.50
WINANS FAMILY	September 22, 1991	Orpheum	$31,562.50
HARRY CONNICK, JR.	October 8, 1991	Orpheum	$202,000.00
NYLONS	October 10, 1991	Orpheum	$29,651.25
NATALIE COLE	October 22, 1991	Orpheum	$75,865.00
MELISSA MANCHESTER	November 1, 1991	State (OPEN)	$-
BRUCE COCKBURN	November 7, 1991	Orpheum	$26,280.00
MOODY BLUES	November 25, 1991	Orpheum	$120,807.50
BARRY MANILOW	November 29, 1991	State Theatre	$178,652.50
ALVIN & CHIPMUNKS	December 3, 1991	Orpheum	$4,180.00
LETTERMEN	December 3, 1991	State Theatre	$16,451.60
ELAYNE BOOSLER	December 7, 1991	Orpheum	$19,840.00
MANNHEIM STEAMROLLER	December 12, 1991	State Theatre	$244,587.50
WIZARD OF OZ	December 20, 1991	State Theatre	$9,890.00
ALABAMA	January 3, 1992	Orpheum	$147,448.00
SAM KINISON	January 17, 1992	State Theatre	$27,970.00
HARRY CONNICK, JR.	January 21, 1992	State Theatre	$291,231.00

CONCERT NAME	CONCERT DATE	CONCERT VENUE	CONCERT GROSS
REO SPEEDWAGON	February 1, 1992	Orpheum	$51,720.50
MARKY MARK	February 14, 1992	Orpheum	$39,530.00
PETER HIMMELMAN	February 15, 1992	State Theatre	$32,672.50
PATTI LABELLE	February 20, 1992	Orpheum	$63,673.00
ROXETTE	February 23, 1992	Orpheum	$46,340.00
LOVE LETTERS	March 21, 1992	State Theatre	$306,391.47
CONWAY T /GEO JONES	March 29, 1992	Orpheum	$73,947.75
ANNIE	April 10, 1992	Orpheum	$166,590.00
SHIRLEY CAESAR	April 19, 1992	State Theatre	$21,257.50
JOHN MCLAUGHLIN	April 23, 1992	State Theatre	$10,156.00
JOHN PRINE	April 24, 1992	Orpheum	$51,689.50
CRASH TEST DUMMIES	April 26, 1992	Orpheum	$37,814.00
NANA MOUSKOURI	May 8, 1992	State Theatre	$24,063.00
ANNE MURRAY	May 9, 1992	State Theatre	$56,265.00
LOU REED	May 9, 1992	Orpheum	$64,782.50
RICKY VAN SHELTON	May 17, 1992	Orpheum	$59,703.50
CATS	May 19, 1992	State Theatre	$915,008.00
SPINAL TAP	May 19, 1992	Orpheum	$55,781.50
YANNI	May 21, 1992	Orpheum	$121,774.00
TRACY CHAPMAN	May 23, 1992	Orpheum	$47,062.50
JERRY SEINFELD	June 4, 1992	Orpheum	$124,951.00
RAY CHARLES	June 4, 1992	State Theatre	$54,247.00
GEORGE WINSTON	June 6, 1992	State Theatre	$30,507.00
PATTI LABELLE	June 14, 1992	Orpheum	$30,325.00
DEF COMEDY JAM	June 19, 1992	Orpheum	$24,125.00
WAYNE NEWTON	June 26, 1992	Orpheum	$43,939.00
WEIRD AL YANKOVIC	June 30, 1992	Orpheum	$29,162.00
RIGHTEOUS BROTHERS	July 9, 1992	Orpheum	$76,775.25
MELISSA ETHERIDGE	July 23, 1992	State Theatre	$46,597.50
BLACK CROWES	July 24, 1992	Orpheum	$152,280.00
GEORGE CARLIN	July 26, 1992	State Theatre	$26,851.50
NATALIE COLE	July 28, 1992	Orpheum	$41,362.50
WARWICK / BACHARACH	July 30, 1992	Orpheum	$49,547.00

CONCERT NAME	CONCERT DATE	CONCERT VENUE	CONCERT GROSS
SEALS & CROFTS / LR BAND	August 4, 1992	State Theatre	$19,764.50
SHIRLEY MCCLAINE	August 21, 1992	State Theatre	$96,450.50
DEF COMEDY JAM	August 23, 1992	State Theatre	$18,007.50
BOB DYLAN	August 27, 1992	Orpheum	$360,938.00
CROSBY STILLS & NASH	August 27, 1992	Orpheum	$171,732.00
DAVID BYRNE	September 4, 1992	Orpheum	$60,225.00
JOAN ARMATRADING	September 15, 1992	Orpheum	$34,358.00
JOSEPH AND THE . . .	September 15, 1992	State Theatre	$6,685,702.22
k.d. lang	October 13, 1992	Orpheum	$125,176.00
TANGERINE DREAM	October 18, 1992	Orpheum	$21,600.50
VICTOR BORGE	October 30, 1992	Orpheum	$79,691.00
BLACK SABBATH	October 31, 1992	Orpheum	$55,341.00
GALLAGHER	November 12, 1992	Orpheum	$114,931.00
KEN HILL PHANTOM	November 18, 1992	Orpheum	$258,640.00
DAVID SANBORN	November 19, 1992	Orpheum	$26,578.00
NEIL YOUNG	November 21, 1992	Orpheum	$154,791.00
PETER HIMMELMAN	November 24, 1992	Orpheum	$25,897.50
SOUNDS OF BLACKNESS	November 27, 1992	Orpheum	$106,850.00
MANHATTAN TRANSFER	December 8, 1992	Orpheum	$66,777.25
PAUL WINTER	December 11, 1992	Orpheum	$28,442.50
FREDDIE JACKSON	December 18, 1992	Orpheum	$34,260.00
JOE SATRIANI	December 20, 1992	Orpheum	$54,382.50
HOWIE MANDEL	January 24, 1993	State Theatre	$92,047.00
HARRY BELAFONTE	February 14, 1993	State Theatre	$61,997.50
EVITA	February 16, 1993	State Theatre	$1,068,578.15
TONY BENNETT	March 6, 1993	State Theatre	$58,729.00
JESUS CHRIST SUPERSTAR	March 9, 1993	State Theatre	$632,554.00
SADE	March 14, 1993	Northrop	$115,597.50
LOST IN YONKERS	March 16, 1993	State Theatre	$418,772.23
ETTA JAMES	March 26, 1993	State Theatre	$26,942.50
DAVID WILCOX	March 27, 1993	State Theatre	$29,861.50
NANCI GRIFFITH	April 2, 1993	State Theatre	$41,174.00
KENNY G	April 6, 1993	Northrop	$235,454.50

CONCERT NAME	CONCERT DATE	CONCERT VENUE	CONCERT GROSS
PHISH	April 9, 1993	State Theatre	$22,687.50
SHIRLEY CAESAR	April 11, 1993	State Theatre	$12,385.00
NINA SIMONE	April 15, 1993	State Theatre	$25,095.00
GORDON LIGHTFOOT	April 21, 1993	Des Moines	$36,315.00
GORDON LIGHTFOOT	April 22, 1993	State Theatre	$90,774.00
GORDON LIGHTFOOT	April 24, 1993	Duluth Aud	$45,379.00
PIRATES OF PENZANCE	April 30, 1993	Orpheum	$180,412.00
GORDON LIGHTFOOT	May 2, 1993	Madison, WI	$36,879.00
RAFFI	May 14, 1993	State Theatre	$61,861.00
SMOTHERS BROTHERS	May 18, 1993	State Theatre	$33,464.26
ANDREW DICE CLAY	May 26, 1993	State Theatre	$53,741.00
LASER LIGHT SPECTACULAR	May 27, 1993	State Theatre	$8,033.40
RICHARD PRYOR	May 29, 1993	State Theatre	$32,222.00
ASPECTS OF LOVE	May 31, 1993	State Theatre	$700,280.90
GORDON LIGHTFOOT	June 5, 1993	Phoenix AZ	$36,799.50
LITTLE FEAT	June 15, 1993	State Theatre	$31,162.50
GORDON LIGHTFOOT	June 16, 1993	Fresno, CA	$21,915.00
LEONARD COHEN	June 22, 1993	State Theatre	$39,912.00
PATTI LABELLE	June 30, 1993	State Theatre	$37,035.00
TEMPTATIONS / FOUR TOPS	July 7, 1993	State Theatre	$51,951.75
RIGHTEOUS BROTHERS	July 15, 1993	State Theatre	$75,127.50
CHICAGO	July 18, 1993	State Theatre	$77,030.00
BILL COSBY	August 7, 1993	State Theatre	$102,650.75
UB40 / GIN BLOSSOMS	August 14, 1993	State Theatre	$41,496.00
CHRIS ISAAK	August 29, 1993	State Theatre	$140,105.00
MARC COHN	September 12, 1993	State Theatre	$48,167.50
MY FAIR LADY	September 22, 1993	State Theatre	$1,125,818.53
GEORGE BENSON	October 5, 1993	State Theatre	$34,952.50
STEVE LAWRENCE / E GORME	October 9, 1993	State Theatre	$95,377.50
JESUS CHRIST SUPERSTAR	October 12, 1993	State Theatre	$1,237,264.00
DAVID LANZ	November 4, 1993	State Theatre	$22,885.50
BRUCE HORNSBY	November 13, 1993	State Theatre	$43,807.50
ROBERT CRAY	November 19, 1993	State Theatre	$41,148.00

CONCERT NAME	CONCERT DATE	CONCERT VENUE	CONCERT GROSS
SOUNDS OF BLACKNESS	November 26, 1993	State Theatre	$100,426.00
PETER HIMMELMAN	November 30, 1993	State Theatre	$23,242.50
HEART	December 1, 1993	Orpheum	$51,158.50
KENNY LOGGINS	December 2, 1993	Orpheum	$54,052.50
JOHN DENVER	December 4, 1993	Orpheum	$168,195.50
MANNHEIM STEAMROLLER	December 9, 1993	Orpheum	$356,123.00
GRUMPY OLD MEN (PREM)	December 10, 1993	State Theatre	$31,000.00
DAVID COPPERFIELD	December 17, 1993	Orpheum	$370,950.50
CRASH TEST DUMMIES	December 31, 1993	State Theatre	$45,600.50
MISS SAIGON	January 11, 1994	Orpheum	$8,322,157.00
CATS	February 1, 1994	State Theatre	$664,954.10
JESUS CHRIST SUPERSTAR	March 1, 1994	State Theatre	$458,685.50
CROSBY STILLS & NASH	March 9, 1994	St Paul CC	$350,000.00
ANDREAS VOLLENWEIDER	March 16, 1994	State Theatre	$25,414.50
GALLAGHER	March 26, 1994	Northrop	$84,720.50
JETHRO TULL	March 28, 1994	Orpheum	$68,160.00
RADIO CITY SPECTACULAR	March 30, 1994	State Theatre	$276,633.00
EVITA	April 5, 1994	State Theatre	$319,658.00
DAVID WILCOX	April 9, 1994	State Theatre	$29,118.00
GREASE	April 12, 1994	Orpheum	$682,085.70
HAIR	April 12, 1994	State Theatre	$376,013.00
FIVE GUYS NAMED MOE	April 19, 1994	State Theatre	$416,547.00
SECRET GARDEN (BWAY)	April 29, 1994	Orpheum	$211,336.30
BRUCE COCKBURN	May 3, 1994	State Theatre	$26,649.00
ODD COUPLE	May 10, 1994	Orpheum	$390,285.25
PETER HIMMELMAN	May 12, 1994	State Theatre	$26,320.00
ELLEN DEGENERES	May 13, 1994	State Theatre	$43,827.00
BLUES TRAVELER	May 14, 1994	State Theatre	$37,888.00
PENN & TELLER	May 25, 1994	State Theatre	$24,888.50
HAL HOLBROOK (M TWAIN)	June 10, 1994	State Theatre	$34,420.00
MIKHAIL BARYSHNIKOV	June 14, 1994	Orpheum	$401,418.00
PHISH	June 16, 1994	State Theatre	$36,452.00
CAMELOT	June 28, 1994	Orpheum	$414,324.20

CONCERT NAME	CONCERT DATE	CONCERT VENUE	CONCERT GROSS
COUNTING CROWS	July 2, 1994	State Theatre	$63,379.50
TORI AMOS	July 14, 1994	State Theatre	$81,960.00
JULIO IGLESIAS	July 24, 1994	Orpheum	$90,420.00
HARRY CHAPIN	August 6, 1994	O'Shaughnessy	$37,000.00
WEIRD AL YANKOVIC	August 6, 1994	State Theatre	$25,024.50
ALL-4-ONE	August 7, 1994	State Theatre	$24,013.00
RICHARD MARX	August 10, 1994	Orpheum	$32,215.50
WOODSTOCK (MOVIE)	August 12, 1994	State Theatre	$15,120.00
LAWRENCE OF A (MOVIE)	August 19, 1994	State Theatre	$14,210.00
RAFFI	August 23, 1994	Orpheum	$61,980.00
SARAH MCLACHLAN	August 23, 1994	State Theatre	$36,914.00
JOHNNY CASH	August 27, 1994	Orpheum	$48,494.50
MELISSA ETHERIDGE	August 31, 1994	Northrop	$95,880.00
BASIA / SPYRO GYRA	September 11, 1994	Orpheum	$47,875.00
SANDRA BERNHARD	September 19, 1994	State Theatre	$17,663.00
HELLO DOLLY (CHANNING)	October 11, 1994	Orpheum	$297,771.00
KITARO	October 16, 1994	State Theatre	$27,820.00
CANDLEBOX	October 18, 1994	State Theatre	$36,702.00
BLOOD BROTHERS	October 25, 1994	Orpheum	$470,541.70
LOREENA MCKENNIT	November 1, 1994	State Theatre	$34,999.00
SHARI LEWIS / LAMBCHOP	November 3, 1994	State Theatre	$10,469.50
BIG HEAD TODD	November 5, 1994	Orpheum	$49,720.00
PRETENDERS	November 6, 1994	Orpheum	$49,380.00
EARTH WIND & FIRE	November 8, 1994	Orpheum	$61,451.50
MARY CHAPIN CARPENTER	November 9, 1994	Orpheum	$57,907.50
SHAWN COLVIN	November 10, 1994	State Theatre	$36,325.00
BRYAN FERRY	November 11, 1994	Orpheum	$50,208.00
SEAL	November 15, 1994	State Theatre	$49,465.00
CRANBERRIES	November 16, 1994	Orpheum	$47,700.00
GONE WITH THE WIND	November 18, 1994	State Theatre	$17,988.00
BO DEANS	November 25, 1994	Orpheum	$57,350.00
PHISH	November 26, 1994	Orpheum	$44,397.50
DEF COMEDY JAM	December 3, 1994	State Theatre	$47,179.50

CONCERT NAME	CONCERT DATE	CONCERT VENUE	CONCERT GROSS
JELLY'S LAST JAM	December 7, 1994	State Theatre	$464,487.20
KENNY RODGERS XMAS	December 17, 1994	State Theatre	$209,457.50
PHANTOM OF THE OPERA	January 14, 1995	Orpheum	$7,876,192.50
JOSEPH AND THE . . .	February 22, 1995	State Theatre	$10,443,510.10
JOHN SECADA	March 2, 1995	Northrop	$72,703.50
GORDON LIGHTFOOT	April 24, 1995	Green Bay WI	$44,584.00
GORDON LIGHTFOOT	April 28, 1995	Milwaukee Pab	$27,840.50
GORDON LIGHTFOOT	April 29, 1995	O'Shaughnessy	$86,657.00
VICTOR VICTORIA	May 23, 1995	Orpheum	$2,996,039.65
GEORGE CARLIN	June 2, 1995	State Theatre	$22,140.00
IAN ANDERSON	June 9, 1995	State Theatre	$33,390.00
RIGHTEOUS BROTHERS	June 12, 1995	State Theatre	$83,467.50
BRETT BUTLER (COMIC)	June 17, 1995	State Theatre	$28,297.50
JOE HENDERSON	June 18, 1995	State Theatre	$7,887.00
DEF COMEDY JAM	June 25, 1995	State Theatre	$32,805.00
ISAAC HAYES	July 7, 1995	Orpheum	$111,150.00
JOHN PRINE	July 15, 1995	Orpheum	$50,129.00
BARRY WHITE	July 25, 1995	Orpheum	$74,220.50
GREGORY PECK	July 30, 1995	State Theatre	$25,163.25
ALAN PARSONS	August 3, 1995	Orpheum	$68,512.50
KISS / SPIDERWOMAN	August 8, 1995	State Theatre	$1,850,000.00
DONNA SUMMER	August 11, 1995	Orpheum	$45,237.50
NANCI GRIFFITH	August 16, 1995	Orpheum	$51,175.00
S. CLARKE/DI MEOLA/PONTY	August 23, 1995	Orpheum	$38,212.50
AIN'T MISPEHAVIN'	September 19, 1995	State Theatre	$300,000.00
C ISAAK / WALLFLOWERS	October 20, 1995	State Theatre	$65,616.50
ALL-4-ONE	October 22, 1995	State Theatre	$18,725.00
DAVID COPPERFIELD	November 3, 1995	State Theatre	$459,706.35
TRISHA YEARWOOD / C RAYE	November 4, 1995	Northrop	$81,529.00
BEAUTY AND THE BEAST	November 7, 1995	Orpheum	$8,565,473.00
RAFFI	November 11, 1995	State Theatre	$57,000.00
JESUS CHRIST SUPERSTAR	November 21, 1995	State Theatre	$495,724.50
CHRIS ISAAK	December 30, 1995	State Theatre	$65,251.00

CONCERT NAME	CONCERT DATE	CONCERT VENUE	CONCERT GROSS
DIAL M FOR MURDER	January 23, 1996	State Theatre	$423,838.25
OAK RIDGE BOYS	February 9, 1996	State Theatre	$36,841.50
RIGHTEOUS BROTHERS	February 14, 1996	Madison CC	$83,586.00
BERNIE MAC	February 16, 1996	Orpheum	$56,143.00
OASIS	February 20, 1996	Orpheum	$41,796.00
ANNE MURRAY	February 24, 1996	State Theatre	$48,121.00
GREASE	February 27, 1996	State Theatre	$1,557,988.74
SWEET HONEY IN THE ROCK	March 9, 1996	Orpheum	$59,620.00
TRACY CHAPMAN	March 14, 1996	State Theatre	$41,920.00
TONY BENNETT	March 17, 1996	Orpheum	$74,096.00
CHIEFTAINS	March 20, 1996	Orpheum	$69,730.50
JACKSON BROWNE	March 21, 1996	Orpheum	$79,807.50
JACKSON BROWNE	March 22, 1996	Des Moines	$82,470.00
JIM BRICKMAN	March 23, 1996	State Theatre	$20,240.50
LOU REED	March 23, 1996	Orpheum	$62,380.00
CEDRIC THE ENTERTAINER	March 24, 1996	State Theatre	$27,450.00
DEL AMITRI	April 9, 1996	Orpheum	$36,366.00
RIGHTEOUS BROTHERS	April 11, 1996	Davenport IA	$73,244.75
MAVERICKS	April 12, 1996	State Theatre	$44,157.00
GORDON LIGHTFOOT	April 14, 1996	Madison CC	$40,359.50
MIKHAIL BARYSHNIKOV	April 25, 1996	State Theatre	$136,627.50
JOE SATRIANI	April 27, 1996	Orpheum	$56,747.50
CATS	May 11, 1996	State Theatre	$812,284.54
JOAN OSBORNE	May 12, 1996	Orpheum	$33,429.50
LITTLE FEAT	May 16, 1996	Orpheum	$53,540.00
RIGHTEOUS BROTHERS	June 8, 1996	Des Moines	$73,079.00
RIGHTEOUS BROTHERS	June 9, 1996	Orpheum	$64,788.50
DICK WHITBECK (MOTOWN)	June 15, 1996	State Theatre	$11,989.50
TRIBUTE TO MOTOWN	June 15, 1996	State Theatre	$11,989.50
MONKEES	June 27, 1996	Orpheum	$57,247.00
HOW TO SUCCEED . . .	July 5, 1996	Orpheum	$796,593.00
AL GREEN	July 23, 1996	State Theatre	$51,059.00
DEAD CAN DANCE	July 26, 1996	Orpheum	$40,704.00

CONCERT NAME	CONCERT DATE	CONCERT VENUE	CONCERT GROSS
LOVE LETTERS (BROADWAY)	August 2, 1996	State Theatre	$28,178.00
SMOKEY JOE'S CAFÉ	August 16, 1996	State Theatre	$1,190,345.20
ELVIS COSTELLO	August 18, 1996	Orpheum	$71,780.00
PAUL WESTERBERG	September 6, 1996	State Theatre	$37,195.00
SHOWBOAT	September 17, 1996	Orpheum	$3,898,623.10
A CHORUS LINE	September 24, 1996	State Theatre	$420,207.80
DAVID COPPERFIELD	October 11, 1996	State Theatre	$294,680.70
CHRIS ISAAK	October 15, 1996	State Theatre	$48,645.50
MANDY PATANKIN	October 18, 1996	State Theatre	$76,241.00
FUNNY GIRL	October 22, 1996	State Theatre	$629,629.43
ZZ TOP	November 4, 1996	State Theatre	$62,816.00
TEMPTATIONS	November 7, 1996	State Theatre	$42,428.00
TEMPTATIONS / SPINNERS	November 7, 1996	State Theatre	$42,428.00
JESUS CHRIST SUPERSTAR	November 9, 1996	State Theatre	$157,712.10
TAP DOGS	November 12, 1996	State Theatre	$483,445.95
JUDY COLLINS	November 29, 1996	State Theatre	$21,462.00
SUNSET BOULEVARD	December 8, 1996	Orpheum	$3,030,117.10
SOUNDS OF BLACKNESS	December 16, 1996	State Theatre	$70,208.81
SOUNDS OF BLACKNESS	December 16, 1996	State Theatre	$70,208.81
FLASH CADILLAC	December 19, 1996	State Theatre	$27,113.26
BARRYMORE	January 28, 1997	State Theatre	$241,823.60
STOMP	February 5, 1997	State Theatre	$886,874.70
RIVERDANCE	February 15, 1997	Orpheum	$1,796,523.50
GREASE	February 25, 1997	State Theatre	$1,390,640.30
JACKIE MASON	March 4, 1997	Music Box Th	$131,000.00
JEWEL	March 18, 1997	Orpheum	$48,580.00
JIM BRICKMAN	March 22, 1997	State Theatre	$26,483.00
SHAWN COLVIN	March 26, 1997	State Theatre	$47,133.50
KING AND I	April 1, 1997	Orpheum	$1,474,325.30
KIRK FRANKLIN	April 17, 1997	Orpheum	$59,478.65
RIGHTEOUS BROTHERS	April 23, 1997	Orpheum	$90,080.00
CHIEFTAINS	April 26, 1997	State Theatre	$70,262.05
CROSBY STILLS & NASH	April 26, 1997	Orpheum	$88,689.00

CONCERT NAME	CONCERT DATE	CONCERT VENUE	CONCERT GROSS
CHRIS ROCK	May 4, 1997	Orpheum	$61,560.00
JOHN TESH	May 4, 1997	State Theatre	$42,621.00
BARRY MANILOW	May 22, 1997	Northrop	$131,290.00
WIZ	May 27, 1997	State Theatre	$124,574.80
MASTER CLASS	June 11, 1997	State Theatre	$396,050.55
GORDON LIGHTFOOT	June 25, 1997	Phoenix CC	$29,816.25
JOHN BERRY	June 26, 1997	State Theatre	$10,772.50
LION KING	July 8, 1997	Orpheum	$6,313,828.75
GRAND FUNK RAILROAD	July 11, 1997	State Theatre	$21,979.50
SAMMY HAGAR	July 11, 1997	Milwaukee	$32,777.50
HARRY BELAFONTE	July 27, 1997	State Theatre	$34,359.50
ELECTRIC LIGHT ORCHESTRA	July 29, 1997	State Theatre	$10,938.50
ELO PART II	July 29, 1997	State Theatre	$10,938.50
RADIOHEAD	August 5, 1997	State Theatre	$32,987.50
MONKEES	August 9, 1997	State Theatre	$51,668.00
DAVID BYRNE	August 23, 1997	State Theatre	$26,150.00
INXS	August 26, 1997	State Theatre	$23,332.50
GIPSY KINGS	August 28, 1997	Northrop	$105,307.50
GORDON LIGHTFOOT	September 10, 1997	Madison CC	$22,903.00
JOHN FOGERTY	September 11, 1997	State Theatre	$52,997.00
DEFENDING THE CAVEMAN	September 16, 1997	State Theatre	$817,675.17
SCOTT THOMPSON	September 19, 1997	Music Box Th	$8,595.00
GORDON LIGHTFOOT	September 20, 1997	Kalamazoo MI	$30,588.00
GORDON LIGHTFOOT	September 21, 1997	Milwaukee WI	$19,237.50
VANDROSS / WILLIAMS	September 23, 1997	Target Center	$168,835.00
GORDON LIGHTFOOT	September 25, 1997	Green Bay WI	$41,262.50
GORDON LIGHTFOOT	September 28, 1997	Des Moines	$32,006.00
GORDON LIGHTFOOT	October 3, 1997	Omaha CC	$30,205.50
JAMIE FOXX	October 3, 1997	Orpheum	$63,652.50
GORDON LIGHTFOOT	October 4, 1997	State Theatre	$74,406.50
NANCI GRIFFITH	October 11, 1997	Orpheum	$33,767.04
42ND STREET (BROADWAY)	October 14, 1997	Orpheum	$491,827.90
TAP DOGS	October 14, 1997	State Theatre	$249,658.40

CONCERT NAME	CONCERT DATE	CONCERT VENUE	CONCERT GROSS
DAN FOGELBERG	October 21, 1997	Orpheum	$43,165.00
MATCHBOX 20	October 22, 1997	Orpheum	$42,997.50
k.d. lang	October 24, 1997	Orpheum	$73,913.00
BIG HEAD TODD	November 1, 1997	Orpheum	$41,827.50
STEVE WINWOOD	November 2, 1997	State Theatre	$55,000.00
JOHN GRAY	November 8, 1997	Orpheum	$5,772.00
PAT MATHENY GROUP	November 9, 1997	State Theatre	$55,679.50
RALPH LEMON (WALKER)	November 15, 1997	State Theatre	$5,053.50
CATS	November 18, 1997	Orpheum	$755,431.50
YES	November 18, 1997	State Theatre	$67,560.00
PATTI LABELLE	December 4, 1997	State Theatre	$63,710.50
JOHNNY MATHIS	December 5, 1997	Orpheum	$299,664.00
DAVE KOZ ET AL	December 6, 1997	State Theatre	$30,334.00
SANDY PATTI	December 9, 1997	State Theatre	$21,915.50
BERNIE MAC	December 12, 1997	Orpheum	$45,523.50
SOUNDS OF BLACKNESS	December 13, 1997	Orpheum	$49,980.83
NOISE / FUNK	December 17, 1997	Orpheum	$1,004,446.30
BOBBY CALDWELL	December 31, 1997	State Theatre	$116,748.50
AUDIO ADRENALINE	February 1, 1998	Orpheum	$34,239.00
PLATTERS, COASTERS . . .	March 7, 1998	State Theatre	$18,397.50
CHICAGO	March 10, 1998	Orpheum	$1,753,619.55
RIVERDANCE	March 12, 1998	Orpheum	$4,129,606.50
STOMP	April 1, 1998	State Theatre	$927,418.60
AIR SUPPLY	April 18, 1998	State Theatre	$56,789.50
HARRY CONNICK, JR.	April 24, 1998	Orpheum	$174,889.50
BONNIE RAITT	May 29, 1998	Orpheum	$160,410.00
MIKHAIL BARYSHNIKOV	June 3, 1998	State Theatre	$131,649.65
GREASE	June 9, 1998	State Theatre	$310,714.90
FOREVER TANGO	June 15, 1998	State Theatre	$167,510.25
BRITISH ROCK SYMPHONY	July 6, 1998	State Theatre	$33,390.00
PHANTOM OF THE OPERA	July 16, 1998	Orpheum	$5,326,277.50
JANET JACKSON	July 29, 1998	Target Center	$577,465.00
BAUHAUS	August 26, 1998	State Theatre	$68,598.50

CONCERT NAME	CONCERT DATE	CONCERT VENUE	CONCERT GROSS
COWBOY JUNKIES	September 2, 1998	State Theatre	$33,730.00
LORD OF THE DANCE	September 11, 1998	Target Center	$368,471.75
JOE COCKER	September 15, 1998	State Theatre	$65,745.50
DENNIS MILLER - M HEDBERG	September 16, 1998	State Theatre	$50,945.00
KENNY ROGERS	September 18, 1998	State Theatre	$41,394.00
TRAGICALLY HIP	September 22, 1998	State Theatre	$30,487.00
WIDESPREAD PANIC	October 2, 1998	State Theatre	$43,171.00
RAGTIME	October 7, 1998	Orpheum	$4,820,496.02
RAT DOG	November 2, 1998	State Theatre	$31,490.00
RATDOG	November 2, 1998	State Theatre	$31,490.00
CHRIS ISAAK	November 3, 1998	State Theatre	$70,041.50
JOE SATRIANI	November 6, 1998	State Theatre	$37,913.00
SQUIRREL NUT ZIPPERS	November 7, 1998	State Theatre	$40,843.00
GULLAH GULLAH ISLAND	November 8, 1998	State Theatre	$64,024.50
DEFENDING THE CAVEMAN	November 10, 1998	State Theatre	$895,155.00
GARBAGE	November 27, 1998	Orpheum	$44,920.00
ANNIE	December 1, 1998	Orpheum	$482,612.00
SMOOTH JAZZ CHRISTMAS	December 3, 1998	State Theatre	$23,368.50
LORI LINE	December 7, 1998	State Theatre	$530,024.00
RUGRATS LIVE	December 9, 1998	Orpheum	$151,917.50
SOUNDS OF BLACKNESS	December 21, 1998	Orpheum	$22,954.00
MANNHEIM ON ICE	December 27, 1998	Target Center	$149,570.25
N'SYNC - BRITTANY SPEARS	December 27, 1998	Orpheum	$49,208.00
JONNY LANG	December 28, 1998	State Theatre	$92,218.00
O'JAYS	December 29, 1998	Orpheum	$40,232.50
SOUL ASYLUM	December 31, 1998	State Theatre	$41,800.00
BLACK CROWES	January 12, 1999	State Theatre	$56,115.50
WIZARD OF OZ	January 14, 1999	Orpheum	$1,211,955.00
MAGIC SCHOOL BUS LIVE	January 16, 1999	State Theatre	$18,596.00
GIN GAME	January 26, 1999	State Theatre	$279,044.85
FAME (BROADWAY)	February 11, 1999	State Theatre	$547,599.00
CATS	March 9, 1999	State Theatre	$624,764.80
LYPSINKA	March 19, 1999	State Theatre	$5,675.00

CONCERT NAME	CONCERT DATE	CONCERT VENUE	CONCERT GROSS
DAVID CROSBY	March 20, 1999	State Theatre	$9,810.00
LASER LIGHT SPECTACULAR	March 26, 1999	State Theatre	$13,641.00
STEVEN WRIGHT	March 28, 1999	State Theatre	$35,736.00
FAITH HILL (DEBUT PERF.)	April 9, 1999	Orpheum	$84,015.00
MANDY PATANKIN	April 21, 1999	State Theatre	$62,436.25
SANDRA BERNHART	April 21, 1999	Womans Club	$38,017.50
JECKYLL & HYDE	May 11, 1999	Orpheum	$623,188.39
ROCKAPELLA	May 14, 1999	State Theatre	$30,626.50
NEIL YOUNG	May 22, 1999	Orpheum	$364,370.00
FOOTLOOSE	June 1, 1999	Orpheum	$631,684.70
TRACY CHAPMAN	June 10, 1999	State Theatre	$69,253.00
HARRY CONNICK, JR.	June 11, 1999	Orpheum	$106,233.00
SEAL	June 11, 1999	State Theatre	$48,600.00
ELVIS COSTELLO	June 13, 1999	State Theatre	$81,240.00
EVITA	June 22, 1999	Orpheum	$492,685.40
SARAH BRIGHTMAN	July 18, 1999	Orpheum	$123,585.00
BERNIE MAC	July 23, 1999	State Theatre	$61,509.00
CHER	August 4, 1999	Target Center	$721,656.25
BARNUM'S KALEIDOSCAPE	August 10, 1999	MOA Lot	$896,270.00
JACKIE MASON	August 13, 1999	State Theatre	$29,868.00
SOUND OF MUSIC	August 24, 1999	Orpheum	$1,488,855.50
LENNY KRAVITZ	August 25, 1999	Target Center	$166,532.50
TOM WAITS	August 29, 1999	State Theatre	$182,592.50
BELA FLECK	September 12, 1999	State Theatre	$37,795.00
BELA FLECK	September 12, 1999	State Theatre	$37,795.00
JOSEPH AND THE . . .	September 14, 1999	State Theatre	$2,056,100.15
MOODY BLUES	September 19, 1999	Northrop	$191,000.50
JAZZ @ LINCOLN CENTER	September 21, 1999	Orpheum	$22,263.02
MUSIC OF DUKE ELLINGTON	September 21, 1999	State Theatre	$12,636.00
RIVERDANCE	October 7, 1999	Orpheum	$2,534,955.34
CELIA CRUZ	October 8, 1999	State Theatre	$26,453.50
BACK STREET BOYS	October 9, 1999	Target Center	$640,077.00
CABARET	October 12, 1999	State Theatre	$1,462,470.15

CONCERT NAME	CONCERT DATE	CONCERT VENUE	CONCERT GROSS
MANDY PATINKIN	October 18, 1999	State Theatre	$76,241.00
SPIRIT (BROADWAY)	October 26, 1999	Orpheum	$150,071.50
NANA MOUSKOURI	November 3, 1999	Orpheum	$28,683.00
MARGARET CHO	November 4, 1999	Womans Club	$44,230.50
LIVE	November 6, 1999	Orpheum	$55,597.50
YES	November 12, 1999	Orpheum	$70,360.00
JACKIE MASON	November 16, 1999	Golden NYC	$5,303,427.00
ARTHUR (BROADWAY)	November 19, 1999	Orpheum	$242,595.00
COUNTING CROWS	November 27, 1999	Orpheum	$58,000.00
MANHATTAN TRANSFER	November 30, 1999	Orpheum	$37,588.90
STING	December 5, 1999	Orpheum	$236,995.00
BLENDERS	December 9, 1999	State Theatre	$27,842.50
LORIE LINE	December 10, 1999	State Theatre	$572,745.00
COLIN RAYE	December 11, 1999	Orpheum	$73,493.25
JANE OLIVOR	December 17, 1999	State Theatre	$20,180.50
STEELES	December 22, 1999	State Theatre	$35,836.25
COUNTING CROWS	January 18, 2000	Orpheum	$63,440.00
FOXWORTHY / ENGVALL	January 22, 2000	Orpheum	$199,983.00
JOSEPH AND THE . . .	January 25, 2000	State Theatre	$460,138.75
JAMIE FOXX	February 4, 2000	Orpheum	$51,502.50
LUIS MIGUEL	February 12, 2000	Orpheum	$113,660.00
ISLEY BROTHERS	February 14, 2000	Orpheum	$75,557.00
ART (BROADWAY)	February 15, 2000	State Theatre	$389,227.20
LORD OF THE DANCE	February 15, 2000	Orpheum	$205,802.00
MARC ANTHONY	February 18, 2000	Orpheum	$80,430.00
TYPE O NEGATIVE	February 22, 2000	Roy Wilkins	$28,710.00
PRETENDERS	February 23, 2000	Orpheum	$64,650.00
KIDS IN THE HALL	February 24, 2000	State Theatre	$256,939.50
CROSBY STILLS NASH YOUNG	February 26, 2000	Target Center	$1,050,617.50
FLATLANDERS	March 3, 2000	State Theatre	$11,315.00
BRIAN MCKNIGHT	March 4, 2000	Orpheum	$79,455.00
Y ADAMS / F HAMMOND	March 7, 2000	Orpheum	$44,768.00
JUDDS	March 12, 2000	Target Center	$358,014.25

CONCERT NAME	CONCERT DATE	CONCERT VENUE	CONCERT GROSS
THIRD EYE BLIND	March 16, 2000	Orpheum	$57,528.00
STEVE HARVEY	March 18, 2000	Orpheum	$69,306.00
TINA TURNER	March 23, 2000	Target Center	$780,656.50
PAT METHENY TRIO	March 25, 2000	State Theatre	$32,369.00
BRYAN ADAMS	March 31, 2000	State Theatre	$71,517.00
DAVID COPPERFIELD	March 31, 2000	Orpheum	$359,373.10
KENNY WAYNE SHEPHERD	April 1, 2000	State Theatre	$39,253.50
TOSHI REAGON	April 1, 2000	400 Bar	$1,494.00
SAVION GLOVER	April 7, 2000	State Theatre	$70,049.75
O.C. SUPERTONES	April 8, 2000	State Theatre	$16,932.00
FOSSE	April 12, 2000	Orpheum	$1,317,641.95
TRACY CHAPMAN	April 12, 2000	State Theatre	$70,929.50
JOE SATRIANI	April 21, 2000	State Theatre	$36,881.50
VIOLENT FEMMES	April 24, 2000	Orpheum	$26,950.50
BIG APPLE CIRCUS	April 27, 2000	State Theatre	$12,576.75
DIANA KRALL	May 3, 2000	State Theatre	$58,337.50
D.L. HUGHLEY	May 6, 2000	Orpheum	$27,571.00
KEVIN JAMES	May 6, 2000	State Theatre	$16,524.50
BLUES CLUES	May 10, 2000	Orpheum	$377,213.50
LORIE LINE (BENEFIT)	May 10, 2000	State Theatre	$45,325.00
MEDESKI MARTIN & WOOD	May 12, 2000	Womans Club	$12,240.00
MICHAEL W. SMITH	May 12, 2000	State Theatre	$53,951.50
LFO	May 16, 2000	State Theatre	$22,860.00
TITANIC	May 16, 2000	Orpheum	$892,115.05
DIANNE REEVES	May 20, 2000	Womans Club	$4,088.00
TRAVIS	May 21, 2000	The Quest	$11,882.50
VIC CHESTNUT KRISTI HERSH	May 21, 2000	Womans Club	$2,600.00
TRISHA YEARWOOD	May 23, 2000	State Theatre	$71,011.50
MAGNETIC FIELDS	May 28, 2000	Womans Club	$7,565.00
MARC COHN (BENEFIT)	June 4, 2000	Rush Creek GC	$-
MACY GRAY	June 8, 2000	Orpheum	$45,637.00
ERIC IDLE	June 9, 2000	Orpheum	$84,765.00
DAVID LANZ	June 10, 2000	Womans Club	$5,415.00

CONCERT NAME	CONCERT DATE	CONCERT VENUE	CONCERT GROSS
ERIC IDLE	June 10, 2000	Madison, WI	$55,178.00
LOU REED	June 12, 2000	Orpheum	$40,185.00
CONTINENTAL DRIFTERS	June 14, 2000	400 Bar	$360.00
INDIGO GIRLS	June 23, 2000	Orpheum	$81,445.00
N SYNC	June 23, 2000	Target Center	$678,713.25
FUNK ALL STARS	June 29, 2000	Orpheum	$20,355.00
ROGER WATERS	July 6, 2000	Target Center	$395,605.50
DIANA ROSS	July 19, 2000	Target Center	$276,751.50
MARY J. BLIGE	August 9, 2000	Orpheum	$94,182.50
D'ANGELO	August 16, 2000	Orpheum	$82,906.50
CIRQUE DU SOLEIL	August 17, 2000	Circus Tent	$1,728,000.00
RIVERDANCE	August 22, 2000	Rside Milwaukee	$1,063,318.90
SANTANA	August 22, 2000	Target Center	$532,152.00
SAW DOCTORS	August 22, 2000	400 Bar	$3,480.00
IRON MAIDEN	August 27, 2000	Roy Wilkins	$134,242.00
ANNIE GET YOUR GUN	September 5, 2000	Orpheum	$525,804.00
BEAR IN BIG BLUE HOUSE	September 13, 2000	State Theatre	$154,209.00
SAVAGE GARDEN	September 13, 2000	Orpheum	$70,372.50
TRAVIS	September 21, 2000	The Quest	$23,159.00
VANDROSS / WILLIAMS	September 23, 2000	Target Center	$335,000.00
TALLULAH	October 1, 2000	State Theatre	$371,133.70
MOBY	October 5, 2000	Roy Wilkins	$95,000.00
VICTORIA WILLIAMS	October 6, 2000	Womans Club	$2,569.00
MAC / HARVEY / CEDRIC	October 7, 2000	Target Center	$397,445.00
VONDA SHEPHARD	October 13, 2000	State Theatre	$31,145.00
INDIGO GIRLS BENEFIT	October 16, 2000	Orpheum	$53,420.00
AIN'T NOTHIN BUT . . . BLUES	October 18, 2000	Orpheum	$29,913.00
DAME EDNA	October 24, 2000	State Theatre	$846,807.67
MARILYN MANSON	October 27, 2000	Orpheum	$78,639.00
NINA GORDON	October 28, 2000	Womans Club	$4,462.50
BEAUTY AND THE BEAST	November 1, 2000	Orpheum	$1,638,792.50
THREE DOORS DOWN	November 7, 2000	Roy Wilkins	$46,720.00
VAGINA MONOLOGUES	November 7, 2000	Womans Club	$221,102.25

CONCERT NAME	CONCERT DATE	CONCERT VENUE	CONCERT GROSS
Y ADAMS / S CAESAR	November 7, 2000	State Theatre	$40,221.50
LIMP BIZKIT / EMINEM	November 9, 2000	Target Center	$567,876.00
GORDON LIGHTFOOT	November 11, 2000	State Theatre	$59,464.00
TINA TURNER	November 11, 2000	Target Center	$843,327.00
DIXIE CHICKS	November 13, 2000	Xcel Center	$1,080,000.00
BOBBY CALDWELL	November 18, 2000	State Theatre	$30,897.50
MANNHEIM STEAMROLLER	November 18, 2000	Target Center	$375,467.00
WIDESPREAD PANIC	November 18, 2000	Roy Wilkins	$90,600.00
KEB MO	November 21, 2000	State Theatre	$38,721.00
BO DEANS	November 22, 2000	Orpheum	$67,358.00
SAMMY HAGAR	November 22, 2000	State Theatre	$37,187.00
PATTY LOVELESS / D WORLEY	November 24, 2000	State Theatre	$13,053.00
WALLFLOWERS	November 24, 2000	Orpheum	$53,742.00
JIM BRICKMAN / D OSMOND	November 25, 2000	State Theatre	$126,633.00
DAVE MATTHEWS BAND	December 3, 2000	Target Center	$773,082.00
MEDESKI MARTIN & WOOD	December 6, 2000	State Theatre	$27,200.00
LORIE LINE	December 8, 2000	State Theatre	$561,551.50
JIMMY SCOTT	December 9, 2000	Womans Club	$7,425.00
INSANE CLOWN POSSE	December 13, 2000	Roy Wilkins	$38,115.00
JOHNNY MATHIS	December 16, 2000	State Theatre	$217,615.50
BLENDERS	December 21, 2000	State Theatre	$41,765.00
BIG WU	December 31, 2000	State Theatre	$47,794.00
JACKIE MASON	January 4, 2001	Womans Club	$26,503.50
RICHARD LEWIS	January 26, 2001	Womans Club	$3,577.00
TENACIOUS D	February 3, 2001	First Avenue	$23,182.00
LOW	February 8, 2001	Womans Club	$7,125.00
JO DEE MESSINA	February 10, 2001	Orpheum	$86,475.50
CINDERELLA	February 13, 2001	State Theatre	$735,724.75
BACK STREET BOYS	February 17, 2001	Target Center	$787,728.50
PANTERA	February 20, 2001	Target Center	$150,370.50
AARON CARTER	February 27, 2001	State Theatre	$46,046.00
MATCHBOX 20	February 27, 2001	Target Center	$383,141.50
JEFF BECK	March 9, 2001	State Theatre	$65,625.00

CONCERT NAME	CONCERT DATE	CONCERT VENUE	CONCERT GROSS
BILL COSBY	March 10, 2001	State Theatre	$192,974.50
CIVIL WAR	March 13, 2001	State Theatre	$422,065.05
MALE INTELLECT	March 13, 2001	Womans Club	$57,059.27
HENRY ROLLINS	March 26, 2001	Womans Club	$12,100.00
AIDA	March 27, 2001	Orpheum	$3,216,571.75
GODSMACK	March 29, 2001	Roy Wilkins	$143,360.00
JOE JACKSON	March 31, 2001	State Theatre	$22,550.00
PERFECT CIRCLE	March 31, 2001	Roy Wilkins	$139,275.00
OVER THE RHINE	April 1, 2001	Womans Club	$2,818.00
AC/DC	April 9, 2001	Xcel Center	$615,420.00
GODSPELL	April 10, 2001	State Theatre	$155,044.25
JERSEY BOYS	April 19, 2001	Orpheum	$3,199,690.00
MARK OLSON / V WILLIAMS	April 20, 2001	Womans Club	$696.00
SEMISONIC	April 21, 2001	State Theatre	$48,697.50
JUDY COLLINS	April 22, 2001	State Theatre	$25,792.00
DAVID SEDARIS	April 24, 2001	State Theatre	$52,360.00
SING ALONG SOUND OF M	April 26, 2001	State Theatre	$100,875.75
WAYNE BRADY	April 28, 2001	Orpheum	$51,698.00
GORDON LIGHTFOOT	April 29, 2001	Green Bay WI	$40,410.00
U2	May 1, 2001	Target Center	$1,465,425.00
MARK KNOPFLER	May 7, 2001	Orpheum	$178,800.00
SATURDAY NIGHT FEVER	May 9, 2001	Orpheum	$575,163.70
RUFUS WAINWRIGHT	May 12, 2001	400 Bar	$5,500.00
NICKEL CREEK	May 13, 2001	Womans Club	$5,523.00
ELTON JOHN / BILLY JOEL	May 15, 2001	Target Center	$3,608,470.72
DONNY OSMOND	May 18, 2001	State Theatre	$231,427.00
JERRY SEINFELD	June 2, 2001	Orpheum	$316,515.00
LYNYRD SKYNYRD	June 10, 2001	Target Center	$146,945.00
IRISH TENORS	June 15, 2001	Orpheum	$116,407.00
N SYNC	June 24, 2001	Metrodome	$2,341,857.50
MYSTICAL / JAHEIM	June 26, 2001	Orpheum	$15,222.50
JIM BAILEY	July 1, 2001	State Theatre	$37,993.50
RALPH'S WORLD	July 1, 2001	Womans Club	$534.00

CONCERT NAME	CONCERT DATE	CONCERT VENUE	CONCERT GROSS
PANTERA	July 5, 2001	Xcel Center	$170,597.50
R. KELLY	July 11, 2001	Orpheum	$137,439.00
JOHN LEGUIZAMO	July 13, 2001	State Theatre	$43,297.50
JANET JACKSON	July 17, 2001	Target Center	$756,324.00
JOURNEY	July 21, 2001	Target Center	$253,130.00
JILL SCOTT	July 22, 2001	Orpheum	$64,704.00
MOBY (ARENA ONE FEST)	July 26, 2001	Midway Stad	$512,650.00
DESTINY'S CHILD	July 30, 2001	Target Center	$317,332.00
MATCHBOX 20	August 1, 2001	Xcel Center	$403,160.00
SADE	August 4, 2001	Target Center	$430,020.00
YES WITH ORCHESTRA	August 7, 2001	State Theatre	$106,550.00
JAMES TAYLOR	August 11, 2001	Target Center	$502,980.00
ERYKAH BADU	August 12, 2001	Orpheum	$93,367.50
GODSMACK	August 13, 2001	Target Center	$159,630.00
JAMIE FOXX	August 17, 2001	Orpheum	$57,523.00
BARENAKED LADIES	August 21, 2001	Xcel Center	$322,394.00
KEB MO / BELA FLECK	August 23, 2001	Orpheum	$66,522.00
BRIGHT EYES	September 7, 2001	Womans Club	$4,762.50
TONY BENNETT / KD LANG	September 8, 2001	Target Center	$132,109.00
RIVERDANCE	September 12, 2001	Orpheum	$1,909,754.00
BRENDA WEILER & BAND	September 15, 2001	Womans Club	$1,920
JIMMY SCOTT	September 21, 2001	Womans Club	$6,185.00
BACK STREET BOYS	September 23, 2001	Target Center	$654,946.00
MAXWELL	September 26, 2001	Orpheum	$123,500.00
SIGUR ROS	September 28, 2001	Womans Club	$11,142.00
TENACIOUS D	October 3, 2001	State Theatre	$47,517.50
RAY DAVIES	October 5, 2001	Womans Club	$13,860.00
BLACK CROWES	October 7, 2001	Orpheum	$73,062.50
BOYS CHOIR OF HARLEM	October 7, 2001	State Theatre	$51,823.50
TRISHA YEARWOOD	October 11, 2001	State Theatre	$44,745.00
ROBERT MIRABAL	October 12, 2001	State Theatre	$13,370.25
TRAVIS	October 13, 2001	State Theatre	$51,892.50
DEFENDING THE CAVEMAN	October 17, 2001	State Theatre	$925,662.28

CONCERT NAME	CONCERT DATE	CONCERT VENUE	CONCERT GROSS
MEDESKI MARTIN & WOOD	October 18, 2001	O'Shaughnessy	$25,315.00
BURN THE FLOOR	October 20, 2001	Orpheum	$64,638.50
TORI AMOS	October 21, 2001	Orpheum	$93,500.00
TIM REYONOLDS	October 26, 2001	Womans Club	$9,005.50
AVALON	October 27, 2001	Orpheum	$20,000.00
ISLEY BROTHERS	October 28, 2001	Orpheum	$85,657.00
TAP DOGS	November 3, 2001	State Theatre	$94,363.00
ACME COMEDY GALA	November 4, 2001	State Theatre	$53,562.50
MAMMA MIA	November 9, 2001	Orpheum	$6,234,369.90
JIMMY BUFFEETT	November 10, 2001	Target Center	$927,406.50
FRANCES MAYES	November 11, 2001	State Theatre	$8,965.50
DWIGHT YOAKAM	November 13, 2001	State Theatre	$31,247.00
MANDY PATINKIN	November 14, 2001	State Theatre	$45,368.50
HARRY CONNICK, JR.	November 29, 2001	State Theatre	$122,317.00
LORIE LINE	November 30, 2001	State Theatre	$784,775.00
LINDA EDER	December 9, 2001	State Theatre	$88,567.50
KWANZAA EVENT	December 11, 2001	Pantages	$-
LORD OF RINGS PREMIERE	December 12, 2001	State Theatre	$40,750.00
ROCKAPELLA	December 13, 2001	Womans Club	$15,566.50
BROTHERS FRANTZICH	December 16, 2001	Womans Club	$1,185.00
SWING (BROADWAY)	January 15, 2002	Orpheum	$620,071.15
JANEANE GAROFALO	January 19, 2002	State Theatre	$59,840.00
BRIAN MCKNIGHT	January 26, 2002	State Theatre	$72,240.00
VEGGIE TALES	January 28, 2002	State Theatre	$354,975.50
FIDDLER ON THE ROOF	January 30, 2002	Orpheum	$1,684,768.55
COEN BROS BLUEGRASS	February 9, 2002	State Theatre	$115,785.00
BARRY MANILOW	February 28, 2002	Orpheum	$319,179.50
CATS	March 4, 2002	Orpheum	$912,004.50
RYAN ADAMS	March 11, 2002	Orpheum	$49,028.00
DIANA KRALL	March 15, 2002	State Theatre	$151,373.00
PROOF	March 19, 2002	State Theatre	$327,346.10
I.C.E. / ZEITGEIST	March 23, 2002	Womans Club	$2,438.00
BLUES CLUES	March 26, 2002	State Theatre	$372,650.50

CONCERT NAME	CONCERT DATE	CONCERT VENUE	CONCERT GROSS
ENRIQUE IGLESIAS	March 27, 2002	Orpheum	$106,468.00
BEST LITTLE WHOREHOUSE	April 9, 2002	Orpheum	$828,100.20
RAY CHARLES	April 10, 2002	State Theatre	$47,237.50
ROBBIE FULKS	April 12, 2002	Womans Club	$1,261.50
WAYNE BRADY	April 13, 2002	State Theatre	$54,007.50
LORD OF THE DANCE	April 19, 2002	Orpheum	$347,314.50
RALPH'S WORLD	April 20, 2002	Womans Club	$478.00
BLAST (BROADWAY)	April 23, 2002	Orpheum	$655,649.00
NICK CAVE & THE BAD SEEDS	April 25, 2002	State Theatre	$55,033.00
DAVID COPPERFIELD	April 26, 2002	State Theatre	$395,290.00
JAYHAWKS	April 26, 2002	Womans Club	$9,730.00
MIKE DOUGHTY	April 27, 2002	Womans Club	$7,638.00
ADDICTED (M LUNDHOLM)	May 1, 2002	Womans Club	$2,920.00
KIDS IN THE HALL	May 1, 2002	State Theatre	$140,212.50
RAVI / ANOUSHKA SHANKAR	May 3, 2002	State Theatre	$67,475.00
SCOOBY-DOO	May 8, 2002	Orpheum	$285,526.50
BJORN AGAIN (ABBA)	May 10, 2002	State Theatre	$76,132.50
BRIGHT EYES	May 10, 2002	Womans Club	$6,754.50
ELLEN DEGENERES	May 17, 2002	State Theatre	$67,597.50
BUDDY (BROADWAY)	May 28, 2002	State Theatre	$119,537.75
BROTHERS FRANTZICH	May 31, 2002	Womans Club	$2,310.00
WINANS FAMILY	June 11, 2002	Orpheum	$33,015.00
MUM (ICELAND)	June 17, 2002	Womans Club	$3,240.00
LOWEN & NAVARRO	June 21, 2002	Womans Club	$3,486.00
DAVE PIRNER	July 28, 2002	Womans Club	$6,285.00
NATIONAL POETRY SLAM	August 17, 2002	Orpheum	$19,780.00
MICHAEL BOLTON	September 5, 2002	Orpheum	$35,964.00
SAW DOCTORS	September 5, 2002	First Avenue	$2,365.00
OLIVIA NEWTON JOHN	September 15, 2002	Orpheum	$61,182.50
TERRY GROSS	September 26, 2002	State Theatre	$9,271.50
SOUTH PACIFIC (R GOULET)	October 1, 2002	Orpheum	$245,218.03
RAFFI	October 5, 2002	State Theatre	$48,231.00
RIVERDANCE	October 15, 2002	Rside Milwaukee	$485,091.50

CONCERT NAME	CONCERT DATE	CONCERT VENUE	CONCERT GROSS
LA BOHEME	October 16, 2002	State Theatre	$28,861.50
GOV'T MULE	October 17, 2002	State Theatre	$17,601.50
JERRY SEINFELD	October 18, 2002	Orpheum	$701,100.00
RYAN ADAMS	October 18, 2002	State Theatre	$47,541.00
NOISE / FUNK	October 22, 2002	State Theatre	$274,412.75
BIG WU	November 2, 2002	State Theatre	$20,951.00
DAVE ATTELL (ACME COM)	November 3, 2002	State Theatre	$34,050.00
FUTURE BIBLE HEROS	November 3, 2002	Womans Club	$2,491.00
DAME EDNA (A NIGHT WITH)	November 5, 2002	State Theatre	$236,768.00
JIM BRICKMAN	November 8, 2002	Pantages	$77,467.50
PRODUCERS	November 12, 2002	Orpheum	$4,722,056.04
SHEDAISY	November 14, 2002	Pantages	$22,120.00
MITCH HEDBERG / L BLACK	November 22, 2002	State Theatre	$57,695.00
LOW	November 23, 2002	Pantages	$11,505.00
YES	November 23, 2002	State Theatre	$105,535.00
RUBEN BLADES	November 24, 2002	Pantages	$16,128.00
BLENDERS	December 4, 2002	State Theatre	$41,665.50
LORIE LINE	December 5, 2002	State Theatre	$792,457.00
PATRICIA BARBER	December 6, 2002	Womans Club	$4,052.00
RADIO CITY CHRISTMAS	December 8, 2002	Orpheum	$4,952,845.30
BLACK NATIVITY	December 12, 2002	Pantages	$324,495.50
HENRY ROLLINS	January 18, 2003	Pantages	$19,440.00
JESUS CHRIST SUPERSTAR	January 28, 2003	Orpheum	$1,015,390.14
JANE MONHEIT	February 1, 2003	Pantages	$12,568.00
RICH LITTLE	February 9, 2003	State Theatre	$39,738.25
LES BALLETS TROCKS	February 11, 2003	Pantages	$72,081.50
SEUSSICAL	February 11, 2003	Orpheum	$578,385.00
SHAOLIN MONKS	February 14, 2003	State Theatre	$74,484.00
LAURIE BERKNER	February 15, 2003	Womans Club	$4,335.00
PRETENDERS	February 16, 2003	State Theatre	$61,233.00
VINCE GILL	February 22, 2003	Pantages	$31,015.50
THREE 'MO TENORS	February 23, 2003	State Theatre	$90,232.50
SPIDERMAN	March 4, 2003	Orpheum	$265,119.50

CONCERT NAME	CONCERT DATE	CONCERT VENUE	CONCERT GROSS
LINDA EDER	March 7, 2003	State Theatre	$65,259.50
tic . . . tic . . . BOOM	March 11, 2003	Pantages	$139,733.83
MADAME BUTTERFLY	March 15, 2003	State Theatre	$55,738.50
MARCEL MARCEAU	March 28, 2003	Pantages	$87,654.00
DAVID COPPERFIELD	March 29, 2003	State Theatre	$295,319.00
DAVID COPPERFIELD	April 1, 2003	Duluth Aud	$96,500.00
DAVID SEDARIS	April 5, 2003	State Theatre	$60,772.00
CHEAP TRICK	April 8, 2003	State Theatre	$22,339.50
ELLEN DEGENERES	April 11, 2003	State Theatre	$73,721.50
GREASE	April 11, 2003	Orpheum	$377,428.14
MEDESKI MARTIN & WOOD	April 15, 2003	Pantages	$21,551.00
CAT POWER	April 18, 2003	Pantages	$13,140.00
MISS SAIGON	April 18, 2003	Orpheum	$559,398.35
IRA GLASS	April 26, 2003	Pantages	$16,920.00
DAN WILSON / M DOUGHTY	April 30, 2003	Womans Club	$10,978.50
BEAR IN THE B. BLUE HOUSE	May 1, 2003	State Theatre	$107,326.50
ELAINE STRITCH AT LIBERTY	June 4, 2003	State Theatre	$92,255.00
EARTH WIND AND FIRE	June 18, 2003	Orpheum	$103,429.00
BILL MAHER	June 28, 2003	Pantages	$23,785.00
MIKHAIL BARYSHNIKOV	July 17, 2003	Pantages	$103,381.50
MICHAEL BUBLE	July 19, 2003	Pantages	$16,327.50
STARLIGHT EXPRESS	July 21, 2003	Orpheum	$575,054.95
FULLY COMMITTED	July 24, 2003	Pantages	$80,060.00
ISLEY BROTHERS	August 3, 2003	Orpheum	$53,196.50
CHRIS ISAAK	August 9, 2003	Orpheum	$108,172.50
A PERFECT CIRCLE	August 11, 2003	Pantages	$27,300.00
BILL COSBY	September 20, 2003	State Theatre	$204,960.00
EDDIE IZZARD	September 26, 2003	Pantages	$95,470.00
URINETOWN	September 30, 2003	Orpheum	$738,863.80
THIRTY DAYS IN FROGTOWN	October 3, 2003	Pantages	$9,021.00
GEORGE CARLIN	October 11, 2003	Orpheum	$136,437.00
JACKSON BROWNE	October 12, 2003	State Theatre	$78,352.00
LUCIA DI LAMMERMOOR	October 14, 2003	Pantages	$12,703.00

CONCERT NAME	CONCERT DATE	CONCERT VENUE	CONCERT GROSS
RANDY NEWMAN	October 19, 2003	Pantages	$31,441.00
BELLE & SEBASTIAN	October 31, 2003	Fitzgerald	$26,274.00
MICHAEL FEINSTEIN	October 31, 2003	Pantages	$9,310.00
D ATTELL / EMO PHILIPS	November 2, 2003	Orpheum	$46,840.00
MICHAEL BUBLE	November 2, 2003	Pantages	$21,717.00
CESARIA EVORA	November 4, 2003	Pantages	$27,441.50
FAME (BROADWAY)	November 7, 2003	Orpheum	$224,256.00
YONDER MT STRING BAND	November 7, 2003	State Theatre	$32,615.50
MAMMA MIA	November 11, 2003	Orpheum	$4,232,820.62
DORA THE EXPLORER	November 12, 2003	State Theatre	$386,811.50
MARTIN SEXTON	November 15, 2003	Pantages	$20,292.00
GRADUATE	November 17, 2003	State Theatre	$469,589.85
ERIC IDLE	November 18, 2003	Madison, WI	$12,320.00
ERIC IDLE	November 19, 2003	Pantages	$33,000.00
FOREIGNER	November 21, 2003	Pantages	$44,569.40
MANNHEIM STEAMROLLER	November 29, 2003	Xcel Center	$488,526.50
BLENDERS	December 5, 2003	Pantages	$65,016.00
COLORS OF CHRISTMAS	December 7, 2003	State Theatre	$59,958.50
JOHN TRONES	December 11, 2003	Pantages	$7,347.00
LINDA EDER	December 13, 2003	State Theatre	$82,236.25
LAST COMIC STANDING	December 14, 2003	Pantages	$22,677.50
LORIE LINE	December 17, 2003	State Theatre	$654,591.00
EXCELSIOR CHOIR / A NESBY	December 21, 2003	Pantages	$7,855.00
MARC COHN	December 31, 2003	Pantages	$58,280.00
ANITA BAKER	January 2, 2004	Orpheum	$165,543.00
OKLAHOMA!	January 5, 2004	Orpheum	$591,333.35
DAVID SANBORN	January 8, 2004	Pantages	$22,656.00
SING-A-LONG WIZ OF OZ	January 16, 2004	State Theatre	$29,867.25
DEF POETRY JAM	February 6, 2004	State Theatre	$48,110.00
JIM BRICKMAN	February 14, 2004	Orpheum	$101,410.00
HAIRSPRAY	February 17, 2004	Orpheum	$2,698,758.90
BRIGHT EYES	February 20, 2004	Pantages	$15,236.50
YAKOV SMIRNOFF	February 21, 2004	Pantages	$21,458.50

CONCERT NAME	CONCERT DATE	CONCERT VENUE	CONCERT GROSS
MARIJUANA-LOGUES	February 25, 2004	Pantages	$73,310.00
EXONERATED	April 6, 2004	State Theatre	$265,000.00
HAIR	July 8, 2004	Pantages	$496,258.50
PHANTOM OF THE OPERA	July 14, 2004	Orpheum	$4,618,262.20
MATTERS / HEART (LU PONE)	October 5, 2004	Orpheum	$232,000.00
CAROL CHANNING	October 16, 2004	Pantages	$37,500.00
WONDERFUL TOWN	October 19, 2004	Orpheum	$335,000.00
MAMMA MIA	January 11, 2005	Orpheum	$1,655,805.59
BRIGHT EYES	January 15, 2005	State Theatre	$41,420.00
TRUMBO	January 25, 2005	Pantages	$68,891.25
SWEET CHARITY	February 8, 2005	Orpheum	$1,060,490.01
DATING IT!	February 12, 2005	Henn Stages	$5,175.00
DANCING HENRY 5	February 17, 2005	Pantages	$3,682.00
NATL ACROBATS TAIWAN	February 24, 2005	State Theatre	$13,617.00
LARRY THE CABLE GUY	February 25, 2005	Orpheum	$224,689.75
CARE BEARS	March 7, 2005	Orpheum	$136,923.50
BRITISH INVASION	March 8, 2005	Pantages	$22,819.00
RALPH LEMON DANCE	March 9, 2005	Pantages	$3,825.00
BORGE OUSLAND (NG)	March 10, 2005	State Theatre	$13,056.25
KATIE MC MAHON	March 18, 2005	Pantages	$7,865.00
ROBERT BALLARD (NG)	March 31, 2005	State Theatre	$18,645.00
LEROME BEL DANCE	April 1, 2005	Pantages	$4,460.00
FRANK CALIENDO	April 2, 2005	Orpheum	$100,772.00
KELLY CLARKSON	April 6, 2005	State Theatre	$72,557.00
LION KING	April 8, 2005	Orpheum	$10,489,818.50
ELIZABETH LONSDORF (NG)	April 14, 2005	State Theatre	$4,818.50
RON WHITE	April 15, 2005	State Theatre	$397,403.50
SECRET GARDEN	April 28, 2005	Pantages	$10,934.00
YONDER MT STRING BAND	April 29, 2005	Pantages	$44,280.50
LENNY KRAVITZ	May 4, 2005	State Theatre	$97,291.00
MIKE EPPS	May 9, 2005	Orpheum	$61,603.00
DORA'S PIRATE ADVEN	May 11, 2005	State Theatre	$410,635.75
JESSE MC CARTNEY	May 16, 2005	State Theatre	$61,628.00

CONCERT NAME	CONCERT DATE	CONCERT VENUE	CONCERT GROSS
MATTAIS KLUM (NG)	May 19, 2005	State Theatre	$10,860.00
AL GREEN	May 20, 2005	State Theatre	$100,856.50
KERI NOBLE	May 20, 2005	Pantages	$20,677.00
MOSAIC (CITY EVENT)	June 4, 2005	Pantages	$-
MADELEINE PEYROUX	June 7, 2005	Pantages	$28,644.50
FUNNIEST MOM	June 11, 2005	Henn Stages	$4,230.00
PUPPETRY OF THE PENIS	June 14, 2005	Henn Stages	$43,839.57
EELS	June 21, 2005	Pantages	$15,427.50
EMMANUEL'S GIFT (CORP)	July 14, 2005	Pantages	$2,818.00
LITTLE SHOP OF HORRORS	July 19, 2005	Orpheum	$557,809.85
MOVIN' OUT	August 3, 2005	Orpheum	$1,929,614.85
RICKIE LEE JONES	August 5, 2005	Pantages	$20,645.00
DAVID GRAY	August 9, 2005	State Theatre	$62,295.00
GIPSY KINGS	August 25, 2005	State Theatre	$120,911.50
JOSEPH AND THE . . .	September 13, 2005	Orpheum	$898,353.60
SIGUR ROS	September 24, 2005	State Theatre	$62,127.00
IVEY AWARDS	September 26, 2005	Pantages	$5,278.00
DEFENDING THE CAVEMAN	October 5, 2005	Henn Stages	$61,000.00
VINCE GILL	October 14, 2005	State Theatre	$49,973.50
JOHNNY MATHIS	October 15, 2005	Orpheum	$86,525.50
KATHLEEN MADIGAN	October 15, 2005	Pantages	$6,298.00
LILY TOMLIN	October 15, 2005	State Theatre	$91,476.00
CELTIC WOMAN	October 22, 2005	Orpheum	$204,643.39
BILL COSBY	October 23, 2005	State Theatre	$82,032.50
BILL ENGVALL	November 5, 2005	Orpheum	$60,957.00
TEN TENORS	November 5, 2005	State Theatre	$32,867.00
AUSSIE PINK FLOYD	November 8, 2005	Orpheum	$140,213.00
ARLECCHINO (GUTHRIE)	November 9, 2005	Pantages	$12,272.50
LINDA EDER	November 18, 2005	State Theatre	$54,478.00
MANNHEIM STEAMROLLER	November 26, 2005	XCEL CENTER	$474,912.25
LORIE LINE	December 2, 2005	State Theatre	$507,580.00
MARTINI & OLIVE	December 3, 2005	Henn Stages	$37,842.90
BLENDERS	December 9, 2005	Pantages	$92,859.25

CONCERT NAME	CONCERT DATE	CONCERT VENUE	CONCERT GROSS
RADIO CITY CHRISTMAS	December 9, 2005	Orpheum	$3,644,915.28
KATHY MATTEA	December 13, 2005	Pantages	$25,226.25
JUDY COLLINS	December 21, 2005	Pantages	$18,067.50
MARC COHN	December 30, 2005	Pantages	$54,370.00
TUESDAYS WITH MORRIE	January 31, 2006	Orpheum	$361,344.23
SWAN LAKE (BOURNE)	February 8, 2006	State Theatre	$213,475.50
LITTLE WOMEN	February 14, 2006	Orpheum	$560,564.25
CARMINA BURANA	March 2, 2006	Pantages	$64,796.00
KATIE MCMAHON	March 17, 2006	Pantages	$10,119.50
ANNIE	March 21, 2006	Orpheum	$919,483.00
JAMES BLUNT	March 27, 2006	State Theatre	$48,762.50
CELTIC WOMAN	April 5, 2006	Orpheum	$165,754.00
ONE MAN STAR WARS	April 18, 2006	Pantages	$51,854.00
KATHY GRIFFIN	April 26, 2006	Pantages	$28,386.00
DAVID COPPERFIELD	May 6, 2006	State Theatre	$246,938.00
CATS	May 30, 2006	Orpheum	$482,166.75
MOSAIC (CITY EVENT)	June 10, 2006	Pantages	$-
RIVERDANCE	June 11, 2006	Orpheum	$465,061.50
KATHY GRIFFIN	June 22, 2006	State Theatre	$61,620.00
DOROTHY THE DINOSAUR	June 24, 2006	State Theatre	$28,322.00
MASON JENNINGS	June 24, 2006	Orpheum	$51,075.00
AWESOME 80S PROM	July 7, 2006	Henn Stages	$93,659.00
GIPSY KINGS	July 12, 2006	State Theatre	$72,693.50
WICKED	July 12, 2006	Orpheum	$2,553,561.56
DANIEL POWTER	July 27, 2006	Pantages	$12,894.50
CHRIS ISAAK	August 5, 2006	State Theatre	$103,947.50
LOVE TAPES	September 13, 2006	Henn Stages	$11,522.94
GORDON LIGHTFOOT	September 17, 2006	State Theatre	$90,750.50
ROSEANNE CASH	September 24, 2006	Pantages	$23,825.00
YONDER MT STRING BAND	September 29, 2006	State Theatre	$29,657.00
CIRQUE DREAMS	October 6, 2006	State Theatre	$144,024.75
SYLVIA	October 11, 2006	Pantages	$98,047.00
MADELEINE PEYROUX	October 13, 2006	State Theatre	$36,634.50

CONCERT NAME	CONCERT DATE	CONCERT VENUE	CONCERT GROSS
TIM CONWAY / KORMAN	October 15, 2006	State Theatre	$138,150.50
DAVID SEDARIS	October 21, 2006	State Theatre	$79,866.50
PILOBOLUS (DANCE)	October 22, 2006	State Theatre	$23,752.00
DRACULA (BALLET)	October 25, 2006	State Theatre	$64,668.00
JAMES BLUNT	October 30, 2006	Northrop	$158,834.50
BELLYDANCE SUPERSTARS	November 5, 2006	Pantages	$12,608.00
25TH ANNUAL . . . SPELLING BEE	November 7, 2006	State Theatre	$474,687.00
SPELLING BEE	November 7, 2006	State Theatre	$234,782.80
VIENNA CHOIR BOYS	November 19, 2006	Pantages	$16,725.00
AUSSIE PINK FLOYD	November 25, 2006	Orpheum	$148,565.00
TWELVE ANGRY MEN	December 5, 2006	State Theatre	$396,245.65
ANITA BAKER	December 8, 2006	Orpheum	$91,554.00
BLENDERS	December 8, 2006	Pantages	$95,993.50
LORIE LINE	December 9, 2006	Orpheum	$457,731.00
BLENDERS	December 17, 2006	Pantages	$93,031.50
ALTAR BOYZ	December 19, 2006	Pantages	$199,762.25
MARC COHN	December 31, 2006	Pantages	$55,760.00
JERRY SEINFELD	February 8, 2007	Orpheum	$534,285.00
JIM BRICKMAN	February 10, 2007	Orpheum	$62,007.50
RAT PACK	February 13, 2007	State Theatre	$471,143.30
DOUBT	March 4, 2007	State Theatre	$315,364.00
RON WHITE	March 9, 2007	Orpheum	$302,231.00
LIGHT IN THE PIAZZA	March 20, 2007	Orpheum	$442,232.00
SOWETO GOSPEL CHOIR	March 22, 2007	State Theatre	$32,860.50
MARTIN SEXTON	April 14, 2007	Pantages	$25,793.00
CELTIC WOMAN	April 17, 2007	Orpheum	$252,719.50
LORENNA MCKENNITT	May 5, 2007	State Theatre	$84,550.00
JON STEWART	May 18, 2007	Orpheum	$319,732.00
NICK SWARDSON	June 9, 2007	State Theatre	$59,408.00
FEIST	June 20, 2007	Pantages	$23,936.50
LYLE LOVETT / KD LANG	July 5, 2007	Orpheum	$105,695.50
CHRIS CORNELL	July 16, 2007	Orpheum	$49,408.00
PATTI SMITH	August 6, 2007	State Theatre	$26,607.00

CONCERT NAME	CONCERT DATE	CONCERT VENUE	CONCERT GROSS
GORDON LIGHTFOOT	September 22, 2007	State Theatre	$84,130.00
WEDDING SINGER	September 25, 2007	Orpheum	$399,389.00
DAVID SEDARIS	October 15, 2007	State Theatre	$78,167.50
LION KING	October 25, 2007	Orpheum	$6,260,935.00
STARS	November 3, 2007	Pantages	$16,191.00
BLENDERS	December 7, 2007	Pantages	$108,217.50
LORIE LINE	December 8, 2007	Orpheum	$382,377.00
TRAMPLED BY TURTLES	December 31, 2007	Orpheum	$39,433.00
ANENUE Q	January 6, 2008	Orpheum	$1,141,158.00
TODD RUNDGREN	January 22, 2008	Pantages	$28,083.00
SWEENEY TODD	February 5, 2008	State Theatre	$499,860.00
SISSEL	February 8, 2008	Pantages	$29,991.00
LORD OF THE DANCE	February 9, 2008	Orpheum	$189,163.00
MY FAIR LADY	February 20, 2008	Orpheum	$1,039,305.00
GREG MARSHALL (NG)	February 21, 2008	State Theatre	$23,000.00
RAIN (BEATLES)	March 3, 2008	Orpheum	$77,441.50
JERSEY BOYS	March 19, 2008	Orpheum	$6,271,742.00
BRADY BARR (NG)	March 20, 2008	State Theatre	$21,000.00
MARY OLIVER	March 30, 2008	State Theatre	$29,338.50
EELS	April 7, 2008	Pantages	$15,465.00
SAM ABELL (NG)	April 17, 2008	State Theatre	$19,000.00
KIDS IN THE HALL	April 26, 2008	Orpheum	$103,327.00
JESUS CHRIST SUPERSTAR	May 4, 2008	Orpheum	$445,037.60
ANNIE GRIFFITHS BELT (NG)	May 8, 2008	State Theatre	$17,000.00
FLIGHT OF CONCHORDS	May 13, 2008	Orpheum	$82,420.00
ARMISTEAD MAUPIN	June 13, 2008	State Theatre	$12,088.50
CROSBY STILLS & NASH	July 11, 2008	Orpheum	$183,988.50
DAVID MCCULLOUGH	October 2, 2008	State Theatre	$49,661.25
MY MORNING JACKET	October 2, 2008	Orpheum	$72,259.50
KATHY GRIFFIN	October 3, 2008	Orpheum	$542,311.50
KHALED HOSSEINI	October 17, 2008	State Theatre	$31,556.75
MASON JENNINGS	October 18, 2008	Orpheum	$41,677.00
RUFUS WAINWRIGHT	October 18, 2008	State Theatre	$59,618.00

CONCERT NAME	CONCERT DATE	CONCERT VENUE	CONCERT GROSS
DAVID SEDARIS	October 19, 2008	State Theatre	$78,494.25
FRANKIE VALLI	October 22, 2008	Orpheum	$209,795.50
ELDAR	October 29, 2008	Dakota	$1,622.00
KINGS OF LEON	November 1, 2008	Orpheum	$83,204.00
WICKED	November 5, 2008	Orpheum	$7,348,217.00
AUSSIE PINK FLOYD	November 14, 2008	State Theatre	$96,668.50
MATT NATHANSON	November 18, 2008	Pantages	$16,611.00
BLENDERS	December 4, 2008	Pantages	$95,000.00
DAN WILSON	December 13, 2008	Pantages	$21,794.00
MANNHEIM STEAMROLLER	December 19, 2008	Orpheum	$354,530.00
GREASE	January 1, 2009	Orpheum	$984,991.00
FROST/NIXON	January 6, 2009	State Theatre	$292,317.00
SPRING AWAKENING	January 6, 2009	State Theatre	$724,386.00
TIM & ERIC	January 22, 2009	Pantages	$24,325.00
ANNIE	February 12, 2009	Orpheum	$93,000.00
FIDDLER ON THE ROOF	February 24, 2009	Orpheum	$1,029,884.00
MOVIN' OUT	March 6, 2009	Orpheum	$310,871.00
GORDON LIGHTFOOT	March 22, 2009	State Theatre	$85,104.50
RAIN (BEATLES)	March 22, 2009	Orpheum	$138,064.00
RENT	March 26, 2009	Orpheum	$779,028.00
MAGIC TREE HOUSE	April 4, 2009	State Theatre	$68,365.00
KRIS KRISTOFFERSON	April 14, 2009	Pantages	$41,796.00
TEN TENORS	April 24, 2009	State Theatre	$19,047.78
TEN TENORS	April 24, 2009	State Theatre	$27,000.00
RIVERDANCE	May 8, 2009	State Theatre	$444,230.50
PHANTOM OF THE OPERA	May 13, 2009	Orpheum	$3,364,671.00
DORA THE EXPLORER	May 15, 2009	State Theatre	$399,000.00
A BRONX TALE	June 2, 2009	State Theatre	$128,252.00
MONTY ALEXANDER	June 12, 2009	State Stage	$21,000.00
A CHORUS LINE	June 16, 2009	Orpheum	$773,639.00
HIPPIEFEST	July 28, 2009	State Theatre	$28,534.50
LOGGINS AND MESSINA	September 1, 2009	State Theatre	$111,330.50
MARY POPPINS	September 3, 2009	Orpheum	$3,834,980.00

CONCERT NAME	CONCERT DATE	CONCERT VENUE	CONCERT GROSS
TODD RUNDGREN	September 15, 2009	State Theatre	$42,555.50
PET SHOP BOYS	September 16, 2009	State Theatre	$59,867.50
BOZ SCAGGS	September 24, 2009	State Theatre	$97,465.50
JOSHUA RADIN	September 25, 2009	Pantages	$14,243.50
AUSSIE PINK FLOYD	October 2, 2009	State Theatre	$110,000.00
101 DALMATIANS	October 13, 2009	Orpheum	$518,700.00
DAVID SEDARIS	October 14, 2009	State Theatre	$77,677.00
RODRIGO Y GABRIELA	October 17, 2009	Pantages	$31,356.00
CELTIC THUNDER	October 29, 2009	State Theatre	$89,000.00
JERRY SEINFELD	November 14, 2009	Orpheum	$528,908.00
WOLFMOTHER	November 14, 2009	State Theatre	$33,148.50
BRETT DENNEN	November 17, 2009	Pantages	$12,284.00
GREASE	November 18, 2009	Orpheum	$357,272.00
IN THE HEIGHTS	December 1, 2009	Orpheum	$684,238.00
BIG BAD VOODOO DADDY	December 6, 2009	Pantages	$27,738.00
KENNY G	December 6, 2009	State Theatre	$46,445.75
BLENDERS	December 11, 2009	Pantages	$91,000.00
DREAMGIRLS	January 17, 2010	Orpheum	$694,743.00
ABBA THE MUSIC	February 6, 2010	Pantages	$55,685.00
YOUNG FRANKENSTEIN	February 9, 2010	Orpheum	$761,582.00
BB KING / BUDDY GUY	February 20, 2010	Orpheum	$196,870.00
STEPHEN SONDHEIM	March 5, 2010	State Theatre	$27,740.00
MAMMA MIA	March 14, 2010	Orpheum	$1,115,858.00
EXPERIENCE HENDRIX	March 17, 2010	Orpheum	$164,845.00
CAROL BURNETT	April 14, 2010	State Theatre	$117,783.40
ANTHONY BOURDAIN	April 23, 2010	State Theatre	$88,465.85
AQUA TEEN	April 29, 2010	Pantages	$6,966.50
MO'NIQUE	May 14, 2010	State Theatre	$42,165.00
STEVE MARTIN BLUEGRASS	June 13, 2010	State Theatre	$103,505.00
DENNIS LEARY	June 15, 2010	State Theatre	$95,667.50
KATHY GRIFFIN	June 26, 2010	Orpheum	$206,971.00
WICKED	August 10, 2010	Orpheum	$9,727,199.00
BUDDY GUY	October 16, 2010	State Theatre	$69,995.50

CONCERT NAME	CONCERT DATE	CONCERT VENUE	CONCERT GROSS
TRAILER PARK BOYS	October 17, 2010	Pantages	$27,780.00
JASON BONHAM LZ	October 19, 2010	State Theatre	$48,885.50
LED ZEPPELIN EXPERIENCE	October 19, 2010	State Theatre	$45,885.50
DAVID SEDARIS	October 21, 2010	State Theatre	$77,939.50
SCRIPT	October 22, 2010	State Theatre	$46,353.00
CELTIC THUNDER	October 24, 2010	State Theatre	$104,802.00
SARA BAREILLES	November 2, 2010	Pantages	$24,100.00
BB KING	November 12, 2010	State Theatre	$114,768.50
TIM & ERIC	November 17, 2010	State Theatre	$33,670.00
BLENDERS	December 3, 2010	Pantages	$85,201.75
MANNHEIM STEAMROLLER	December 3, 2010	Orpheum	$230,590.00
LINDA EDER	December 21, 2010	Pantages	$47,750.45
LYLE LOVETT / HIATT	February 7, 2011	State Theatre	$103,985.00
BOZ SCAGGS	February 12, 2011	State Theatre	$100,499.00
LILY TOMLIN	February 13, 2011	State Theatre	$57,503.00
CLAY AIKEN	March 5, 2011	State Theatre	$26,984.50
RIVERDANCE	March 18, 2011	State Theatre	$349,708.00
CELTIC WOMAN	April 22, 2011	State Theatre	$185,075.00
ROBERT CRAY	May 19, 2011	Pantages	$20,280.00
GIPSY KINGS	May 24, 2011	State Theatre	$88,032.00
JACKSON BROWNE	May 29, 2011	State Theatre	$118,636.00
BRETT DENNEN	June 5, 2011	Pantages	$16,380.00
ELVIS COSTELLO	June 29, 2011	State Theatre	$97,502.00
STEVE EARLE	July 23, 2011	Pantages	$38,342.00
RHYTHMIC CIRCUS	August 12, 2011	Pantages	$40,148.80
CHRIS ISAAK	August 13, 2011	State Theatre	$66,721.00
JANET JACKSON	August 19, 2011	Orpheum	$256,556.00
RETURN TO FOREVER	August 24, 2011	Orpheum	$70,521.50
SCRIPT	August 30, 2011	Orpheum	$71,537.50
YO GABBA GABBA	September 15, 2011	State Theatre	$66,110.00
LINDSEY BUCKINGHAM	September 16, 2011	Pantages	$40,226.50
GORDON LIGHTFOOT	September 17, 2011	State Theatre	$70,799.50
PETER FRAMPTON	September 30, 2011	State Theatre	$103,394.50

CONCERT NAME	CONCERT DATE	CONCERT VENUE	CONCERT GROSS
TRAILER PARK BOYS	October 4, 2011	Pantages	$29,278.00
FRAN LEBOWITZ	October 14, 2011	Pantages	$9,241.00
AUSSIE PINK FLOYD	October 20, 2011	Orpheum	$125,860.50
DAVID SEDARIS	November 13, 2011	State Theatre	$79,818.50
CAKE BOSS	November 15, 2011	Orpheum	$45,014.30
AL JARREAU	November 16, 2011	Pantages	$39,271.00
JERRY SEINFELD	November 18, 2011	Orpheum	$491,182.00
LINDA EDER	December 2, 2011	Pantages	$36,611.50
BLENDERS	December 9, 2011	Pantages	$84,889.00
BUDDY GUY	March 2, 2012	State Theatre	$83,300.00
RAIN (BEATLES)	March 3, 2012	Orpheum	$199,804.25
WILLIAM SHATNER	March 15, 2012	Orpheum	$103,791.40
RICKIE LEE JONES	April 13, 2012	Pantages	$12,195.00
FLORENCE & THE MACHINE	April 27, 2012	State Theatre	$98,961.00
GIPSY KINGS	April 28, 2012	State Theatre	$54,135.00
WEIRD AL YANKOVIC	May 3, 2012	State Theatre	$86,634.50
BB KING	May 18, 2012	State Theatre	$121,615.00
UNDER THE STREETLAMP	June 17, 2012	Pantages	$18,914.00
DAN SAVAGE	June 22, 2012	Pantages	$34,722.50
RHYTHMIC CIRCUS	July 20, 2012	Pantages	$40,422.00
MERLE HAGGARD/KRIS K	July 28, 2012	State Theatre	$137,301.00
CROSBY STILLS & NASH	August 6, 2012	Orpheum	$196,747.50
HUGH LAURIE	August 18, 2012	Pantages	$46,684.50
MASTERS OF ILLUSION	September 21, 2012	State Theatre	$30,439.50
FRANKIE VALLI	September 22, 2012	State Theatre	$113,483.50
ED SHEERAN	September 26, 2012	State Theatre	$44,955.50
VINCE GILL	October 13, 2012	State Theatre	$88,003.50
SCRIPT	October 26, 2012	Orpheum	$67,911.50
JACKSON BROWNE	October 28, 2012	State Theatre	$124,674.00
DAVID SEDARIS	November 10, 2012	State Theatre	$82,270.00
BRIAN SETZER ORCHESTRA	November 17, 2012	Orpheum	$124,930.65
AUSSIE PINK FLOYD	November 18, 2012	Orpheum	$100,899.00
MANNHEIM STEAMROLLER	November 23, 2012	Orpheum	$185,258.00

CONCERT NAME	CONCERT DATE	CONCERT VENUE	CONCERT GROSS
CHRIS ISAAK	November 27, 2012	State Theatre	$68,069.00
KATHY GRIFFIN	December 1, 2012	State Theatre	$179,337.00
BLENDERS	December 14, 2012	Pantages	$83,724.00
TRAILER PARK BOYS	December 14, 2012	State Theatre	$69,787.00
TONY BENNETT	January 20, 2013	State Theatre	$172,687.00
JOHN DENVER TRIBUTE	February 17, 2013	State Theatre	$44,216.00
LORD OF THE DANCE	February 23, 2013	State Theatre	$80,496.00
BUDDY GUY / JONNY LANG	March 10, 2013	State Theatre	$125,494.50
MAVERICKS	April 3, 2013	Pantages	$38,372.00
BOZ SCAGGS	April 11, 2013	State Theatre	$107,310.00
GAITHER VOCAL BAND	April 12, 2013	Orpheum	$87,051.50
CELTIC WOMAN	April 13, 2013	Orpheum	$149,138.05
CHICAGO	April 27, 2013	State Theatre	$152,960.50
GORDON LIGHTFOOT	April 29, 2013	State Theatre	$76,569.00
JESSE COOK	May 9, 2013	Pantages	$9,058.50
ANTHONY BOURDAIN	May 11, 2013	State Theatre	$136,175.00
CAROL BURNETT	May 17, 2013	State Theatre	$129,650.50
CHRIS MANN	June 4, 2013	The Dakota	$6,647.00
TENORS	June 14, 2013	State Theatre	$69,295.50
ALICE COOPER	July 14, 2013	State Theatre	$174,648.50
MERLE HAGGARD	July 19, 2013	State Theatre	$75,185.50
PETER FRAMPTON	July 21, 2013	State Theatre	$67,146.50
STEVE MARTIN BLUEGRASS	July 22, 2013	State Theatre	$134,423.00
BJ THOMAS	July 27, 2013	Pantages	$12,080.50
KENNY LOGGINS	July 30, 2013	State Theatre	$32,280.00
ABBA THE CONCERT	August 3, 2013	Pantages	$36,136.00
JIM JEFFERIES	August 24, 2013	State Theatre	$33,449.00
LINDA EDER	August 24, 2013	Pantages	$29,785.00
DIANA ROSS	August 28, 2013	Orpheum	$199,041.00
JONNY LANG	September 18, 2013	State Theatre	$45,779.50
HUGH LAURIE	October 15, 2013	Pantages	$47,375.00
GHOST BRO. MUSICAL	October 31, 2013	State Theatre	$41,570.90
BILLY COLLINS	November 1, 2013	Pantages	$19,927.50

CONCERT NAME	CONCERT DATE	CONCERT VENUE	CONCERT GROSS
DAVID SEDARIS	November 3, 2013	State Theatre	$71,045.00
IRA GLASS (DANCE)	November 10, 2013	State Theatre	$95,557.00
BRIAN SETZER ORCHESTRA	November 15, 2013	Orpheum	$114,724.50
BOB NEWHART	November 22, 2013	State Theatre	$72,720.00
MARTINA MCBRIDE	December 6, 2013	State Theatre	$98,619.00
MANHATTAN TRANSFER	December 11, 2013	Pantages	$29,268.50
BLENDERS	December 12, 2013	Pantages	$101,604.00
JOHN TRONES / BRICKMAN	December 23, 2013	Pantages	$15,986.50
JERRY SEINFELD	January 16, 2014	Orpheum	$532,489.00
MIKE BIRBIGLIA	February 22, 2014	Pan/Fitz	$70,853.00
MAVERICKS	March 9, 2014	Pantages	$45,447.50
DAVID GARRETT	March 12, 2014	State Theatre	$43,421.00
RICK SPRINGFIELD	March 23, 2014	Pantages	$34,050.00
AMY SCHUMER	March 27, 2014	Orpheum	$91,809.00
JILIAN MICHAELS	March 29, 2014	Pantages	$43,800.00
MASON JENNINGS	April 5, 2014	State Theatre	$31,092.50
EXPERIENCE HENDRIX	April 8, 2014	State Theatre	$94,584.00
RAIN (BEATLES)	April 11, 2014	State Theatre	$144,183.50
CHICAGO	April 26, 2014	State Theatre	$165,462.00
JESSE COOK	May 3, 2014	Pantages	$18,164.00
NICKEL CREEK	May 11, 2014	State Theatre	$94,003.00
RODRIGUEZ	May 17, 2014	State Theatre	$82,105.00
BILL MAHER	May 30, 2014	State Theatre	$149,409.00
MAXWELL	June 15, 2014	State Theatre	$90,934.00
RODRIGO Y GABRIELA	July 15, 2014	State Theatre	$64,469.00
JACKSON BROWNE	July 18, 2014	State Theatre	$135,145.50
JEFF BRIDGES	July 24, 2014	Pantages	$51,327.50
DENNIS DEYOUNG	September 6, 2014	Pantages	$28,518.50
BUDDY GUY	September 7, 2014	State Theatre	$70,535.00
IMPRACTICAL JOKERS	September 26, 2014	Orpheum	$143,379.00
TIM & ERIC	September 26, 2014	State Theatre	$59,295.00
AUSSIE PINK FLOYD	September 30, 2014	Orpheum	$84,554.50
BOZ SCAGGS	September 30, 2014	State Theatre	$103,837.50

CONCERT NAME	CONCERT DATE	CONCERT VENUE	CONCERT GROSS
OLD CROW MED. SHOW	October 2, 2014	State Theatre	$41,842.50
DAVID SEDARIS	October 29, 2014	State Theatre	$77,357.00
BRIAN SETZER ORCHESTRA	November 14, 2014	Orpheum	$119,229.00
FRESH BEAT BAND	November 18, 2014	State Theatre	$29,394.68
CELTIC THUNDER	November 28, 2014	State Theatre	$106,614.00
JOHNNY MATHIS	December 4, 2014	State Theatre	$150,694.50
BIG BAD VOODOO DADDY	December 7, 2014	Pantages	$32,875.50
MANNHEIM STEAMROLLER	December 7, 2014	Orpheum	$143,802.50
TRAILER PARK BOYS	December 7, 2014	State Theatre	$92,480.00
BLENDERS	December 12, 2014	Pantages	$91,440.50
DEMETRI MARTIN	February 7, 2015	State Theatre	$61,110.00
WHOSE LINE IS IT . . .	February 18, 2015	State Theatre	$83,618.00
PENTATONIX	March 7, 2015	Orpheum	$121,291.50
GREGG ALLMAN	March 27, 2015	Pantages	$65,722.50
MAVERICKS	April 4, 2015	Pantages	$51,783.00
STEVE WINWOOD	April 17, 2015	State Theatre	$125,466.50
KEVIN SMITH	May 1, 2015	State Theatre	$42,815.00
MARY CHAPIN CARPENTER	May 2, 2015	State Theatre	$63,942.50
CHICAGO	May 19, 2015	State Theatre	$155,214.00
JEFF BECK	May 23, 2015	State Theatre	$110,742.00
SCRIPT	June 5, 2015	State Theatre	$63,624.50
GORDON LIGHTFOOT	June 20, 2015	State Theatre	$91,234.00
BOZ SCAGGS	July 18, 2015	State Theatre	$88,565.00
ANTHONY BOURDAIN	July 24, 2015	State Theatre	$167,482.02
WOODY ALLEN	August 2, 2015	State Theatre	$69,128.50
DIANA KRALL	August 7, 2015	State Theatre	$166,415.00
STEVE EARLE	September 5, 2015	Pantages	$31,279.00
BOBBY CALDWELL	September 19, 2015	Pantages	$23,779.00
RINGO STARR	October 16, 2015	State Theatre	$213,260.00
RODNEY CARRINGTON	October 16, 2015	Pantages	$21,888.00
LYLE LOVETT / HIATT	October 17, 2015	State Theatre	$115,198.50
MATISYAHU	October 24, 2015	Pantages	$19,443.00
BILL BURR	October 28, 2015	Orpheum	$195,615.00

CONCERT NAME	CONCERT DATE	CONCERT VENUE	CONCERT GROSS
DAVID SEDARIS	November 1, 2015	State Theatre	$80,669.74
AMERICA'S TEST KITCHEN	November 4, 2015	Pantages	$96,128.00
JIM GAFFIGAN	November 4, 2015	State Theatre	$791,859.50
JACKSON BROWNE	November 10, 2015	State Theatre	$142,929.50
JIM JEFFERIES	November 11, 2015	Pantages	$69,751.50
BRIAN SETZER ORCHESTRA	November 14, 2015	Orpheum	$124,544.50
IMPRACTICAL JOKERS	November 14, 2015	State Theatre	$204,287.50
ALICE COOPER	December 6, 2015	State Theatre	$103,031.00
BLENDERS	December 11, 2015	Pantages	$96,282.50
R5	March 11, 2016	State Theatre	$74,460.00
LARRY THE CABLE GUY	March 19, 2016	Orpheum	$240,451.00
MAVERICKS	March 19, 2016	State Theatre	$88,972.00
RIVERDANCE	March 25, 2016	State Theatre	$401,291.75
IRA GLASS	April 9, 2016	State Theatre	$91,868.00
TONY BENNETT	May 6, 2016	State Theatre	$176,288.00
MICHAEL CARBONARO	May 7, 2016	State Theatre	$57,756.30
HARRY CONNICK, JR.	May 12, 2016	State Theatre	$198,730.00
LINDSEY VONN EVENT	June 3, 2016	Orpheum	$-
PETER FRAMPTON	July 13, 2016	State Theatre	$74,320.50
CHRIS ISAAK	July 19, 2016	Pantages	$61,440.00
LYLE LOVETT / HIATT	July 22, 2016	State Theatre	$118,703.50
WEIRD AL YANKOVIC	August 19, 2016	State Theatre	$111,826.50
AUSSIE PINK FLOYD	September 6, 2016	State Theatre	$82,130.00
CELTIC THUNDER	September 30, 2016	State Theatre	$99,347.00
BILL MAHER	October 8, 2016	State Theatre	$156,265.50
HERB ALPERT	October 12, 2016	Pantages	$32,332.00
GORDON LIGHTFOOT	October 16, 2016	State Theatre	$94,560.50
DAVID SEDARIS	October 28, 2016	State Theatre	$85,673.25
STEVE EARLE	November 5, 2016	Pantages	$48,800.50
MANNHEIM STEAMROLLER	December 4, 2016	State Theatre	$202,140.10
NICHOLAS DAVID	December 4, 2016	Pantages	$13,316.00
BO DEANS	December 30, 2016	Pantages	$35,534.50
ART GARFUNKEL	January 12, 2017	Pantages	$63,729.00

CONCERT NAME	CONCERT DATE	CONCERT VENUE	CONCERT GROSS
KRIS KRISTOFFERSON	January 14, 2017	Pantages	$57,348.00
PATTI LABELLE	January 14, 2017	State Theatre	$78,181.00
JERRY SEINFELD	January 18, 2017	Orpheum	$651,952.00
STEVE WINWOOD	February 23, 2017	State Theatre	$149,680.50
JIM JEFFERIES	February 24, 2017	Orpheum	$113,163.50
LYLE LOVETT / HIATT	February 25, 2017	State Theatre	$124,742.50
RAIN (BEATLES)	March 11, 2017	State Theatre	$90,155.50
IL VOLO	March 20, 2017	State Theatre	$126,702.00
GEORGE THOROGOOD	March 26, 2017	State Theatre	$77,781.50
STEVE MARTIN / SHORT	May 18, 2017	Orpheum	$680,115.00
ABBA THE CONCERT	May 21, 2017	Pantages	$45,071.00
SEBASTIN MANASCALCO	May 21, 2017	State Theatre	$106,466.00
MOVE LIVE	May 28, 2017	State Theatre	$148,992.50
DIANA KRALL	June 2, 2017	State Theatre	$156,602.50
DANIEL O'DONNELL	June 4, 2017	State Theatre	$82,766.00
CELTIC WOMAN	June 13, 2017	Orpheum	$93,114.40
SETH MEYERS	June 16, 2017	State Theatre	$83,939.32
DEMETRI MARTIN	June 17, 2017	State Theatre	$58,980.50
MOODY BLUES	June 27, 2017	Orpheum	$238,161.00
TIM & ERIC	July 26, 2017	State Theatre	$60,098.50
DANCING W STARS	July 30, 2017	State Theatre	$148,672.50
TAJ MAHAL / KEB MO	September 6, 2017	State Theatre	$114,073.00
MAVERICKS	September 29, 2017	State Theatre	$104,449.00
PETER YARROW/P STOCKEY	October 7, 2017	Pantages	$50,442.00
MICHAEL McDONALD / COHN	November 2, 2017	State Theatre	$111,968.50
DAVID SEDARIS	November 5, 2017	State Theatre	$97,939.00
BRIAN SETZER ORCHESTRA	November 10, 2017	State Theatre	$122,224.50
HIP HOP NUTCRACKER	November 21, 2017	State Theatre	$165,483.00
CELTIC THUNDER	December 9, 2017	State Theatre	$109,271.00
ILLUSIONISTS	March 23, 2018	Orpheum	$349,402.60
MAX RAABE (LAST SHOW)	April 21, 2018	Pantages	$31,959.50

$394,331,896.40
GROSS

APPENDIX 2

LIVE SHOWS PRESENTED BY FRED KROHN

JANUARY 23, 1972 THROUGH APRIL 21, 2018

TOTAL GROSS: $394,331,896.40

(ALPHABETICAL ORDER)

CONCERT NAME	CONCERT DATE	CONCERT VENUE	CONCERT GROSS
101 DALMATIANS	October 13, 2009	Orpheum	$518,700.00
25TH ANNUAL . . . SPELLING BEE	November 7, 2006	State Theatre	$474,687.00
42ND STREET (BROADWAY)	October 14, 1997	Orpheum	$491,827.90
A BRONX TALE	June 2, 2009	State Theatre	$128,252.00
A CHORUS LINE	July 3, 1979	Orpheum	$835,877.50
A CHORUS LINE	September 9, 1980	Northrop	$689,482.04
A CHORUS LINE	June 15, 1982	Orpheum	$480,000.00
A CHORUS LINE	January 8, 1991	Orpheum	$276,564.00
A CHORUS LINE	September 24, 1996	State Theatre	$420,207.80
A CHORUS LINE	June 16, 2009	Orpheum	$773,639.00
A PERFECT CIRCLE	August 11, 2003	Pantages	$27,300.00
AARON CARTER	February 27, 2001	State Theatre	$46,046.00
ABBA THE CONCERT	August 3, 2013	Pantages	$36,136.00
ABBA THE CONCERT	May 21, 2017	Pantages	$45,071.00
ABBA THE MUSIC	February 6, 2010	Pantages	$55,685.00
AC/DC	April 9, 2001	Xcel Center	$615,420.00
ACME COMEDY GALA	November 4, 2001	State Theatre	$53,562.50
ADDICTED (M LUNDHOLM)	May 1, 2002	Womans Club	$2,920.00
AIDA	March 27, 2001	Orpheum	$3,216,571.75
AIN'T MISBEHAVIN'	June 10, 1980	Orpheum	$40,000.00
AIN'T MISPEHAVIN'	September 19, 1995	State Theatre	$300,000.00

CONCERT NAME	CONCERT DATE	CONCERT VENUE	CONCERT GROSS
AIN'T NOTHIN BUT . . . BLUES	October 18, 2000	Orpheum	$29,913.00
AIR SUPPLY	March 9, 1990	Orpheum	$21,000.00
AIR SUPPLY	July 26, 1991	Orpheum	$16,029.65
AIR SUPPLY	April 18, 1998	State Theatre	$56,789.50
AL GREEN	July 23, 1996	State Theatre	$51,059.00
AL GREEN	May 20, 2005	State Theatre	$100,856.50
AL JARREAU	October 9, 1977	O'Shaughnessy	$10,999.00
AL JARREAU	November 24, 1978	Orpheum	$18,716.00
AL JARREAU	May 22, 1982	Northrop	$45,000.00
AL JARREAU	November 16, 2011	Pantages	$39,271.00
ALABAMA	January 3, 1992	Orpheum	$147,448.00
ALAN PARSONS	August 3, 1995	Orpheum	$68,512.50
ALICE COOPER	July 14, 2013	State Theatre	$174,648.50
ALICE COOPER	December 6, 2015	State Theatre	$103,031.00
ALL-4-ONE	August 7, 1994	State Theatre	$24,013.00
ALL-4-ONE	October 22, 1995	State Theatre	$18,725.00
ALLMAN BROTHERS	July 24, 1971	Midway Stad	$175,000.00
ALTAR BOYZ	December 19, 2006	Pantages	$199,762.25
ALVIN & CHIPMUNKS	December 3, 1991	Orpheum	$4,180.00
AMAZING RHYTHM ACES	July 10, 1977	O'Shaughnessy	$4,282.00
AMERICA	February 6, 1973	Northrop	$12,500.00
AMERICA'S TEST KITCHEN	November 4, 2015	Pantages	$96,128.00
AMY SCHUMER	March 27, 2014	Orpheum	$91,809.00
ANDRAE CROUCH	August 26, 1979	Orpheum	$9,620.68
ANDREAS VOLLENWEIDER	October 13, 1989	Orpheum	$23,000.00
ANDREAS VOLLENWEIDER	March 16, 1994	State Theatre	$25,414.50
ANDREW DICE CLAY	May 26, 1993	State Theatre	$53,741.00
ANDY WILLIAMS	November 27, 1989	Orpheum	$107,325.00
ANENUE Q	January 6, 2008	Orpheum	$1,141,158.00
ANITA BAKER	January 2, 2004	Orpheum	$165,543.00
ANITA BAKER	December 8, 2006	Orpheum	$91,554.00
ANNE MURRAY	March 8, 1974	O'Shaughnessy	$8,292.98
ANNE MURRAY	August 16, 1974	Duluth Aud	$11,720.00

CONCERT NAME	CONCERT DATE	CONCERT VENUE	CONCERT GROSS
ANNE MURRAY	August 17, 1974	O'Shaughnessy	$15,488.00
ANNE MURRAY	March 21, 1975	Northrop	$14,683.00
ANNE MURRAY	March 22, 1975	Duluth Aud	$10,158.00
ANNE MURRAY	May 17, 1990	Orpheum	$67,000.00
ANNE MURRAY	May 9, 1992	State Theatre	$56,265.00
ANNE MURRAY	February 24, 1996	State Theatre	$48,121.00
ANNIE	October 16, 1980	Orpheum	$157,449.00
ANNIE	April 10, 1992	Orpheum	$166,590.00
ANNIE	December 1, 1998	Orpheum	$482,612.00
ANNIE	March 21, 2006	Orpheum	$919,483.00
ANNIE	February 12, 2009	Orpheum	$93,000.00
ANNIE GET YOUR GUN	September 5, 2000	Orpheum	$525,804.00
ANNIE GRIFFITHS BELT (NG)	May 8, 2008	State Theatre	$17,000.00
ANTHONY BOURDAIN	April 23, 2010	State Theatre	$88,465.85
ANTHONY BOURDAIN	May 11, 2013	State Theatre	$136,175.00
ANTHONY BOURDAIN	July 24, 2015	State Theatre	$167,482.02
AQUA TEEN	April 29, 2010	Pantages	$6,966.50
ARLECCHINO (GUTHRIE)	November 9, 2005	Pantages	$12,272.50
ARMISTEAD MAUPIN	June 13, 2008	State Theatre	$12,088.50
ART (BROADWAY)	February 15, 2000	State Theatre	$389,227.20
ART GARFUNKEL	January 12, 2017	Pantages	$63,729.00
ARTHUR (BROADWAY)	November 19, 1999	Orpheum	$242,595.00
ASPECTS OF LOVE	May 31, 1993	State Theatre	$700,280.90
AUDIO ADRENALINE	February 1, 1998	Orpheum	$34,239.00
AUSSIE PINK FLOYD	November 8, 2005	Orpheum	$140,213.00
AUSSIE PINK FLOYD	November 25, 2006	Orpheum	$148,565.00
AUSSIE PINK FLOYD	November 14, 2008	State Theatre	$96,668.50
AUSSIE PINK FLOYD	October 2, 2009	State Theatre	$110,000.00
AUSSIE PINK FLOYD	October 20, 2011	Orpheum	$125,860.50
AUSSIE PINK FLOYD	November 18, 2012	Orpheum	$100,899.00
AUSSIE PINK FLOYD	September 30, 2014	Orpheum	$84,554.50
AUSSIE PINK FLOYD	September 6, 2016	State Theatre	$82,130.00
AVALON	October 27, 2001	Orpheum	$20,000.00

CONCERT NAME	CONCERT DATE	CONCERT VENUE	CONCERT GROSS
AWESOME 80S PROM	July 7, 2006	Henn Stages	$93,659.00
BACK STREET BOYS	October 9, 1999	Target Center	$640,077.00
BACK STREET BOYS	February 17, 2001	Target Center	$787,728.50
BACK STREET BOYS	September 23, 2001	Target Center	$654,946.00
BAND (THE BAND)	June 26, 1971	Midway Stad	$174,300.00
BARENAKED LADIES	August 21, 2001	Xcel Center	$322,394.00
BARNUM'S KALEIDOSCAPE	August 10, 1999	MOA Lot	$896,270.00
BARRY MANILOW	November 29, 1991	State Theatre	$178,652.50
BARRY MANILOW	May 22, 1997	Northrop	$131,290.00
BARRY MANILOW	February 28, 2002	Orpheum	$319,179.50
BARRY WHITE	July 25, 1995	Orpheum	$74,220.50
BARRYMORE	January 28, 1997	State Theatre	$241,823.60
BASIA / SPYRO GYRA	September 11, 1994	Orpheum	$47,875.00
BAUHAUS	August 26, 1998	State Theatre	$68,598.50
BB KING	November 12, 2010	State Theatre	$114,768.50
BB KING	May 18, 2012	State Theatre	$121,615.00
BB KING / BUDDY GUY	February 20, 2010	Orpheum	$196,870.00
BEAR IN BIG BLUE HOUSE	September 13, 2000	State Theatre	$154,209.00
BEAR IN THE B. BLUE HOUSE	May 1, 2003	State Theatre	$107,326.50
BEATLEMANIA	July 30, 1979	Orpheum	$900,000.00
BEAUTY AND THE BEAST	November 7, 1995	Orpheum	$8,565,473.00
BEAUTY AND THE BEAST	November 1, 2000	Orpheum	$1,638,792.50
BELA FLECK	September 12, 1999	State Theatre	$37,795.00
BELA FLECK	September 12, 1999	State Theatre	$37,795.00
BELLE & SEBASTIAN	October 31, 2003	Fitzgerald	$26,274.00
BELLYDANCE SUPERSTARS	November 5, 2006	Pantages	$12,608.00
BERNIE MAC	February 16, 1996	Orpheum	$56,143.00
BERNIE MAC	December 12, 1997	Orpheum	$45,523.50
BERNIE MAC	July 23, 1999	State Theatre	$61,509.00
BEST LITTLE WHOREHOUSE	August 19, 1980	Orpheum	$250,000.00
BEST LITTLE WHOREHOUSE	April 9, 2002	Orpheum	$828,100.20
BIG APPLE CIRCUS	April 27, 2000	State Theatre	$12,576.75
BIG BAD VOODOO DADDY	December 6, 2009	Pantages	$27,738.00

CONCERT NAME	CONCERT DATE	CONCERT VENUE	CONCERT GROSS
BIG BAD VOODOO DADDY	December 7, 2014	Pantages	$32,875.50
BIG HEAD TODD	November 5, 1994	Orpheum	$49,720.00
BIG HEAD TODD	November 1, 1997	Orpheum	$41,827.50
BIG WU	December 31, 2000	State Theatre	$47,794.00
BIG WU	November 2, 2002	State Theatre	$20,951.00
BILL BURR	October 28, 2015	Orpheum	$195,615.00
BILL COSBY	October 13, 1974	O'Shaughnessy	$7,564.00
BILL COSBY	August 7, 1993	State Theatre	$102,650.75
BILL COSBY	March 10, 2001	State Theatre	$192,974.50
BILL COSBY	September 20, 2003	State Theatre	$204,960.00
BILL COSBY	October 23, 2005	State Theatre	$82,032.50
BILL ENGVALL	November 5, 2005	Orpheum	$60,957.00
BILL GAITHER TRIO	July 29, 1989	Orpheum	$37,000.00
BILL MAHER	June 28, 2003	Pantages	$23,785.00
BILL MAHER	May 30, 2014	State Theatre	$149,409.00
BILL MAHER	October 8, 2016	State Theatre	$156,265.50
BILLY COLLINS	November 1, 2013	Pantages	$19,927.50
BILLY SQUIRE	June 23, 1991	Orpheum	$23,000.00
BJ THOMAS	July 27, 2013	Pantages	$12,080.50
BJORN AGAIN (ABBA)	May 10, 2002	State Theatre	$76,132.50
BLACK CROWES	July 24, 1992	Orpheum	$152,280.00
BLACK CROWES	January 12, 1999	State Theatre	$56,115.50
BLACK CROWES	October 7, 2001	Orpheum	$73,062.50
BLACK NATIVITY	December 12, 2002	Pantages	$324,495.50
BLACK SABBATH	October 31, 1992	Orpheum	$55,341.00
BLACKSTONE (MAGICIAN)	July 30, 1989	Orpheum	$61,000.00
BLAST (BROADWAY)	April 23, 2002	Orpheum	$655,649.00
BLENDERS	December 9, 1999	State Theatre	$27,842.50
BLENDERS	December 21, 2000	State Theatre	$41,765.00
BLENDERS	December 4, 2002	State Theatre	$41,665.50
BLENDERS	December 5, 2003	Pantages	$65,016.00
BLENDERS	December 9, 2005	Pantages	$92,859.25
BLENDERS	December 8, 2006	Pantages	$95,993.50

CONCERT NAME	CONCERT DATE	CONCERT VENUE	CONCERT GROSS
BLENDERS	December 17, 2006	Pantages	$93,031.50
BLENDERS	December 7, 2007	Pantages	$108,217.50
BLENDERS	December 4, 2008	Pantages	$95,000.00
BLENDERS	December 11, 2009	Pantages	$91,000.00
BLENDERS	December 3, 2010	Pantages	$85,201.75
BLENDERS	December 9, 2011	Pantages	$84,889.00
BLENDERS	December 14, 2012	Pantages	$83,724.00
BLENDERS	December 12, 2013	Pantages	$101,604.00
BLENDERS	December 12, 2014	Pantages	$91,440.50
BLENDERS	December 11, 2015	Pantages	$96,282.50
BLOOD BROTHERS	October 25, 1994	Orpheum	$470,541.70
BLUES CLUES	May 10, 2000	Orpheum	$377,213.50
BLUES CLUES	March 26, 2002	State Theatre	$372,650.50
BLUES TRAVELER	May 14, 1994	State Theatre	$37,888.00
BO DEANS	September 21, 1989	Orpheum	$49,000.00
BO DEANS	May 2, 1991	Orpheum	$51,000.00
BO DEANS	November 25, 1994	Orpheum	$57,350.00
BO DEANS	November 22, 2000	Orpheum	$67,358.00
BO DEANS	December 30, 2016	Pantages	$35,534.50
BOB DYLAN	August 27, 1992	Orpheum	$360,938.00
BOB GOLDTHWAIT	September 28, 1989	Orpheum	$27,000.00
BOB NEWHART	November 22, 2013	State Theatre	$72,720.00
BOB WEIR	May 17, 1991	Orpheum	$59,085.00
BOBBY CALDWELL	December 31, 1997	State Theatre	$116,748.50
BOBBY CALDWELL	November 18, 2000	State Theatre	$30,897.50
BOBBY CALDWELL	September 19, 2015	Pantages	$23,779.00
BONNIE RAITT	May 10, 1989	Orpheum	$87,000.00
BONNIE RAITT	May 29, 1998	Orpheum	$160,410.00
BORGE OUSLAND (NG)	March 10, 2005	State Theatre	$13,056.25
BOYS CHOIR OF HARLEM	October 7, 2001	State Theatre	$51,823.50
BOZ SCAGGS	September 24, 2009	State Theatre	$97,465.50
BOZ SCAGGS	February 12, 2011	State Theatre	$100,499.00
BOZ SCAGGS	April 11, 2013	State Theatre	$107,310.00

CONCERT NAME	CONCERT DATE	CONCERT VENUE	CONCERT GROSS
BOZ SCAGGS	September 30, 2014	State Theatre	$103,837.50
BOZ SCAGGS	July 18, 2015	State Theatre	$88,565.00
BRADY BARR (NG)	March 20, 2008	State Theatre	$21,000.00
BRENDA WEILER & BAND	September 15, 2001	Womans Club	$1,920.00
BRETT BUTLER (COMIC)	June 17, 1995	State Theatre	$28,297.50
BRETT DENNEN	November 17, 2009	Pantages	$12,284.00
BRETT DENNEN	June 5, 2011	Pantages	$16,380.00
BRIAN MCKNIGHT	March 4, 2000	Orpheum	$79,455.00
BRIAN MCKNIGHT	January 26, 2002	State Theatre	$72,240.00
BRIAN SETZER ORCHESTRA	November 17, 2012	Orpheum	$124,930.65
BRIAN SETZER ORCHESTRA	November 15, 2013	Orpheum	$114,724.50
BRIAN SETZER ORCHESTRA	November 14, 2014	Orpheum	$119,229.00
BRIAN SETZER ORCHESTRA	November 14, 2015	Orpheum	$124,544.50
BRIAN SETZER ORCHESTRA	November 10, 2017	State Theatre	$122,224.50
BRIGHT EYES	September 7, 2001	Womans Club	$4,762.50
BRIGHT EYES	May 10, 2002	Womans Club	$6,754.50
BRIGHT EYES	February 20, 2004	Pantages	$15,236.50
BRIGHT EYES	January 15, 2005	State Theatre	$41,420.00
BRITISH INVASION	March 8, 2005	Pantages	$22,819.00
BRITISH ROCK SYMPHONY	July 6, 1998	State Theatre	$33,390.00
BROTHERS FRANTZICH	December 16, 2001	Womans Club	$1,185.00
BROTHERS FRANTZICH	May 31, 2002	Womans Club	$2,310.00
BRUCE COCKBURN	March 14, 1989	Orpheum	$21,000.00
BRUCE COCKBURN	November 7, 1991	Orpheum	$26,280.00
BRUCE COCKBURN	May 3, 1994	State Theatre	$26,649.00
BRUCE HORNSBY	July 21, 1991	Orpheum	$41,867.50
BRUCE HORNSBY	November 13, 1993	State Theatre	$43,807.50
BRYAN ADAMS	March 31, 2000	State Theatre	$71,517.00
BRYAN FERRY	November 11, 1994	Orpheum	$50,208.00
BUDDY (BROADWAY)	May 28, 2002	State Theatre	$119,537.75
BUDDY GUY	October 16, 2010	State Theatre	$69,995.50
BUDDY GUY	March 2, 2012	State Theatre	$83,300.00
BUDDY GUY	September 7, 2014	State Theatre	$70,535.00

CONCERT NAME	CONCERT DATE	CONCERT VENUE	CONCERT GROSS
BUDDY GUY / JONNY LANG	March 10, 2013	State Theatre	$125,494.50
BUNNY WAILER	April 20, 1989	Orpheum	$12,000.00
BURN THE FLOOR	October 20, 2001	Orpheum	$64,638.50
BURT REYNOLDS	June 5, 1991	Orpheum	$49,220.00
BUTTERFIELD BLUES BAND	June 26, 1971	Midway Stad	SEE THE BAND
C ISAAK / WALLFLOWERS	October 20, 1995	State Theatre	$65,616.50
CAB CALLOWAY	April 28, 1990	Orpheum	$24,000.00
CABARET	October 12, 1999	State Theatre	$1,462,470.15
CAKE BOSS	November 15, 2011	Orpheum	$45,014.30
CAMELOT	June 28, 1994	Orpheum	$414,324.20
CANDLEBOX	October 18, 1994	State Theatre	$36,702.00
CARE BEARS	March 7, 2005	Orpheum	$136,923.50
CARMINA BURANA	March 2, 2006	Pantages	$64,796.00
CAROL BURNETT	April 14, 2010	State Theatre	$117,783.40
CAROL BURNETT	May 17, 2013	State Theatre	$129,650.50
CAROL CHANNING	October 16, 2004	Pantages	$37,500.00
CAROLE KING	November 16, 1975	Northrop	$28,000.00
CAROLE KING	February 1, 1976	Northrop	$41,538.14
CAT POWER	April 18, 2003	Pantages	$13,140.00
CATS	May 19, 1992	State Theatre	$915,008.00
CATS	February 1, 1994	State Theatre	$664,954.10
CATS	May 11, 1996	State Theatre	$812,284.54
CATS	November 18, 1997	Orpheum	$755,431.50
CATS	March 9, 1999	State Theatre	$624,764.80
CATS	March 4, 2002	Orpheum	$912,004.50
CATS	May 30, 2006	Orpheum	$482,166.75
CEDRIC THE ENTERTAINER	March 24, 1996	State Theatre	$27,450.00
CELIA CRUZ	October 8, 1999	State Theatre	$26,453.50
CELTIC THUNDER	October 29, 2009	State Theatre	$89,000.00
CELTIC THUNDER	October 24, 2010	State Theatre	$104,802.00
CELTIC THUNDER	November 28, 2014	State Theatre	$106,614.00
CELTIC THUNDER	September 30, 2016	State Theatre	$99,347.00
CELTIC THUNDER	December 9, 2017	State Theatre	$109,271.00

CONCERT NAME	CONCERT DATE	CONCERT VENUE	CONCERT GROSS
CELTIC WOMAN	October 22, 2005	Orpheum	$204,643.39
CELTIC WOMAN	April 5, 2006	Orpheum	$165,754.00
CELTIC WOMAN	April 17, 2007	Orpheum	$252,719.50
CELTIC WOMAN	April 22, 2011	State Theatre	$185,075.00
CELTIC WOMAN	April 13, 2013	Orpheum	$149,138.05
CELTIC WOMAN	June 13, 2017	Orpheum	$93,114.40
CESARIA EVORA	November 4, 2003	Pantages	$27,441.50
CHEAP TRICK	January 3, 1989	Orpheum	$51,000.00
CHEAP TRICK	April 8, 2003	State Theatre	$22,339.50
CHER	August 4, 1999	Target Center	$721,656.25
CHICAGO	July 18, 1993	State Theatre	$77,030.00
CHICAGO	March 10, 1998	Orpheum	$1,753,619.55
CHICAGO	April 27, 2013	State Theatre	$152,960.50
CHICAGO	April 26, 2014	State Theatre	$165,462.00
CHICAGO	May 19, 2015	State Theatre	$155,214.00
CHIEFTAINS	March 20, 1996	Orpheum	$69,730.50
CHIEFTAINS	April 26, 1997	State Theatre	$70,262.05
CHRIS CORNELL	July 16, 2007	Orpheum	$49,408.00
CHRIS ISAAK	August 29, 1993	State Theatre	$140,105.00
CHRIS ISAAK	December 30, 1995	State Theatre	$65,251.00
CHRIS ISAAK	October 15, 1996	State Theatre	$48,645.50
CHRIS ISAAK	November 3, 1998	State Theatre	$70,041.50
CHRIS ISAAK	August 9, 2003	Orpheum	$108,172.50
CHRIS ISAAK	August 5, 2006	State Theatre	$103,947.50
CHRIS ISAAK	August 13, 2011	State Theatre	$66,721.00
CHRIS ISAAK	November 27, 2012	State Theatre	$68,069.00
CHRIS ISAAK	July 19, 2016	Pantages	$61,440.00
CHRIS MANN	June 4, 2013	The Dakota	$6,647.00
CHRIS ROCK	May 4, 1997	Orpheum	$61,560.00
CINDERELLA	February 13, 2001	State Theatre	$735,724.75
CIRQUE DREAMS	October 6, 2006	State Theatre	$144,024.75
CIRQUE DU SOLEIL	August 17, 2000	Circus Tent	$1,728,000.00
CIVIL WAR	March 13, 2001	State Theatre	$422,065.05

CONCERT NAME	CONCERT DATE	CONCERT VENUE	CONCERT GROSS
CLAY AIKEN	March 5, 2011	State Theatre	$26,984.50
COCTEAU TWINS	November 28, 1990	Orpheum	$23,000.00
COEN BROS BLUEGRASS	February 9, 2002	State Theatre	$115,785.00
COLIN RAYE	December 11, 1999	Orpheum	$73,493.25
COLORS OF CHRISTMAS	December 7, 2003	State Theatre	$59,958.50
CONTINENTAL DRIFTERS	June 14, 2000	400 Bar	$360.00
CONWAY T /GEO JONES	March 29, 1992	Orpheum	$73,947.75
COUNTING CROWS	July 2, 1994	State Theatre	$63,379.50
COUNTING CROWS	November 27, 1999	Orpheum	$58,000.00
COUNTING CROWS	January 18, 2000	Orpheum	$63,440.00
COWBOY JUNKIES	September 2, 1998	State Theatre	$33,730.00
CRANBERRIES	November 16, 1994	Orpheum	$47,700.00
CRASH TEST DUMMIES	April 26, 1992	Orpheum	$37,814.00
CRASH TEST DUMMIES	December 31, 1993	State Theatre	$45,600.50
CROSBY STILLS & NASH	August 27, 1992	Orpheum	$171,732.00
CROSBY STILLS & NASH	March 9, 1994	St Paul CC	$350,000.00
CROSBY STILLS & NASH	April 26, 1997	Orpheum	$88,689.00
CROSBY STILLS & NASH	July 11, 2008	Orpheum	$183,988.50
CROSBY STILLS & NASH	August 6, 2012	Orpheum	$196,747.50
CROSBY STILLS NASH YOUNG	February 26, 2000	Target Center	$1,050,617.50
CROW	June 26, 1971	Midway Stad	SEE THE BAND
CROWDED HOUSE	September 18, 1991	Orpheum	$34,835.50
CRYSTAL GAYLE	November 19, 1977	O'Shaughnessy	$12,359.00
CRYSTAL GAYLE	July 27, 1979	Orpheum	$21,193.00
CULT	March 14, 1990	Orpheum	$68,000.00
D ATTELL / EMO PHILIPS	November 2, 2003	Orpheum	$46,840.00
D.L. HUGHLEY	May 6, 2000	Orpheum	$27,571.00
D'ANGELO	August 16, 2000	Orpheum	$82,906.50
DAME EDNA	October 24, 2000	State Theatre	$846,807.67
DAME EDNA (A NIGHT WITH)	November 5, 2002	State Theatre	$236,768.00
DAN FOGELBERG	October 21, 1997	Orpheum	$43,165.00
DAN SAVAGE	June 22, 2012	Pantages	$34,722.50
DAN WILSON	December 13, 2008	Pantages	$21,794.00

CONCERT NAME	CONCERT DATE	CONCERT VENUE	CONCERT GROSS
DAN WILSON / M DOUGHTY	April 30, 2003	Womans Club	$10,978.50
DANCING HENRY 5	February 17, 2005	Pantages	$3,682.00
DANCING W STARS	July 30, 2017	State Theatre	$148,672.50
DANIEL O'DONNELL	June 4, 2017	State Theatre	$82,766.00
DANIEL POWTER	July 27, 2006	Pantages	$12,894.50
DATING IT!	February 12, 2005	Henn Stages	$5,175.00
DAVE ATTELL (ACME COM)	November 3, 2002	State Theatre	$34,050.00
DAVE BRUBECK (RECORD)	May 7, 1979	Orpheum	$-
DAVE KOZ ET AL	December 6, 1997	State Theatre	$30,334.00
DAVE MATTHEWS BAND	December 3, 2000	Target Center	$773,082.00
DAVE PIRNER	July 28, 2002	Womans Club	$6,285.00
DAVID BYRNE	September 4, 1992	Orpheum	$60,225.00
DAVID BYRNE	August 23, 1997	State Theatre	$26,150.00
DAVID COPPERFIELD	December 11, 1988	Orpheum	$160,000.00
DAVID COPPERFIELD	May 19, 1990	Orpheum	$155,025.00
DAVID COPPERFIELD	December 17, 1993	Orpheum	$370,950.50
DAVID COPPERFIELD	November 3, 1995	State Theatre	$459,706.35
DAVID COPPERFIELD	October 11, 1996	State Theatre	$294,680.70
DAVID COPPERFIELD	March 31, 2000	Orpheum	$359,373.10
DAVID COPPERFIELD	April 26, 2002	State Theatre	$395,290.00
DAVID COPPERFIELD	March 29, 2003	State Theatre	$295,319.00
DAVID COPPERFIELD	April 1, 2003	Duluth Aud	$96,500.00
DAVID COPPERFIELD	May 6, 2006	State Theatre	$246,938.00
DAVID CROSBY	March 20, 1999	State Theatre	$9,810.00
DAVID GARRETT	March 12, 2014	State Theatre	$43,421.00
DAVID GRAY	August 9, 2005	State Theatre	$62,295.00
DAVID LANZ	November 4, 1993	State Theatre	$22,885.50
DAVID LANZ	June 10, 2000	Womans Club	$5,415.00
DAVID MCCULLOUGH	October 2, 2008	State Theatre	$49,661.25
DAVID SANBORN	August 8, 1991	Orpheum	$41,341.50
DAVID SANBORN	November 19, 1992	Orpheum	$26,578.00
DAVID SANBORN	January 8, 2004	Pantages	$22,656.00
DAVID SEDARIS	April 24, 2001	State Theatre	$52,360.00

CONCERT NAME	CONCERT DATE	CONCERT VENUE	CONCERT GROSS
DAVID SEDARIS	April 5, 2003	State Theatre	$60,772.00
DAVID SEDARIS	October 21, 2006	State Theatre	$79,866.50
DAVID SEDARIS	October 15, 2007	State Theatre	$78,167.50
DAVID SEDARIS	October 19, 2008	State Theatre	$78,494.25
DAVID SEDARIS	October 14, 2009	State Theatre	$77,677.00
DAVID SEDARIS	October 21, 2010	State Theatre	$77,939.50
DAVID SEDARIS	November 13, 2011	State Theatre	$79,818.50
DAVID SEDARIS	November 10, 2012	State Theatre	$82,270.00
DAVID SEDARIS	November 3, 2013	State Theatre	$71,045.00
DAVID SEDARIS	October 29, 2014	State Theatre	$77,357.00
DAVID SEDARIS	November 1, 2015	State Theatre	$80,669.74
DAVID SEDARIS	October 28, 2016	State Theatre	$85,673.25
DAVID SEDARIS	November 5, 2017	State Theatre	$97,939.00
DAVID WILCOX	March 27, 1993	State Theatre	$29,861.50
DAVID WILCOX	April 9, 1994	State Theatre	$29,118.00
DEAD CAN DANCE	July 26, 1996	Orpheum	$40,704.00
DEF COMEDY JAM	June 19, 1992	Orpheum	$24,125.00
DEF COMEDY JAM	August 23, 1992	State Theatre	$18,007.50
DEF COMEDY JAM	December 3, 1994	State Theatre	$47,179.50
DEF COMEDY JAM	June 25, 1995	State Theatre	$32,805.00
DEF POETRY JAM	February 6, 2004	State Theatre	$48,110.00
DEFENDING THE CAVEMAN	September 16, 1997	State Theatre	$817,675.17
DEFENDING THE CAVEMAN	November 10, 1998	State Theatre	$895,155.00
DEFENDING THE CAVEMAN	October 17, 2001	State Theatre	$925,662.28
DEFENDING THE CAVEMAN	October 5, 2005	Henn Stages	$61,000.00
DEL AMITRI	April 9, 1996	Orpheum	$36,366.00
DELANEY & BONNIE	June 26, 1971	Midway Stad	SEE THE BAND
DELANEY & BONNIE	February 22, 1972	O'Shaughnessy	$5,115.92
DEMETRI MARTIN	February 7, 2015	State Theatre	$61,110.00
DEMETRI MARTIN	June 17, 2017	State Theatre	$58,980.50
DENNIS DEYOUNG	September 6, 2014	Pantages	$28,518.50
DENNIS LEARY	June 15, 2010	State Theatre	$95,667.50
DENNIS MILLER	April 28, 1991	Orpheum	$43,683.00

CONCERT NAME	CONCERT DATE	CONCERT VENUE	CONCERT GROSS
DENNIS MILLER - M HEDBERG	September 16, 1998	State Theatre	$50,945.00
DESTINY'S CHILD	July 30, 2001	Target Center	$317,332.00
DIAL M FOR MURDER	January 23, 1996	State Theatre	$423,838.25
DIANA KRALL	May 3, 2000	State Theatre	$58,337.50
DIANA KRALL	March 15, 2002	State Theatre	$151,373.00
DIANA KRALL	August 7, 2015	State Theatre	$166,415.00
DIANA KRALL	June 2, 2017	State Theatre	$156,602.50
DIANA ROSS	August 12, 1991	Orpheum	$86,140.00
DIANA ROSS	July 19, 2000	Target Center	$276,751.50
DIANA ROSS	August 28, 2013	Orpheum	$199,041.00
DIANNE REEVES	May 20, 2000	Womans Club	$4,088.00
DICK WHITBECK (MOTOWN)	June 15, 1996	State Theatre	$11,989.50
DIXIE CHICKS	November 13, 2000	Xcel Center	$1,080,000.00
DOLLY PARTON	August 15, 1977	O'Shaughnessy	$12,260.00
DOLLY PARTON	August 17, 1977	Duluth Aud	$14,459.50
DOLLY PARTON	August 19, 1977	S Bend, Ind	$12,112.00
DOLLY PARTON	October 26, 1977	Fargo Aud	$15,856.50
DOLLY PARTON	October 27, 1977	Rochester Aud	$17,249.00
DOLLY PARTON	June 27, 1978	Duluth Aud	$19,066.00
DONNA SUMMER	August 11, 1995	Orpheum	$45,237.50
DONNY OSMOND	May 18, 2001	State Theatre	$231,427.00
DORA THE EXPLORER	November 12, 2003	State Theatre	$386,811.50
DORA THE EXPLORER	May 15, 2009	State Theatre	$399,000.00
DORA'S PIRATE ADVEN	May 11, 2005	State Theatre	$410,635.75
DOROTHY HAMILL NUT ICE	December 4, 1989	Orpheum	$643,000.00
DOROTHY HAMILL NUT ICE	December 6, 1990	Orpheum	$420,000.00
DOROTHY THE DINOSAUR	June 24, 2006	State Theatre	$28,322.00
DOUBT	March 4, 2007	State Theatre	$315,364.00
DOUG HENNING MAGIC	June 22, 1979	Orpheum	$90,646.00
DRACULA (BALLET)	October 25, 2006	State Theatre	$64,668.00
DREAMGIRLS	January 17, 2010	Orpheum	$694,743.00
DUELING BANJOS	May 5, 1973	O'Shaughnessy	$3,401.91
DURAN DURAN	March 17, 1989	Orpheum	$65,000.00

CONCERT NAME	CONCERT DATE	CONCERT VENUE	CONCERT GROSS
DWIGHT YOAKAM	November 13, 2001	State Theatre	$31,247.00
EARTH WIND & FIRE	November 8, 1994	Orpheum	$61,451.50
EARTH WIND AND FIRE	June 18, 2003	Orpheum	$103,429.00
ED SHEERAN	September 26, 2012	State Theatre	$44,955.50
EDDIE IZZARD	September 26, 2003	Pantages	$95,470.00
EDIE BRICKELL	May 3, 1989	Orpheum	$36,000.00
EDIE BRICKELL	April 9, 1991	Orpheum	$45,454.50
EELS	June 21, 2005	Pantages	$15,427.50
EELS	April 7, 2008	Pantages	$15,465.00
ELAINE STRITCH AT LIBERTY	June 4, 2003	State Theatre	$92,255.00
ELAYNE BOOSLER	June 23, 1990	Orpheum	$17,000.00
ELAYNE BOOSLER	December 7, 1991	Orpheum	$19,840.00
ELDAR	October 29, 2008	Dakota	$1,622.00
ELECTRIC LIGHT ORCHESTRA	July 29, 1997	State Theatre	$10,938.50
ELIZABETH LONSDORF (NG)	April 14, 2005	State Theatre	$4,818.50
ELLA FITZGERALD	September 13, 1974	O'Shaughnessy	$16,512.00
ELLA FITZGERALD / OSCAR P	August 21, 1989	Northrop	$57,000.00
ELLEN DEGENERES	May 13, 1994	State Theatre	$43,827.00
ELLEN DEGENERES	May 17, 2002	State Theatre	$67,597.50
ELLEN DEGENERES	April 11, 2003	State Theatre	$73,721.50
ELO PART II	July 29, 1997	State Theatre	$10,938.50
ELTON JOHN / BILLY JOEL	May 15, 2001	Target Center	$3,608,470.72
ELVIS COSTELLO	August 18, 1996	Orpheum	$71,780.00
ELVIS COSTELLO	June 13, 1999	State Theatre	$81,240.00
ELVIS COSTELLO	June 29, 2011	State Theatre	$97,502.00
EMMANUEL'S GIFT (CORP)	July 14, 2005	Pantages	$2,818.00
EMMY LOU HARRIS/GOODMN	April 21, 1979	Orpheum	$22,030.00
ENRIQUE IGLESIAS	March 27, 2002	Orpheum	$106,468.00
ERASURE	February 26, 1990	Orpheum	$31,000.00
ERIC IDLE	June 9, 2000	Orpheum	$84,765.00
ERIC IDLE	June 10, 2000	Madison, WI	$55,178.00
ERIC IDLE	November 18, 2003	Madison, WI	$12,320.00
ERIC IDLE	November 19, 2003	Pantages	$33,000.00

CONCERT NAME	CONCERT DATE	CONCERT VENUE	CONCERT GROSS
ERYKAH BADU	August 12, 2001	Orpheum	$93,367.50
ETTA JAMES	June 29, 1990	Orpheum	$29,000.00
ETTA JAMES	March 26, 1993	State Theatre	$26,942.50
EVERLY BROS	August 5, 1989	Orpheum	$57,000.00
EVERLY BROS/C PERKINS	August 3, 1990	Orpheum	$89,000.00
EVITA	February 16, 1993	State Theatre	$1,068,578.15
EVITA	April 5, 1994	State Theatre	$319,658.00
EVITA	June 22, 1999	Orpheum	$492,685.40
EXCELSIOR CHOIR / A NESBY	December 21, 2003	Pantages	$7,855.00
EXONERATED	April 6, 2004	State Theatre	$265,000.00
EXPERIENCE HENDRIX	March 17, 2010	Orpheum	$164,845.00
EXPERIENCE HENDRIX	April 8, 2014	State Theatre	$94,584.00
FAITH HILL (DEBUT PERF.)	April 9, 1999	Orpheum	$84,015.00
FAME (BROADWAY)	February 11, 1999	State Theatre	$547,599.00
FAME (BROADWAY)	November 7, 2003	Orpheum	$224,256.00
FEIST	June 20, 2007	Pantages	$23,936.50
FIDDLER ON THE ROOF	January 30, 2002	Orpheum	$1,684,768.55
FIDDLER ON THE ROOF	February 24, 2009	Orpheum	$1,029,884.00
FIDDLER ROOF(TOPOL)	February 20, 1990	Orpheum	$532,624.00
FIVE GUYS NAMED MOE	April 19, 1994	State Theatre	$416,547.00
FLASH CADILLAC	December 19, 1996	State Theatre	$27,113.26
FLATLANDERS	March 3, 2000	State Theatre	$11,315.00
FLIGHT OF CONCHORDS	May 13, 2008	Orpheum	$82,420.00
FLORENCE & THE MACHINE	April 27, 2012	State Theatre	$98,961.00
FOOTLOOSE	June 1, 1999	Orpheum	$631,684.70
FOREIGNER	November 21, 2003	Pantages	$44,569.40
FOREVER TANGO	June 15, 1998	State Theatre	$167,510.25
FOSSE	April 12, 2000	Orpheum	$1,317,641.95
FOXWORTHY / ENGVALL	January 22, 2000	Orpheum	$199,983.00
FRAN LEBOWITZ	October 14, 2011	Pantages	$9,241.00
FRANCES MAYES	November 11, 2001	State Theatre	$8,965.50
FRANK CALIENDO	April 2, 2005	Orpheum	$100,772.00
FRANKIE VALLI	October 22, 2008	Orpheum	$209,795.50

CONCERT NAME	CONCERT DATE	CONCERT VENUE	CONCERT GROSS
FRANKIE VALLI	September 22, 2012	State Theatre	$113,483.50
FRED PENNER	May 18, 1991	Orpheum	$3,755.50
FREDDIE JACKSON	December 18, 1992	Orpheum	$34,260.00
FRESH BEAT BAND	November 18, 2014	State Theatre	$29,394.68
FROST/NIXON	January 6, 2009	State Theatre	$292,317.00
FULLY COMMITTED	July 24, 2003	Pantages	$80,060.00
FUNK ALL STARS	June 29, 2000	Orpheum	$20,355.00
FUNNIEST MOM	June 11, 2005	Henn Stages	$4,230.00
FUNNY GIRL	October 22, 1996	State Theatre	$629,629.43
FUTURE BIBLE HEROS	November 3, 2002	Womans Club	$2,491.00
GAITHER VOCAL BAND	April 12, 2013	Orpheum	$87,051.50
GALLAGHER	November 9, 1990	Orpheum	$129,000.00
GALLAGHER	November 12, 1992	Orpheum	$114,931.00
GALLAGHER	March 26, 1994	Northrop	$84,720.50
GARBAGE	November 27, 1998	Orpheum	$44,920.00
GATO BARBIERI	October 14, 1977	O'Shaughnessy	$8,791.00
GEORGE BENSON	July 15, 1981	Northrop	$108,000.00
GEORGE BENSON	October 5, 1993	State Theatre	$34,952.50
GEORGE CARLIN	June 2, 1990	Orpheum	$31,000.00
GEORGE CARLIN	July 26, 1992	State Theatre	$26,851.50
GEORGE CARLIN	June 2, 1995	State Theatre	$22,140.00
GEORGE CARLIN	October 11, 2003	Orpheum	$136,437.00
GEORGE THOROGOOD	April 28, 1991	Orpheum	$98,300.00
GEORGE THOROGOOD	March 26, 2017	State Theatre	$77,781.50
GEORGE WINSTON	June 6, 1992	State Theatre	$30,507.00
GHOST BRO. MUSICAL	October 31, 2013	State Theatre	$41,570.90
GIN GAME	January 26, 1999	State Theatre	$279,044.85
GIPSY KINGS	August 28, 1997	Northrop	$105,307.50
GIPSY KINGS	August 25, 2005	State Theatre	$120,911.50
GIPSY KINGS	July 12, 2006	State Theatre	$72,693.50
GIPSY KINGS	May 24, 2011	State Theatre	$88,032.00
GIPSY KINGS	April 28, 2012	State Theatre	$54,135.00
GLADYS KNIGHT	November 2, 1989	Orpheum	$43,000.00

CONCERT NAME	CONCERT DATE	CONCERT VENUE	CONCERT GROSS
GODSMACK	March 29, 2001	Roy Wilkins	$143,360.00
GODSMACK	August 13, 2001	Target Center	$159,630.00
GODSPELL	April 10, 2001	State Theatre	$155,044.25
GONE WITH THE WIND	November 18, 1994	State Theatre	$17,988.00
GORDON LIGHTFOOT	January 23, 1972	O'Shaughnessy	$18,668.80
GORDON LIGHTFOOT	February 11, 1973	O'Shaughnessy	$17,998.68
GORDON LIGHTFOOT	February 16, 1974	Duluth Aud	$11,516.66
GORDON LIGHTFOOT	February 17, 1974	O'Shaughnessy	$27,178.89
GORDON LIGHTFOOT	February 8, 1975	Duluth Aud	$24,101.50
GORDON LIGHTFOOT	February 9, 1975	O'Shaughnessy	$47,567.00
GORDON LIGHTFOOT	April 24, 1976	Northrop	$48,075.00
GORDON LIGHTFOOT	October 22, 1976	Duluth Aud	$30,000.50
GORDON LIGHTFOOT	April 15, 1977	Northrop	$58,922.00
GORDON LIGHTFOOT	April 17, 1977	Fargo NDSU	$22,983.50
GORDON LIGHTFOOT	March 10, 1978	Northrop	$59,139.00
GORDON LIGHTFOOT	March 11, 1978	Duluth Aud	$30,491.00
GORDON LIGHTFOOT	April 27, 1979	Northrop	$73,517.00
GORDON LIGHTFOOT	April 28, 1979	Duluth Aud	$24,118.00
GORDON LIGHTFOOT	October 2, 1981	Northrop	$42,997.00
GORDON LIGHTFOOT	October 3, 1981	Duluth Aud	$20,102.00
GORDON LIGHTFOOT	October 4, 1981	Madison CC	$19,891.00
GORDON LIGHTFOOT	October 15, 1982	Madison CC	$21,387.00
GORDON LIGHTFOOT	October 16, 1982	Duluth Aud	$15,874.50
GORDON LIGHTFOOT	October 17, 1982	Northrop	$45,570.50
GORDON LIGHTFOOT	March 18, 1983	Milwaukee	$27,017.00
GORDON LIGHTFOOT	April 20, 1984	Madison CC	$20,238.57
GORDON LIGHTFOOT	April 21, 1984	Duluth Aud	$14,108.50
GORDON LIGHTFOOT	April 22, 1984	Northrop	$46,844.00
GORDON LIGHTFOOT	April 23, 1984	Milwaukee	$24,975.47
GORDON LIGHTFOOT	June 9, 1984	Kansas City MO	$20,899.00
GORDON LIGHTFOOT	August 19, 1985	Milwaukee	$21,321.24
GORDON LIGHTFOOT	June 6, 1987	Milwaukee Riv	$31,323.15
GORDON LIGHTFOOT	June 7, 1987	Northrop	$58,966.00

CONCERT NAME	CONCERT DATE	CONCERT VENUE	CONCERT GROSS
GORDON LIGHTFOOT	November 5, 1988	Milwaukee Riv	$34,202.09
GORDON LIGHTFOOT	November 6, 1988	Northrop	$59,439.00
GORDON LIGHTFOOT	October 22, 1989	Chicago Symp	$36,578.00
GORDON LIGHTFOOT	November 2, 1989	Milwaukee Riv	$20,688.13
GORDON LIGHTFOOT	November 3, 1989	Duluth Aud	$22,595.52
GORDON LIGHTFOOT	November 4, 1989	Orpheum	$71,604.00
GORDON LIGHTFOOT	June 27, 1990	TEMPE AZ	$33,041.00
GORDON LIGHTFOOT	April 21, 1993	Des Moines	$36,315.00
GORDON LIGHTFOOT	April 22, 1993	State Theatre	$90,774.00
GORDON LIGHTFOOT	April 24, 1993	Duluth Aud	$45,379.00
GORDON LIGHTFOOT	May 2, 1993	Madison, WI	$36,879.00
GORDON LIGHTFOOT	June 5, 1993	Phoenix AZ	$36,799.50
GORDON LIGHTFOOT	June 16, 1993	Fresno, CA	$21,915.00
GORDON LIGHTFOOT	April 24, 1995	Green Bay WI	$44,584.00
GORDON LIGHTFOOT	April 28, 1995	Milwaukee Pab	$27,840.50
GORDON LIGHTFOOT	April 29, 1995	O'Shaughnessy	$86,657.00
GORDON LIGHTFOOT	April 14, 1996	Madison CC	$40,359.50
GORDON LIGHTFOOT	June 25, 1997	Phoenix CC	$29,816.25
GORDON LIGHTFOOT	September 10, 1997	Madison CC	$22,903.00
GORDON LIGHTFOOT	September 20, 1997	Kalamazoo MI	$30,588.00
GORDON LIGHTFOOT	September 21, 1997	Milwaukee WI	$19,237.50
GORDON LIGHTFOOT	September 25, 1997	Green Bay WI	$41,262.50
GORDON LIGHTFOOT	September 28, 1997	Des Moines	$32,006.00
GORDON LIGHTFOOT	October 3, 1997	Omaha CC	$30,205.50
GORDON LIGHTFOOT	October 4, 1997	State Theatre	$74,406.50
GORDON LIGHTFOOT	November 11, 2000	State Theatre	$59,464.00
GORDON LIGHTFOOT	April 29, 2001	Green Bay WI	$40,410.00
GORDON LIGHTFOOT	September 17, 2006	State Theatre	$90,750.50
GORDON LIGHTFOOT	September 22, 2007	State Theatre	$84,130.00
GORDON LIGHTFOOT	March 22, 2009	State Theatre	$85,104.50
GORDON LIGHTFOOT	September 17, 2011	State Theatre	$70,799.50
GORDON LIGHTFOOT	April 29, 2013	State Theatre	$76,569.00
GORDON LIGHTFOOT	June 20, 2015	State Theatre	$91,234.00

CONCERT NAME	CONCERT DATE	CONCERT VENUE	CONCERT GROSS
GORDON LIGHTFOOT	October 16, 2016	State Theatre	$94,560.50
GOV'T MULE	October 17, 2002	State Theatre	$17,601.50
GRADUATE	November 17, 2003	State Theatre	$469,589.85
GRAND FUNK RAILROAD	July 11, 1997	State Theatre	$21,979.50
GREASE	April 12, 1994	Orpheum	$682,085.70
GREASE	February 27, 1996	State Theatre	$1,557,988.74
GREASE	February 25, 1997	State Theatre	$1,390,640.30
GREASE	June 9, 1998	State Theatre	$310,714.90
GREASE	April 11, 2003	Orpheum	$377,428.14
GREASE	January 1, 2009	Orpheum	$984,991.00
GREASE	November 18, 2009	Orpheum	$357,272.00
GREG MARSHALL (NG)	February 21, 2008	State Theatre	$23,000.00
GREGG ALLMAN	March 27, 2015	Pantages	$65,722.50
GREGORY PECK	July 30, 1995	State Theatre	$25,163.25
GRUMPY OLD MEN (PREM)	December 10, 1993	State Theatre	$31,000.00
GULLAH GULLAH ISLAND	November 8, 1998	State Theatre	$64,024.50
GYPSY (TYNE DALY)	June 27, 1989	Orpheum	$429,000.00
HAIR	February 24, 1991	Orpheum	$46,690.50
HAIR	April 12, 1994	State Theatre	$376,013.00
HAIR	July 8, 2004	Pantages	$496,258.50
HAIRSPRAY	February 17, 2004	Orpheum	$2,698,758.90
HAL HOLBROOK (M TWAIN)	June 10, 1994	State Theatre	$34,420.00
HALL AND OATES	March 12, 1991	Orpheum	$38,947.50
HARRY BELAFONTE	July 27, 1990	Orpheum	$77,000.00
HARRY BELAFONTE	February 14, 1993	State Theatre	$61,997.50
HARRY BELAFONTE	July 27, 1997	State Theatre	$34,359.50
HARRY CHAPIN	September 8, 1977	O'Shaughnessy	$13,710.00
HARRY CHAPIN	August 6, 1988	O'Shaughnessy	$33,000.00
HARRY CHAPIN	August 6, 1994	O'Shaughnessy	$37,000.00
HARRY CONNICK, JR.	October 21, 1990	Orpheum	$162,000.00
HARRY CONNICK, JR.	October 8, 1991	Orpheum	$202,000.00
HARRY CONNICK, JR.	January 21, 1992	State Theatre	$291,231.00
HARRY CONNICK, JR.	April 24, 1998	Orpheum	$174,889.50

CONCERT NAME	CONCERT DATE	CONCERT VENUE	CONCERT GROSS
HARRY CONNICK, JR.	June 11, 1999	Orpheum	$106,233.00
HARRY CONNICK, JR.	November 29, 2001	State Theatre	$122,317.00
HARRY CONNICK, JR.	May 12, 2016	State Theatre	$198,730.00
HEART	December 1, 1993	Orpheum	$51,158.50
HELLO DOLLY (CHANNING)	October 11, 1994	Orpheum	$297,771.00
HENRY ROLLINS	March 26, 2001	Womans Club	$12,100.00
HENRY ROLLINS	January 18, 2003	Pantages	$19,440.00
HERB ALPERT	October 12, 2016	Pantages	$32,332.00
HIP HOP NUTCRACKER	November 21, 2017	State Theatre	$165,483.00
HIPPIEFEST	July 28, 2009	State Theatre	$28,534.50
HOW TO SUCCEED . . .	July 5, 1996	Orpheum	$796,593.00
HOWIE MANDEL	May 1, 1991	Orpheum	$46,450.00
HOWIE MANDEL	January 24, 1993	State Theatre	$92,047.00
HUGH LAURIE	August 18, 2012	Pantages	$46,684.50
HUGH LAURIE	October 15, 2013	Pantages	$47,375.00
I.C.E. / ZEITGEIST	March 23, 2002	Womans Club	$2,438.00
IAN ANDERSON	June 9, 1995	State Theatre	$33,390.00
ICE CUBE / TOO SHORT	November 29, 1990	Orpheum	$63,000.00
IL VOLO	March 20, 2017	State Theatre	$126,702.00
ILLUSIONISTS	March 23, 2018	Orpheum	$349,402.60
IMPRACTICAL JOKERS	September 26, 2014	Orpheum	$143,379.00
IMPRACTICAL JOKERS	November 14, 2015	State Theatre	$204,287.50
IN THE HEIGHTS	December 1, 2009	Orpheum	$684,238.00
INDIGO GIRLS	June 23, 2000	Orpheum	$81,445.00
INDIGO GIRLS BENEFIT	October 16, 2000	Orpheum	$53,420.00
INSANE CLOWN POSSE	December 13, 2000	Roy Wilkins	$38,115.00
INXS	August 26, 1997	State Theatre	$23,332.50
IRA GLASS	April 26, 2003	Pantages	$16,920.00
IRA GLASS	April 9, 2016	State Theatre	$91,868.00
IRA GLASS (DANCE)	November 10, 2013	State Theatre	$95,557.00
IRISH TENORS	June 15, 2001	Orpheum	$116,407.00
IRON MAIDEN	August 27, 2000	Roy Wilkins	$134,242.00
ISAAC HAYES	July 7, 1995	Orpheum	$111,150.00

CONCERT NAME	CONCERT DATE	CONCERT VENUE	CONCERT GROSS
ISLEY BROTHERS	February 14, 2000	Orpheum	$75,557.00
ISLEY BROTHERS	October 28, 2001	Orpheum	$85,657.00
ISLEY BROTHERS	August 3, 2003	Orpheum	$53,196.50
IT'S A BEAUTIFUL DAY	July 24, 1971	Midway Stad	SEE ALLMAN BRO
IVEY AWARDS	September 26, 2005	Pantages	$5,278.00
JACKIE MASON	March 4, 1997	Music Box Th	$131,000.00
JACKIE MASON	August 13, 1999	State Theatre	$29,868.00
JACKIE MASON	November 16, 1999	Golden NYC	$5,303,427.00
JACKIE MASON	January 4, 2001	Womans Club	$26,503.50
JACKSON BROWNE	March 21, 1996	Orpheum	$79,807.50
JACKSON BROWNE	March 22, 1996	Des Moines	$82,470.00
JACKSON BROWNE	October 12, 2003	State Theatre	$78,352.00
JACKSON BROWNE	May 29, 2011	State Theatre	$118,636.00
JACKSON BROWNE	October 28, 2012	State Theatre	$124,674.00
JACKSON BROWNE	July 18, 2014	State Theatre	$135,145.50
JACKSON BROWNE	November 10, 2015	State Theatre	$142,929.50
JAMES BLUNT	March 27, 2006	State Theatre	$48,762.50
JAMES BLUNT	October 30, 2006	Northrop	$158,834.50
JAMES TAYLOR	September 16, 1989	Orpheum	$148,000.00
JAMES TAYLOR	August 11, 2001	Target Center	$502,980.00
JAMIE FOXX	October 3, 1997	Orpheum	$63,652.50
JAMIE FOXX	February 4, 2000	Orpheum	$51,502.50
JAMIE FOXX	August 17, 2001	Orpheum	$57,523.00
JANE MONHEIT	February 1, 2003	Pantages	$12,568.00
JANE OLIVOR	March 17, 1979	Orpheum	$13,000.00
JANE OLIVOR	December 17, 1999	State Theatre	$20,180.50
JANEANE GAROFALO	January 19, 2002	State Theatre	$59,840.00
JANET JACKSON	July 29, 1998	Target Center	$577,465.00
JANET JACKSON	July 17, 2001	Target Center	$756,324.00
JANET JACKSON	August 19, 2011	Orpheum	$256,556.00
JASON BONHAM LZ	October 19, 2010	State Theatre	$48,885.50
JAYHAWKS	April 26, 2002	Womans Club	$9,730.00
JAZZ @ LINCOLN CENTER	September 21, 1999	Orpheum	$22,263.02

CONCERT NAME	CONCERT DATE	CONCERT VENUE	CONCERT GROSS
JECKYLL & HYDE	May 11, 1999	Orpheum	$623,188.39
JEFF BECK	March 9, 2001	State Theatre	$65,625.00
JEFF BECK	May 23, 2015	State Theatre	$110,742.00
JEFF BRIDGES	July 24, 2014	Pantages	$51,327.50
JELLY'S LAST JAM	December 7, 1994	State Theatre	$464,487.20
JERRY JEFF WALKER	April 7, 1977	Duluth Aud	$14,013.78
JERRY JEFF WALKER	April 8, 1977	Northrop	$27,754.00
JERRY JEFF WALKER	May 5, 1979	Orpheum	$38,262.00
JERRY JEFF WALKER	March 28, 1980	St. Paul CC Th	$37,000.00
JERRY SEINFELD	June 9, 1990	Orpheum	$41,000.00
JERRY SEINFELD	June 7, 1991	Orpheum	$45,144.00
JERRY SEINFELD	June 4, 1992	Orpheum	$124,951.00
JERRY SEINFELD	June 2, 2001	Orpheum	$316,515.00
JERRY SEINFELD	October 18, 2002	Orpheum	$701,100.00
JERRY SEINFELD	February 8, 2007	Orpheum	$534,285.00
JERRY SEINFELD	November 14, 2009	Orpheum	$528,908.00
JERRY SEINFELD	November 18, 2011	Orpheum	$491,182.00
JERRY SEINFELD	January 16, 2014	Orpheum	$532,489.00
JERRY SEINFELD	January 18, 2017	Orpheum	$651,952.00
JERSEY BOYS	April 19, 2001	Orpheum	$3,199,690.00
JERSEY BOYS	March 19, 2008	Orpheum	$6,271,742.00
JESSE C YOUNG / P CRUISE	April 9, 1976	Northrop	$26,677.00
JESSE COLIN YOUNG	April 8, 1976	Duluth UMD	$6,472.00
JESSE COLIN YOUNG	April 3, 1977	Northrop	$18,914.00
JESSE COLIN YOUNG	November 11, 1978	Orpheum	$13,896.00
JESSE COOK	May 9, 2013	Pantages	$9,058.50
JESSE COOK	May 3, 2014	Pantages	$18,164.00
JESSE MC CARTNEY	May 16, 2005	State Theatre	$61,628.00
JESUS CHRIST SUPERSTAR	March 9, 1993	State Theatre	$632,554.00
JESUS CHRIST SUPERSTAR	October 12, 1993	State Theatre	$1,237,264.00
JESUS CHRIST SUPERSTAR	March 1, 1994	State Theatre	$458,685.50
JESUS CHRIST SUPERSTAR	November 21, 1995	State Theatre	$495,724.50
JESUS CHRIST SUPERSTAR	November 9, 1996	State Theatre	$157,712.10

CONCERT NAME	CONCERT DATE	CONCERT VENUE	CONCERT GROSS
JESUS CHRIST SUPERSTAR	January 28, 2003	Orpheum	$1,015,390.14
JESUS CHRIST SUPERSTAR	May 4, 2008	Orpheum	$445,037.60
JETHRO TULL	March 28, 1994	Orpheum	$68,160.00
JEWEL	March 18, 1997	Orpheum	$48,580.00
JILIAN MICHAELS	March 29, 2014	Pantages	$43,800.00
JILL SCOTT	July 22, 2001	Orpheum	$64,704.00
JIM BAILEY	July 1, 2001	State Theatre	$37,993.50
JIM BRICKMAN	March 23, 1996	State Theatre	$20,240.50
JIM BRICKMAN	March 22, 1997	State Theatre	$26,483.00
JIM BRICKMAN	November 8, 2002	Pantages	$77,467.50
JIM BRICKMAN	February 14, 2004	Orpheum	$101,410.00
JIM BRICKMAN	February 10, 2007	Orpheum	$62,007.50
JIM BRICKMAN / D OSMOND	November 25, 2000	State Theatre	$126,633.00
JIM GAFFIGAN	November 4, 2015	State Theatre	$791,859.50
JIM JEFFERIES	August 24, 2013	State Theatre	$33,449.00
JIM JEFFERIES	November 11, 2015	Pantages	$69,751.50
JIM JEFFERIES	February 24, 2017	Orpheum	$113,163.50
JIMMY BUFFEETT	November 10, 2001	Target Center	$927,406.50
JIMMY SCOTT	December 9, 2000	Womans Club	$7,425.00
JIMMY SCOTT	September 21, 2001	Womans Club	$6,185.00
JO DEE MESSINA	February 10, 2001	Orpheum	$86,475.50
JOAN ARMATRADING	September 15, 1992	Orpheum	$34,358.00
JOAN BAEZ	July 14, 1979	Northrop	$35,159.00
JOAN JETT	March 23, 1990	Orpheum	$37,000.00
JOAN OSBORNE	May 12, 1996	Orpheum	$33,429.50
JOE COCKER	September 15, 1998	State Theatre	$65,745.50
JOE HENDERSON	June 18, 1995	State Theatre	$7,887.00
JOE JACKSON	September 13, 1989	Orpheum	$32,000.00
JOE JACKSON	March 31, 2001	State Theatre	$22,550.00
JOE SATRIANI	March 18, 1990	Orpheum	$49,000.00
JOE SATRIANI	December 20, 1992	Orpheum	$54,382.50
JOE SATRIANI	April 27, 1996	Orpheum	$56,747.50
JOE SATRIANI	November 6, 1998	State Theatre	$37,913.00

CONCERT NAME	CONCERT DATE	CONCERT VENUE	CONCERT GROSS
JOE SATRIANI	April 21, 2000	State Theatre	$36,881.50
JOHN BALDRY	July 24, 1971	Midway Stad	SEE ALLMAN BRO
JOHN BERRY	June 26, 1997	State Theatre	$10,772.50
JOHN DENVER	December 4, 1993	Orpheum	$168,195.50
JOHN DENVER TRIBUTE	February 17, 2013	State Theatre	$44,216.00
JOHN FOGERTY	September 11, 1997	State Theatre	$52,997.00
JOHN GRAY	November 8, 1997	Orpheum	$5,772.00
JOHN LEGUIZAMO	July 13, 2001	State Theatre	$43,297.50
JOHN MCLAUGHLIN	April 23, 1992	State Theatre	$10,156.00
JOHN PRINE	October 31, 1976	O'Shaughnessy	$10,554.50
JOHN PRINE	September 30, 1979	Orpheum	$24,000.00
JOHN PRINE	April 24, 1992	Orpheum	$51,689.50
JOHN PRINE	July 15, 1995	Orpheum	$50,129.00
JOHN PRINE / L. REDBONE	September 22, 1978	O'Shaughnessy	$25,055.50
JOHN SEBASTIAN	June 26, 1971	Midway Stad	SEE THE BAND
JOHN SECADA	March 2, 1995	Northrop	$72,703.50
JOHN TESH	May 4, 1997	State Theatre	$42,621.00
JOHN TRONES	December 11, 2003	Pantages	$7,347.00
JOHN TRONES / BRICKMAN	December 23, 2013	Pantages	$15,986.50
JOHNNY CASH	August 27, 1994	Orpheum	$48,494.50
JOHNNY MATHIS	December 5, 1997	Orpheum	$299,664.00
JOHNNY MATHIS	December 16, 2000	State Theatre	$217,615.50
JOHNNY MATHIS	October 15, 2005	Orpheum	$86,525.50
JOHNNY MATHIS	December 4, 2014	State Theatre	$150,694.50
JON STEWART	May 18, 2007	Orpheum	$319,732.00
JONNY LANG	December 28, 1998	State Theatre	$92,218.00
JONNY LANG	September 18, 2013	State Theatre	$45,779.50
JOSEPH AND THE . . .	September 15, 1992	State Theatre	$6,685,702.22
JOSEPH AND THE . . .	February 22, 1995	State Theatre	$10,443,510.10
JOSEPH AND THE . . .	September 14, 1999	State Theatre	$2,056,100.15
JOSEPH AND THE . . .	January 25, 2000	State Theatre	$460,138.75
JOSEPH AND THE . . .	September 13, 2005	Orpheum	$898,353.60
JOSHUA RADIN	September 25, 2009	Pantages	$14,243.50

CONCERT NAME	CONCERT DATE	CONCERT VENUE	CONCERT GROSS
JOURNEY	July 21, 2001	Target Center	$253,130.00
JOY OF COOKING	July 24, 1971	Midway Stad	SEE ALLMAN BRO
JUDDS	March 12, 2000	Target Center	$358,014.25
JUDY COLLINS	December 6, 1972	O'Shaughnessy	$17,837.00
JUDY COLLINS	October 19, 1973	O'Shaughnessy	$19,302.00
JUDY COLLINS	July 31, 1976	Northrop	$23,379.85
JUDY COLLINS	July 16, 1977	Northrop	$28,123.00
JUDY COLLINS	April 1, 1979	Northrop	$33,723.00
JUDY COLLINS	November 29, 1996	State Theatre	$21,462.00
JUDY COLLINS	April 22, 2001	State Theatre	$25,792.00
JUDY COLLINS	December 21, 2005	Pantages	$18,067.50
JULIO IGLESIAS	July 24, 1994	Orpheum	$90,420.00
K. T. OSLIN	August 17, 1990	Orpheum	$43,000.00
K. T. OSLIN	July 18, 1991	Orpheum	$38,752.50
k.d. lang	August 19, 1989	Orpheum	$63,000.00
k.d. lang	October 13, 1992	Orpheum	$125,176.00
k.d. lang	October 24, 1997	Orpheum	$73,913.00
KATHLEEN MADIGAN	October 15, 2005	Pantages	$6,298.00
KATHY GRIFFIN	April 26, 2006	Pantages	$28,386.00
KATHY GRIFFIN	June 22, 2006	State Theatre	$61,620.00
KATHY GRIFFIN	October 3, 2008	Orpheum	$542,311.50
KATHY GRIFFIN	June 26, 2010	Orpheum	$206,971.00
KATHY GRIFFIN	December 1, 2012	State Theatre	$179,337.00
KATHY MATTEA	December 13, 2005	Pantages	$25,226.25
KATIE MC MAHON	March 18, 2005	Pantages	$7,865.00
KATIE MCMAHON	March 17, 2006	Pantages	$10,119.50
KEB MO	November 21, 2000	State Theatre	$38,721.00
KEB MO / BELA FLECK	August 23, 2001	Orpheum	$66,522.00
KEITH JARRETT	November 14, 1977	Northrop	$15,193.00
KELLY CLARKSON	April 6, 2005	State Theatre	$72,557.00
KEN HILL PHANTOM	October 3, 1989	Orpheum	$523,640.00
KEN HILL PHANTOM	November 16, 1990	Orpheum	$364,640.00
KEN HILL PHANTOM	November 18, 1992	Orpheum	$258,640.00

CONCERT NAME	CONCERT DATE	CONCERT VENUE	CONCERT GROSS
KENNY G	April 6, 1993	Northrop	$235,454.50
KENNY G	December 6, 2009	State Theatre	$46,445.75
KENNY LOGGINS	November 17, 1988	Orpheum	$48,000.00
KENNY LOGGINS	December 2, 1993	Orpheum	$54,052.50
KENNY LOGGINS	July 30, 2013	State Theatre	$32,280.00
KENNY RODGERS XMAS	December 17, 1994	State Theatre	$209,457.50
KENNY ROGERS	September 18, 1998	State Theatre	$41,394.00
KENNY WAYNE SHEPHERD	April 1, 2000	State Theatre	$39,253.50
KERI NOBLE	May 20, 2005	Pantages	$20,677.00
KEVIN JAMES	May 6, 2000	State Theatre	$16,524.50
KEVIN SMITH	May 1, 2015	State Theatre	$42,815.00
KHALED HOSSEINI	October 17, 2008	State Theatre	$31,556.75
KIDS IN THE HALL	February 24, 2000	State Theatre	$256,939.50
KIDS IN THE HALL	May 1, 2002	State Theatre	$140,212.50
KIDS IN THE HALL	April 26, 2008	Orpheum	$103,327.00
KING AND I	April 1, 1997	Orpheum	$1,474,325.30
KINGS OF LEON	November 1, 2008	Orpheum	$83,204.00
KIRK FRANKLIN	April 17, 1997	Orpheum	$59,478.65
KISS / SPIDERWOMAN	August 8, 1995	State Theatre	$1,850,000.00
KITARO	April 12, 1990	Orpheum	$29,000.00
KITARO	October 16, 1994	State Theatre	$27,820.00
KRIS KRISTOFFERSON	March 31, 1973	O'Shaughnessy	$17,792.70
KRIS KRISTOFFERSON	November 30, 1973	O'Shaughnessy	$18,078.00
KRIS KRISTOFFERSON	September 27, 1974	Milwaukee	$20,080.00
KRIS KRISTOFFERSON	September 28, 1974	Duluth Aud	$16,304.50
KRIS KRISTOFFERSON	September 29, 1974	O'Shaughnessy	$19,409.00
KRIS KRISTOFFERSON	August 13, 1977	Northrop	$32,444.00
KRIS KRISTOFFERSON	April 14, 2009	Pantages	$41,796.00
KRIS KRISTOFFERSON	January 14, 2017	Pantages	$57,348.00
KWANZAA EVENT	December 11, 2001	Pantages	$-
LA BOHEME	October 16, 2002	State Theatre	$28,861.50
LARRY THE CABLE GUY	February 25, 2005	Orpheum	$224,689.75
LARRY THE CABLE GUY	March 19, 2016	Orpheum	$240,451.00

CONCERT NAME	CONCERT DATE	CONCERT VENUE	CONCERT GROSS
LASER LIGHT SPECTACULAR	January 26, 1990	Orpheum	$12,000.00
LASER LIGHT SPECTACULAR	May 27, 1993	State Theatre	$8,033.40
LASER LIGHT SPECTACULAR	March 26, 1999	State Theatre	$13,641.00
LAST COMIC STANDING	December 14, 2003	Pantages	$22,677.50
LAURA NYRO	August 9, 1988	Childrens Th	$27,117.00
LAURIE ANDERSON	February 27, 1990	Orpheum	$23,000.00
LAURIE BERKNER	February 15, 2003	Womans Club	$4,335.00
LAWRENCE OF A (MOVIE)	August 19, 1994	State Theatre	$14,210.00
LED ZEPPELIN EXPERIENCE	October 19, 2010	State Theatre	$45,885.50
LENINGRAD MUSIC HALL	June 8, 1990	Orpheum	$73,736.25
LENNY KRAVITZ	August 25, 1999	Target Center	$166,532.50
LENNY KRAVITZ	May 4, 2005	State Theatre	$97,291.00
LEO KOETTKE	November 8, 1975	Duluth Aud	$8,214.00
LEO KOETTKE	February 25, 1977	Duluth UMD	$6,302.00
LEO SAYER	July 27, 1977	Northrop	$11,361.29
LEON RUSSELL	April 21, 1978	Northrop	$18,089.00
LEONARD COHEN	June 22, 1993	State Theatre	$39,912.00
LEROME BEL DANCE	April 1, 2005	Pantages	$4,460.00
LES BALLETS TROCKS	February 11, 2003	Pantages	$72,081.50
LETTERMEN	December 3, 1991	State Theatre	$16,451.60
LFO	May 16, 2000	State Theatre	$22,860.00
LIGHT IN THE PIAZZA	March 20, 2007	Orpheum	$442,232.00
LILY TOMLIN	May 2, 1975	O'Shaughnessy	$10,083.00
LILY TOMLIN	October 15, 2005	State Theatre	$91,476.00
LILY TOMLIN	February 13, 2011	State Theatre	$57,503.00
LIMP BIZKIT / EMINEM	November 9, 2000	Target Center	$567,876.00
LINDA EDER	December 9, 2001	State Theatre	$88,567.50
LINDA EDER	March 7, 2003	State Theatre	$65,259.50
LINDA EDER	December 13, 2003	State Theatre	$82,236.25
LINDA EDER	November 18, 2005	State Theatre	$54,478.00
LINDA EDER	December 21, 2010	Pantages	$47,750.45
LINDA EDER	December 2, 2011	Pantages	$36,611.50
LINDA EDER	August 24, 2013	Pantages	$29,785.00

CONCERT NAME	CONCERT DATE	CONCERT VENUE	CONCERT GROSS
LINDSEY BUCKINGHAM	September 16, 2011	Pantages	$40,226.50
LINDSEY VONN EVENT	June 3, 2016	Orpheum	$-
LION KING	July 8, 1997	Orpheum	$6,313,828.75
LION KING	April 8, 2005	Orpheum	$10,489,818.50
LION KING	October 25, 2007	Orpheum	$6,260,935.00
LITTLE FEAT	March 31, 1989	Orpheum	$25,000.00
LITTLE FEAT	May 16, 1990	Orpheum	$44,000.00
LITTLE FEAT	June 15, 1993	State Theatre	$31,162.50
LITTLE FEAT	May 16, 1996	Orpheum	$53,540.00
LITTLE RICHARD	July 24, 1971	Midway Stad	SEE ALLMAN BRO
LITTLE SHOP OF HORRORS	July 19, 2005	Orpheum	$557,809.85
LITTLE WOMEN	February 14, 2006	Orpheum	$560,564.25
LIVE	November 6, 1999	Orpheum	$55,597.50
LIZA MINNELLI	October 13, 1979	Orpheum	$490,000.00
LOGGINS AND MESSINA	September 1, 2009	State Theatre	$111,330.50
LORD OF RINGS PREMIERE	December 12, 2001	State Theatre	$40,750.00
LORD OF THE DANCE	September 11, 1998	Target Center	$368,471.75
LORD OF THE DANCE	February 15, 2000	Orpheum	$205,802.00
LORD OF THE DANCE	April 19, 2002	Orpheum	$347,314.50
LORD OF THE DANCE	February 9, 2008	Orpheum	$189,163.00
LORD OF THE DANCE	February 23, 2013	State Theatre	$80,496.00
LOREENA MCKENNIT	November 1, 1994	State Theatre	$34,999.00
LORENNA MCKENNITT	May 5, 2007	State Theatre	$84,550.00
LORI LINE	December 7, 1998	State Theatre	$530,024.00
LORIE LINE	December 10, 1999	State Theatre	$572,745.00
LORIE LINE	December 8, 2000	State Theatre	$561,551.50
LORIE LINE	November 30, 2001	State Theatre	$784,775.00
LORIE LINE	December 5, 2002	State Theatre	$792,457.00
LORIE LINE	December 17, 2003	State Theatre	$654,591.00
LORIE LINE	December 2, 2005	State Theatre	$507,580.00
LORIE LINE	December 9, 2006	Orpheum	$457,731.00
LORIE LINE	December 8, 2007	Orpheum	$382,377.00
LORIE LINE (BENEFIT)	May 10, 2000	State Theatre	$45,325.00

CONCERT NAME	CONCERT DATE	CONCERT VENUE	CONCERT GROSS
LOST IN YONKERS	March 16, 1993	State Theatre	$418,772.23
LOU REED	April 7, 1989	Orpheum	$55,000.00
LOU REED	May 9, 1992	Orpheum	$64,782.50
LOU REED	March 23, 1996	Orpheum	$62,380.00
LOU REED	June 12, 2000	Orpheum	$40,185.00
LOVE LETTERS	March 21, 1992	State Theatre	$306,391.47
LOVE LETTERS (BROADWAY)	August 2, 1996	State Theatre	$28,178.00
LOVE TAPES	September 13, 2006	Henn Stages	$11,522.94
LOW	February 8, 2001	Womans Club	$7,125.00
LOW	November 23, 2002	Pantages	$11,505.00
LOWEN & NAVARRO	June 21, 2002	Womans Club	$3,486.00
LUCIA DI LAMMERMOOR	October 14, 2003	Pantages	$12,703.00
LUIS MIGUEL	February 12, 2000	Orpheum	$113,660.00
LYLE LOVETT / HIATT	February 7, 2011	State Theatre	$103,985.00
LYLE LOVETT / HIATT	October 17, 2015	State Theatre	$115,198.50
LYLE LOVETT / HIATT	July 22, 2016	State Theatre	$118,703.50
LYLE LOVETT / HIATT	February 25, 2017	State Theatre	$124,742.50
LYLE LOVETT / KD LANG	July 5, 2007	Orpheum	$105,695.50
LYNYRD SKYNYRD	June 10, 2001	Target Center	$146,945.00
LYPSINKA	March 19, 1999	State Theatre	$5,675.00
MAC / HARVEY / CEDRIC	October 7, 2000	Target Center	$397,445.00
MACY GRAY	June 8, 2000	Orpheum	$45,637.00
MADAME BUTTERFLY	March 15, 2003	State Theatre	$55,738.50
MADELEINE PEYROUX	June 7, 2005	Pantages	$28,644.50
MADELEINE PEYROUX	October 13, 2006	State Theatre	$36,634.50
MAGIC SCHOOL BUS LIVE	January 16, 1999	State Theatre	$18,596.00
MAGIC TREE HOUSE	April 4, 2009	State Theatre	$68,365.00
MAGNETIC FIELDS	May 28, 2000	Womans Club	$7,565.00
MALE INTELLECT	March 13, 2001	Womans Club	$57,059.27
MAMMA MIA	November 9, 2001	Orpheum	$6,234,369.90
MAMMA MIA	November 11, 2003	Orpheum	$4,232,820.62
MAMMA MIA	January 11, 2005	Orpheum	$1,655,805.59
MAMMA MIA	March 14, 2010	Orpheum	$1,115,858.00

CONCERT NAME	CONCERT DATE	CONCERT VENUE	CONCERT GROSS
MAN OF LA M (KILEY)	May 15, 1979	Orpheum	$750,000.00
MANDY PATANKIN	October 18, 1996	State Theatre	$76,241.00
MANDY PATANKIN	April 21, 1999	State Theatre	$62,436.25
MANDY PATINKIN	October 18, 1999	State Theatre	$76,241.00
MANDY PATINKIN	November 14, 2001	State Theatre	$45,368.50
MANHATTAN TRANSFER	October 24, 1976	O'Shaughnessy	$11,568.00
MANHATTAN TRANSFER	July 21, 1978	O'Shaughnessy	$22,236.00
MANHATTAN TRANSFER	December 8, 1992	Orpheum	$66,777.25
MANHATTAN TRANSFER	November 30, 1999	Orpheum	$37,588.90
MANHATTAN TRANSFER	December 11, 2013	Pantages	$29,268.50
MANNHEIM ON ICE	December 27, 1998	Target Center	$149,570.25
MANNHEIM STEAMROLLER	November 24, 1989	Orpheum	$202,000.00
MANNHEIM STEAMROLLER	December 12, 1991	State Theatre	$244,587.50
MANNHEIM STEAMROLLER	December 9, 1993	Orpheum	$356,123.00
MANNHEIM STEAMROLLER	November 18, 2000	Target Center	$375,467.00
MANNHEIM STEAMROLLER	November 29, 2003	Xcel Center	$488,526.50
MANNHEIM STEAMROLLER	November 26, 2005	XCEL CENTER	$474,912.25
MANNHEIM STEAMROLLER	December 19, 2008	Orpheum	$354,530.00
MANNHEIM STEAMROLLER	December 3, 2010	Orpheum	$230,590.00
MANNHEIM STEAMROLLER	November 23, 2012	Orpheum	$185,258.00
MANNHEIM STEAMROLLER	December 7, 2014	Orpheum	$143,802.50
MANNHEIM STEAMROLLER	December 4, 2016	State Theatre	$202,140.10
MARC ANTHONY	February 18, 2000	Orpheum	$80,430.00
MARC COHN	September 12, 1993	State Theatre	$48,167.50
MARC COHN	December 31, 2003	Pantages	$58,280.00
MARC COHN	December 30, 2005	Pantages	$54,370.00
MARC COHN	December 31, 2006	Pantages	$55,760.00
MARC COHN (BENEFIT)	June 4, 2000	Rush Creek GC	$-
MARCEL MARCEAU	March 28, 2003	Pantages	$87,654.00
MARGARET CHO	November 4, 1999	Womans Club	$44,230.50
MARIJUANA-LOGUES	February 25, 2004	Pantages	$73,310.00
MARILYN MANSON	October 27, 2000	Orpheum	$78,639.00
MARK KNOPFLER	May 7, 2001	Orpheum	$178,800.00

CONCERT NAME	CONCERT DATE	CONCERT VENUE	CONCERT GROSS
MARK OLSON / V WILLIAMS	April 20, 2001	Womans Club	$696.00
MARKY MARK	February 14, 1992	Orpheum	$39,530.00
MARLENE DIETRICH	May 26, 1974	O'Shaughnessy	$13,396.75
MARTIN SEXTON	November 15, 2003	Pantages	$20,292.00
MARTIN SEXTON	April 14, 2007	Pantages	$25,793.00
MARTINA MCBRIDE	December 6, 2013	State Theatre	$98,619.00
MARTINI & OLIVE	December 3, 2005	Henn Stages	$37,842.90
MARY CHAPIN CARPENTER	November 9, 1994	Orpheum	$57,907.50
MARY CHAPIN CARPENTER	May 2, 2015	State Theatre	$63,942.50
MARY J. BLIGE	August 9, 2000	Orpheum	$94,182.50
MARY OLIVER	March 30, 2008	State Theatre	$29,338.50
MARY POPPINS	September 3, 2009	Orpheum	$3,834,980.00
MASON JENNINGS	June 24, 2006	Orpheum	$51,075.00
MASON JENNINGS	October 18, 2008	Orpheum	$41,677.00
MASON JENNINGS	April 5, 2014	State Theatre	$31,092.50
MASTER CLASS	June 11, 1997	State Theatre	$396,050.55
MASTERS OF ILLUSION	September 21, 2012	State Theatre	$30,439.50
MATCHBOX 20	October 22, 1997	Orpheum	$42,997.50
MATCHBOX 20	February 27, 2001	Target Center	$383,141.50
MATCHBOX 20	August 1, 2001	Xcel Center	$403,160.00
MATISYAHU	October 24, 2015	Pantages	$19,443.00
MATT NATHANSON	November 18, 2008	Pantages	$16,611.00
MATTAIS KLUM (NG)	May 19, 2005	State Theatre	$10,860.00
MATTERS / HEART (LU PONE)	October 5, 2004	Orpheum	$232,000.00
MAVERICKS	April 12, 1996	State Theatre	$44,157.00
MAVERICKS	April 3, 2013	Pantages	$38,372.00
MAVERICKS	March 9, 2014	Pantages	$45,447.50
MAVERICKS	April 4, 2015	Pantages	$51,783.00
MAVERICKS	March 19, 2016	State Theatre	$88,972.00
MAVERICKS	September 29, 2017	State Theatre	$104,449.00
MAX RAABE (LAST SHOW)	April 21, 2018	Pantages	$31,959.50
MAXWELL	September 26, 2001	Orpheum	$123,500.00
MAXWELL	June 15, 2014	State Theatre	$90,934.00

CONCERT NAME	CONCERT DATE	CONCERT VENUE	CONCERT GROSS
MAZE	May 13, 1990	Orpheum	$41,000.00
MEDESKI MARTIN & WOOD	May 12, 2000	Womans Club	$12,240.00
MEDESKI MARTIN & WOOD	December 6, 2000	State Theatre	$27,200.00
MEDESKI MARTIN & WOOD	October 18, 2001	O'Shaughnessy	$25,315.00
MEDESKI MARTIN & WOOD	April 15, 2003	Pantages	$21,551.00
MEL TORME	March 17, 1988	Radisson Mpls	$45,098.00
MELISSA ETHERIDGE	February 10, 1990	Orpheum	$39,000.00
MELISSA ETHERIDGE	July 23, 1992	State Theatre	$46,597.50
MELISSA ETHERIDGE	August 31, 1994	Northrop	$95,880.00
MELISSA MANCHESTER	November 1, 1991	State (OPEN)	$-
MERLE HAGGARD	July 19, 2013	State Theatre	$75,185.50
MERLE HAGGARD/KRIS K	July 28, 2012	State Theatre	$137,301.00
MICHAEL BOLTON	September 5, 2002	Orpheum	$35,964.00
MICHAEL BUBLE	July 19, 2003	Pantages	$16,327.50
MICHAEL BUBLE	November 2, 2003	Pantages	$21,717.00
MICHAEL CARBONARO	May 7, 2016	State Theatre	$57,756.30
MICHAEL FEINSTEIN	October 31, 2003	Pantages	$9,310.00
MICHAEL JOHNSON	November 25, 1977	O'Shaughnessy	$20,285.00
MICHAEL JOHNSON	October 6, 1978	Duluth Aud	$7,476.00
MICHAEL JOHNSON	October 14, 1978	Northrop	$24,151.00
MICHAEL McDONALD / COHN	November 2, 2017	State Theatre	$111,968.50
MICHAEL W. SMITH	May 12, 2000	State Theatre	$53,951.50
MICHELLE SHOCKED	May 15, 1990	Orpheum	$38,000.00
MICKEY ROONEY	May 5, 1989	Orpheum	$28,000.00
MIDNIGHT OIL	October 20, 1988	Orpheum	$29,000.00
MIDNIGHT OIL	September 12, 1990	Orpheum	$31,000.00
MIKE & THE MECHANICS	April 22, 1989	Orpheum	$14,000.00
MIKE BIRBIGLIA	February 22, 2014	Pan/Fitz	$70,853.00
MIKE DOUGHTY	April 27, 2002	Womans Club	$7,638.00
MIKE EPPS	May 9, 2005	Orpheum	$61,603.00
MIKE QUATRO JAM BAND	July 24, 1971	Midway Stad	SEE ALLMAN BRO
MIKHAIL BARYSHNIKOV	June 14, 1994	Orpheum	$401,418.00
MIKHAIL BARYSHNIKOV	April 25, 1996	State Theatre	$136,627.50

CONCERT NAME	CONCERT DATE	CONCERT VENUE	CONCERT GROSS
MIKHAIL BARYSHNIKOV	June 3, 1998	State Theatre	$131,649.65
MIKHAIL BARYSHNIKOV	July 17, 2003	Pantages	$103,381.50
MILES DAVIS	April 27, 1990	Orpheum	$55,000.00
MISS SAIGON	January 11, 1994	Orpheum	$8,322,157.00
MISS SAIGON	April 18, 2003	Orpheum	$559,398.35
MITCH HEDBERG / L BLACK	November 22, 2002	State Theatre	$57,695.00
MO'NIQUE	May 14, 2010	State Theatre	$42,165.00
MOBY	October 5, 2000	Roy Wilkins	$95,000.00
MOBY (ARENA ONE FEST)	July 26, 2001	Midway Stad	$512,650.00
MONKEES	June 27, 1996	Orpheum	$57,247.00
MONKEES	August 9, 1997	State Theatre	$51,668.00
MONTY ALEXANDER	June 12, 2009	State Stage	$21,000.00
MOODY BLUES	November 25, 1991	Orpheum	$120,807.50
MOODY BLUES	September 19, 1999	Northrop	$191,000.50
MOODY BLUES	June 27, 2017	Orpheum	$238,161.00
MOSAIC (CITY EVENT)	June 4, 2005	Pantages	$-
MOSAIC (CITY EVENT)	June 10, 2006	Pantages	$-
MOVE LIVE	May 28, 2017	State Theatre	$148,992.50
MOVIN' OUT	August 3, 2005	Orpheum	$1,929,614.85
MOVIN' OUT	March 6, 2009	Orpheum	$310,871.00
MUDDY WATERS	June 26, 1971	Midway Stad	SEE THE BAND
MUM (ICELAND)	June 17, 2002	Womans Club	$3,240.00
MUSIC OF A L WEBER	May 27, 1989	Northrop	$201,000.00
MUSIC OF DUKE ELLINGTON	September 21, 1999	State Theatre	$12,636.00
MY FAIR LADY	September 22, 1993	State Theatre	$1,125,818.53
MY FAIR LADY	February 20, 2008	Orpheum	$1,039,305.00
MY MORNING JACKET	October 2, 2008	Orpheum	$72,259.50
MYSTICAL / JAHEIM	June 26, 2001	Orpheum	$15,222.50
N SYNC	June 23, 2000	Target Center	$678,713.25
N SYNC	June 24, 2001	Metrodome	$2,341,857.50
N'SYNC - BRITTANY SPEARS	December 27, 1998	Orpheum	$49,208.00
NANA MOUSKOURI	May 8, 1992	State Theatre	$24,063.00
NANA MOUSKOURI	November 3, 1999	Orpheum	$28,683.00

CONCERT NAME	CONCERT DATE	CONCERT VENUE	CONCERT GROSS
NANCI GRIFFITH	April 2, 1993	State Theatre	$41,174.00
NANCI GRIFFITH	August 16, 1995	Orpheum	$51,175.00
NANCI GRIFFITH	October 11, 1997	Orpheum	$33,767.04
NANCY W / D LETTERMAN	October 7, 1984	Orpheum	$23,000.00
NAPOLEON (MOVIE)	July 14, 1989	Orpheum	$18,000.00
NATALIE COLE	July 28, 1977	Northrop	$29,417.00
NATALIE COLE	June 30, 1979	Orpheum	$15,436.00
NATALIE COLE	October 22, 1991	Orpheum	$75,865.00
NATALIE COLE	July 28, 1992	Orpheum	$41,362.50
NATIONAL POETRY SLAM	August 17, 2002	Orpheum	$19,780.00
NATL ACROBATS TAIWAN	February 24, 2005	State Theatre	$13,617.00
NEIL YOUNG	November 21, 1992	Orpheum	$154,791.00
NEIL YOUNG	May 22, 1999	Orpheum	$364,370.00
NELSON	February 19, 1991	Orpheum	$43,067.50
NELSON	July 24, 1991	Orpheum	$28,175.00
NICHOLAS DAVID	December 4, 2016	Pantages	$13,316.00
NICK CAVE & THE BAD SEEDS	April 25, 2002	State Theatre	$55,033.00
NICK SWARDSON	June 9, 2007	State Theatre	$59,408.00
NICKEL CREEK	May 13, 2001	Womans Club	$5,523.00
NICKEL CREEK	May 11, 2014	State Theatre	$94,003.00
NINA GORDON	October 28, 2000	Womans Club	$4,462.50
NINA SIMONE	April 15, 1993	State Theatre	$25,095.00
NITTY GRITTY DIRT BAND	July 9, 1976	O'Shaughnessy	$7,637.00
NOISE / FUNK	December 17, 1997	Orpheum	$1,004,446.30
NOISE / FUNK	October 22, 2002	State Theatre	$274,412.75
NYLONS	November 11, 1988	Orpheum	$31,000.00
NYLONS	October 10, 1991	Orpheum	$29,651.25
O.C. SUPERTONES	April 8, 2000	State Theatre	$16,932.00
O'JAYS	December 29, 1998	Orpheum	$40,232.50
O'JAYS / REGINA BELLE	October 13, 1990	Orpheum	$63,000.00
OAK RIDGE BOYS	February 9, 1996	State Theatre	$36,841.50
OASIS	February 20, 1996	Orpheum	$41,796.00
ODD COUPLE	May 10, 1994	Orpheum	$390,285.25

CONCERT NAME	CONCERT DATE	CONCERT VENUE	CONCERT GROSS
OKLAHOMA!	June 23, 1981	Northrop	$425,000.00
OKLAHOMA!	January 5, 2004	Orpheum	$591,333.35
OLD CROW MED. SHOW	October 2, 2014	State Theatre	$41,842.50
OLIVIA NEWTON JOHN	September 15, 2002	Orpheum	$61,182.50
ONE MAN STAR WARS	April 18, 2006	Pantages	$51,854.00
OVER THE RHINE	April 1, 2001	Womans Club	$2,818.00
PANTERA	February 20, 2001	Target Center	$150,370.50
PANTERA	July 5, 2001	Xcel Center	$170,597.50
PAT MATHENY GROUP	November 9, 1997	State Theatre	$55,679.50
PAT METHENY TRIO	March 25, 2000	State Theatre	$32,369.00
PATRICIA BARBER	December 6, 2002	Womans Club	$4,052.00
PATTI LABELLE	February 11, 1990	Orpheum	$67,000.00
PATTI LABELLE	February 20, 1992	Orpheum	$63,673.00
PATTI LABELLE	June 14, 1992	Orpheum	$30,325.00
PATTI LABELLE	June 30, 1993	State Theatre	$37,035.00
PATTI LABELLE	December 4, 1997	State Theatre	$63,710.50
PATTI LABELLE	January 14, 2017	State Theatre	$78,181.00
PATTI SMITH	August 6, 2007	State Theatre	$26,607.00
PATTY LOVELESS / D WORLEY	November 24, 2000	State Theatre	$13,053.00
PAUL WESTERBERG	September 6, 1996	State Theatre	$37,195.00
PAUL WINTER	December 11, 1992	Orpheum	$28,442.50
PEGGY LEE	August 15, 1987	Radisson Mpls	$50,000.00
PENN & TELLER	November 21, 1990	Orpheum	$60,000.00
PENN & TELLER	May 25, 1994	State Theatre	$24,888.50
PENTATONIX	March 7, 2015	Orpheum	$121,291.50
PERFECT CIRCLE	March 31, 2001	Roy Wilkins	$139,275.00
PET SHOP BOYS	April 3, 1991	Orpheum	$29,960.00
PET SHOP BOYS	September 16, 2009	State Theatre	$59,867.50
PETER FRAMPTON	September 30, 2011	State Theatre	$103,394.50
PETER FRAMPTON	July 21, 2013	State Theatre	$67,146.50
PETER FRAMPTON	July 13, 2016	State Theatre	$74,320.50
PETER HIMMELMAN	February 15, 1992	State Theatre	$32,672.50
PETER HIMMELMAN	November 24, 1992	Orpheum	$25,897.50

CONCERT NAME	CONCERT DATE	CONCERT VENUE	CONCERT GROSS
PETER HIMMELMAN	November 30, 1993	State Theatre	$23,242.50
PETER HIMMELMAN	May 12, 1994	State Theatre	$26,320.00
PETER PAUL & MARY	October 3, 1981	Northrop	$67,000.00
PETER YARROW/P STOCKEY	October 7, 2017	Pantages	$50,442.00
PHANTOM OF THE OPERA	January 14, 1995	Orpheum	$7,876,192.50
PHANTOM OF THE OPERA	July 16, 1998	Orpheum	$5,326,277.50
PHANTOM OF THE OPERA	July 14, 2004	Orpheum	$4,618,262.20
PHANTOM OF THE OPERA	May 13, 2009	Orpheum	$3,364,671.00
PHISH	April 9, 1993	State Theatre	$22,687.50
PHISH	June 16, 1994	State Theatre	$36,452.00
PHISH	November 26, 1994	Orpheum	$44,397.50
PILOBOLUS (DANCE)	October 22, 2006	State Theatre	$23,752.00
PINK FLOYD LASER SHOW	January 26, 1990	Orpheum	$17,000.00
PIRATES OF PENZANCE	April 30, 1993	Orpheum	$180,412.00
PLATTERS, COASTERS . . .	March 7, 1998	State Theatre	$18,397.50
POCO	July 24, 1971	Midway Stad	SEE ALLMAN BRO
PRETENDERS	November 6, 1994	Orpheum	$49,380.00
PRETENDERS	February 23, 2000	Orpheum	$64,650.00
PRETENDERS	February 16, 2003	State Theatre	$61,233.00
PRODUCERS	November 12, 2002	Orpheum	$4,722,056.04
PROOF	March 19, 2002	State Theatre	$327,346.10
PUPPETRY OF THE PENIS	June 14, 2005	Henn Stages	$43,839.57
R. E. M.	July 5, 1984	Orpheum	$79,000.00
R. KELLY	July 11, 2001	Orpheum	$137,439.00
R5	March 11, 2016	State Theatre	$74,460.00
RADIO CITY CHRISTMAS	December 8, 2002	Orpheum	$4,952,845.30
RADIO CITY CHRISTMAS	December 9, 2005	Orpheum	$3,644,915.28
RADIO CITY SPECTACULAR	March 30, 1994	State Theatre	$276,633.00
RADIOHEAD	August 5, 1997	State Theatre	$32,987.50
RAFFI	May 14, 1993	State Theatre	$61,861.00
RAFFI	August 23, 1994	Orpheum	$61,980.00
RAFFI	November 11, 1995	State Theatre	$57,000.00
RAFFI	October 5, 2002	State Theatre	$48,231.00

CONCERT NAME	CONCERT DATE	CONCERT VENUE	CONCERT GROSS
RAGTIME	October 7, 1998	Orpheum	$4,820,496.02
RAIN (BEATLES)	March 3, 2008	Orpheum	$77,441.50
RAIN (BEATLES)	March 22, 2009	Orpheum	$138,064.00
RAIN (BEATLES)	March 3, 2012	Orpheum	$199,804.25
RAIN (BEATLES)	April 11, 2014	State Theatre	$144,183.50
RAIN (BEATLES)	March 11, 2017	State Theatre	$90,155.50
RALPH LEMON (WALKER)	November 15, 1997	State Theatre	$5,053.50
RALPH LEMON DANCE	March 9, 2005	Pantages	$3,825.00
RALPH'S WORLD	July 1, 2001	Womans Club	$534.00
RALPH'S WORLD	April 20, 2002	Womans Club	$478.00
RANDY NEWMAN	October 19, 2003	Pantages	$31,441.00
RAT DOG	November 2, 1998	State Theatre	$31,490.00
RAT PACK	February 13, 2007	State Theatre	$471,143.30
RATDOG	November 2, 1998	State Theatre	$31,490.00
RAVI / ANOUSHKA SHANKAR	May 3, 2002	State Theatre	$67,475.00
RAY CHARLES	August 11, 1988	State Theatre	$37,925.50
RAY CHARLES	September 15, 1989	Orpheum	$47,000.00
RAY CHARLES	June 4, 1992	State Theatre	$54,247.00
RAY CHARLES	April 10, 2002	State Theatre	$47,237.50
RAY DAVIES	October 5, 2001	Womans Club	$13,860.00
RED ARMY CHORUS	October 12, 1989	Orpheum	$71,000.00
REDEYE	July 24, 1971	Midway Stad	SEE ALLMAN BRO
RENT	March 26, 2009	Orpheum	$779,028.00
REO SPEEDWAGON	February 1, 1992	Orpheum	$51,720.50
REPLACEMENTS	February 7, 1991	Orpheum	$97,832.00
RETURN TO FOREVER	August 24, 2011	Orpheum	$70,521.50
RHYTHMIC CIRCUS	August 12, 2011	Pantages	$40,148.80
RHYTHMIC CIRCUS	July 20, 2012	Pantages	$40,422.00
RICH LITTLE	February 9, 2003	State Theatre	$39,738.25
RICHARD LEWIS	January 26, 2001	Womans Club	$3,577.00
RICHARD MARX	August 10, 1994	Orpheum	$32,215.50
RICHARD PRYOR	May 29, 1993	State Theatre	$32,222.00
RICK SPRINGFIELD	March 23, 2014	Pantages	$34,050.00

CONCERT NAME	CONCERT DATE	CONCERT VENUE	CONCERT GROSS
RICKIE LEE JONES	August 5, 2005	Pantages	$20,645.00
RICKIE LEE JONES	April 13, 2012	Pantages	$12,195.00
RICKY VAN SHELTON	May 17, 1992	Orpheum	$59,703.50
RIGHTEOUS BROTHERS	July 9, 1992	Orpheum	$76,775.25
RIGHTEOUS BROTHERS	July 15, 1993	State Theatre	$75,127.50
RIGHTEOUS BROTHERS	June 12, 1995	State Theatre	$83,467.50
RIGHTEOUS BROTHERS	February 14, 1996	Madison CC	$83,586.00
RIGHTEOUS BROTHERS	April 11, 1996	Davenport IA	$73,244.75
RIGHTEOUS BROTHERS	June 8, 1996	Des Moines	$73,079.00
RIGHTEOUS BROTHERS	June 9, 1996	Orpheum	$64,788.50
RIGHTEOUS BROTHERS	April 23, 1997	Orpheum	$90,080.00
RINGO STARR	October 16, 2015	State Theatre	$213,260.00
RIVERDANCE	February 15, 1997	Orpheum	$1,796,523.50
RIVERDANCE	March 12, 1998	Orpheum	$4,129,606.50
RIVERDANCE	October 7, 1999	Orpheum	$2,534,955.34
RIVERDANCE	August 22, 2000	Rside Milwaukee	$1,063,318.90
RIVERDANCE	September 12, 2001	Orpheum	$1,909,754.00
RIVERDANCE	October 15, 2002	Rside Milwaukee	$485,091.50
RIVERDANCE	June 11, 2006	Orpheum	$465,061.50
RIVERDANCE	May 8, 2009	State Theatre	$444,230.50
RIVERDANCE	March 18, 2011	State Theatre	$349,708.00
RIVERDANCE	March 25, 2016	State Theatre	$401,291.75
ROBBIE FULKS	April 12, 2002	Womans Club	$1,261.50
ROBERT BALLARD (NG)	March 31, 2005	State Theatre	$18,645.00
ROBERT CRAY	September 6, 1988	State Theatre	$38,110.50
ROBERT CRAY	November 13, 1990	Orpheum	$55,000.00
ROBERT CRAY	November 19, 1993	State Theatre	$41,148.00
ROBERT CRAY	May 19, 2011	Pantages	$20,280.00
ROBERT MIRABAL	October 12, 2001	State Theatre	$13,370.25
ROBERT PALMER	November 26, 1988	Orpheum	$61,000.00
ROBERTA FLACK	July 29, 1979	Orpheum	$17,500.00
ROCKAPELLA	May 14, 1999	State Theatre	$30,626.50
ROCKAPELLA	December 13, 2001	Womans Club	$15,566.50

CONCERT NAME	CONCERT DATE	CONCERT VENUE	CONCERT GROSS
RODNEY CARRINGTON	October 16, 2015	Pantages	$21,888.00
RODRIGO Y GABRIELA	October 17, 2009	Pantages	$31,356.00
RODRIGO Y GABRIELA	July 15, 2014	State Theatre	$64,469.00
RODRIGUEZ	May 17, 2014	State Theatre	$82,105.00
ROGER WATERS	July 6, 2000	Target Center	$395,605.50
RON WHITE	April 15, 2005	State Theatre	$397,403.50
RON WHITE	March 9, 2007	Orpheum	$302,231.00
ROSEANNE BARR	July 25, 1991	Orpheum	$35,249.00
ROSEANNE CASH	September 24, 2006	Pantages	$23,825.00
ROXETTE	February 23, 1992	Orpheum	$46,340.00
RUBEN BLADES	November 24, 2002	Pantages	$16,128.00
RUFUS WAINWRIGHT	May 12, 2001	400 Bar	$5,500.00
RUFUS WAINWRIGHT	October 18, 2008	State Theatre	$59,618.00
RUGRATS LIVE	December 9, 1998	Orpheum	$151,917.50
RYAN ADAMS	March 11, 2002	Orpheum	$49,028.00
RYAN ADAMS	October 18, 2002	State Theatre	$47,541.00
S. CLARKE/DI MEOLA/PONTY	August 23, 1995	Orpheum	$38,212.50
SADE	March 14, 1993	Northrop	$115,597.50
SADE	August 4, 2001	Target Center	$430,020.00
SAM ABELL (NG)	April 17, 2008	State Theatre	$19,000.00
SAM KINISON	March 25, 1990	Orpheum	$43,000.00
SAM KINISON	January 17, 1992	State Theatre	$27,970.00
SAMMY HAGAR	July 11, 1997	Milwaukee	$32,777.50
SAMMY HAGAR	November 22, 2000	State Theatre	$37,187.00
SANDRA BERNHARD	September 19, 1994	State Theatre	$17,663.00
SANDRA BERNHART	April 21, 1999	Womans Club	$38,017.50
SANDY PATTI	December 9, 1997	State Theatre	$21,915.50
SANTANA	August 22, 2000	Target Center	$532,152.00
SARA BAREILLES	November 2, 2010	Pantages	$24,100.00
SARAH BRIGHTMAN	July 18, 1999	Orpheum	$123,585.00
SARAH MCLACHLAN	August 23, 1994	State Theatre	$36,914.00
SARAH VAUGHN	May 7, 1989	Orpheum	$37,000.00
SATURDAY NIGHT FEVER	May 9, 2001	Orpheum	$575,163.70

CONCERT NAME	CONCERT DATE	CONCERT VENUE	CONCERT GROSS
SAVAGE GARDEN	September 13, 2000	Orpheum	$70,372.50
SAVION GLOVER	April 7, 2000	State Theatre	$70,049.75
SAW DOCTORS	August 22, 2000	400 Bar	$3,480.00
SAW DOCTORS	September 5, 2002	First Avenue	$2,365.00
SCOOBY-DOO	May 8, 2002	Orpheum	$285,526.50
SCOTT THOMPSON	September 19, 1997	Music Box Th	$8,595.00
SCRIPT	October 22, 2010	State Theatre	$46,353.00
SCRIPT	August 30, 2011	Orpheum	$71,537.50
SCRIPT	October 26, 2012	Orpheum	$67,911.50
SCRIPT	June 5, 2015	State Theatre	$63,624.50
SEAL	November 15, 1994	State Theatre	$49,465.00
SEAL	June 11, 1999	State Theatre	$48,600.00
SEALS & CROFTS / LR BAND	August 4, 1992	State Theatre	$19,764.50
SEBASTIN MANASCALCO	May 21, 2017	State Theatre	$106,466.00
SECRET GARDEN	April 28, 2005	Pantages	$10,934.00
SECRET GARDEN (BWAY)	April 29, 1994	Orpheum	$211,336.30
SEMISONIC	April 21, 2001	State Theatre	$48,697.50
SETH MEYERS	June 16, 2017	State Theatre	$83,939.32
SEUSSICAL	February 11, 2003	Orpheum	$578,385.00
SHAOLIN MONKS	February 14, 2003	State Theatre	$74,484.00
SHARI LEWIS / LAMBCHOP	November 3, 1994	State Theatre	$10,469.50
SHARON LOIS & BRAM	April 27, 1989	Orpheum	$24,000.00
SHARON LOIS & BRAM	April 21, 1990	Orpheum	$22,000.00
SHAWN COLVIN	November 10, 1994	State Theatre	$36,325.00
SHAWN COLVIN	March 26, 1997	State Theatre	$47,133.50
SHAWN PHILLIPS	April 11, 1975	Duluth Aud	$11,764.00
SHAWN PHILLIPS / HALL & O	November 3, 1975	Duluth Aud	$9,317.00
SHEDAISY	November 14, 2002	Pantages	$22,120.00
SHIRLEY CAESAR	April 19, 1992	State Theatre	$21,257.50
SHIRLEY CAESAR	April 11, 1993	State Theatre	$12,385.00
SHIRLEY MCCLAINE	August 21, 1992	State Theatre	$96,450.50
SHOWBOAT	September 17, 1996	Orpheum	$3,898,623.10
SIGUR ROS	September 28, 2001	Womans Club	$11,142.00

CONCERT NAME	CONCERT DATE	CONCERT VENUE	CONCERT GROSS
SIGUR ROS	September 24, 2005	State Theatre	$62,127.00
SINBAD	July 7, 1990	Orpheum	$43,000.00
SING ALONG SOUND OF M	April 26, 2001	State Theatre	$100,875.75
SING-A-LONG WIZ OF OZ	January 16, 2004	State Theatre	$29,867.25
SISSEL	February 8, 2008	Pantages	$29,991.00
SLAYER	January 30, 1991	Orpheum	$44,400.00
SMOKEY JOE'S CAFÉ	August 16, 1996	State Theatre	$1,190,345.20
SMOOTH JAZZ CHRISTMAS	December 3, 1998	State Theatre	$23,368.50
SMOTHERS BROTHERS	May 18, 1993	State Theatre	$33,464.26
SOUL ASYLUM	December 31, 1998	State Theatre	$41,800.00
SOUND OF MUSIC	August 24, 1999	Orpheum	$1,488,855.50
SOUNDS OF BLACKNESS	November 27, 1992	Orpheum	$106,850.00
SOUNDS OF BLACKNESS	November 26, 1993	State Theatre	$100,426.00
SOUNDS OF BLACKNESS	December 16, 1996	State Theatre	$70,208.81
SOUNDS OF BLACKNESS	December 16, 1996	State Theatre	$70,208.81
SOUNDS OF BLACKNESS	December 13, 1997	Orpheum	$49,980.83
SOUNDS OF BLACKNESS	December 21, 1998	Orpheum	$22,954.00
SOUTH PACIFIC (R GOULET)	February 21, 1989	Orpheum	$220,000.00
SOUTH PACIFIC (R GOULET)	October 1, 2002	Orpheum	$245,218.03
SOWETO GOSPEL CHOIR	March 22, 2007	State Theatre	$32,860.50
SPELLING BEE	November 7, 2006	State Theatre	$234,782.80
SPIDERMAN	March 4, 2003	Orpheum	$265,119.50
SPINAL TAP	May 19, 1992	Orpheum	$55,781.50
SPIRIT (BROADWAY)	October 26, 1999	Orpheum	$150,071.50
SPRING AWAKENING	January 6, 2009	State Theatre	$724,386.00
SQUIRREL NUT ZIPPERS	November 7, 1998	State Theatre	$40,843.00
STARLIGHT EXPRESS	July 21, 2003	Orpheum	$575,054.95
STARS	November 3, 2007	Pantages	$16,191.00
STEELES	December 22, 1999	State Theatre	$35,836.25
STEPHEN SONDHEIM	March 5, 2010	State Theatre	$27,740.00
STEVE EARLE	July 23, 2011	Pantages	$38,342.00
STEVE EARLE	September 5, 2015	Pantages	$31,279.00
STEVE EARLE	November 5, 2016	Pantages	$48,800.50

CONCERT NAME	CONCERT DATE	CONCERT VENUE	CONCERT GROSS
STEVE GOODMAN	November 6, 1976	UMD Kirby	$1,869.90
STEVE GOODMAN	October 7, 1977	O'Shaughnessy	$7,592.00
STEVE HARVEY	March 18, 2000	Orpheum	$69,306.00
STEVE LAWRENCE / E GORME	October 23, 1990	Orpheum	$107,000.00
STEVE LAWRENCE / E GORME	October 9, 1993	State Theatre	$95,377.50
STEVE MARTIN	February 27, 1977	O'Shaughnessy	$9,320.00
STEVE MARTIN / SHORT	May 18, 2017	Orpheum	$680,115.00
STEVE MARTIN BLUEGRASS	June 13, 2010	State Theatre	$103,505.00
STEVE MARTIN BLUEGRASS	July 22, 2013	State Theatre	$134,423.00
STEVE WINWOOD	November 2, 1997	State Theatre	$55,000.00
STEVE WINWOOD	April 17, 2015	State Theatre	$125,466.50
STEVE WINWOOD	February 23, 2017	State Theatre	$149,680.50
STEVEN WRIGHT	March 28, 1999	State Theatre	$35,736.00
STING	December 5, 1999	Orpheum	$236,995.00
STOMP	February 5, 1997	State Theatre	$886,874.70
STOMP	April 1, 1998	State Theatre	$927,418.60
STYX	June 25, 1991	Orpheum	$53,527.50
SUGAR BABIES	July 30, 1985	Northrop	$260,000.00
SUNSET BOULEVARD	December 8, 1996	Orpheum	$3,030,117.10
SWAN LAKE (BOURNE)	February 8, 2006	State Theatre	$213,475.50
SWEENEY TODD	February 5, 2008	State Theatre	$499,860.00
SWEET CHARITY	February 8, 2005	Orpheum	$1,060,490.01
SWEET HONEY IN THE ROCK	March 9, 1996	Orpheum	$59,620.00
SWING (BROADWAY)	January 15, 2002	Orpheum	$620,071.15
SYLVIA	October 11, 2006	Pantages	$98,047.00
TAJ MAHAL	February 5, 1977	UM W Bank	$6,860.00
TAJ MAHAL	October 29, 1977	O'Shaughnessy	$17,708.00
TAJ MAHAL	March 26, 1978	O'Shaughnessy	$7,151.00
TAJ MAHAL / KEB MO	September 6, 2017	State Theatre	$114,073.00
TALLULAH	October 1, 2000	State Theatre	$371,133.70
TANGERINE DREAM	October 18, 1992	Orpheum	$21,600.50
TAP DOGS	November 12, 1996	State Theatre	$483,445.95
TAP DOGS	October 14, 1997	State Theatre	$249,658.40

CONCERT NAME	CONCERT DATE	CONCERT VENUE	CONCERT GROSS
TAP DOGS	November 3, 2001	State Theatre	$94,363.00
TEMPTATIONS	November 7, 1996	State Theatre	$42,428.00
TEMPTATIONS / FOUR TOPS	July 7, 1993	State Theatre	$51,951.75
TEMPTATIONS / SPINNERS	November 7, 1996	State Theatre	$42,428.00
TEN TENORS	November 5, 2005	State Theatre	$32,867.00
TEN TENORS	April 24, 2009	State Theatre	$19,047.78
TEN TENORS	April 24, 2009	State Theatre	$27,000.00
TENACIOUS D	February 3, 2001	First Avenue	$23,182.00
TENACIOUS D	October 3, 2001	State Theatre	$47,517.50
TENORS	June 14, 2013	State Theatre	$69,295.50
TERRY GROSS	September 26, 2002	State Theatre	$9,271.50
THIRD EYE BLIND	March 16, 2000	Orpheum	$57,528.00
THIRTY DAYS IN FROGTOWN	October 3, 2003	Pantages	$9,021.00
THREE 'MO TENORS	February 23, 2003	State Theatre	$90,232.50
THREE DOORS DOWN	November 7, 2000	Roy Wilkins	$46,720.00
tic . . . tic . . . BOOM	March 11, 2003	Pantages	$139,733.83
TIM & ERIC	January 22, 2009	Pantages	$24,325.00
TIM & ERIC	November 17, 2010	State Theatre	$33,670.00
TIM & ERIC	September 26, 2014	State Theatre	$59,295.00
TIM & ERIC	July 26, 2017	State Theatre	$60,098.50
TIM ALLEN	March 23, 1991	Orpheum	$47,196.00
TIM CONWAY / KORMAN	October 15, 2006	State Theatre	$138,150.50
TIM REYONOLDS	October 26, 2001	Womans Club	$9,005.50
TIMBUKTU! (ERTHA KITT)	November 7, 1979	Orpheum	$350,000.00
TINA TURNER	March 23, 2000	Target Center	$780,656.50
TINA TURNER	November 11, 2000	Target Center	$843,327.00
TITANIC	May 16, 2000	Orpheum	$892,115.05
TODD RUNDGREN	May 5, 1991	Orpheum	$28,700.00
TODD RUNDGREN	January 22, 2008	Pantages	$28,083.00
TODD RUNDGREN	September 15, 2009	State Theatre	$42,555.50
TOM WAITS	October 11, 1979	Orpheum	$37,000.00
TOM WAITS	November 1, 1987	Orpheum	$39,391.50
TOM WAITS	August 29, 1999	State Theatre	$182,592.50

CONCERT NAME	CONCERT DATE	CONCERT VENUE	CONCERT GROSS
TONY BENNETT	March 6, 1993	State Theatre	$58,729.00
TONY BENNETT	March 17, 1996	Orpheum	$74,096.00
TONY BENNETT	January 20, 2013	State Theatre	$172,687.00
TONY BENNETT	May 6, 2016	State Theatre	$176,288.00
TONY BENNETT / KD LANG	September 8, 2001	Target Center	$132,109.00
TONY GLOVER	June 26, 1971	Midway Stad	SEE THE BAND
TORI AMOS	July 14, 1994	State Theatre	$81,960.00
TORI AMOS	October 21, 2001	Orpheum	$93,500.00
TOSHI REAGON	April 1, 2000	400 Bar	$1,494.00
TRACY CHAPMAN	May 23, 1992	Orpheum	$47,062.50
TRACY CHAPMAN	March 14, 1996	State Theatre	$41,920.00
TRACY CHAPMAN	June 10, 1999	State Theatre	$69,253.00
TRACY CHAPMAN	April 12, 2000	State Theatre	$70,929.50
TRAGICALLY HIP	September 22, 1998	State Theatre	$30,487.00
TRAILER PARK BOYS	October 17, 2010	Pantages	$27,780.00
TRAILER PARK BOYS	October 4, 2011	Pantages	$29,278.00
TRAILER PARK BOYS	December 14, 2012	State Theatre	$69,787.00
TRAILER PARK BOYS	December 7, 2014	State Theatre	$92,480.00
TRAMPLED BY TURTLES	December 31, 2007	Orpheum	$39,433.00
TRAVIS	May 21, 2000	The Quest	$11,882.50
TRAVIS	September 21, 2000	The Quest	$23,159.00
TRAVIS	October 13, 2001	State Theatre	$51,892.50
TRIBUTE TO MOTOWN	June 15, 1996	State Theatre	$11,989.50
TRISHA YEARWOOD	May 23, 2000	State Theatre	$71,011.50
TRISHA YEARWOOD	October 11, 2001	State Theatre	$44,745.00
TRISHA YEARWOOD / C RAYE	November 4, 1995	Northrop	$81,529.00
TRUMBO	January 25, 2005	Pantages	$68,891.25
TUESDAYS WITH MORRIE	January 31, 2006	Orpheum	$361,344.23
TWELVE ANGRY MEN	December 5, 2006	State Theatre	$396,245.65
TYPE O NEGATIVE	February 22, 2000	Roy Wilkins	$28,710.00
U2	May 1, 2001	Target Center	$1,465,425.00
UB40 / GIN BLOSSOMS	August 14, 1993	State Theatre	$41,496.00
UNDER THE STREETLAMP	June 17, 2012	Pantages	$18,914.00

CONCERT NAME	CONCERT DATE	CONCERT VENUE	CONCERT GROSS
URINETOWN	September 30, 2003	Orpheum	$738,863.80
VAGINA MONOLOGUES	November 7, 2000	Womans Club	$221,102.25
VANDROSS / WILLIAMS	September 23, 1997	Target Center	$168,835.00
VANDROSS / WILLIAMS	September 23, 2000	Target Center	$335,000.00
VANILLA ICE	February 3, 1991	Orpheum	$45,860.00
VEGGIE TALES	January 28, 2002	State Theatre	$354,975.50
VIC CHESTNUT KRISTI HERSH	May 21, 2000	Womans Club	$2,600.00
VICTOR BORGE	October 30, 1992	Orpheum	$79,691.00
VICTOR VICTORIA	May 23, 1995	Orpheum	$2,996,039.65
VICTORIA WILLIAMS	October 6, 2000	Womans Club	$2,569.00
VIENNA CHOIR BOYS	November 19, 2006	Pantages	$16,725.00
VINCE GILL	February 22, 2003	Pantages	$31,015.50
VINCE GILL	October 14, 2005	State Theatre	$49,973.50
VINCE GILL	October 13, 2012	State Theatre	$88,003.50
VIOLENT FEMMES	April 24, 2000	Orpheum	$26,950.50
VONDA SHEPHARD	October 13, 2000	State Theatre	$31,145.00
WALLFLOWERS	November 24, 2000	Orpheum	$53,742.00
WARWICK / BACHARACH	July 30, 1992	Orpheum	$49,547.00
WAYLON JENNINGS	July 15, 1977	Met Center	$72,500.50
WAYLON JENNINGS	October 29, 1977	Ann Arbor MI	$32,179.00
WAYLON JENNINGS	October 30, 1977	Grand Rapids MI	$31,184.00
WAYLON JENNINGS	July 21, 1978	Duluth Aud	$35,111.00
WAYLON JENNINGS	July 22, 1978	St. Paul CC	$109,499.00
WAYLON JENNINGS	June 7, 1980	Met Center	$111,000.00
WAYNE BRADY	April 28, 2001	Orpheum	$51,698.00
WAYNE BRADY	April 13, 2002	State Theatre	$54,007.50
WAYNE NEWTON	June 26, 1992	Orpheum	$43,939.00
WEDDING SINGER	September 25, 2007	Orpheum	$399,389.00
WEIRD AL YANKOVIC	June 30, 1992	Orpheum	$29,162.00
WEIRD AL YANKOVIC	August 6, 1994	State Theatre	$25,024.50
WEIRD AL YANKOVIC	May 3, 2012	State Theatre	$86,634.50
WEIRD AL YANKOVIC	August 19, 2016	State Theatre	$111,826.50
WHOSE LINE IS IT . . .	February 18, 2015	State Theatre	$83,618.00

CONCERT NAME	CONCERT DATE	CONCERT VENUE	CONCERT GROSS
WICKED	July 12, 2006	Orpheum	$2,553,561.56
WICKED	November 5, 2008	Orpheum	$7,348,217.00
WICKED	August 10, 2010	Orpheum	$9,727,199.00
WIDESPREAD PANIC	October 2, 1998	State Theatre	$43,171.00
WIDESPREAD PANIC	November 18, 2000	Roy Wilkins	$90,600.00
WILLIAM SHATNER	March 15, 2012	Orpheum	$103,791.40
WINANS FAMILY	September 22, 1991	Orpheum	$31,562.50
WINANS FAMILY	June 11, 2002	Orpheum	$33,015.00
WIZ	May 27, 1997	State Theatre	$124,574.80
WIZARD OF OZ	December 20, 1991	State Theatre	$9,890.00
WIZARD OF OZ	January 14, 1999	Orpheum	$1,211,955.00
WOLFMOTHER	November 14, 2009	State Theatre	$33,148.50
WONDERFUL TOWN	October 19, 2004	Orpheum	$335,000.00
WOODSTOCK (MOVIE)	August 12, 1994	State Theatre	$15,120.00
WOODY ALLEN	August 2, 2015	State Theatre	$69,128.50
Y ADAMS / F HAMMOND	March 7, 2000	Orpheum	$44,768.00
Y ADAMS / S CAESAR	November 7, 2000	State Theatre	$40,221.50
YAKOV SMIRNOFF	February 21, 2004	Pantages	$21,458.50
YANNI	May 21, 1991	Orpheum	$99,321.00
YANNI	May 21, 1992	Orpheum	$121,774.00
YES	November 18, 1997	State Theatre	$67,560.00
YES	November 12, 1999	Orpheum	$70,360.00
YES	November 23, 2002	State Theatre	$105,535.00
YES WITH ORCHESTRA	August 7, 2001	State Theatre	$106,550.00
YO GABBA GABBA	September 15, 2011	State Theatre	$66,110.00
YONDER MT STRING BAND	November 7, 2003	State Theatre	$32,615.50
YONDER MT STRING BAND	April 29, 2005	Pantages	$44,280.50
YONDER MT STRING BAND	September 29, 2006	State Theatre	$29,657.00
YOUNG FRANKENSTEIN	February 9, 2010	Orpheum	$761,582.00
YVONNE ELLIMAN	July 19, 1978	O'Shaughnessy	$2,698.00
ZZ TOP	November 4, 1996	State Theatre	$62,816.00

$394,331,896.40
GROSS

APPENDIX 3

MINNEAPOLIS BROADWAY SEASONS

1992/1993 THROUGH 2009/2010

SEASON	PRESENTERS	MINNNEAPOLIS SHOWS	ST. PAUL SHOWS
1992-1993	Ordway / Jujamcyn	Joseph and the . . . (Orpheum)	The Secret Garden
		Evita (Orpheum)	Richard III
		Lost in Yonkers (Orpheum)	City of Angels
		Cats (State)	Lettice & Lovage
			Phantom of the Opera
			Shear Madness
1993-1994	Ordway / Jujamcyn	Miss Saignon (Orpheum)	Guys and Dolls
		Aspects of Love (State)	Les Miserables
		My Fair Lady (State)	Annie Get Your Gun
		Five Guys Named Moe (State)	Camelot
			Will Rogers Follies
1994 - 1995	Ordway / Jujamcyn	Camelot (Orpheum)	The Sound of Music
		Hello Dolly (Orpheum)	Crazy for You
		Blood Brothers (Orpheum)	Cats
		Jelly's Last Jam (State)	Fiddler on the Roof
		Phantom of the Opera (Orpheum)	The Sisters Rosensweig
		Cats (State)	Les Miserables
1995 - 1996	Ordway / Jujamcyn	Kiss of the Spider Woman (State)	Show Boat
		Ain't Misbehavin' (State)	Damn Yankees
		Dial "M" For Murder (State)	West Side Story
		Beauty and the Beast (Orpheum)	An Inspector Calls
1996 - 1997	Theatre Live! / Jujamcyn	How to Succeed in Busness (Orpheum)	
		Smokey Joe's Café (State)	

SEASON	PRESENTERS	MINNNEAPOLIS SHOWS	ST. PAUL SHOWS
		Funny Girl (Orpheum)	
		Carousel (Orpheum)	
		Sunset Boulevard (Orpheum)	
		The King & I (Orpheum)	
		Show Boat (Orpheum)	
		Barrymore (State)	
1997 - 1998	Theatre Live! / Jujamcyn	The Lion King (Orpheum)	
		Master Class (State)	
		Defending the Caveman (State)	
		42nd Street (Orpheum)	
		Noise / Funk (Orpheum)	
		Chicago (State)	
1998 / 1999	Theatre Live! / Jujamcyn	Ragtime (Orpheum)	
		The Civil War (Orpheum)	
		The Gin Game (State)	
		Jekyll & Hyde (Orpheum)	
		Footloose (Orpheum)	
1999-2000	Theatre Live / Jujamcyn	The Sound of Music (Orpheum)	
		Joseph and the . . . (State)	
		Cabaret (State)	
		Art (State)	
		Fosse (Orpheum)	
		Titanic (Orpheum)	
2000 - 2001	Theatre Live! / Jujancyn	Annie Get Your Gun (Orpheum)	
		Tallulah (State)	
		Dame Edna (State)	
		Beauty & The Beast (Orpheum)	
		Saturday Night Fever (Orpheum)	
		Cinderella (Orpheum)	
		The Civil War (State)	
		Aida (Orpheum)	
2001 - 2002	Theatre Live! / Jujamcyn	Mamma Mia (Orpheum)	
		Swing! (Orpheum)	

SEASON	PRESENTERS	MINNNEAPOLIS SHOWS	ST. PAUL SHOWS
		Fifflrt on the Roof (Orpheum)	
		Best Little Whorehouse (Orpheum)	
		Blast! (State)	
		Defending the Caveman (State)	
2002 - 2003	Theatre Live! / Jujamcyn	The Producers (Orpheum)	
		Radio City Chrstmas (Orpheum)	
		Jesus Christ Superstar (Orpheum)	
		Seussical the Musical (Orpheum)	
		Starlight Express (Orpheum)	
		Urinetown the Musical (Orpheum)	
2003 - 2004	Theatre Live! / Jujamcyn	The Graduate (State)	
		Oklahoma! (Oroheum)	
		Hairspray (Orpheum)	
		The Exonerated (State)	
		Phantom of the Opera (Orpheum)	
2004 - 2005	Henn. Th Trust / BAA	Patti LaPone (Orpheum)	
		Wonderful Town (Orpheum)	
		Sweet Charity (Orpheum)	
		The Lion King (Orpheum)	
		Little Shop of Horrors (Orpheum)_	
		Movin' Out (Orpheum)_	
2005 - 2006	Henn Th Trust / BAA	Joseph and the . . . (Orpheum)	
		Radio City Christmas (Orpheum)	
		Little Women (Orpheum)	
		Tuesdays with Morrie (State)	
		Annie (Orpheum)	
		Wicked (Orpheum)	
2006 - 2007	Henn Th Trust / BAA	Spelling Bee (State)	
		Altar Boyz (Pantages)	
		Doubt (State)	
		Hairspray (Orpheum)	
		Twelve Angry Men (State)	
		The Rat Pack (Orpheum)	

SEASON	PRESENTERS	MINNNEAPOLIS SHOWS	ST. PAUL SHOWS
		Light in the Piazza (Orpheum)	
		Cats (Orpheum)	
2007 - 2008	Henn Th Trust / BAA	The Wedding Singer (Orpheum)	
		The Lion King (Orpheum)	
		Avenue Q (State)	
		Sweeny Todd (State)	
		My Fair Lady (Orpheum)	
		Jersey Boys (Orpheum)	
2008 - 2009	Henn Th Trust / BAA	Wicked (Orpheum)	
		Grease (Orpheum)	
		Frost / Nixon (State)	
		Spring Awakening (Orpheum)	
		Fidler on the Roof (Orpheum)	
		A Chorsu Line (Orpheum)	
		Phantom of the Opera (Orpheum)	
		A Brons Tale (State)	
		Rent (Orpheum)	
		Annie (Orpheum)	
2009 - 2010	Henn Th Trust / BAA	Mary Poppins (Orpheum)	
		101 Dalmatians (Orpheum)	
		In the Heights (Orpheum)	
		Dreamgirls (Orpheum)	
		Young Frankenstein (Orpheum)	
		Dirty Dancing (Orpheum)	
		Mamma Mia (Orpheum)	
		Avenue Q (Orpheum)	

INDEX

Page numbers in **bold** indicate illustrations.

Abbott Northwestern Hospital, 131–132, 133, 134
Aida, 168
Alk, Howard, 72, **72**
Allen, Ralph, 175
Allen, Woody, 236–237
Allman, Duane, 27–28, 33
Allman, Gregg, 28, 33
The Allman Brothers, 27–28, **29**, 33
Anderson, Loni, 140
Anderson, Marian, 19
Andrews, Julie, 164
Applegate, Christina, 164
Aquatennial (1970s), 202
"Aquatennial Spectacular" (1968), 24–25
"Aretha Franklin Review," 24–25, **25**
Armstrong, Louis, 4–5, **5**
Artspace Projects
    saving Pantages and, 186–187
    Schubert and, 195–198
Asleep at the Wheel, 181

Bacharach, Burt, 6, 112, 113, 144–147, **145**
Baez, Joan, 70
Bailey, F. Lee, 181
Bailey, Jim, 218–219
Baker, Anita, 227–229
Baldry, Long John, 28
The Band, 25
Barclay, Steven, 215–216
Barrymore, 153
Baryshnikov, Mikhail "Misha," 149, **150**, 151–152
Bay City Rollers, 142
Beacom, Harry, **30**
    basic facts about, 25
    Bennett and, 202
    Chad Mitchell Trio and, 148
    Ellis and, 105

    end of promotions by, 30–31
    finances, 29, 30–31, 105
    The First Edition and The Foundations show,
       21, 22
    "Open Air Celebration," 25–27
    "Open Air Celebration II 'Superball,'" 27–29
    staff, **31**
    Warwick and, 146
    Zimmerman and, 69
Beatles, 24, 237–238
Beauty and the Beast, 164
Becker, Rob, 159–160, **160**
Belafonte, Harry, 138–139
Belton, Sharon Sayles, 92, 128, 188
Bennett, Michael, 50
Bennett, Tony, 201–203, **202**
Benson, George, 147–148
Betts, Dickey, 28, 33
Betts, Keter, 120
Binger, James
    clout of, 91, 130
    Joseph and The Amazing Technicolor Dreamcoat, 96
    Fred Krohn and, 251
    Ordway and, 127, 128
    Shubert Theater and, 197
    See also Jujamcyn Productions
Blackstone, Harry, 135
Blackstone, Harry, Jr., 135
Blair, Dennis, 176
Blakey, Art, 18
The Blenders, 223
Block E and Shubert Theatre, 192–193, 195
Blue Condition, 157, 158
Boehlke, Bain, 219
Bohlander, Fred, 44
Boschwitz, Rudy, 144
"boss," 120
Bourdain, Anthony, 233–234
Boyce, Tommy, 180

Bramlett, Bonnie, 32
Bramlett, Delaney, 32
Brand, Mike, 161
Bream, Jon, 143, 220
Brookfield Management, 192–193
Brubeck, Dave, 47–48
Bublé, Michael, 226–227
The Buckinghams, 44
Buffy (dog), 7
Burnett, Carol, 231, **232**, 233
Bush, Walter, 105, 178
Butterfield Blues Band, 25

Caesar, Shirley, 143
Caldwell, Bobby, 157–158
Calhoun Beach Club, 147
Campbell, Glen, 180
"Canadian songbird." *See* Murray, Anne
Cannes Film Festival, 70, 72, **72**, **73**
Carleton College
    Fred Krohn as student at, 62–66, **66**
    Lord of the Rings premiere to benefit, 220–222,
        221
    shows run by Fred Krohn, 18–22, 25
Carlson, Arne, 68, 167, **167**
Carlson, Barbara, 68, 137
Carlson, Susan, 68, 167, **167**
Carroll, Leo G., 7–8, **8**
Chad Mitchell Trio, 148
Chalfen, Morris "Morrie," 29–30
Champion, Gower, 50–51, 81
Channing, Carol, 203–205, **204**
Chapin, Harry, 46
Charles, Ray, 89–90
Cheap Trick, 87
Chelseth, Archie D., 63
Cherryhomes, Jackie, 186, 188
Chicago Tribune, 14, **14**
Children's Theatre, 55
Chiodini, John, 124
A Chorus Line, 49–51, **51**, 75–78, 79, 80–81
"Christmas Card from a Hooker in Minneapolis"
    (song), 54
Christmas This Way (Krohn), 3–4
Circuit Films, 70
Cirque du Soleil, 206–207
City Pages, 189
CityBusiness, 187
Clear Channel Entertainment, 244, 245, 246, 247, 250
Clements, Terry, 110
Cliburn, Van, 19

Close, Glenn, 166
Coca, Imogene, 10, **12**
Cole, Natalie, 157
Coleman, Laurie, 213–214
Coleman, Norm, 213–214
Collins, Judy, 18–19, **19**, 33–34
Colter, Jessi, 41, 43, 181
Connor, Bill, 128, 129
Coolidge, Rita, 34
Cooper, Alice, 235–236
Copperfield, David, 87, 135–136
COVID shutdown, 260–261
Crenshaw, Stephen, 49, 51, **51**

Dale Warland Singers, 47–48
Dame Edna, 155–157, **156**, 164
Dave Brubeck and his Trio, 47–48
Davies, Dennis Russell, 47–48
Davis, Chip, 134
Davis, Miles, 134–135
Dayton's Department Store
    Line, 200
    The Lion King world premiere, 165, 168
    pop stars at, 146
Defending the Caveman, 159–160, **161**
Delaney & Bonnie & Friends, 25, **27**, 32
Denver, John, 148
Dickinson, Angie, 144
Dietrich, Marlene, xiii, **xiii**, 111–116, **117**, 118
Disney University, 164, **164**
Dittmar, John, 235
"The Divine One," 58
Dochtermann, Kevin, **182**, **183**
Don Ellis Orchestra, 30–31
Donovan, Deborah, 10–12
Donovan, Josh, 10–12
Donovan, Mark, 10–12
Dorothy Hamill's Nutcracker On Ice, 131–134, **132**
Drabinsky, Garth, 94–96, 252
Durenberger, David, 63
Durham, Bobby, 120
Dylan, Bob, **71**
    "Open Air Celebration" and, 25
    Orpheum and, 76–80, 82–83, 85–86
    Renaldo & Clara, 70, 72, 74
    Zimmerman as conduit to, 69
Dylan, Maria, 75
Dziedzic, Walter, 131

Edelstein, Mel, 70, 73
Eder, Linda, 229

Eisler, Chuck, 48–49
Eisner, Michael, 164, 167
Elaine Stritch at Liberty, 225–226
Eldridge, Roy, 120
Ellis, Don, 30–31, 105
Esther (assistant of Mann), 78
Evans, Linda, 139–140
Expo 67, 23

Felder, Raoul, 174, 175
"Fever," 124, 125
The First Edition, 21–22
"The First Lady of Song." *See* Fitzgerald, Ella
Fitzgerald, Ella, **119**, **120**
    characteristics, 120
    concert poster problem, 120–121
    daytime soap operas and, 119–120
    death, 122
    fur coat, 121, 122
    moniker, 58
    nightcap with Fred Krohn, 121–122
Fjelstad, Ralph, 62, 63
Flanagan, Tommy, 120
Flatley, Michael, 154
folk music, 111, 148
    See also specific artists
Foster, David, 227
The Foundations, 21–22
Francis, Michael, 168
Frankie Valli and the Four Seasons, 180
Franklin, Aretha, 24–25, 58, 143
Fraser, Don, 91
Frasier, Joe, 148
Frauenshuh, David, 91, 92–93
Freeman, Stan, 114, 115
Fuller, Buckminster, 21

Garland, Judy, **14**, 14–15, **16**, 17, 218
Gelder, Lawrence Van, 173
Gigi, 12–13
Ginell, Richard, 48
Glover, Tony, 25
"Godmother of Soul," 58, 141–142
The Good Brothers, 108
Gore, John
    Historic Theatre Group, Ltd. and, 255–256
    Live Nation and, 250, 254–255
The Gospel According to Scrooge, 89
gospel music, 143
    See also specific artists
Goulet, Robert, 55–56, **56**, 87

Griffin, Kathy, 230
Grunseth, John, 68

Hamill, Dorothy, 131–134, **132**
Hammel Green and Abrahamson, 93, 100
Harris, Emmylou, 87
Hart, Bobby, 180
Harvey, Barry, 110
Haynes, Rick, 110
Head, Douglas, 64, 91
Hedberg, Mitch, 158–159, **159**
Heinsbergen, Tony, Jr., 94, 100
Heltzer, Jim
    Orpheum Theatre, 84–85
    positions held by, 83, 186
    State Theater and, 92
Hennepin Avenue, condition of (1988), 84, 87
Hennepin Theatre District, 91, 185
Hennepin Theatre Trust
    Historic Theatre Group, Ltd. and, 243–244, 245, 247
    Hoch and Lisa Krohn, 257, 259
Henning, Doug, 135
Herbert, Maureen, 63
"Here You Come Again" (album), 44
Heritage Preservation Award, 191
Hill, Faith, 199
Hinsdale Doings (newspaper), 7
Hinsdale Health Museum, 2–3
Hinsdale Junior High School, 1–2
Hinsdale Youth Center, 4–5
Historic Theatre Group, Ltd.
    Dorothy Hamill's Nutcracker On Ice, 131–132, 133, 134
    financial success of, 251–253
    Gore and, 255–256
    Hennepin Theatre Trust and, 243–244, 245
    Fred Krohn's resignation as president and CEO, 256
    Fred Krohn's responsibilities as president and CEO, 252
    Live Nation and, 247
    management agreements for theatres, 243–247, **246**
    PACE and, 253–254
    Pantages Theatre and, 189, 191–192
    State Theatre opening with Manchester, 141
Hively, Jan, 91
Hoch, Tom, **93**
    Hennepin Theatre Trust, 257
    with MCDA, 84

Orpheum restoration, 100
   Pantages and, 185, 188, 191
   Theatre Live! Inc. and, 161
The Hollies, 180
Horne, Lena, 82
Houston, Cissy, 24
Houston, Whitney, 143
Hudson, Garth, **27**
Humphries, Barry, 155–157, **156**

"I'll Be Seeing You," 125
Intermission Lounge, 85
"Is That All There Is," 125
Isherwood, Charles, 176, 213
It's A Beautiful Day, 28
"It's a Good Day," 125

Jarreau, Al, 46–47
Jass, Mel, 69
jazz. *See* specific artists
Jefferson Airplane, 28
Jekyll & Hyde, 229
Jennings, Waylon, 41, **42**, 43–44, 181
Jesus People Church, 89
Joel, Billy, 183–184
John, Elton, 149, 183–184
John Golden Theatre, 172, **173**, **174**
Johnson, Jamoe, 28, 33
Joseph and The Amazing Technicolor Dreamcoat,
   96–98, 127, 161
Joy of Cooking, 28
Jujamcyn Productions
   basic facts about, 99
   Broadway partnership with Ordway, 127, 128
   Broadway partnership with Theatre Live! Inc.,
      128–129, 243
   Clear Channel Entertainment and, 250
   Dame Edna, 155–157
   Minneapolis Broadway market, 161
   pre-Broadway tryouts and, 163–164
   SFX and, 250
Juno Award, 36

Kaplan, Sam, 241
Kaplan, Sylvia, 241
Kapp, Joe, **67**
Kasper, Tim, 223
Katsaros, Doug, 176
Keane, Barry, 110
Key Brand Entertainment, 250, 255, 256, 257
Kids in the Hall, 203

Kildow, Allan, 141
Kiley, Richard, 48–49
"Kind of a Drag" (song), 44
King, Carole, 37–38
King, Donovan, 10, **12**
King, Jean LeVander, 63, **64**
Kinken, Sam, 203
KJZI-FM, 157, 158
Kobluk, Mike, 148
Koerner, Ray, and Glover, 21
Kottke, Leo, 37
Kristofferson, Kris, 34–35, **35**, 107
Krohn, Frank (brother), vii–viii, **viii**, 6, 106
Krohn, Fred, **8**, **35**, **36**, **41**, **45**, **59**, **64**, **65**, **67**, **72**, **73**,
   93, **100**, **107**, **109**, **159**, **179**, **182**, **183**, **204**, **206**,
   209, **215**, **239**, **246**
   appearance of, xiii
   Binger and, 251
   booking Broadway shows with Rawley, 81–82
   as Broadway producer, 171–174, 176
   characteristics, 3, 6
   as child playwright, 3–4
   childhood, 1–6
   in college, 18–22, 25, 62–66, **66**
   corporate entities worked with, 248
   as deputy state auditor, 68
   Disney University graduation, 164, **164**
   friendship with Mason, 169, 176, 177
   in *Gigi*, 12–13
   grandparents, 5–6
   intended career, 22, 23
   as lawyer, 66–67
   on LeVander staff, 63–65
   as movie producer, **72**, 72–74, **73**
   pets, 6–7
   "press pass" use, **23**, 23–24, 146, 237
   retirement, 259
   role with artists, xiv
   in *Under The Sycamore Tree*, 10–12, **11**
   as teenager, 6–13, 14–15, 17
   travels by, 259
   University of Minnesota law school, 66
Krohn, Herb (father), 115
Krohn, Linda "Lindy" (sister)
   Beatles, 237–238
   Lightfoot and, 110
   Nhork Syndicate press pass and, 23–24
   "Open Air Celebration" and, 26
   Pecks, 209
Krohn, Lisa (sister), **viii**, **215**
   Baryshnikov and, 151

Bennett, 202
The Blenders, 223
Bourdain, 234
Fitzgerald and, 121
Hennepin Theatre Trust, 257, 259
importance of, viii
"Open Air Celebration" and, 26
Pecks, 209–211
Riverdance, 155
Vonn, 239–240
Krohn, Lucy (mother), **vii**, **7**
Fitzgerald and, 119
importance of, vii
Lightfoot and, 110
nickname, 5
Krohn, Randy (brother), 26–27
Kullijian, Harry, 205
Kupcinet, Irv, 17

La Fiesta de la Posada, 47–48
LaBelle, Patti, 58, 141–142
Lady and the Tramp (movie), 125
Lady Buffington of Scottwell (dog), 7
Lance, Ryan, 223
Landesman, Rocco, 174
Larson, Jack, 178
LaSalle project, 91, 93
Laughing Room Only, 176
Lee, Peggy, 68, 123–126, **124**
Leonhart, Jay, 124
Letterman, David, **53**, 53–54
LeVander, Harold, 23, 63, **65**, 65–66, **66**, **67**
Lightfoot, Bev, 109
Lightfoot, Gordon, **107**, **109**
characteristics, 109, 110
financial backing for first show with, 106
Juno Award, 36
on Fred Krohn, xi–xii
Lucy and Lindy Krohn and, 110
at O'Shaughnessy Auditorium, 106–107
total number of concerts with, 107
Upper Midwest concerts beyond Twin cities,
108–109
Weil and, 149
Lindquist, Kelly, 186–187
Line, Lorie, 200–201
Line, Tim, 200–201
The Lion King world premiere, xi, 103, 161, **162**,
163, 164–168, **168**
Little Richard, 26–27, 28, **30**
Live at the Guthrie, 149

Live Nation, 246, 247, 250, 254
Loggins, Kenny, 87
Lonn, Jerry, 83
Lord of the Rings, 222
Lowe, Rudy, 49
Lynch, Lee, **246**
Baryshnikov and, 151
clout of, 91, 92
Hamill and, 132–133, 134
importance to Fred Krohn of, ix
Nirvana Health Club sauna and, 88
PACE negotiations, 253–254
Lynch, Terry, ix

Mackintosh, Cameron, **100**
Malo, Raul, 219–220
Man of La Mancha, 48–49
Manchester, Melissa, 141
The Manhattan Transfer, 38–39
Manilow, Barry, 140
Mann, Ted
characteristics, 78
Pantages's landmark designation, 187–188
plans to demolish Mann Theatre, 185
sale of Orpheum, 77, 78–79
Mann Theatre. *See* Pantages Theatre
Mannheim Steamroller, 134
Marceau, Marcel, **224**, 224–225
Mariucci, John, 178
Martell, Annie, 148
Martin, Steve, 40, **41**
Mason, Jackie, **170**
award-winning shows, 171
friendship with Fred Krohn, 169, 176, 177
Laughing Room Only, 176
Much Ado About Everything, 171–174, **173**, **174**,
175
at Music Box Theatre, 169, 170–171
Prune Danish, 176
Mathis, Johnny, 214, **215**
The Mavericks, 219–220
Max (dog), 87
Maynard, Cary, **59**, 62
McCarty, Charlie, 28–29
McCullum, Kevin, 130, 187
McFadden, Jerry Dale, 220
McGraw, Tim, 199
McNab, Horace Greeley, 80
Merrick, David, 51, 81
Met Center/Metropolitan Sports Center
Jennings and The Waylors, 41, 43

Fred Krohn's shadowing of Reid, 178
shows at during 1960s, 180–181
Waylon Jennings, Jessi Colter, and Asleep at
    the Wheel, 181
The Who, 181
Metropolitan Stadium
    Beatles, 237–238
    Williams, 61
Midler, Bette, 241–242
Midway Stadium
    "Open Air Celebration I," 25–27, **28**
    "Open Air Celebration II 'Superball,'" 27–29,
        29, **30**
    "Open Air Celebration III," 28–29
    "Waylon's North Country Jamboree," 43
Mike Quatro Jam Band, 28
Miller, Ann, 56–58, 249
Miller, Barbara, 63
Minneapolis Auditorium
    The Allman Brothers, 32
    "Aquatennial Spectacular," 24–25
    Beacom and, 25
Minneapolis Community Development Agency
    (MCDA), 128–129
    Cirque du Soleil, 206–207
    Hoch at, 84
    Fred Krohn as manager of Orpheum, 86–87
    leadership, 83, 186, 191
    Orpheum upgrades, 86
    Pantages and, 189, 191–192
Minneapolis Energy Center, 103
Minnelli, Liza, 51–52
Miss Saigon, 100, 103–104, 127
Mitchell, Chad, 148
Mitchell, Clint, 154
Mondale, Eleanor, 213
Mondale, Joan, 68, 213
Monk, Thelonious, 19–21
Monterey Peninsula Artists, 44
Montoya, Carlos, 21
Morrison, Bradley, 189
Mr. Las Vegas, 144
Much Ado About Everything, 171–174, **173**, **174**, 175
Munderloh, Otts, 152
Murray, Anne, 34, **36**, 36–37, 107
Music Box Theatre, 169, 170–171
Musser, Laura Jane, 19
Musser, Richard Drew, 19

Nason, John, 21, 65
Nelson, Nancy, 207–208, 231, 233

New York Times, 173, 176, 213
Newhart, Bob, 205–206, **206**
Newton, Wayne, 144
Nhork Syndicate press pass, **23**, 23–24, 146, 237
Nirvana Health Club (sauna), 87–88, **88**
Nixon, Richard, 65, **65**
Nordyke, Tom, 186–187
North Oaks, Minnesota, 62
Northrop Auditorium
    Woody Allen, 236–237
    Benson, 147–148
    Fitzgerald, 122
    Jarreau, 47
    Carole King, 37
    The Lion King world premiere, xi
    Sugar Babies, 56–58, 249
    Youngbloods, 38
Novak, Vera, 55–56, **56**
N'SYNC, 181–182, **183**
The Nylons, 87
Nyro, Laura, 55

Oakley, Berry, 28, 33
O'Brien, Margaret, **12**, 13
"Open Air Celebration I," 25–27, **28**
"Open Air Celebration II 'Superball,'" 27–29, **29**, **30**
"Open Air Celebration III," 28–29
Ordway Music Theatre
    Binger and, 128
    as economic development tool for downtown
        Minneapolis, 129
    Jujamcyn Productions and, 127, 128
    management of Pantages, State, and Orpheum
        as "The Twin Cities Theatre Alliance,"
        244–246
    Joan Mondale, 68
    Show Boat, 127–128
    St. Paul-only Broadway season and, 129–130
Orpheum Theatre, **101**, **102**
    Aida, 168
    air conditioning and, 82
    Bacharach, 147
    Baryshnikov, 151
    Bay City Rollers, 142
    Beauty and the Beast, 164
    Belafonte, 138
    Blackstone, 135
    "bus and truck" and "split-week" shows, 81
    Chad Mitchell Trio, 148
    Channing, 204–205
    A Chorus Line, 49–51, **51**, 75–78, 79, 80–81

condition of, 87
Dylan and, 76–79, 82–83
Griffin, 230
Heltzer and MCDA, 83, 84–86
Henning, 135
Hill, 199
Historic Theatre Group, Ltd. management
    agreements, 243–247
Horne, 82
Jarreau, 47
Jekyll & Hyde, 229
Kids in the Hall, 203
Fred Krohn as manager, 86–87
LaBelle, 141–142
legendary vaudeville acts, 135
Letterman, **53**, 53–54
The Lion King world premiere, 103, 164–168, **168**
Man of La Mancha, 48–49
Minneapolis's purchase of, 85–86
Minnelli, 51–52
Miss Saigon, 100, 103–104, 127
neighborhood surrounding, 84
Newton, 144
N'SYNC and Brittany Spears, 181–182
recording of *La Fiesta de la Posada*, 47–48
rehab of, to accommodate "mega" touring
    shows, 99, 100, 103
Reynolds's *Conversation*, 140
Riverdance, 154–155
Show Boat, 127–128, 129
South Pacific, 87
Sunset Boulevard, 129
upgrades by Fred Krohn and Dylan, 79–80
upgrades by MCDA, 86
Vaughan, 58
Waits, 54
Warwick, 147
Wilson, **53**, 53–54
Yanni, 139–140
Osborne, Barrie, **221**, 222
O'Shaughnessy Auditorium
    Delaney & Bonnie & Friends, 32
    Dietrich, xiii, **xiii**, 111, 112–116, **117**, 118
    Fitzgerald, 120–121
    Jarreau, 47
    Lightfoot, xi, 106–107
    The Manhattan Transfer, 39
    Martin, 40, **41**
    Parton, 44
    Shirt, 137
Osmond, Donny, 96–98

Oszustowicz, Dick, 131–132

PACE Theatrical Group, 250, 252–253
Palast Orchester, 258
Palme, Emile, 124
Palmer, Robert, 87
Pantages Theatre, **186**, **190**, **196**
    The Blenders, 223
    Bublé, 226–227
    Eder, 229
    Griffin, 230
    Historic Theatre Group, Ltd. and, 189, 191–
        192, 243–247
    Jarreau, 47
    landmark designation and award, 187–188, 191
    Marceau, **224**, 224–225
    The Mavericks, 220
    Minneapolis purchase of, 188–189
    plans to demolish, 185
    saving of, 186–189, 191–192
    Shubert and, 193, 195
Papp, Joe, 75–78
Parton, Dolly, 44, **45**, 46
Pass, Joe, 122
Pat (dog), 6–7
Patinkin, Mandy, 46, **152**, 152–153
Paul Butterfield Blues Band, 21
Peck, Carey, 210–211
Peck, Gregory, 207–211, **209**
Peck, Veronique, 208–210
Peer, Beverly, 137
Perez, Eddie, 220
Perpich, Rudy, 68
Perry, Dein, 212
Peter, Paul and Mary, 52–53
Peters, Jon, **35**
Peterson, Oscar, 122
Pickett, Wilson, 180
Plummer, Christopher, 153–154
Poco, 28
Pomus, Doc, 175
poster problem, 120–121
Pride Rock, 165–166
Prince, 141, 142
Protzman, Bob, 119, 120
Prune Danish, 176

"Queen of Soul," 24–25, 58, 143

Raabe, Max, 258
Radisson Hotel, 123–126, **124**

Raelettes, 89–90
Raize, Jason, **167**
Rawley, Ernie, 81–82
Reagan, Ronald, 65
Redeye, 28
Reid, Bob, 23, 178
Renaldo & Clara (movie), 70, **71**, **72**, 72–74
Reynolds, Burt, 140
Richert, Wanda, 50–51, **51**, 81
Ringo Starr and His All-Starr Band, 238
Riverdance, 154–155
The Robert Cray Band, 90
Robinson, Robert, 200
Rockefeller, Nelson, 65
Rogers, Kenny, 22
Roise, Charlene K., 187–188, 193
"The Role of Harold LeVander as Legislative
    Leader of the 65th Session of the Minnesota
    Legislature," 63
Rolvaag, Karl, 63
Rooney, Mickey, 56–58, 249
Rosenfeld, Jyll, 171, 172, 174, 176
Ross, Diana, 140
Roth, Susan, 195
Rubinoff, David, 1–2
Russo, Aaron, 38
Rust, Allan, 223
Rust, Darren, 223

"Sally" awards, 68
Salt Creek Playhouse
    Carroll, Leo G., 7, 8, **8**
    Coca and King Donovan, 10
    Gigi, 12–13
    location, 9
    Under The Sycamore Tree, 10–12
Saltzman, Ben, 79
Saltzman, Naomie, 79
Satchmo, 4–5, **5**
Scandinavian Ballroom (Radisson Hotel),
    123–126, **124**
Schiller, Wellington du, 6
Schneider, Peter, 167
Schumacher, Tom, 167
Scott, Robert, 137
Sebastian, John, 25
Sedaris, David, 216–218, **217**
Sergio Mendes and Brazil '66, 180
SFX Entertainment, 249, 250, 252–253
Shankar, Anoushka, 222–223
Shankar, Ravi, 18, 222–223

Shapiro, Dick, 249
Shattuck Military Academy, 21
Shea, Red, 149
Sheeley, Jim, 161
Sheeran, Ed, 235
Shepardson, Ray, 92, 93, **93**, 100
Sherman, Mark, 124
Short, Bobby, 68, 137, **137**
Show Boat, 81, 127–128, 129
Shubert Theatre, **194**, **197**
    Artspace and, 195–198
    Block E and, 192–193, 195
    Pantages and, 193, 195
Siegel, Jeffrey, **107**
Sillerman, Robert F.X., 249–250
Simon, Carly, 149
Sinatra, Frank, 52, 160, 180
Skyway News, 187
Smith, Brett, 91
Smokey Joe's Cafe, 164
smoking in theaters, 108
Snyder, Corson (grandfather), 5–6, **8**, 23
Snyder, Lucy, "Big Lucy" (grandmother), 5–6, **8**,
    23
Sondheim, Stephen, 9
Songbook (CD), 110
South Pacific, 55–56, 87
Spears, Brittany, 181–182
The Spencer Davis Group, 240
St. Paul Chamber Orchestra, 47–48
St. Paul Civic Center, 43–44
Stage Magazine, 176
A Star is Born (movie), 34–35
Star Tribune, 156, 167
Starr, Ringo, 237–238
State Theatre
    acoustics and sightlines, 90–91
    Becker, Rob, 159–160
    Bennett, 202–203
    booking shows, 94, 99
    Burnett, 233
    Caesar, 143
    Caldwell, Bobby, 158
    Charles and Raelettes, 89–90
    Cooper, 235–236
    Dame Edna, 155–157, 164
    as economic development tool for downtown
        Minneapolis, 129
    Eder, 229
    Griffin, 230
    Historic Theatre Group, Ltd. and, 243–247

Jesus People Church, 89
Joseph and The Amazing Technicolor Dreamcoat, 96–98, 127, 161
Line, 200–201
Lord of the Rings, 222
Manchester, 141
Manilow, 140
Mason, 172
Newhart, 205–206, **206**
Patinkin, **152**, 152–153
Plummer, 153
restoration and reopening, 93–94, **95**
Ringo Starr and His All-Starr Band, 238
The Robert Cray Band, 90
Sedaris, 216–218
Sheeran, 235
Stritch, 225–226
Vonn, 239–240
"The State Theatre Group," 86, 91–93
Steele, Mike, 151, 167
Stern, Isaac, 21
Stimson Building, 189, 191
Stoll, Jon, 176
Stookey, Noel Paul, 52–53
Stout, John, 221–222
Strawberry Alarm Clock, 180
Stritch, Elaine, 225–226
Sugar Babies, 56–58, 249
Sunset Boulevard, 129
"supply pastors," 5–6
Sutton, Ward, 172
Sweet Charity, 164
The Sweet Inspirations, 24

Taj Mahal, 39–40
Tap Dogs, 212
Tapestry (album), 37, 38
Target Center
    Cooper, 236
    Dorothy Hamill's Nutcracker On Ice, 134
    Sinatra, 180
    Theatre Live! Inc. and, 182–183
Tate, Grady, 124
Taylor, James, 149
Taymor, Julie, 165, 166
Tex, Joe, 180
Theatre Live! Inc.
    Broadway partnership with Jujamcyn Productions, 128–129, 243
    Cirque du Soleil, 206–207
    Hoch and, 161

Riverdance, 155
    Target Center and, 182–183
Tiny Tim, **179**, 180
Topper (television program), 7–8, 9
Towers, Terrell, 187
"Trash Day" (song), 54
Travers, Mary, 52–53
Trucks, Butch, 33
Tucker, Forest, 81
"The Twin Cities Theatre Alliance," 244–246

Under The Sycamore Tree, 10–12
University of Minnesota law school, 23, 66
University of Minnesota West Bank lecture hall, 39–40

The Vagina Monologues, 213–214
Valeda The Transparent Lady, 3, **3**
Vallie, Frankie, 180
Variety, 157, 174, 176
Varsity Theater, 72
Vaughan, Sarah, 58
Ventura, Jesse, **182**, 201
Ventura, Terry, **182**, 201
Victor/Victoria, 164
Vonn, Lindsey, 9, 168, 238–240, **239**

Waggoner, Porter, 44
Waits, Tom, 54
Warg, Dana, 182, **182**, 183, **183**
Warwick, Dionne, 145, 146, **146**, 147
Wasser, Alan, 249
Waters, Muddy, 25
"Waylon's North Country Jamboree," 43
The Waylors, 41, 43
Webber, Sir Andrew Lloyd, 96–97, **97**
Weber, Bruce, 176
Weil, Sue
    Baryshnikov and, 149, 151
    as booker, 59, 106, 111
    career after leaving Twin Cities, 149, 151
    Miles Davis and, 134
    Live at the Guthrie, 149
    Midler, 241
Weisman, Eliot, 52
Weiss, Steve, **159**
"What You Won't Do For Love," 157
The Who, 181
Wildhorn, Frank, 229
Williams, Andy, **59**, 60, 61
Wilson, Laurel Ann, 76, 77

Wilson, Nancy, **53**, 53–54
Wilson, Pamela Ann, 50, 51
Winwood, Steve, 240–241
Wolf, Henry, 60–61
Wolfe, Digby, 176
Woman's Club Theatre, 213–214
Woody Allen and His New Orleans Jazz Band, 237
The World According to Me, 171

Xcel Center, 182–183

Yanisch, Rebecca, 128–129
Yanni, 139–140
Yarrow, Peter, 52–53
Young, Jesse Colin, 38

The Young Rascals, **179**, 180
Youngbloods, 38
Yvette on the Mississippi, 137

Zelenovich, Mark, Jr., "Junior," 53, 69, 70
Zelenovich, Mark, Sr., "Senior," 69, 70
Zimmerman, David, **69**
    as conduit to Dylan, 69
    Fred Krohn and, 69–70
    "Open Air Celebration" and, 25
    Orpheum and, 76–77, 83
    Renaldo & Clara and, 70
Zimmerman, Gayle, 77
Zimmern, Andrew, 234